PRAISE FOR *IN THE CARDS*

"Infused with . . . fresh detail. Between the sweetness of the relationship and the summery beach setting, romance fans will find this a warming winter read."

—*Publishers Weekly*

"Fans will love the frank honesty of her characters. [Beck's] scenery is richly detailed and the story engaging."

—*RT Book Reviews*

"[A] realistic and heartwarming story of redemption and love . . . Beck's understanding of interpersonal relationships and her flawless prose make for a believable romance and an entertaining read."

—*Booklist*

PRAISE FOR *WORTH THE WAIT*

"[A] poignant and heartwarming story of young love and redemption and will literally make your heart ache . . . Jamie Beck has a real talent for making the reader feel the sorrow, regret, and yearning of this young character."

—*Fresh Fiction*

PRAISE FOR *WORTH THE TROUBLE*

"Beck takes readers on a journey of self-reinvention and risky investments, in love and in life . . . With strong family ties, loyalty, playful banter, and sexual tension, Beck has crafted a beautiful second-chances story."

—*Publishers Weekly* (starred review)

PRAISE FOR *SECRETLY HERS*

"[I]n Beck's ambitious, uplifting second Sterling Canyon contemporary . . . Conflicting views and family drama lay the foundation for emotional development in this strong Colorado-set contemporary."

—*Publishers Weekly*

"[W]itty banter and the deepening of the characters and their relationship, along with some unexpected plot twists and a lovable supporting cast . . . will keep the reader hooked . . . A smart, fun, sexy, and very contemporary romance."

—*Kirkus Reviews*

PRAISE FOR *UNEXPECTEDLY HERS*

"Character-driven, sweet, and chock-full of interesting secondary characters."

—*Kirkus Reviews*

PRAISE FOR *WORTH THE RISK*

"An emotional read that will leave you reeling at times and hopeful at others."

—*Books & Boys Book Blog*

PRAISE FOR *BEFORE I KNEW*

"A tender romance rises from the tragedy of two families—a must read!"

—Robyn Carr, #1 *New York Times* bestselling author

"A multilayered and tightly plotted journey that's sure to tug at the heartstrings."

—*Publishers Weekly*

"Jamie Beck's deeply felt novel hits all the right notes, celebrating the power of forgiveness, the sweetness of second chances, and the heady joy of reaching for a dream. Don't miss this one!"

—Susan Wiggs, #1 *New York Times* bestselling author

"*Before I Knew* kept me totally enthralled as two compassionate, relatable characters, each in search of forgiveness and fulfillment, turn a recipe for heartache into a story of love, hope, and some really good menus!"

—Shelley Noble, *New York Times* bestselling author of *Whisper Beach*

PRAISE FOR *ALL WE KNEW*

"[A] moving story about the flux of life and the steadfastness of family."

—*Publishers Weekly*

"[A]n impressively crafted and deftly entertaining read from first page to last."

—*Midwest Book Review*

"*All We Knew* is compelling, heartbreaking, and emotional."

—*Harlequin Junkie*

PRAISE FOR *JOYFULLY HIS*

"A quick and sweet read that is perfect for the holidays."

—*Harlequin Junkie*

when you knew

ALSO BY JAMIE BECK

In the Cards

The St. James Novels

Worth the Wait

Worth the Trouble

Worth the Risk

The Sterling Canyon Novels

Accidentally Hers

Secretly Hers

Unexpectedly Hers

Joyfully His

The Cabot Novels

Before I Knew

All We Knew

when you knew

A CABOT NOVEL

JAMIE BECK

This is a work of fiction. Names, characters, organizations, places, events, and incidents are either products of the author's imagination or are used fictitiously.

Published by Montlake Romance, Seattle

www.apub.com

ISBN-13: 9781503902503
ISBN-10: 1503902501

Cover design by Rachel Adam Rogers

Printed in the United States of America

For Aunt Teeky, Uncle Bill, Billy, and Laurie

—my second family.

This above all: to thine own self be true

—*William Shakespeare*

Chapter One

Colic

According to *Merriam-Webster*: a condition marked by recurrent episodes of prolonged and uncontrollable crying and irritability in an otherwise healthy infant that is of unknown cause and usually subsides after three to four months of age

According to me: karmic payback for reneging on my offer to let Hunter and Sara adopt my baby

Colt had been screaming all evening, as usual. Colic, they said, although labeling it did nothing at all to help Gentry's infant son or her to live with the never-ending fussing. No amount of soothing, bouncing, rocking, or walking quieted him if his eyes were open.

Alone, and on the verge of a nervous breakdown, Gentry questioned her sanity. Her thoughts slid like quicksilver, fueling the stress headache pulsating behind her eyes. Her son's screeching response to the doorbell, which echoed off the vaulted ceiling and plate glass windows, didn't help.

With her unhappy child bristling in her arms, Gentry raced across the living room—sidestepping a growing stack of unread parenting magazines—to reach the door before the visitor rang again. If she'd actually succeeded in getting Colt to sleep this evening, she might've shot the fool on the other side of her door for having risked waking him. In fact, she might shoot him anyway just because it had been that kind of day and her frustration needed a target.

She flung her door open, baby pressed to her chest, and gawked at her half brother, Hunter. "You?"

Hunter and his wife, Sara, stood there against the backdrop of a dusky summer sunset. Wide eyes and slack jaws contrasted with their elegant Saturday-night attire. Were they stunned by her impolite greeting, or by her shabby appearance? Probably both, she conceded.

Seconds ticked by before Hunter found his voice. "You're alive."

"Depends on your definition." Gentry retreated into the house, knowing they'd follow even though she hadn't invited them to visit. She couldn't shoo them away, but she didn't want them to see her strung out, either.

Expecting Gentry to fail was something of a Cabot family tradition. For most of her life, she'd been happy to live "down" to their expectations. In rare moments of self-honesty, she could admit that, at times, she'd even turned it into a game. An immature dynamic, for sure, but one that hurt less than being ignored or than trying and failing. She didn't, however, want to be seen as a failure of a mother. Especially not by them.

Colton was the only perfect, innocent, precious thing she'd ever produced in her entire life. She didn't regret her decision to keep him, but unlike Sara, she had no idea how to be a mom, let alone be a good one. Hadn't exactly had a great role model. But for his sake, she now had to build bridges with her family instead of burning them down.

"We just left A CertainTea." Sara held up a to-go bag that smelled like curried seafood. Her signature smile returned, which complemented her simple summer sheath and shiny hair. Confronted by that glamour, Gentry smoothed the loose hairs that had pulled free from her ponytail, scarcely able to recall the last time *she* had looked as sharp.

"No one has seen or heard from you in almost three days. We thought we'd check in on our way home and drop off some food."

Hunter and Sara lived about a half mile up the road. Their proximity had been one of the reasons Gentry had purchased this unit. Its oversize deck and lake views didn't hurt, either. The only flaw was the cliff of a backyard, which descended more than one hundred feet to Lake Sandy. Not the *best* play space, but that view! She'd figured the flat front yard and neighborhood park would suffice.

Sara set the takeout bag on the entry table, her gaze homing in on Colt. Gentry almost wished her sister-in-law had held a grudge against her for keeping Colt, because Sara's graciousness inflicted far worse guilt. The look of love she now gave Colt only made it harder.

"Thanks." Gentry's stomach gurgled at the whiff of real food. Getting to the grocery store had become harder than climbing Mount Everest, so she'd been making do with Ritz crackers, oatmeal, and eggs. A fact underscored by the empty red-and-yellow box tipped over on the coffee table.

Hunter stood, legs apart, hands on his hips. His owlish gaze roamed the living room, taking inventory of the remnants of what had once been a lovely, contemporary condominium.

Baby blankets lay strewn on several surfaces, including over the outrageously pricey Roche Bobois sofa cushions now tipped askew. Two half-empty baby bottles sat on various tabletops—sans coasters—and brightly colored baby play gyms, bouncy seats, and other necessities ate up a majority of the floor space. The pièce de résistance? The hideous white plastic sculpture—otherwise known as the Diaper Genie—looming in one corner.

The look on Hunter's face confirmed what Gentry already guessed. His house never looked ravaged by a monsoon, despite his hectic life with their foster son, Ty. "What the hell happened?"

"Nothing." Gentry rhythmically jostled Colt, brushing Quackers—her ancient, love-worn Beanie Baby duck—against his arm. Her son fussed, heedless of her wish that he'd stop long enough to convince Hunter and Sara that she knew what she was doing. Colt's tiny head bobbled against her collarbone.

She tucked her nose against his cheek to smell his sweet skin and then looked into those inky-blue eyes—the color of a moonless night sky—and swore she'd do right by him. Somehow she'd learn, on her own, to be what he needed and give him everything he deserved.

Someday. As soon as his constant crying ended and her mental fog lifted. *Then* she'd finally experience the bliss reflected in most other young mothers' faces. Tonight, however, there'd be no bliss. Right now she'd settle for thirty minutes of peace and quiet.

Hunter winced as she touched Quackers to Colt's nose, showing no recognition of the plush toy he'd given her for her fifth birthday.

When he'd bought it for her with his own money all those years ago, she'd believed, for the first time, he might love her like he did Colby. Growing up alone, she'd envied her siblings' closeness. Every time they'd gone home to their mother, Gentry had run to her room to cuddle her surrogate, Quackers, which explained his worn condition.

Sara reached both hands toward Colt, soft smile on display. "Can I hold the little pumpkin while you eat?"

"And shower," Hunter muttered, earning himself a sharp look of disapproval from Sara. He raised his hands in surrender.

Hunter and Sara probably thought they'd make better parents for Colt than Gentry did. As much as she wanted to prove them wrong, right now she wanted that curry shrimp more. "Sure."

Gentry handed her son to Sara, whose entire face lit up with adoration. Would there come a day when wondering if Sara coveted him a bit would no longer be Gentry's first thought? It wasn't charitable or fair of her, considering how quickly her sister-in-law had forgiven her.

Forcing her uneasiness aside, Gentry retrieved the to-go bag from the entry table. Anything from their sister, Colby's, restaurant qualified as the best food in the Greater Portland area. Colby's boyfriend,

Alec, was A CertainTea's chef and had spent years training in Mougins, France.

Gentry practically skipped to the kitchen, clutching the bag with greedy hands. Her brother followed her and waited while she reheated the food in the microwave—the one appliance her mom had taught her how to use.

"Gentry." He then waved his hand up and down, obviously unimpressed by her formula-stained robe, UGG slippers, and ponytail. "Are you okay? You seem a little . . . overwhelmed."

"You caught me at a bad moment." She turned away, pretending to study the plate spinning in the microwave. He didn't need to know that the so-called bad moment repeated over and over, minute by minute, day by day, like a hellish version of *Groundhog Day*.

He tipped his head, narrowing his eyes a shade. "Will you be back at work starting Monday? I hate to pressure you, but the new product launch is around the corner. We need *all* hands on deck in the marketing department, even entry-level employees like you."

The family business, Cabot Tea Company, had entered into a joint venture with King Cola to produce and distribute ready-to-drink iced tea. Hunter had pretty much gambled the family fortune on the venture. He'd been growing more intense by the day in an effort to ensure the launch's success. Although none of Gentry's low-level responsibilities would make or break it, she had to do her best. She'd only gone to work at CTC this year to ditch her black sheep status so that her son could be proud and have a real place among the Cabots.

"I thought the launch wasn't until October," she deadpanned.

His brows rode up his forehead. "What?"

"Oh, for God's sake, Hunter. I'm joking." She snatched the plate from the microwave and grabbed a fork. He was lucky she was starving or he'd have gotten an earful. "I know the schedule. I've been on some calls with my mom and the team."

Just not Facetime or Skype—*God forbid!*

The first too-hot bite of shrimp burned the roof of her mouth, but hunger kept her chewing. She heard herself purring the kinds of sounds that, in another context, might come from the bedroom—not that she could remember *that* feeling. "Alec's the best chef *ev-ah*."

"Colby would agree." Hunter smiled for the first time since he'd arrived.

Gentry had taken her third bite when Sara came into the kitchen with Colt, forehead creased with concern. "I think he's a little warm. And this cough. Have you been to the doctor?"

Gentry loved Sara but thought her worrywart reflex and preference to parent "by the book" added unnecessary stress to motherhood. Whenever Ty's adoption went through, the poor tyke's childhood would be a series of well-intentioned and warmly enforced rules and expectations, tutors, and lessons. Sara probably googled every little boo-boo, too.

Gentry didn't believe in all that. Rules had never helped her. Too many of them boxed a person in. And too many expectations resulted in dozens of ways to fail. She wanted Colt to be a free spirit. To explore without limitations, so he'd become a confident, interesting, "outside the box" kind of man.

"I don't need a doctor. Colt's warm from crying all evening." She chomped another shrimp. Honestly, it tasted orgasmically good. Was that a word? Well, it should be. *Note to self—check* Merriam-Webster.

"His cough sounds wet, but I can't tell if he's wheezing. You know, preemies are more susceptible to respiratory illnesses like RSV. Maybe you should have him checked just to be sure." Sara patted Colt while swaying with him, cuddling him like a beloved, if squealing, teddy bear.

Sara often brought up the preemie thing, but Gentry hated labels. Colt had been born three weeks ahead of his due date without significant complications. End of story.

"At eight thirty on a Friday night?" Gentry made a face. "The pediatrician's office is closed, Sara."

"What about pediatric urgent care?" Sara suggested with a hopeful smile.

"This isn't urgent. And look at me. I'm in no state to leave the house." Gentry ate the last shrimp with a bit of despair now that the plate was empty. If Hunter and Sara would look away for three seconds, she could lick the plate. "Besides, the people in that waiting room are *really* sick. Why expose Colt to those germs when it isn't necessary?"

"Good point." Hunter's surprised expression irked Gentry. As if her common sense was as rare as snow in Florida.

"What if I call Ian?" Sara kept Gentry locked in her sights, calm and determined, as usual. "He's in town . . . at a motel, actually. He can listen to Colt's lungs and make sure there isn't a problem."

Ian, the humanitarian EMT Sara had wanted to fix Gentry up with many moons ago, *before* Gentry had decided to keep her baby. The same EMT who'd arrived on the scene downtown less than nine weeks ago, when Gentry's water had broken well ahead of schedule, and Sara's flat tire had prevented them from heading to the hospital. How fitting that her second run-in with him might be as humiliating as the first.

"Why's he at a motel?" Gentry wondered aloud. She recalled thinking him handsome, which said a lot considering the Freddy Krueger–caliber labor pains stabbing her belly when they'd met. Not that it mattered. Handsome men weren't a priority. The last time she'd dived into that pool—her one-night stand in Napa with a gorgeous man she knew only as "Smith"—she'd ended up with Colt. Now she hadn't the interest in or time for men or, sadly, sex.

"Gloria said something about his fiancée breaking things off, and him coming home to get his things." Sara had met Ian's mother, Gloria, because that woman ran the Angel House, a homeless shelter for women and children where Sara volunteered. "It's possible he hasn't got the security deposit to rent someplace new."

"Why'd he bother with that when he could've had his things boxed and shipped?" Gentry conjured his unforgettable green eyes, wavy umber hair, a smattering of freckles across the bridge of his nose. A "boy next door" type with a dash of sexy.

"Maybe he hoped to save his relationship." Sara kissed Colt and stroked his silky hair, clearly less interested in Ian's story than Gentry was. "Let's see if he'll come take a listen."

Gentry shot Hunter a look. He shrugged, which meant he knew that Sara wouldn't let up, and he wasn't going to argue.

"You're totally overreacting." Gentry placed the back of her hand on Colt's forehead, which did feel a little warm. Not scary hot or anything. She rummaged through the kitchen drawer stuffed with 1,001 infant gizmos. When she located the baby thermometer, she held it up and almost cried, "Eureka!" Instead, she stuck it in Colt's ear until it beeped. "Ninety-nine point six. Nothing a little baby Tylenol can't handle."

"That won't help his lungs. Wouldn't you rather be safe than sorry?" Sara shrugged a shoulder.

A quiet stare-down ensued for four seconds, maybe five. *Fiddle-flippin'-sticks.*

"Fine. Call Ian." Hopefully, the guy would laugh, and Sara would back down. Gentry reached for her son. Once she had him in her arms, she said, "Excuse me."

While Sara called Ian and conferred with Hunter, Gentry took Colt to the bathroom and dabbed a cool washcloth across his forehead. She checked his writhing body for a rash but found none. Clearish fluid—not green gunk—ran from his nose.

Sara's concern niggled, even though Gentry seriously doubted the need to call in reinforcements. While she changed Colt's diaper, she was struck by his absolute dependence on her judgment. His utter trust. *In her.*

Her poor son.

If he could speak, she'd know what he needed. Instead, she remained stymied, trying to decipher one cry from another. Trying to determine if his head, ears, or belly caused the ache that kept him crying. What? What? *What?*

She lifted him and swayed, humming softly in a fruitless attempt to comfort them both. In all honesty, at any second she could fall apart or asleep—a real toss-up. In the privacy of the bathroom, she closed her eyes while clinging to her child. *It's us against the world, baby.*

Either God took pity on her or Colt had finally worn himself out, because his crying subsided to a dull kind of whine. Gentry inhaled deeply and rolled her shoulders back. By the time she returned to the living room, Ian was knocking on the door.

An inadvertent glance in the mirror set off a new shock wave of horror. Who *was* that anxious, depleted soul staring back at her? No wonder Hunter and Sara had been stunned into silence when they'd first arrived.

Gentry closed her eyes again, momentarily imagining herself in her normal clothes: Gaultier, perhaps? Trendy, high-heeled shoes that drew attention to her long legs and ankle tattoo. A multitude of bracelets on her arm. Her auburn hair artfully woven in a waterfall braid. The image of her old self enabled her to tip up her chin and pretend spit-up didn't coat her robe.

She opened her eyes just as Sara escorted Ian inside. At least her messy apartment would still look like a palace compared with the disaster zones he'd navigated.

◆ ◆ ◆

Ian hadn't known what to make of Sara's call. They'd spoken only on a few brief occasions, but his mother held her in high regard. He remembered their first encounter, when she'd been hurt by a resident's abusive husband, who'd barged into the Angel House in search of his wife. Once Ian had made sure neither woman was hurt, Sara had shifted to the role of matchmaker, pimping the very sister-in-law who now needed help.

The same one he'd met months ago, when she'd unexpectedly gone into labor.

He suspected part of Sara's current agenda once again involved playing Cupid, otherwise they could've taken the infant to an urgent care facility. Whether or not Gentry was a coconspirator had yet to be determined.

He stepped inside the swanky, newly constructed unit, with its picture-perfect views framed by massive plate glass windows. This joint probably cost upwards of a million bucks. Like a reflex, his mind immediately calculated other uses for that kind of money: medicine, water, clothes . . . food. Or a donation to the EMT training facility he was founding in Haiti, in his father's name, with the help of his dad's old friend Dr. Archer Cooke.

"Thank you for coming out of your way tonight." Sara led him into the living room. She gestured to the imposing man on her left. "This is my husband, Hunter, and his sister Gentry, whom you might remember. And that little bundle is Colt."

Ian shook Hunter's hand, reminding himself not to nitpick. Sara volunteered at the shelter, and the Cabot family had started a foundation that supported a number of community-outreach programs. If they also thought monogrammed dress shirts and gold watches were important, who was he to judge? "Nice to meet you."

He then turned to Gentry, who didn't look particularly grateful to see him despite the polite smile on her face. She sure hadn't primped for his arrival, he thought, holding back a wry smile. Clearly, she was no more interested in Sara's matchmaking than he was. *Good.*

Ian had zero interest in being fixed up with any woman so soon after his breakup with Farrah. His disinterest went doubly so with respect to an heiress to the Cabot Tea fortune, who'd likely drive him up the wall with her oblivious privileged complaints.

"Sorry. I asked Sara not to bother you." Despite the circles under her eyes, the ratty ponytail, and bathrobe in need of a serious washing,

Gentry Cabot was tall and proud, with striking green eyes and a naturally flirtatious smile. Even her grimy robe didn't hamper a sudden tug of attraction—an untimely and unwelcome response—leaving him strangely thunderstruck.

"It's fine. I wasn't busy."

"Well, now that you're here, these two can go home with a clear conscience." Gentry's pointed look and quick nod toward the door left no doubt about her dismissal. In less than five minutes and twenty-five words, she seemed like a modern-day Scarlett O'Hara, but hopefully not *that* manipulative. She patted her brother's cheek. "Thanks for bringing me dinner, but I think we've got this little situation under control."

"But—" Sara began.

"I promise I'll call you with a full report. I'll even type it up and highlight the bullet points if that makes you feel better." Gentry affected a playful smirk.

Oh yeah. Her sarcasm confirmed his quick assessment.

"Smart-ass." Hunter kissed his sister's forehead. With a final scan of her unkempt apartment and Ian's emergency bag, he said, "Come on, Sara. Let's go before we get cooties and end up getting Ty sick."

Sara stroked Colt's head and drew a deep inhalation of his baby scent before kissing his face. "Okay. Thanks again, Ian." She glanced around the disaster area that was Gentry's living room, her nose wrinkling with empathy. "Gentry, I'll check in tomorrow."

Hunter spun her toward the door before she'd find an excuse to stay. As they left, he waved at Ian. "Nice to meet you."

"Same." Ian nodded, curious about the whiff of tension between Gentry and the others.

Gentry closed the door and faced him, shrugging a bit too nonchalantly. "Well, what next?"

Some might admire her tough-girl routine, but he'd seen genuine mettle up close often enough to know the difference. Natalia, in Macao,

Colombia, who'd lost a child in a massive mudslide but soldiered on to care for her others. Children like Makenly, Lise, and Richo, who were students at Marie Ormont's school in Haiti and remained curious despite a lack of adequate food, resources, or water. Those traits proved real strength.

Lucky for her, Gentry Cabot's strength would probably never be tested.

Ian reached for the child. "Why don't I take a listen? Sara mentioned a concern about wheezing."

Gentry carefully handed her son to him. For a moment, her guarded expression softened—eyes shining with a mother's devotion. "I'm sure this isn't necessary, but if I didn't let Sara call you, she wouldn't have slept all night from worry."

That might be true, but he suspected Gentry wouldn't mind reassurance, either.

"It's not an inconvenience." Taking fifteen minutes out of his life to do a stranger a favor took about as much thought as breathing.

"We took his temperature ten minutes ago. Ninety-nine point six." Gentry hovered over his shoulder as he laid the baby on the suede sofa and pulled out a stethoscope.

Gentry's pinched brow and drawn mouth didn't look all that different from that of other young mothers he'd witnessed in fieldwork. He supposed a mother's worry transcended race and socioeconomic status.

Ian's thoughts then flitted to the acceptance he'd seen in other parents' eyes when illness and food shortages wreaked havoc on their lives. Those memories made it tough to consider "everyday problems" as being grave. But life experience shaped perspective, and Gentry's sheltered existence didn't make her motherhood worries less troubling to her than anyone else's were to them.

"Has he thrown up or had excessive diarrhea?" Ian asked. He listened to Colt's rapid heartbeat, which he could barely hear, thanks to the baby's fussing.

"No."

"Any rashes?" He cast a quick look at her.

"No." Gentry brushed her hand across her scalp and stroked her ponytail. "Honestly, he's been colicky since that first week. He gets all fired up, and nothing calms him down. Even those 'drops' I read about don't do shit—squat. Sorry."

She flicked her hand in a way that suggested she wasn't very sorry.

"Curse away—it's your place." He offered a smile meant to comfort, but she started chewing on her thumbnail.

From the looks of things, Gentry had no help around the house. She didn't wear a ring on her left hand, either, so her baby's dad might not be overly involved.

He knew a little something about the hardship faced by a single mom. Although his parents had been married, his father had traveled the world, saving others, leaving Ian's mother alone to raise him for long stretches of time. "Does he have reflux?"

"Not that I know of." She frowned. "The doctor never tested for it or anything. Is that even something an eight-week-old can get?"

"It's possible."

She continued biting her nails.

Ian examined Colt's chest and watched him breathe, seeing no overt signs of respiratory distress—no sucking in under the ribs, no blue-tinted skin. Still, Sara had mentioned Colt's preemie status, and Ian knew enough to know that, with infants, things could change quickly.

The other thing he knew—Gentry wasn't as calm and collected as she wanted to appear. Few new mothers were, and this one looked like she'd barely survived a zombie apocalypse. Dealing with any infant, let alone a colicky one, was challenging.

An unexpected swell of empathy arose, softening the edges of his harsh opinions.

"Nothing's setting off alarms, but there's a slight chest rattle you should monitor tonight."

She closed her eyes and tucked her chin. "So Sara was right?"

He watched her defeated expression pinch with worry even as she stifled a yawn. Without rest, she'd end up sick, too. "You look like you could use a little break. Go lie down for a bit. I'll keep an eye on Colt."

"Why would you do that?" Just like that, her guard went back up.

"Because that's what I do." From the time he could walk, his mom and dad had taught him how to read a situation and offer assistance. And anytime he thought of his dad, who'd died trying to save others, his heart washed in a mix of pride and sorrow.

"Sara says that about you. She thinks you're a superhero." Gentry narrowed her eyes a tad, hip already cocked. "I don't believe in superheroes."

The hint of coyness in her husky voice affected him in a primal way he couldn't escape. "I'm no superhero. Perhaps Prince Charming, though."

Her lips quirked; her eyes glittered with humor. Tickling her funny bone made him feel . . . something. Something better than he'd been feeling these past couple of days while he'd been trying to regroup. Something he didn't quite understand.

"Since Sara vouches for you, I guess I can trust you."

"An Eagle Scout at your service." When he lifted Colt up to his chest, Gentry's cocky expression slipped. "You can trust me."

She came close enough that he could feel her warmth. She kissed Colt's head and then looked Ian in the eye. "I'll take a quick shower and maybe rest for fifteen minutes."

"Take your time."

She wandered toward the hallway. Before she disappeared around the corner, she stopped, hand on the wall, and turned toward him. Despite her dirty robe and unwashed hair, her posture and bearing rivaled any princess. "Thank you."

He nodded.

Thirty minutes later, with Gentry's catnap having turned into a deep slumber, Ian had found the formula and bottles—which hadn't been difficult because they were sitting out on the counter along with almost everything else. He fed the boy, burped him, and changed his diaper. When the kid wouldn't keep still against his chest, Ian strolled onto the deck, hoping a change of temperature and scenery might do some good.

Even in June, nighttime temperatures around Lake Sandy often dipped into the fifties. Tonight was no exception. A gentle breeze seemed to catch Colt by surprise, causing him to go still and stop whining. Surrounded by the music of a thousand crickets, Ian swayed back and forth like a human cradle as he looked down the hill toward the lake.

The murky-blue light from the half moon cast the forested slope in animated shadows. Leafy trees murmured in the summer wind, calming the infant, who seemed to be burrowing into Ian's soft chambray shirt. The million-dollar view had to be beautiful in daylight, but Ian preferred the peacefulness of nighttime. He didn't get much peace and quiet in Haiti, where he'd spent the majority of his time this past year training others for disaster preparedness and, more recently, working with Archer, Stanley Delbeau, and Sainte Michel Hospital administrators to structure their venture.

There he spent muggy nights huddled on a net-covered bed, listening to the tinny buzz of mosquitoes and the eerie beat of the distant drumming from mysterious, off-limits voodoo ceremonies. Those things might've made sleep impossible if it hadn't been for the effects of overwhelming exhaustion.

Here in Oregon, he never experienced that bone-deep kind of tired, which wasn't a surprise. If anything, whenever stateside, he felt a bit twitchy, like he knew he had someplace more important to be. Someplace where he had a million chances to improve others' lives and carry out his father's mission.

His father's legacy called to him on a constant basis. And when he was out there serving others, his nightmare—the memory of the last time he'd seen his father, when he'd lost him in the aftermath of the Haitian earthquake—always subsided.

Farrah had never gotten that. She'd pretended to in the beginning, but she'd grown tired of being alone so often. Impatient to begin the future and family she wanted. Now that Ian was single again, he could fully commit to memorializing the man who'd meant everything to him, without guilt.

Somewhere beneath the deck, he heard a wild animal foraging. A raccoon, perhaps. He realized then that Colt had actually fallen asleep against his chest. He opened the door and stepped back inside. Guessing that the baby's bassinet was in Gentry's room, he settled Colt in the playpen set up in the space between the living and dining rooms.

Had the slight rattle he'd heard earlier been temporarily been relieved by the cold air? He gently touched the back of his hand to Colt's head. Still warm despite having just been outside.

He frowned and looked over his shoulder toward Gentry's bedroom. She was bushed. He should let her sleep.

With nothing better to do, he began folding the various blankets and stacking the photographs of Colt and empty frames scattered across the massive glass dining table. A little unexpected help went a long way toward lightening the load for people under stress. Although this Lake Sandy condo was far from a true disaster zone, he had no doubt that Gentry Cabot was in over her head.

Chapter Two

Baffling

According to *Merriam-Webster*: extremely confusing or difficult to understand

According to me: Ian Crawford

Gentry bolted upright in her bed and gasped as if she'd broken through Lake Sandy's surface in search of oxygen. The red numbers of the digital clock read 5:36. Eight-plus hours of uninterrupted sleep. What the hell had happened to Colt?

She tossed the covers aside and bounded to his bassinet. *Empty!* Without another thought, she ran—bare feet chilled by the cold walnut floors—to the living room, then stopped short.

Was it possible to be disoriented and confused because of *more* sleep? She shook her head to wake herself up.

The barest light in the sky came through the huge windows, giving her a clear view of the space. The *clean* space. Blankets neatly folded beside the sofa. Half-empty bottles removed. Playthings tucked away behind an oversize chair. The aroma of freshly brewed coffee wafting through the air.

Mm-mm.

Wait . . . what?

The hairs on her arms tingled all at once as she became aware of someone's presence. She spun slowly to her left, breath held, as if she'd been dropped into a bizarre dream. One that smelled good.

Ian stood in her kitchen—her spotless kitchen—pouring himself a cup of coffee. Rumpled shirt and hair, sleepy eyes. The early-morning moment thrust an unexpected intimacy upon them even as she tried to process the fact that he'd stayed the night.

In a tone that barely rose above a whisper, he said, "Good morning."

He wouldn't quite look at her, though. An odd duck, that one. No judgment there. She'd always liked odd ducks, being one herself.

"Where's my son?" The muscles in her neck tightened with impatience and a touch of panic.

He held his index finger to his lips to remind her to keep quiet. "Sleeping," he said, pointing toward the playpen.

She tiptoed into the living room and peeked into the Pack 'n Play, where her cherub lay on his back, eyes closed. Although she heard a slight hiss with each breath, he looked so angelic. Her heart swelled from the rush of love filling it like a water balloon.

She leaned over the railing, almost brushing his velvety cheek with her fingers, but caught herself before accidentally waking him.

Her heart rate slowed just enough for her thoughts to settle. The quiet moment in her newly cleaned condo—an unbelievable luxury—prompted the urge to yawn and stretch. Another incredible extravagance.

Her entire body felt nimble, thanks to the much-needed rest. Only after she scratched her side did she realize she'd raced out of her bedroom wearing nothing but a silky tank top and underpants. Super-skimpy ones.

She tried to glance down at her chest without moving her head. It took about half a second to see clear evidence of the morning chill in the air. If the coffee hadn't yet awakened Ian, her "headlights" and tattoos probably had.

Gentry wasn't falsely modest. Most of the time she would happily preen half-naked in front of a guy. She admitted, without shame, that she liked turning them on, too. But in this case, she hadn't meant to shock or seduce Ian. The fact that he might think she had, embarrassed her, which was sort of remarkable in itself. Not that she'd let him know.

She strolled into the kitchen, head held high, gaze direct. "Prince Charming *and* a fairy godmother. Rarer than a purple unicorn."

"Huh?" He scratched the back of his neck and then pretended to find something interesting to stare at in his coffee mug.

Most men she'd known would ogle her and then proposition her. Not this one. Ian's eyes darted all around the kitchen in a chivalrous attempt *not* to stare at her boobs. How endearing.

"Thank you"—she waved around the kitchen—"for all this. For cleaning and, it seems, taking care of my son all night."

"You're welcome." He looked into her eyes again, but not before his gaze dipped—for an instant—to her chest. Finally, he gave up and gestured up and down with his hand. "Maybe you want to put your robe on?"

"If it makes you more comfortable." She shrugged and turned away, only releasing a relieved sigh and breaking into a trot once he couldn't see her. After pulling on a pair of pajama pants and a T-shirt, she returned. "I didn't mean to fall asleep and stick you with Colt all night."

"I know." He set his empty mug in the sink. "It's fine. It seemed like you could use the help."

Great. Now he, like everyone else, thought her inept.

She imagined his running internal commentary all night: Didn't take her kid to the doctor—check. Messy house—check. Abandoned her son for a few hours' sleep—check. Before she could form a reply, he said, "My mom was sort of a single mom for long stretches, so I know how hard it can be."

Oh. Better. So much so that, if she were a different kind of woman, she might've become teary from that validation, however inflated it might be.

Gentry cleared her throat, teetering like a paddleboarder on rough water. "Well, can I tell Sara she inconvenienced you for nothing?"

He rubbed his jaw before crossing his arms. "I wouldn't call it an emergency, but you should probably take him to the doctor. There's still a slight rattle in his chest, and his temperature is still elevated."

"Shoot." She glanced over her shoulder. "Is it serious?"

"I wouldn't ignore it and give it a chance to become a bigger problem."

"I'd planned to put him in day care starting tomorrow." She said it aloud, talking to herself more than to him. Hunter and her mom probably anticipated a last-minute excuse for pushing back her start date at work. She'd hate to prove them right.

That said, she hadn't fully reconciled returning to work when she herself had resented being raised by nannies. At the same time, she wanted to be a good role model of ambition and goal setting for Colt. Although a corporate career required her to subdue herself for eight hours each day, it also regularly involved her with her family—a real first for her, and a "must" for Colt's sake.

"Well, I'll get out of your hair." Ian scrubbed his face while yawning.

"Wait!" Gentry exclaimed without thinking. Speaking with an adult in the morning—especially one with kind eyes and a broad chest—had been a pleasurable change of pace. "Can I make you breakfast?"

"No need. I ought to go." He grinned.

As if he had to be somewhere important by six o'clock in the morning. She supposed he was sick of babysitting. Or likely needed to catch up on some sleep. Her sofa's sleek style kicked ass, but it wouldn't make for the most comfortable mattress for someone his height.

"Okay. Can I pay you for everything you did? I hear the going rate for sitters is, like, twenty dollars an hour. And you cleaned!"

"No, thanks. I'm good."

His frowny-faced response made her feel stupid. She hadn't meant to insult him, but she didn't want to be a leech, either. "Sorry, I just . . . a full night's sleep was an amazing gift. I feel so good I might finally get around to framing my photos today. I don't know how to repay you, but let me try."

Tit for tat. Give and take.

She didn't like owing a debt.

A little sparkle lit his eye. "Well, I did see you in your undies. How about we call it even?"

Her cheeks got hot. Flustering people was *her* job, not the other way around. She wasn't sure if she liked being taunted, although her tummy fluttered in a not-unpleasant way. *That* made her more embarrassed. Since when had she become so hard up for attention?

"Wait a sec. Now I think you got the better end of the deal." Ego salved by a quick comeback. Good. Balance restored.

"It's possible." He smiled fully for the first time since they'd met. He had nice lips and exactly the right amount of scruff around his jaw. Maybe even the start of a dimple on his left cheek. His sage-green eyes had an "old soul" quality.

She doubted that the sun at her back caused her intense warmth. Then Colt woke with a start, and the sudden spark between Ian and her fizzled.

"That's my cue," Ian sighed. She recognized that tired sigh, because her son, while adorable, wore everyone out. A lot like his mother.

"Chicken." She smirked, desperately wishing for another option. Ian intrigued her, and that never happened. She wished he'd hang out for longer than ten minutes.

But she'd better get used to life as a single mom, because the number of men who'd line up to date her in her present circumstances would be about zero. She turned to lift Colt out of the playpen and then kissed his head and cheeks.

"Good morning, bugaboo. Are we going to have a nice day today? Mommy wants to go for a walk by the lake. Will be you be a good boy in the stroller? No crying, please? Pretty please?" She rubbed her nose against his belly and reveled in his gurgling coos.

Ian had made his way to the entry but had stopped to watch her.

Taking hold of Colt's little arm, she waved it. "Say 'bye-bye' to Ian. Bye-bye!"

Ian nodded and then, without another word, walked out the door.

Bye-bye.

The condo dimmed in his absence.

She could feel sorry for herself, or she could leave a message with the pediatrician to schedule an appointment. Resigned to her fate, she went to the kitchen to fix Colt a bottle, left a message with the doctor, then changed Colt's diaper and prayed she could get a little morning walk in before he started fussing.

On her way out the door, her mother called. Gentry answered mostly to prevent an uninvited drop-in. "Hi, Mom."

"Good morning." The surprise in her mother's voice was no doubt intended to make Gentry feel bad for not having returned her recent call. In truth, Gentry couldn't take any more of her mom's parenting advice.

Her mom, who'd been ghostlike during Gentry's childhood, suddenly thought herself an expert on mothering. It took every ounce of Gentry's patience—which, granted, wasn't much to begin with—to keep sarcasm from her voice.

Nasty barbs had been their preferred mode of communication for most of their relationship. But since becoming a mother herself, Gentry was trying to be more mature, even if it killed her.

"I'm literally on my way out the door with Colt."

"Why don't you swing by the house? Your father and I would love to see the little button . . . and you, of course."

Of course.

"We'll see. I'm waiting to hear from the doctor's office. Colt's got a bit of a cold, and I want to take him in to get checked."

"Is it serious?" Genuine concern colored her tone.

"I can't tell. That's why I want to go."

"If he's sick, you can't put him in day care tomorrow." Her mom clucked. "I wish you'd have gotten a nanny like I suggested."

Gentry closed her eyes and drew a deep breath. *One. Two. Three. Release . . .* "Miss Linda's will be like a home away from home. I want him to be with other kids, not alone most of the day."

She'd specifically picked Miss Linda's for its intimate in-home setting.

"He's an infant, Gentry." It sounded as if her mother had rolled her eyes when she said that. "A fussy one. He'll be in a crib all day."

Gentry shook her head even though no one but Colt would see her. "So-o-o, like I said, I'm on my way out. I'll call you after the doctor appointment and let you know if I'll be at work tomorrow."

"Another reason to hire a nanny. Kids get sick often. You won't get ahead if you call out all the time. You need someone at home to manage Colt so you can earn everyone's respect at work."

At least this time she hadn't added a quip about Smith. Gorgeous, charming, half-drunk Smith. To be fair, Gentry had been drunk, too.

Thinking of him always made her stop for a second. Who, and where, was he, and would he want to know about his son? Was he a good guy who *deserved* to know Colt? Should she try to find him to give her son more family? Naturally, she never voiced those thoughts to a soul, let alone her mother.

"I'll manage my son fine, thanks. Tell Dad hi." Gentry pressed "End" and tossed her phone in the back of the stroller.

Nothing got under her skin and drove up her spine faster than her mother's unsolicited advice. The worst part, though? Her mom wasn't exactly wrong. A nanny who could also help around the house like Ian had would certainly make Gentry's life a little easier. But she felt sure Colt would be happier in the long run with the other kids at Miss Linda's.

Whatever brief respite her morning had offered, every cell in her body now buzzed with negative energy. She adjusted her lululemon cropped pants and neon Jogbra, then fastened Colt into the stroller.

He, however, had reached the limit of his ability to be awake without fussing, and began to wriggle and cry when she adjusted the buckles. For what she'd spent on this contraption, it should be able to buckle her son in on its own and solve her other problems, too.

She didn't know if her anxiety caused Colt's cycle of tears or if, like her, he naturally rebelled against being told what to do. Either way, she was screwed.

◆ ◆ ◆

Whenever visiting Portland, which wasn't often or ever for very long, Ian made a point of meeting his mother at the Clackamas United Church of Christ on Sundays. The building's funky shape—resembling a sort of towering but warped tepee—reached right up to heaven. Inside, its wood plank and beamed ceilings lent a cozy feel to the lofty space. A narrow, modern stained-glass window that had to be at least twenty-some-feet high filtered pale-blue light onto the altar.

Sitting in those pews reminded him of his youth. Of the hours he'd spent here with his parents, who'd volunteered to help with every function and fund-raiser, always reaching out to assist people in need. His dad might as well have been a king for how well loved and respected he'd been in this congregation. Ian presumed his father now watched over it like a guardian angel. Exactly the way the man had approached life on earth, too.

"Can I crash in the basement for a week or two?" Ian asked his mom, who'd taken him to lunch after the service. He shoved a french fry in his mouth, having craved comfort food while in Haiti. Going months at a time without it excused his current gluttony.

"I wish you could, but the shelter is strictly for women and children. Even if it weren't a rule, your presence might make some residents uncomfortable." She patted his jaw like she'd done since he was about six. "Can't you stay at the motel until you return to Haiti?"

"Guess I don't have a choice." Ninety bucks a night added up quickly when one didn't have an income or savings to speak of. He needed a quick influx of cash so he could return to his project.

He'd blown the very last of his savings on the ticket home to collect his things from Farrah's place. He didn't own much, but he couldn't risk her tossing the baseball he'd caught with his dad at the inaugural Mariners game at Safeco Field, or the handwoven wool *mochila* he'd been given by a young girl in Colombia after he'd assisted her family following that massive mudslide.

"If you need a little extra cash, I can help." His mom narrowed her gaze like she did whenever she thought she'd read his mind. Years of practice made her pretty damn good at it.

"Nah." Ian dragged another fry through the glob of ketchup on his plate, wishing that had been easier to say. Being broke sucked, but he wouldn't tax his mom, either. He'd figure it out on his own. While here in the States, he'd seek some new donors for his project, too.

On a personal level, he'd never much cared about money, preferring the freedom to fly off to the next natural disaster whenever possible. To make ends meet, he'd routinely taken short-term home-care gigs and done volunteer EMT shifts for a small stipend—enough to cover rent on a tiny studio in a lousy part of town.

Then Farrah had invited him to live with her, which had been a nice upgrade. He'd contributed what he could when he could. Her initial attitude toward his priorities had lasted long enough for him to get comfortable and believe she was a woman like his mom, who could handle a relationship with a man much like his dad. But once Farrah had realized she'd never change him—never persuade him to take a full-time job stateside—she'd handed him walking papers. Via text, no less.

"You sure?" His mom tilted her head to the left, gentle smile in place.

"You know me. I'll scrounge up some cash to get by till I leave."

She nodded, her gaze growing distant. "I think Farrah will regret her decision."

"Doubtful. I let her down. I missed a lot of things that she asked me to attend, like her cousin's wedding and her family's Easter brunch." He carried some shame about that because Farrah had been good to him and deserved better.

"It's not like she was alone, Ian. She would've been surrounded by family at those events." His mother reached out and squeezed his hand. Although only sixty, she looked older. She'd never had an easy life. The years of honest but hard work had crisscrossed her face and neck with fine wrinkles and turned her brown hair a pretty shade of silver.

"I shouldn't have made promises I couldn't keep." Flying back and forth every six weeks had been expensive and exhausting. Farrah couldn't join him because of her teaching job, which included summer school programs. "If I'd only been doing regular relief work, we might've made it work. But once I hooked up with Archer and Stanley and got serious about founding the Crawford Volunteer Ambulance Corps, the writing was on the wall." Of course, he had no intention of giving up those plans now. C-VAC would be a reality soon, south of Port-au-Prince, in Jacmel.

Looking back, his biggest mistake had been trying to make her happy by sinking the bulk of his meager savings into a ring this past winter. A ring she'd kept even after she'd kicked him out. The fact that the wasted money distressed him more than the breakup said a lot about that relationship. About him, too, if he was being honest.

The whole experience taught him that long distances and love don't mix.

As if reading his thoughts, his mom said, "When you feel lonely or have doubts, remember, with the right partner, you *can* have a home and a family, just like your father did." She shot him a mother-knows-best look before taking her first bite of apple pie.

The warm pie's cinnamon aroma made his mouth water.

"There aren't many women like you, Mom." He grabbed a fork and snatched a bite of her pie for himself. *Oh man, that was good.*

She reached across the table to pat his hand. "I'm no paragon. I had my moments, especially when you were very young. But when you love someone, you make sacrifices."

The tone of her voice struck him sideways. Both of his parents had preached about sacrifice since Ian could walk. He enjoyed helping others, but sometimes a selfish side of him dreamed of indulgence. Of freedom from "the Crawford way." In fact, those thoughts had spurred the argument he'd had with his dad just before his father had died. That he'd died being bitterly disappointed in Ian haunted him.

"Your dad would be so proud of what you're doing in Haiti. I know I am. After everything he gave to the world, it's wonderful to think that his name and mission will go on." Her eyes misted with memories, but Ian didn't deserve her praise. Not when he'd kept the argument between his father and him those final forty-eight hours a secret all these years.

"I've got big shoes to fill." He recalled the trips they'd taken to Central America, South America, and the Caribbean. Then his thoughts circled back to their last one.

It should've been him, not his dad, who'd rushed back into that unstable building in search of more survivors. If they hadn't been locked in their own cold war—if he had acted instead—his mom wouldn't have been a young widow. She wouldn't be so alone in the world, and Ian wouldn't live with such regret. He winced, shying away from the shame.

"Let's change the subject." He took a long swallow of soda through a straw. "I saw your friend Sara last night."

"Oh?" She sat back after pushing the remains of her pie toward him. "Where?"

Ian polished off her pie while explaining the circumstances behind Sara's call, and how he'd spent his night. Naturally, he omitted some details, like Gentry's lacy panties that left almost nothing to the imagination. He'd been trying not to think of those all morning, actually. At one point during church, he'd been trying so hard not to think about them he was sure the devil himself would reach up and pull him under.

"Oh, the poor thing. New moms are overwhelmed. And a single mom, well, she's also desperate." Gloria smiled at her son. She'd said it so sincerely it almost made him believe there'd been a time when she hadn't been competent and assured . . . if a little weary. "You're a good man, Ian Crawford."

He winked at her. "Thanks to you, maybe."

"No maybes. For sure." She set forty dollars on the table. "Sorry to rush off, but I need to get back to the Angel House. You okay?"

"Yeah." He stood, reluctant to return to the no-man's-land of the lonely motel, with its stiff polyester bedding and vinyl chair. A stark contrast to the suede sofa and walnut floors in Gentry's condo, but an upgrade from most of the makeshift accommodations he'd called home while out in the field. "No worries. I'll talk to you tomorrow."

His mom kissed him goodbye when they reached her nine-year-old red Honda. After she put-putted away, he wandered next door to the convenience store and bought himself a local paper.

A bunch of older kids wandered the aisles, grabbing candy, chips, and soda while horsing around, oblivious to the advantages of these stores. Within arm's length, you could buy first-aid supplies, nourishment, and oil for your car. People in impoverished countries might literally kill for this stuff that everyone here took for granted.

He shook off the thought and then strolled several blocks, newspaper tucked under his arm, enjoying the summer sunshine. He paused at Bilquist Elementary. The single-story brick-and-glass building hadn't changed much, other than a new coat of royal-blue paint on sections of its exterior. He suspected the inside smelled exactly as it had decades ago and that those scents could unlock many memories.

How many schoolmates still lived around here? What might his life be like if his parents hadn't indoctrinated him into the Crawford way? Questions without answers.

He sighed before continuing his stroll, unsure what had him so keyed up this morning. He didn't miss Farrah—at least, not the way he should. In truth, they'd spent more time apart than they had together, which was why she'd dumped him, and probably why he didn't mourn the loss like he should.

Ian mourned a different loss—that of the hope that he *could* have it all, like his mom believed.

He kept walking until he got to Heddie Notz Park, then took a seat at a picnic table shaded by a copse of maples. Forty feet away, several young kids scaled the jungle gym. Their moms conversed on the nearby benches or sat with their noses practically touching their smartphones.

A gentle summer breeze whistled through the leaves overhead, its peaceful sound often punctured by a child's laughter or shout. None of those cheerful sounds drowned out the voices of two chatty moms.

"I'm glad Cindy's not here droning on about her diet and yoga obsessions. For God's sake, let me eat my brownie in peace, right?" The blonde sipped something topped with whipped cream, from Starbucks.

The brunette nodded. "She should focus her energy on Bobby. That kid needs help. He's such a loner."

"Not my problem. I've got enough to deal with at home with my three." The blonde set her now-empty cup on the ground beside her feet. "Hey, who cleans your house? I need to find someone new, but I hate that search process."

Ian snorted before he could stop himself, which drew a sharp look from the blonde.

"Is there a problem?" she asked.

He shook his head, his gaze steady but pleasant. "No, ma'am. Allergies."

She looked skeptical of his white lie, proving she wasn't an idiot even if she seemed like a pill. She turned back to her friend, but not before he heard her mutter "Asshole."

Yeah, well . . . maybe. Like many of his humanitarian compatriots, he struggled with an intolerance for whining, because he'd witnessed years of high-stakes pain and suffering. He might be a little worse than most, but come *on*, people.

The mothers in low-income and disaster-stricken countries didn't have smartphones and cleaning crews. Yet somehow he knew they'd appreciate a sunny, carefree day enough to stay present rather than complain or scroll through Facebook.

Whatever. He had to focus on his own situation so he could get back to where he belonged. Turning his back on the women, he unfolded the newspaper on the tabletop and perused the headlines.

Not much had changed since the last time he'd been home. Another article about the much-debated coal terminal project along the Columbia River. A suspicious warehouse fire that, fortunately, hadn't injured anyone. The seller-friendly residential real estate market. A typical week in a typical American city.

He tried to imagine staying put and reading that same news every day. Keeping a steady job at a local hospital. Waking up to an alarm clock instead of a rooster, rushing asthmatics to the ER, and making small talk at a cocktail party with women like the ones at his back. So-called normalcy had been something he'd wished for in the weeks before his father had died. Then his world had turned upside down, and he'd assumed his father's mantle to cope with his grief. Now he could barely recall the young man he'd been or remember why he'd thought he'd be happier with a quiet life.

He flipped to the classifieds.

Hard to say what was more depressing—the lack of overall jobs or the lack of options for a guy like him. He'd hoped for a temporary home health-care position—sadly, those few ads sought at least a three-month commitment. That would kill the momentum he, Stanley, and Archer had going now. One month—max—would be ideal. He'd amass some money and do some networking, then head back to Jacmel.

He refolded the paper and tossed it in the trash. From the corner of his eye, he saw a redhead with a toddler enter the playground from the opposite side from which he was leaving. They reminded him of Gentry and Colt.

Gentry Cabot. He'd thought he had her pegged, but she'd surprised him in the nanoseconds she let her guard down. Or maybe her underwear had blinded him to her flaws. Guys were easy that way, and he wouldn't pretend to be above those baser instincts when it came to women and sex.

He smiled, remembering the firm curve of her ass. That image would stay with him for quite some time, considering the lacy thong didn't leave much to the imagination. Her legs were probably as long as his, too. And as stellar as her backside had been, it had been her chest that had made him nearly fall to his knees. Maybe because the too-small tank had covered just enough to allow his imagination to run wild. Or maybe because the cup of her breasts perfectly matched the curve of her bottom. Heavy, yet pert. He could almost feel them in his hands now.

He stopped and shook his head, stunned by the effect of the vivid daydream.

Now *that*—not his earlier snort—was the jerkiest thing he'd thought today. Objectifying a poor woman who could barely fend for herself, let alone deal with her fussy kid.

He wondered about Colt's diagnosis, then wondered why he cared. In all probability, he'd never see them again. As much as curiosity poked at his conscience, he had his own troubles to sort out, and Gentry Cabot wasn't one of them.

Chapter Three

Ingenious

According to *Merriam-Webster*: marked by originality, resourcefulness, and cleverness in conception or execution

According to me: me!

Dr. Evans—or the "Cucumber," as Gentry thought of her, thanks to her cool temperament—kept one hand pressed to Colt's head and peered into his left ear through her otoscope. She didn't frown or hasten her examination despite his spastic wailing. "Mm."

"'Mm,' what?" Gentry hovered, chewing her thumbnail, desperate for a diagnosis with a cure, unlike his colic. Seeing Colt shivering in pain, or fear—or both—made her want to scoop him into her arms. Did all babies look so cold in a doctor's office?

The Cucumber remained focused, turning Colt's tiny head to inspect his other ear, acting as if he weren't causing a chain reaction of screams among the children in the adjoining exam rooms. Gentry half expected the life-size giraffe wall sticker to start curling at the edges.

Oh, Colt. What can we do for you, Boo?

"He's got an ear infection." Dr. Evans tossed the throwaway plastic tip in the trash before returning the instrument to the wall unit that housed that blood pressure cuff and other stuff. "You can dress him now."

She then sank onto the black vinyl swivel stool and rolled to her desk where she retrieved a prescription pad.

Thank God. Medicine meant a cure. A cure promised some measure of relief for Colt . . . and possibly for her, too.

She managed to get Colt's frenzied limbs back into his onesie, then cradled him to her chest and swayed. "How'd he get it? He's hardly exposed to other people."

"Babies are susceptible to a lot of things. He has a little cold, and that could've caused the infection. Infants are on their backs a lot, and because their canals are so small, they don't drain as well. Given his colic, it's no surprise you didn't notice unusual crankiness sooner." She tore the script from the pad and smiled.

Perhaps the Cucumber had intended to make Gentry feel less incompetent with that excuse, but it had the opposite effect. Other mothers—ones like Sara—would've known right away. Just like every day since he'd been born, Gentry had failed him in some way. Each day it became harder to stop second-guessing herself and her choices.

She glanced at the handwriting on the prescription. "I thought antibiotics weren't good for kids."

"If Colt were six months or older, I might recommend other options. But with infants, we like to knock it out before it gets worse. Hopefully, he won't be prone to these infections in the coming years." She placed Colt's chart in the bin the nurses managed. "Antibiotics for ten days. He should start feeling better in a day or two. If you can raise one side of his mattress, that will help with the drainage."

A day or two? Dear God, that sounded brutally long. She nuzzled her son's fine hair, her heart sore from his pain. "So I guess I shouldn't put him in day care until he's better, huh?"

That meant no work for her. An image of Hunter's disappointed scowl flashed. Gentry kissed Colt's head, rocking him to no avail. Did he feed off *her* anxiety, or was it the other way around?

"Most centers prohibit kids with fevers. Colt's temperature is still elevated, so I'd keep him home for a few days." Dr. Evans's tight grip on the doorknob subtly revealed that, despite her serene voice, her nerves were frayed from spending ten minutes with Colt. "Infants in day care tend to catch more colds than those at home. Some argue that it can build the immune system faster, but you want to take precautions, like disinfecting anything he plays with and such. Also, be on the lookout for sick kids when you go there. If the center you chose doesn't manage that well, you might want to switch."

Oh joy. Perfect setup for at least one "I told you so" from her mom.

"Thanks." Gentry followed Dr. Evans out of the exam room, cradling her wailing son, and walked directly into the sight line of three other moms and their kids.

The women, dressed in stretchy yoga pants, and busy wrestling toddlers who were acting more like monkeys than kids, wore expressions ranging from contempt to pity.

Well, screw them. Colt may be loud, but he was still perfect.

She forced herself to smile, grateful that she'd managed to wear a chic summer Rag & Bone halter dress and kick-ass platform sandals. Chin up, she breezed by, beaming at Colt as if his cries were akin to Beethoven's "Ode to Joy," and then headed directly to CVS.

After suffering through a Muzak rendition of George Michael's "Father Figure" during a painful wait in the miles-long line at the pharmacy counter, she finally got home and administered the first dose. Thankfully, Colt had worn himself out. She put him down in his bassinet after raising one side.

Grabbing the remote from her nightstand, she then rolled down the blackout shades. Her eyes adjusted to the darkened room enough to allow her to enjoy watching Colt's body and mouth twitch as he fell off to sleep.

The bottomless love in her heart terrified her. She'd never cared this much for anything. That made her fear of screwing up—something she'd never much worried about before—unbearable. Between Colt's chronic pain and constant crying, she had yet to experience the sustained joyfulness that motherhood brought others. Someday. Soon. *Please.*

For now, she'd try to escape her bedroom without waking him. Something of a quandary, actually. Maybe she should nap instead of risk the door click waking him. Having slept well last night, she didn't need a nap. She needed to solve her work problem pronto, and then finally frame those photos.

She crept from the bedroom on her tiptoes. Once she reached the living room, she flopped onto the sofa cushions, sprawling out like a lazy teen, and enjoyed the debris-free space.

Ian had been a godsend, and a gorgeous one at that. One that had stirred up all kinds of unsettling sensations. Like her son's tummy trouble, hers she'd suffer without any cure. How long did one have to go without sex to be considered a virgin again? Now *that* was something to cry about. *Abstinence-induced colic.* She snickered.

Thinking of Ian reminded her of her promise to give Sara an update. Gentry might as well embrace the productive way to procrastinate about telling Hunter she wouldn't be back at work tomorrow.

"Gentry, how's Colt?" Sara answered without preamble.

"Ear infection." Gentry closed her eyes, determined to sound confident instead of contrite, even in the face of proof that Colt might've been better off under Sara's care. "You were right to suggest calling Ian. Thanks."

"I'm glad he could help."

Gentry doubted Ian had followed up with Sara or told her that he'd spent the night. "He was very helpful."

It had been beyond wonderful to have an extra set of eyes and ears . . . and hands. Women with husbands or partners were lucky. She'd kill for that kind of support.

"I'll tell him you said so," Sara said.

"Oh?" Gentry sat up, alert and slightly hot. "You're seeing him today?"

"Maybe." A shuffling noise came through the phone, and Gentry could hear Ty in the background. "Hunter's home to watch Ty, so I'm running errands, getting a haircut. I plan to swing by the Angel House with some donations, too. Ian might be there visiting his mom. If not, I can pass the message along."

Ian's cool green eyes and scruffy jaw from this morning flickered in Gentry's memory. Her mouth went kind of dry. *How stupid!* Ian Crawford was a reputable man—almost too good—and in no way the right guy for her.

She'd detected a hint of wry humor beneath that serious demeanor, but he didn't seem like a man who liked to have fun. Gentry craved fun and hopefully would have some, one day soon, before she forgot how.

Ian also had no sense of fashion. No money. And no interest in her—well, no real interest. He *had* been a little affected by her near-naked body. But a man would have to be dead not to, she conceded. In any case, she'd be a fool to pine for a guy so obviously ill-suited to her lifestyle.

If she *were* to bring a man into Colt's life, it should probably be Smith. But finding him when she had no idea where to begin could prove impossible. And there were risks. Normally, risks wouldn't bother her, but when it came to her son, she couldn't afford to be impulsive.

In the meantime, she could use help. If she recalled, Ian could use housing.

"Sara, do you have Ian's number? I promised him an update, too." A harmless white lie.

"Sure. I'll text it to you." Another loud noise rang out, followed by the sound of Hunter's scolding voice. Ty must've broken something. A hint of things to come in Gentry's life a year or two from now. Perhaps she should've decorated her condo with foam padding and shag carpets instead of glass and stone. "Oh, shoot. Gentry, I've got to go. If you need anything, let me know. I'm happy to help."

"I'm good. Don't forget to text me!" Gentry wasn't sure if Sara heard that last part until five minutes later, when her phone pinged.

She stared at the number. It'd be bold—rarely a deterrent. He'd be shocked, which she usually enjoyed. Yet Ian was honest *and* an EMT. The best possible temporary nanny until Colt was well enough to go to Miss Linda's.

Decision made, she dialed him. To her surprise, he answered, despite not recognizing the caller. What kind of person answered anonymous calls these days?

"Hello?"

His rich voice sounded sexier than she remembered, probably because she wasn't distracted by her own appearance or embarrassment. Her gut responded with a chorus of flutters. She flexed her toes. "Hi, Ian. It's Gentry Cabot."

"Oh, hi." His voice jumped a key or two. "Is something wrong with Colt?"

Gentry grinned at his concern. "No. He has a cold and an ear infection. Nothing respiratory."

"That's good."

She paused because she didn't know how to begin. Ian struck her as a guy's guy, unlikely to consider himself perfect nanny material. With each millisecond, she felt more foolish sitting there tongue-tied. No one who knew her would believe it.

"Is there something else?" he asked when the silence dragged on.

"Actually, yes." *Deep breath and then go for it.* "I'm supposed to return to work tomorrow, but with Colt's fever, I can't drop him at day care. Sara had mentioned that you were temporarily stuck in a motel. I can offer you seven hundred fifty dollars per week and a free place to live if you'll watch Colt while I'm at work. It'd be temporary—like a few weeks—until he can safely go to day care."

She closed her eyes and held her breath, picturing Ian's face. He'd probably grimaced in horror. She opened her eyes when that vision made her stomach twist in an unpleasant way. "Ian?"

"Um," he hesitated, blowing out a breath and a derisive chuckle. "Sure. Why not?"

On the surface, she should be thrilled. She would be, in fact, if it weren't for his self-mocking tone.

"Gee, don't be too excited." She covered her mouth, shaking her head. She needed his help more than he wanted hers.

"Sorry." He cleared his throat. "It's perfect, actually. I need something temporary. I'm returning to Haiti at the first opportunity."

That wasn't exactly news to her. It shouldn't matter at all, yet the living room seemed suddenly gloomy despite the sunlight pouring in through the windows. "Great. Come over anytime today. The guest room is upstairs, so you'll have some privacy. Er, to a degree, anyway. There's no escaping Colt's crying."

"I picked up on that already." His tone shifted, sounding almost warm, like he didn't deem her son a nightmarish devil.

"Guess I'll see you a little later."

"I'll come by around six, if that works."

"Perfect. I'll try to get Colt down before then so we can talk. Thanks." She hung up and slunk back down into the cushions, one arm over her eyes.

As impulsive moves went, this was nothing new, yet her erratic heartbeat had only now resumed a normal rhythm. She smiled, welcoming the kind of eager anticipation she hadn't experienced in months. Help was on the way, and its packaging was no hardship.

Spirits renewed, she checked the baby monitor, then grabbed a yogurt, banana, and the mirror frames. Once she'd finished eating, she sorted through the photos and began to separate them while also thinking through a list of rules for Ian.

While framing, her thoughts turned toward the handsome rescuer on the way, and her devious, sex-depraved mind started to spin all kinds of scenarios that had nothing at all to do with Ian's abilities as a childcare giver. This could be trouble, or fun . . . or both. Before she had Colt, that combination had always been something Gentry relished. Her mischievousness came rushing back, like lyrics to an old song she hadn't sung in far too long.

◆ ◆ ◆

It took Ian less than ten minutes to pack his duffel bag. He then sat on the motel bed, blinking into space.

A nanny, no . . . a *manny*, for chrissakes. Not something he'd ever considered, but Gentry's offer had been otherwise perfect.

Temporary. Housing. Ready cash.

He'd do anything for that, including saddle himself to a colicky infant and his high-maintenance mother. In less than a month he'd have enough money for airfare and a little extra. Per his discussions with Archer, he'd go straight to Jacmel and oversee Stanley and the renovations to the cheap commercial property they'd recently leased. While still in Oregon, Ian would work on acquiring basic life-support ambulances.

This nanny gig would be fine as long as he and Gentry worked out boundaries in advance. Boundaries that should include a rule against waltzing around the house in underwear. Of course, he'd be lying if he pretended he wouldn't like to see that again. The recollection once again made him semihard.

He smirked at himself and shook his head. *Keep your cool.* If Farrah couldn't deal with Ian's choices, a woman like Gentry definitely couldn't put up with him and his lifestyle.

He'd approach this job like he did when training others for disaster work. Teach her some basics and establish systems she could maintain without him. At that point, he'd leave her and Colt better off than he'd found them, and then move on with his life.

Feeling better about his decision, he heaved the duffel over his shoulder and took an Uber to Lake Sandy.

As he approached the glossy black door, it occurred to him that he'd never lived anyplace this posh. An uncomfortable sensation took root, which seemed ironic, that something might be wrong with him, because he felt less anxious in a foreign land ravaged by disaster and disease than he did in an upper-class neighborhood in his hometown.

A memory of his father and him surfaced. Ian had been about eight. They'd been trolling a local neighborhood, knocking on doors to ask for pledge money for some walkathon, when they'd arrived at a newer home with a red Corvette parked in the driveway.

"Whoa!" Ian broke free of his dad's hold, ran to the shiny car, and peered in its window. He imagined its engine roaring to life, then bounced on his toes. "Dad, let's get a car like this one!"

His father watched him, wearing a slight frown. "Come on back. Let's remember our mission."

Ian returned to his father's side, but not without stealing several more glances at that Vette and picturing himself in it with its roof removed. So cool!

A woman answered the door, polite smile fixed on her face.

Ian's father had barely begun his spiel when she raised her hand. "Sorry, but I don't want to waste your time. We donate to other charities already. Can't do them all, you know."

"Of course. Have a nice day," Ian's father said before she closed the door.

He took Ian's hand and walked down the front walkway, then stopped on the sidewalk and turned toward the ruby-red stunner Ian so admired.

Together they stared at it just long enough for Ian to fantasize that his father might want one, too. Then his dad said, "Think about how many meals or clothes the money for that showy car might've purchased for the Burnside Shelter."

Without another word, his father ruffled Ian's hair and tugged him along to the next house.

Ian hadn't remembered that incident in years. Now he knocked on Gentry's door and waited, wondering—with an uneasy kind of anticipation—what life with Gentry Cabot would bring. It wouldn't be boring; that much was certain.

As soon as she opened the door, he heard Colt's whining in the distance. It didn't shock him that she'd failed to get him to sleep. On top of being sick, the kid seemed willful. "Hey."

She backed up and waved him in, her crooked, forced smile suggesting it had been another long day. "Welcome."

"Thanks." He stepped inside and looked around. In less than ten hours, the living room had nearly reverted to its former state. Gentry must have pulled out every toy and blanket in an effort to entertain her son. He also noted a half-eaten slice of pizza and open soda can on an end table.

She stepped around the stroller she'd parked in the entry and crossed to Colt. "I wish the medicine worked faster. This is torture!"

"Sorry." He stood there, awkwardly, unsure how to begin this new job. Then he remembered: establish trust—always step one. "Couldn't get him down?"

"No. He's not sleepy." She cuddled her son and looked at Ian with no small amount of exasperation.

"What if you put him in the bassinet and let him cry a bit? He'd eventually give up and pass out."

"No!" Her eyes widened. "Then he'll think I don't care."

She might not have noticed the way she covered Colt's ears, as if she didn't even want him to hear Ian's suggestion. So much for "step one."

The truth was that Ian knew very little about raising kids other than the two basic parenting styles: tough love or indulgence. He'd been raised with a bit of both—his father being tough, his mom being soft. Obviously, Gentry took after his mom, so perhaps his role should provide balance. "I doubt he'll remember when he grows up. In the meantime, you'd get a little break now and then."

"I'm not so wimpy that I need to torment my son just to give myself a break." She frowned, staring at him now with some doubt. "We'd better talk through our expectations."

"Don't worry, I'll follow your rules. I'm only making a suggestion." He stood in place, scanning the room, uncertain about what he should do next. "Maybe I should put my things away?"

Her gaze landed on his medium-size canvas duffel. "That's *all* your stuff?"

He patted it. "I travel light."

Gentry's features blanked for a second, like she couldn't process having so little. When she came to, she pointed to the open wood-and-iron staircase to his left. "Your room's upstairs on the right. Take your time. I'll go rock Colt awhile. When he wears out, we can talk."

She held herself high and strutted toward her bedroom. Although her dress covered her ass—barely—he couldn't help but recall the way she'd looked this morning. He watched her hips sway, long legs eating up the floor until she disappeared from view.

On his way upstairs, he passed by several black-and-white photos that hung on the wall in the substantial square mirrored frames he'd piled in the corner last night. He paused to take a closer look. Most were taken while Colt slept. One caught the baby awake with his face in repose.

The collection was extensive for a kid who was only a couple of months old. At this rate, she'd have the place decked out in the world's most expensive wallpaper by Colt's first birthday.

He continued up the stairs and found the bedroom on the right. The Taj Mahal compared with the motel and any other place he'd ever slept. It smelled of lavender and lemon.

Like the rest of the condo, its walls were dove-gray. The room featured a huge plate glass window, providing him his own lake view. Sunrise would be pretty amazing tomorrow, and stargazing wouldn't be too bad, either.

A platform bed with stark-white linens and a gray leather headboard dominated the room. The dark wood floors were partly covered by low-pile gray-and-white carpet. Shimmery gauze drapes framed either side of the window, and LED pendant lights hung low over the nightstands flanking the massive bed.

Along the opposite wall stood a small dresser—more than adequate for his few belongings, especially with the closet that had been outfitted with shelving and hanging rods.

After unpacking, he wandered into the bathroom, with its slate floors, modern-style vanity, and large glass-encased shower. It was almost too fancy to mess up, he thought. This bedroom suite exceeded the standards of most homes he'd ever seen.

He shook his head to clear his guilt and then decided to test the mattress.

A mistake.

A pillow top with the perfect firmness for support. He let himself fall back and stretch his arms overhead. Closing his eyes, he marveled a bit at the situation: him, in a fancy condo, babysitting. No one would believe it.

He could die on this mattress and be happy; it felt that good. No bugs or lumps. Heaven. Then, he being a guy, and a redheaded bombshell being only a few rooms away, he thought of other uses for this monster-size bed. His mind conjured a reverse-babysitter fantasy, this one featuring Gentry in the panties and tank top she'd worn this morning.

Maybe she'd come knocking in the wee hours because she couldn't sleep. He pictured her standing against the doorjamb, hip cocked, hair piled up on her head except for a stray tendril or two.

A familiar smoky voice interrupted his answering grin.

"What in the world are *you* thinking?"

His eyes popped open as he sprang upright. There she was, almost like in his fantasy, except she was still wearing the halter dress.

"Nothing." He stood, eager to move away from that conversation and those thoughts. "This room's amazing."

She crossed to the window and glanced down toward the lake, hands linked behind her back. "When I first saw this condo, all the trees and water views made it seem like a peaceful haven where I could raise my son. Guess the joke's on me."

"How so?"

She turned and shot him a "Give me a break" look. "After meeting Colt, you don't really think I have any *peace* here, do you?"

"Not yet, but you will soon. Babies grow up and stop fussing."

"So they say, but unlike other moms, I find myself wishing time away to get there, and that doesn't feel so good." She pressed her lips together in a tight line, as if regretting what she'd confessed. Looking through the window once more, she said, "Let's go downstairs and talk about how this will work."

"Whatever you want."

"Look at you. Already a star pupil." She grinned and twirled toward the door, walking out ahead of him.

He couldn't help but chuckle and admit, despite it all, he liked her feisty humor. Thank God he wouldn't be here long enough to do anything stupid.

Chapter Four

Quandary

According to *Merriam-Webster*: a state of perplexity or doubt

According to me: the state of my decision about Colt's childcare

Gentry held the railing on her way down the steps, grasping at anything to steady herself. It was one thing to take impulsive risks when she'd been single, quite another to do so where her son was concerned.

Ian tromped behind her. A stranger in her home. One she'd hired on a whim, probably because he'd revived her spirit by giving her a solid night's sleep. Meanwhile, she hadn't asked for references (other than Sara), and had relied on the fact that he knew how to handle health-care emergencies. What had she been thinking? Guilty heat warmed her cheeks when the devil on her shoulder whispered reminders about his other fine attributes.

When they reached the living room, she asked, "How about a drink?"

"Sure." He stood with his hands in his pockets, calm and still. Not ruffled at all. Another quandary to ponder: had he acquired that special skill because of working in disaster zones, or was he able to work those jobs because of a natural state of Zen?

Either way, she needed to vet this guy, ASAP. "Cool."

She walked to the refrigerator to see if she had any beer. He looked more like a beer guy than a wine guy, and it seemed important to get that right. "Beer?"

"Actually, water's fine." He rocked back on his heels.

Water?

"I've got wine . . ." She stood with the refrigerator door still open, the cold air keeping her rising body temperature in check.

He shook his head. "I promise, I'm good with water."

She kept from rolling her eyes. Eagle Scout—or something worse, she suddenly thought. "Are you a recovering alcoholic?" She slapped her hand across her mouth as soon as she blurted out the worrisome thought.

"No!" For the first time since he'd arrived tonight, it seemed like she'd flustered him. He recovered quickly, though. *Good.* He'd need that skill. She doubted that would be the one and only time she said something that shocked him.

"Sorry. I wouldn't judge, though. I only wanted to know because of Colt."

"I understand, but don't worry. I've never been much of a drinker."

"What a shame." She grinned.

He smiled in kind, his eyes crinkling in a way that suggested he was trying to figure her out. *Good luck with that!*

She pointed to the narrow cupboard above the dishwasher. "Glasses are over there. You might as well start learning where stuff is."

For a split second she debated the wine, then got irked. Hell if she'd let anyone make her feel like she shouldn't drink wine in her own house. She'd adopt a conservative role at Cabot Tea in order to bond with her family, but she needed her freedom at home.

She retrieved the opened bottle of Arneis from the refrigerator—a perfect, light white wine for summer. She poured herself a bit, then reconsidered and filled the entire glass. "Let's sit on the deck and talk about how this will work."

"After you." He gestured for her to lead, water glass in hand.

On her way through the living room, she grabbed the baby monitor and a throw from the sofa to pull over her shoulders in case a breeze made it too cool.

Ian stood on the deck, waiting for her to choose a seat. His formality would not do. This guy needed to loosen up. She decided to mess with him a little—make him laugh. Earlier this morning she'd glimpsed a hint of good humor buried under all his manners. Manners were nice, but she preferred playfulness, especially in a roommate.

Donning the blanket like a cape, she started for one chair, then circled it and headed for another, cape flowing behind her, before stepping away from both. With one arm across her chest and the other bringing her wineglass to her lips, she watched him.

His brows pinched together in confusion; then one quirked upward. He looked her in the eye, mimicked her position—down to her extended pinkie finger—and sipped his water.

She lost the battle against smiling, at which point he chuckled.

"How about we sit at the same time?" she offered.

"Sure." He reached for the chair nearest to him.

"Nope, that's mine." She used her hip to bump him out of the way. The brief contact—her first physical contact with any man in months, excluding family—caused her body to reverberate like a gong. She dropped onto the seat, tucked the blanket around her cool feet, and took a long swallow of wine so he wouldn't see her blush.

He sat, stretching his long, muscular legs out, while letting his gaze take in the wooded hillside and glittering lake below. His boyishly handsome face held her attention. In another life, she might have leaped across the table and licked those freckles scattered across the bridge of his nose and then bitten his shapely bottom lip. "Nice view."

"Worth every penny." As soon as those words left her mouth, she noticed *his* mouth twitch, like he'd squashed a thought—an impolite one. *Huh.* Her ice-breaking silliness hadn't quite eased the tension. Time to lay it on the table. "Let's start by getting all the awkwardness out of the way. Otherwise living together for two minutes, let alone two weeks or more, will be torture."

He shrugged. "Fire away."

"In case you were wondering, I'm not crazy, despite the fact that I hired a virtual stranger to watch my son."

She made sure to keep her gaze steady, although that was harder than it should've been. He possessed the kind of calm assuredness that made her think he could read her mind. If he could, he'd know she was fighting an inexplicable crush.

"Not crazy. Got it," he said, his expression neutral except for a glimmer of humor in his eyes. His captivating eyes. The only part of himself that he didn't keep on a tight leash. Now the part of *her* that liked to crack people open tingled with anticipation.

"I'm just desperate." Then, because that sounded bad, she corrected herself, saying, "In a bind, I mean. I *have* to go back to work tomorrow. Given your connection to Sara, your expertise, and what you did last night, you seem trustworthy."

"I am." He sipped more water like he was rationing it or something. Very odd duck, this one. "Why the urgency to go to work, though? Don't you work for your family's company?"

"I do, but everyone's stretched thin because of the new product launch." She straightened her chair, unwilling to admit that she also didn't want her family and coworkers to think she couldn't hack juggling motherhood and work. "Besides, if I no-show, I'll never hear the end of it from Hunter or my mom. That'd be worse than death."

He nodded, but that constipated expression returned, like he was thinking something he shouldn't say.

"What?" she demanded.

"Sorry?"

"That's the second time you've repressed some snarky thought. Just spit it out. You'll soon learn I rarely keep my opinions to myself, so make free with yours," she teased. And then, because that might've sounded a bit obnoxious, she added, "Please."

He leaned forward, pushing his water glass aside, eyes assessing, the tiniest uptick at the corners of his mouth. "As long as you're asking nicely."

In the silence that stretched, the crickets grew louder, almost drowning out the sound of her bare foot tapping against the wood deck. She stilled herself and chugged a bit more of her wine, then flipped her palm up in question. "Well?"

"I was thinking that people throw around that phrase—'worse than death'—way too easily."

"It's only a saying. It doesn't mean anything."

"Exactly." He shrugged.

"Well, hello, Mr. McJudgy-Pants." She cocked her head, waiting for his comeback.

"You asked." He tucked his chin for an instant and rapped his thumbs on the table. "Why don't we talk about the job? Am I only on from eight to five, or do you want to mix it up some nights and have me handle Colt so you can sleep well?"

"I'm thinking eight forty-five to six during the week, and maybe a few hours on the weekend if you're free. I'm used to being awakened at night, so I'll deal with that on my own."

"Sounds fine."

"I've made a list of important numbers, like my cell, my work line, the pediatrician, and so on. I'll leave money in case you need it to get something for Colt. Also, Colt's feeding and nap schedule are written down—not that he follows it much. But I don't want you letting him cry it out or anything barbaric. I know it's exhausting, but he must feel safe and loved so he knows he's the most important thing to me. Can you handle that?"

His expression screamed "I've handled so much worse," but he didn't say it. At least he was consistent.

"I can. I doubt day care will cater to his whims, though. Why not hire a permanent nanny?" He gestured around. "Clearly, you can afford one."

"Day care will be better for socialization. Of course, this situation with his ears makes me consider waiting until he's old enough to actually socialize." She finished her wine and muttered, "I hate when my mom is right."

His expression remained passive, as if he wasn't all that interested in her answer. Only his eyes—sparkling and attentive—gave him away.

Questions percolated in her mind. Did he regret this decision? What did he think of her? Did he miss his ex?

"One last thing," she said. "I'd prefer if you didn't have overnight guests."

He bit his lip, cocking his head. The sexy expression caused her to squeeze her thighs together. "Shouldn't be a problem."

"Really? I'd hate that rule if I were young and single."

He leaned closer. "You *are* young and single."

Was it her overactive imagination, or was he flirting with her? She wished she'd brought the whole wine bottle outside. "Colt's a magician. When he's around, men disappear."

Ian laughed. He had a hearty laugh that made her tingle, but too soon he ruined the little buzz. "Will Colt's dad be stopping in to visit?"

"No." That was all she'd say about that. She wasn't ashamed of her one-night stand, but she wasn't exactly proud, either. Mostly because now her son might grow up with questions about his father that she couldn't answer.

"Sorry."

"Don't be. I'm not." She swirled her wineglass, staring at what was left. "Being a single mom isn't all bad. Plus, it's spawned my blog, Apron Strings and Mommy Things. I've already built a little readership. People like my pictures and humor. Some poor souls even ask for *my* advice."

Before she wiped the sarcastic smirk off her face, a movement from inside snagged her attention. Through the sliding glass door, she caught her parents using their key to enter the condo without knocking. "Oh, great."

Hopefully, Ian heard the warning in her voice. He sat back, turning to see them before they reached the deck.

Gentry's insides tensed, having been unprepared for the intrusion and her mother's inevitable judgment. "Mom, Dad, didn't expect to see you."

Ian immediately stood and extended his hand. "Mr. and Mrs. Cabot. I'm Ian Crawford." Then Gentry watched him fight a grimace as he finished with "the nanny."

She couldn't help it. She giggled.

He should have been miffed at Gentry for laughing in his face, but instead he struggled not to grin. When was the last time he'd had to smother a laugh? Her parents' shocked expressions made that battle even harder. He'd never met anyone quite like Gentry, whose moods and thoughts ricocheted in all kinds of unexpected directions. If someone had asked, he wouldn't have guessed he'd enjoy it so much.

"Ian," Mrs. Cabot said, shooting her daughter a queer look. "I'm Jenna."

Jenna physically resembled Gentry, but her stiff, self-conscious manner and sharper features made her less attractive.

Mr. Cabot, on the other hand, flashed a welcoming grin while offering a warm handshake. "Call me Jed."

"Sure thing." Ian nodded. "Nice to meet you both."

Gentry rose from her chair and kissed her mom hello, then hugged her dad. "By the way, that key isn't an invitation to barge in without warning. It's a good thing we're dressed."

Ian choked on his water, but Jenna clearly knew one of her daughter's jokes when she heard it. She rolled her eyes, waving a bejeweled hand. "It's past seven o'clock. I thought, if you were lucky enough to get Colt down, you wouldn't appreciate us waking him by knocking."

"Thanks," Gentry conceded, twirling a lock of hair around her finger until its tip turned white. Interesting. Especially when paired with a tone of bored nonchalance. "So what brings you by?"

"We wanted to hear about Colt's doctor visit." Jenna sounded perturbed that she hadn't already received an update.

"He's got an ear infection and will be fine in a few days," Gentry assured her.

"Oh, poor baby." Jenna frowned. "Now I wish he was still awake so I could see him for myself."

"Sorry, but if you go in there to peek, you'll wake him," Gentry said.

"I love that little honeybee," Jenna sighed. "What if I take off my shoes and don't make a peep?"

"Mom, *please*."

"Fine." She gave Ian another quick head-to-toe assessment before asking Gentry, "I assume you'll show up at work tomorrow now that you've taken my advice?"

Gentry's eyes flickered her irritation. No wonder. Jenna didn't give off a warm, fuzzy vibe, and Ian experienced a profound moment of gratitude for his own mother's gentler nature.

"Ian's only here until the infection clears and I can send Colt to day care as planned."

"Because your childhood was so terrible despite having had the best nannies." Jenna cast a weary gaze at Ian, as if looking for an ally.

Ian was certain Jenna would've said more, but Jed pulled out a chair and pushed her onto it.

"Let's not rehash all that." Jed took a seat beside his wife. "So, Ian, how'd you get roped into this so quickly?"

"Sara called me last night to come check on Colt because I'm an EMT, I guess. When Gentry got the doctor's advice, she asked for some help." He kept his gaze on Jed but could feel Jenna's stare assessing his every move.

"Do you have experience with infants?" Jenna leaned forward, ramping up for what promised to be quite an inquisition.

"Mom, Ian works for me, not you," Gentry interrupted. "And he's taking care of *my* son."

"Who is *my* grandson."

"Jenna, honey." Jed patted her hand, then resumed speaking with Ian. "How do you know Sara? Did you go to school with Hunter?"

Ian shook his head. "My mother runs the Angel House. I met Sara there last fall."

Jed's smile broadened. "We have a special place in our hearts for that shelter. Sara and Hunter wouldn't have Ty without it."

Ian immediately liked the genuine man. "My mother speaks highly of Sara, too. Admittedly, I don't know her well."

Jenna waved her index finger back and forth between Gentry and him. "So you two barely know each other?"

She shot Gentry a pointed look before either answered.

"Dad." Gentry closed her eyes.

"Ian, do you work with Portland Med Center or Shriners?" Jed asked.

"Neither, actually. I'm only in Portland for a few weeks. Then I'm heading back to Haiti—"

"Haiti?" Jenna interrupted.

"Yes. I've spent the majority of my career working in developing nations, assisting with disaster relief and providing training." Ian now wished that he'd joined Gentry in drinking that bottle of wine.

"I see." Jenna's shoulders relaxed upon learning this information, which he guessed she'd add to the "Ian Crawford" mental file she was clearly compiling. "I suppose if you can do all that, one little baby shouldn't be a problem. Maybe having help in the house will finally convince my daughter to do so on a more permanent basis."

"Disaster relief? You must see some terrible tragedies." Jed's expression revealed empathy, even as he artfully steered the conversation away from a mother-daughter showdown.

"Yes, but also tremendous resilience and hope," Ian said, aware of Gentry's riveted attention. He didn't hate it, either. "It's very rewarding."

"Your parents must be proud," Jed said.

"Or terrified," Jenna insisted. "What mother wants her child living in constant danger?"

Ian's mom had never objected, but he chose not to correct Jenna.

"How'd you get involved in that kind of work?" Jed asked.

"My parents. I grew up helping my mom locally. In my teens, my father started taking me with him to other countries when possible."

"Does your dad still globe-trot?" Gentry asked.

"No," he responded, hoping to end that line of questioning. Gentry's raised brow prodded further response. "He died several years ago."

"Oh! Sorry." Gentry grimaced and covered her mouth with her hand for the second time tonight. Given her propensity for blurting out her thoughts, he doubted it would be the last. As usual, his dad's death halted conversation for an awkward moment. Apparently, Gentry sensed Ian's reluctance to divulge more, because instead of grilling him, as he suspected she wanted to, she popped off her chair. "I need more wine. Anyone else?"

"No, honey. We wanted to check in, but we'll get out of your hair and let Ian get settled." Her dad tapped his reluctant wife on the shoulder before smiling at Gentry. "See you at the office tomorrow. Busy weeks ahead."

"I know, I know." Gentry hugged him again, stiffening slightly when her mom kissed her cheek. "See you in the morning."

Ian stood. "Nice meeting you both."

He watched Gentry lead them out, only then becoming aware of the slight perspiration that dotted his upper lip. He didn't want her prodding for more information about his dad or the circumstances leading to his death.

Glancing upward, he wondered what his dad might think of him now, staying here in such luxury. Worse, how he'd feel if Ian admitted that he looked forward to sleeping in that bed? Would he call it selling out, or say the ends justified the means? He doubted his dad would approve of Ian's instacrush on a woman like Gentry, who couldn't be more different from his mother or Farrah, or any of the women he'd ever known.

As long as C-VAC got off the ground, surely this brief detour couldn't hurt.

Gentry returned with the bottle and an extra glass. "Don't think about turning this down. *Everyone* needs a glass of wine after meeting my mother."

He couldn't help himself. He laughed, although she hadn't been joking.

"He laughs. Good," she teased, taking her seat and covering herself with the blanket. She didn't quiz him about his past—thank God. The wind whipped through the trees, adding a chorus of whistling leaves to their conversation. "I was beginning to wonder."

Her observation bothered him. He knew he didn't laugh often, or at least not often enough. To be fair, most days he didn't experience much humor in life. Lots of struggle and pain and injustice. Very little merriment.

But maybe, for right now, he could hit "Pause" on all that and enjoy the break. A peaceful time to remember, once he returned to Jacmel, where he'd have plenty of grave situations to handle. "It's been known to happen."

"Cheers." She raised her glass and clinked his.

He took a prolonged sip, letting the cool drink warm his throat and stomach. They sat for another moment or two, drinking their wine in comfortable silence. Then, as if on cue, the baby monitor squawked.

Gentry's eyes fluttered closed, and she finished her glassful in one swallow. "My hour of rest is over. Here's your chance to run for cover tonight."

He could. He wasn't on the clock for another twelve or so hours. But something about the way she stood there—breath held in her chest—kept him in place. "I should probably shadow you and Colt tonight so I get to know him and see how you like things done."

A quick smile lit up her face.

"Glutton for punishment, I see." Gentry grabbed the monitor and other things, then started for the door, glancing back over her shoulder. "I suspect you think my life is easy compared with most, but we'll revisit that opinion in a week or two."

"Challenge accepted." He followed her into the house. Whether it was the wine or Gentry's playful jabs, he wasn't sure, but he relaxed for the first time since he'd returned to Oregon.

Chapter Five

Regression

According to *Merriam-Webster*: a trend or shift toward a lower or less perfect state: such as . . . **c :** reversion to an earlier mental or behavioral level

According to me: a less-than-triumphant return to work

"You're running late." Ian stood—his wavy hair still damp from his shower—with his arms reaching for Colt.

He might be ready to take over, but Gentry couldn't release her son. For the past eight weeks, she'd spent most of each day nuzzling him, inhaling his intoxicating scent, feeling the weight of him against her chest and shoulder. The sudden realization that, by leaving, she'd miss out on all those moments—even the fussy ones—rooted her in place. Not even her desire to prove herself to her family made her budge.

8:47. If she hit all the green lights, she could make it to CTC in ten minutes. She snuggled her son and smothered his head with kisses, willing him to remember each one. "Mommy loves you, Boo. I'll be home soon. You won't even miss me, I bet. I love you. Love you lots."

Ian gently pried Colt from her grip. "He'll be fine. I promise. Go to work and enjoy the break from all this. Your son knows you love him."

But would he? If she left him every day, how would he understand that her heart now beat for him?

"Gentry, trust me." He waved her off with one hand while bouncing Colt with one arm. "Go!"

Her son squealed, but that was nothing new. It had nothing to do with her or Ian. Little Boo didn't understand the significance of her conservative attire or anticipate the impending change in their normal routine. It wouldn't be until later, when he wanted her and was stuck with a stranger, that he might be confused and afraid and . . .

Ian stared at her, head tilted, eyes fathomless and pitying. *Oh no. Pity!* Had she sunk *that* low?

Dabbing her eyes, she nodded. "Okay. I'm going. But keep your phone with you at all times. And send pictures or call me if anything is weird. Do we need a quick review of where everything is—and all the numbers?"

"No. I've got it under control."

She'd prefer for him to be a little flustered—anxious, even—instead of so calm. At least then she'd know he understood that caring for Colt wasn't an easy undertaking. This might not be an earthquake or hurricane zone, but that ten pounds of flesh and bone in Ian's arms could wreak as much havoc. "I'll call in a while."

"You don't need to check in. I'll call you if there's any problem."

8:50. *No more stalling.* She leaned in and kissed Colt's head one last time. "Bye-bye, bugaboo."

Before letting Ian see the new tears forming, she spun around and raced out the door.

She tossed her bag into the passenger seat of the "Volcanic Orange" convertible Mini Cooper—the car she refused to give up in favor of a more practical car—and sped off to work, blowing through at least one yellow light. She cranked the Julia Michaels tune about issues and sang aloud, determined to pull herself together.

She could do this. She could be a single, working mother who stunned her coworkers with her brilliance *and* made her son happy and secure. She could have it all, just like society—and her family—promised. But she'd do it better than her parents because, when push came to shove, Colt would be her priority.

It'd been a while since she'd worn such tailored clothing and spiky heels, so her race from the parking lot to the elevator was less than graceful.

9:05. *Shoot.*

She strode down the hall to her cubicle and dumped her bag on the floor beneath her desk. The ten-by-ten workstation had never looked so neat. Proof of her extended absence. After turning on her computer, she decided a cup of tea might be better than slapping herself in the face to wake up. Preferably the Earl Grey with double bergamot. On her way to the break room, she passed her mom's office. Lights on, but empty.

Just as well. Her brain needed a shot or two of caffeine to shift gears before doing battle. She'd use the five or ten minutes to get herself organized before wowing her mom with her new slogan idea. It wasn't until she was walking back to her desk, sipping her tea—sweetened with three packs of sugar—that she noticed the other empty offices and workstations. Even Miss Perfect, Becky, wasn't around.

She sat at her desk to open her calendar when her phone pinged.

Where are you? came a text from her mom.

At my desk. Where r u?

Conference room meeting with your brother and the rest of the team. 9 weeks to launch.

Ten minutes in and she'd already screwed up. Way to burn through the goodwill she'd built up prior to maternity leave. She sprang from her seat, spilling hot tea on herself. *Fuck all, that was hot!* And now a pale-brown stain slowly bled across her cream-colored Alexander McQueen silk top. Perfect. *Hello, everyone, meet the American Bridget Jones. Better dressed, but just as clumsy.*

After ducking into the bathroom to dab her shirt so the stain wouldn't set, she dashed up the steps to the conference room. At least she'd remembered a notepad.

Before she drew near the glass-walled meeting room, she slowed her pace. She'd never be as smart as Hunter or Colby, but she had her own talents to offer. She also knew enough to project the illusion of having her shit together.

It'd all be fine once they applauded her latest contribution. She'd e-mailed it to Hunter last night in a moment of pure genius—because pure genius always strikes at three a.m. when one is burping an infant.

Hunter stood at the head of the table, still speaking, so he simply gestured toward an open chair. His eyes momentarily strayed to her tea stain before he continued his train of thought. "We've got to stay on point with the branding. So let's take another look at some of these marketing messages. For instance, this tagline, 'The tea you know, on the go.'"

"That's mine," Gentry announced, beaming. The cleverness of that tagline sounded even better today than it had last night. When her smile was met with blank stares, she added, "What?"

"It's off point." Hunter's face pinched the way it always did when he concentrated.

Gentry kept her eyes on his, mostly because everyone else, including Becky, now stared at her like she'd shown up in a bikini. "It goes to our established reputation and the new product's convenience."

"We're entering a billion-dollar market and need to distinguish ourselves from the established big players. The fact that ten percent of every purchase of Cabot's ChariTea will be donated to the Maverick Foundation makes *our* bottled iced tea different. It'll make people feel good about the purchase." Hunter's hands went to his hips. He wasn't nasty, just direct. Like always. Imposing and well dressed, with laser-focused eyes that weren't the least bit softened by his wire-rim glasses. "Your idea doesn't highlight that."

"But it's catchy." Like a castaway grasping at a leaky dinghy, Gentry desperately fought to salvage her idea. "'ChariTea begins with you' is boring—"

"It's on message," her mother interrupted. She darted a look around the table, then chose her words carefully. "I know you've been . . . distracted. But the weekly updates you should've been reviewing explained the charitable USP."

Unique selling proposition. Yeah, fine. But the slogan they'd chosen was lame. No way would it resonate widely.

"Millennials make up the majority of this product market. Like me, they actually buy convenience products for two dollars per bottle rather than brew a pitcher at home. Like me, they'll prefer *my* tagline," Gentry said. "The tags aren't on the labels, so we can still change it on ads and social media campaigns."

She noticed Becky raise her brows, and not in a good way.

"Research and experience say we stick with one distinct message," her mom insisted. As chief marketing officer, she pretty much had the final say.

Gentry's phone buzzed in her pocket. She knew she shouldn't look, but it could be about Colt. Unable to stop herself, she glanced at the screen. Not Ian. A comment notification from her blog, which she'd respond to later. She set the phone aside, but not before drawing her brother's attention.

"May we proceed?" he asked.

Everyone's gaze now carefully avoided hers. No doubt sweat had added new stains to her silk blouse.

"Sorry." She shrank back in her seat after being scorched by her mother's perturbed expression.

"Nine weeks from today we soft-launch in Oregon, Washington, California, and Nevada, with a national rollout next summer." Hunter looked across the table at Jenna. "You've got the influencers in these spaces teed up, right?"

"Yes. Becky has the full report on that." Jenna looked at Becky, who preened whenever she got attention.

This was no surprise. Becky fit in better with Gentry's family than she did. Gentry rarely received public accolades. She told herself it was because her family couldn't risk annoying the other employees by heaping praise on her.

The sad truth was that taking maternity leave had set her back to square one. Meanwhile, Colt was at home without her. Not an acceptable trade-off. Her idea had merit. "Can we revisit the slogan thing?"

"Sis, no one's saying your slogan isn't catchy," Hunter said, his patience fraying. "It just doesn't fit."

"But—"

"Gentry, move on." Her mom's tight voice interrupted.

The others, including Becky, stirred uncomfortably. Her mom had a reputation for resisting change once a decision had been made. On the other hand, Gentry saw no point in rejecting a fresh idea. Sometimes it took time for the right proposal to bubble to the surface. She did, however, realize that now wasn't the time to push.

Hunter laid his hands on the table. "We have to get through the agenda. Let's move on to discussing our distribution partners in the various markets, and what we're doing to get prime placement in those outlets."

The conversation turned to boring business aspects that fell outside the scope of her responsibility, so Gentry's mind wandered. She hadn't planned on the teary start to her day, let alone being summarily dismissed in front of a dozen coworkers. Not the triumphant return she'd envisioned, and that didn't make it easier to be here instead of at home with her son.

The image of Colt nestled in Ian's strong arms resurfaced, tugging at a needy spot in her chest like it had thirty minutes ago. She then tried to picture Smith with their son but couldn't.

Colt resembled Smith, though. A daily reminder of the fact that he was growing up fatherless. She wished she knew more about Smith so she'd also know what to expect from Colt. With the exception of his stubborn streak, her son didn't seem to have inherited any of *her* traits.

That thought made her wonder how many ways he'd already found to torment Ian.

Suddenly people around her were standing and making their way out of the room. She rose, but Hunter held his hand up. Her mom didn't budge, either. *Perfect.* A not-so-private scolding coming her way. Unlike praise, *these* kinds of talks did *not* stir employee discontent.

Once the room had emptied, Hunter shut the heavy glass door and took a seat. He shrugged in an uncharacteristically resigned manner. "Sis, how's Colt?"

"I told Sara yesterday that he's fine. It's an ear infection."

"Good. That's good." Most days Hunter took seriousness to new heights, so his forced smile made her suspicious. "I'm sure it's tough being away from him for the first time. I know I said we needed you back, but not if you can only give us half of your attention. If you need more time, tell us now so we can redistribute the work and hit all our targets."

She supposed the softball-size tea stain and her slogan screwup justified his concerns, but the fact that she'd lost the ground—the respect—she'd been earning this year embarrassed her like a pie in the face.

When Colby had an off day, she got the benefit of the doubt. Granted, Colby had finished college, become a lawyer and, unlike Gentry, hadn't reneged on a promise to let Hunter adopt her baby. Then again, Colby did marry someone she barely knew the first time around, and that ended with two major disasters. In Gentry's mind, *both* Cabot sisters had made some big mistakes, but Gentry never got out from under the weight of hers.

She knew in her bones that, no matter how hard she tried, she'd always be the "half" sib. But she'd suck it up and work with her family, hoping to build a personal bridge her son could cross to belong, because she never wanted *Colt* to feel left out or "less than."

"I'm fine. I'll *be* fine. It's only the first day. First hour, really." Gentry kept her chin up, pretending she didn't already look like the disaster they believed her to be. "It may take a couple of days to nail down the juggling routine, but I will. I promise."

Her mom and Hunter exchanged a look. Then her brother said, "You know, if you need an extra hand, Sara's available."

Saint Sara, the perfect wife and mother. Competence personified. No doubt everyone thought Colt would've been better off with Sara and Hunter than with her. Sometimes even Gentry wondered.

"I have Ian." Gentry avoided her mom's gaze.

"What?" Hunter sat back, surprised.

"She hired a temporary nanny." Her mother's tone was uncommonly neutral, drawing Gentry's ire.

She almost preferred her brother and mother in their natural state—intense and aggressive—instead of coddling. This patient act freaked Gentry out. If she didn't know better, she'd believe the conference room had transported her to a virtual-reality version of her life.

"I couldn't drop Colt at day care with a fever," Gentry added.

"True. He's still colicky, too, which would be tough for anyone managing more than one kid." Hunter grimaced.

Her mom's brows shot up as she glanced at Hunter. "I'd take colic over the stunts your sister pulled." Then she raised a brow at Gentry. "You'd better hope Colt doesn't test you the same way."

"He won't." Gentry stopped herself from saying more. Colt wouldn't rebel because she wouldn't treat him as an afterthought or a possession to be trotted out when convenient. He'd never be "half" of anything, either. He would be whole. Gentry would make sure of that. "If that's all, let me go get myself organized."

"Good idea," they both said in unison. Unaccustomed to agreeing on much, they each made an uncomfortable face and moved away from each other.

Gentry grabbed her empty notepad and left the room, ducking into the bathroom to call Ian.

"Hello?" Ian answered.

Gentry didn't hear her son in the background. "Why can't I hear Colt crying?"

"He's got a bottle in his mouth."

"Oh." She pictured Colt in Ian's lap, sucking away. The image made her smile, then frown. Colt didn't care who fed him as long as someone did. Even her own son didn't need her and only her. Would anyone, ever?

She stifled a self-pitying sigh. "So you're fine? He's fine?"

"Everyone's fine." Ian paused. "Anything else?"

Well, now she felt foolish. "No."

"Have a good day." Ian's warm voice lingered in her mind after he'd hung up.

When Gentry arrived at her desk, Becky swung by to drop off a stack of research. In her typical pedantic tone, she said, "If you recall, we've taken a brand molecule–mapping approach. This compilation includes all the research supporting the focus on ChariTea's charitable aspect. Now we need to incorporate environmental information into the process and build consumer anticipation."

Becky stared at Gentry as if waiting for some acknowledgment. Gentry stifled the urge to break into a golf clap, choosing a polite nod instead. "Got it."

"Good. I'm tasking you with pushing the social media campaigns. Matt and I will work with traditional advertisers and distributors. Use this research to identify unique outreach opportunities on our online platforms. Contests, giveaways, competitions, and so on. All of our target market data is in there to help." Becky crossed her arms, her expression prim. They'd worked together this past year, but Gentry was sure Becky never wanted to be stuck training her. "Start with what we've begun, but I'd like some fresh ideas by Wednesday. We don't have a lot of time, and unlike you, I don't have job security."

It'd been a while since Gentry had been hit with a blatant dig about nepotism. In truth, nepotism wasn't the right term, because she *owned* a chunk of CTC, like her parents and siblings. That had come about years earlier when her dad's tax adviser had made some estate planning suggestions.

Unlike her family, Gentry had never aspired to climb the corporate ladder. She'd preferred less conventional work, like when she'd been a live mannequin, professional cuddler, and dog walker. She'd thrived on those unusual adventures, although she quit the cuddler job because the loneliness of some of those clients would cling to her for days.

Even now, photography and her blog were more engaging than pushing iced tea. But her family didn't understand any of that. They'd considered all those other jobs as stunts or whims. Not options befitting a Cabot. Now she sat, working in a cubicle with no view or adventure, still waiting for acceptance.

Becky cleared her throat.

Hunter's warnings about earning her peers' respect rang in her head, so Gentry let Becky's dig pass. "You'll have an outline by Wednesday."

"Good." Becky relaxed a bit. "Thanks, Gentry. Welcome back."

Welcome back. Wouldn't it be nice if Becky were sincere?

◆ ◆ ◆

Gentry walked through the front door and dropped her bag on the floor without looking at him. Ian watched her shuck off her shoes, which she flung into the corner, where they lay piled atop each other like blue silk firewood.

Expensive shoes, no doubt. He'd learned a bit more about her today when he'd had sixteen free minutes to scroll through her blog. Replete with photos of—and stories about—Colt, it also showcased clothes and accessories, baby and beauty products, and evidenced an endearing mix of enthusiasm, hubris, clever observation, and a fair amount of empathetic commiseration with her followers.

The last few paragraphs of the post she'd written last night had caught his eye.

> I swore I'd *never* hire a nanny. I had my reasons, none of which matter to anyone but me. Still, they mattered to me as much as air and water, and yet…now I've gone and hired a nanny.
>
> I could make excuses. He's a temporary fix. Desperate times and all that blah, blah, blah. But why bother with explanations?
>
> If I begin with a truth—the fact that, like all new moms, I don't know what the heck I'm doing—then there's no good reason to stick to preconceived ideas about what I should or shouldn't do. That kind of mindless adherence to things that sound good in concept but don't work well in real life won't help me or my son.

No siree.

We're all winging it, so we might as well roll with it and, in this particular case, enjoy the perks of being proven wrong.

He'd wondered what caused her anti-nanny stance to begin with, and then he'd wondered exactly what perks she intended to enjoy.

Now, though, Gentry's stained shirt and drawn expression warned him to tread with caution.

He braced to be the target of her dark mood. Farrah had given him some practice in this department. He used to point out the harsh realities he'd seen in his work to give her a different perspective on her problems. Turns out that tactic had only made him seem unsympathetic. Today he'd be careful not to make comparisons.

Gentry forced her frown into a weak smile. "Thanks for watching him later than our deal. I promise I won't make it a habit."

Six forty-five. Not horribly late. Not like he had anything, or anyone, else waiting on him, either.

She arched her spine, hands clasped behind her back, as she walked farther into the living room. Even a conservative—if stained—top and pencil skirt couldn't hide that sinfully sexy body when her hips and chest were thrust into that position. Not that he should be thinking about that now—or ever.

Still, he couldn't help but smile at the contrast between her attire and her ankle and forearm tattoos.

"No problem." He pointed at the faint beige spot on her blouse. "Rough first day?"

She glanced at her chest; then her chin rose above a half shrug. "Some people are clumsy."

Some people? A sufficiently vague response. He'd noticed this about her in the short time they'd spent together. Evasive when it came to admitting to any imperfection or lack of control. He wanted to know what happened, but she craned her neck in search of Colt. "Where's my son?"

"Asleep." The little fusspot had kept him hopping. Countless dirty diapers, hours of crying, and two spit-ups. But Ian still managed to keep the place clean and throw something together for dinner. His success made him grin.

She bugged her eyes. "Already?"

"Yes." Was she pissed off? "A few minutes ago."

"How?" Her posture deflated. "He's usually ramping up into a good evening fit right about now."

"Guess I wore him out." Ian hadn't considered that she might want to spend time with him. "Sorry. Did you want me to keep him up to see you?"

"No. I'm sure he'll wake up before long, anyway." As her gaze roamed the spick-and-span condo, it grew even gloomier.

Good thing he'd never needed much praise. He glanced around, unable to guess the source of her mood. When he looked back at her, her dewy eyes stopped him cold. "Is something wrong?"

"Of course not. What could possibly be wrong? Everything here is *perfect*." She marched into the kitchen and yanked a fresh bottle of wine from the refrigerator, then paused with the door open. "What's *this*?"

She removed the kale and quinoa chicken salad he'd tossed together.

"Dinner." He rested his hands on his hips, confused. Would this state be his new norm until he returned to Haiti?

The Tupperware landed with a plunk on the counter as tears pooled in her eyes. "Excuse me."

She brushed past him in a blur of confusing fury and sorrow, racing into the powder room.

He froze. Contrary to her claims from last night, maybe Gentry Cabot *was* crazy. Closing his eyes, he considered some options. A: bolt to his room to avoid what promised to be a weird cyclone of emotion, because if Gentry was anything like Farrah, he was in a lose-lose situation no matter what he said to soothe her. B: attempt to validate whatever problem had sent her running. Not his strong suit, but surely the nicer thing to do.

He drew a breath before padding over to the powder room and tapping on the door. "Gentry? You okay?"

She opened it almost immediately, unable to mask her red-rimmed eyes. "Sorry."

Ian didn't know a single man who didn't falter in the face of a teary woman, and he was no exception. "Did I do something wrong?"

"Nope." She slipped past him and returned to the kitchen, where she filled her wineglass.

She hadn't bitten his head off or blamed him—a positive sign that perhaps he'd picked the right option. He'd roll with it and try to help her relax.

"It's nice out." He approached her with caution. "Go sit on the deck and get some fresh air. I'll fix you a plate."

She kept her eyes on her wineglass, which remained on the counter, and nodded. She must've needed the pampering, because he doubted she caved often. "Okay."

He arranged the chopped chicken salad on a plate, sprinkled it with pomegranate arils and goat cheese, then went to the deck. Gentry had her chin on her knees, like a young girl who'd lost her best friend. He wanted to help but didn't think he'd be welcome. He set the plate in front of her. "Would you prefer to be alone?"

"No." She picked up the fork, flashing a sheepish grin while still not quite meeting his gaze. "But *you* might."

Another surprise, but not even as big as finding himself in want of a little adult company as well. Specifically, hers. Her unpredictability intrigued him. He didn't want to examine that too closely, but he took a seat.

"Thanks," she said, before trying her first bite. Her brows rose. "This is good."

"Whole Foods makes it pretty easy to throw together a dinner salad," he confessed.

"Easy for some." Her gloomy expression returned.

"It was a joke, Gentry." Their conversation reminded him of the mirror hall in a fun house, where nothing appeared as it was.

"How'd you even get there without a car? It's like two miles from here." She continued eating.

"I took Colt out in the stroller and used its bottom rack to carry the bags."

She attacked that salad like a refugee who hadn't eaten in days. The mysterious emotions rumbling behind her green eyes turned them as gray as storm clouds.

He could sit here guessing, or he could ask. "It seems like I've upset you somehow . . ."

"Look at the place," she said, having barely swallowed her last bite before snatching another with her fork. A pomegranate seed fell off the fork onto her shirt, adding a pink stain to the beige one.

He held his breath, expecting more tears.

Instead, she plucked it off her chest and flicked it into the woods, snickering as if that seed had proved some point. She finally finished her thought, her voice filled with discouragement. "It's spotless, and Colt's sleeping."

"And that's a problem?"

"First, I screw up at work. Then I come home to all this. Either you and Sara are some kind of super-parenting geniuses, or I'm inept. Either way, Colt's stuck with a crappy mother." A dry chuckle emerged, but she kept her gaze on her plate. "The fact that I'm spilling my guts to you proves I'm totally losing it."

Her ruddy cheeks told him she immediately regretted her confession. If he thought she was throwing a pity party, he might've been annoyed. Instead, her sincerity shone through like a flashlight.

Without thinking, he clasped her hand in a firm grip. Her gaze dropped to their intertwined fingers, but she didn't withdraw. He held her hand longer than he'd planned. Another thing he didn't want to think too hard about. Reluctantly, he released his hold. "You're a good mother. I've seen you with Colt. Your love is obvious."

"Love's the bare minimum he deserves. I can count on one hand the number of days where I showered, kept the house clean, ate well, and dealt with him all day." She stabbed at her salad.

"I'm glad I'm not that kale." When his poor joke didn't work, he said, "It's easier for me because I'm *not* his mother."

Her expression turned to panic. "Did you let him cry himself to sleep?"

"No. I promised I wouldn't." He sat forward. "But you love him so much his crying probably paralyzes you."

"Gee, thanks." A wry cover. She did *that* often, too.

"All I'm saying is that if you spend all your time cuddling and soothing him, it makes it harder to get other things done."

She sighed and looked down at the lake for a moment before returning her attention to him. "What did *you* do?"

"Distracted him with activities—reaching games and rolling him over out here on a blanket. Texture stimulation. Whatever I could think of to surprise him and keep him moving."

"And he stopped crying long enough to enjoy it?"

"Not really. He's fussy, but he's curious, too. He'd interact for a few minutes here and there before starting up again. He napped pretty well, though, which is when I straightened up." He shrugged. "Remember, I sleep all night, unlike you, so I didn't need to nap when he did."

Gentry's brows pinched together as she pushed the remnants of her salad around the plate. "Thank you, Ian. Maybe I'd be happier that you did such a good job if *I'd* kicked ass at work."

"Sorry you had a tough start."

She sipped more of her wine. "The thing is, I still think I'm right. They just won't listen."

"Right about what?" He welcomed the change of subject, having never been particularly adept at intimate conversation.

Gentry explained the slogan debate.

Corporate America and profit had never been his motivation. "I don't know squat about advertising, but I like your slogan better."

"Thanks, but it's out. It doesn't highlight the USP."

"USB?"

"US*P*—unique selling proposition. It's what makes our ready-made teas special. Sort of the main reason someone would choose us over other brands. We're charging a little more, too—we've got to prove we're worth it. Kind of like with people."

"What?" Her free-flowing thoughts spun like a potter's wheel, making them tough to follow. And yet he was certain that, when pieced together, the pattern would be more colorful and complex than Haitian mosaic artwork.

"Marketing a product isn't all that different from marketing ourselves."

"You think people need to sell themselves?"

She laughed in his face. "Of course *you* wouldn't think so. Mr. Humanitarian-devoting-his-life-to-saving-the-world. *You* don't need to think about what makes you special. You just are." Gentry swigged more wine and averted her eyes.

The unspoken implication—that she was unlike him—rang out as if she'd shouted through a bullhorn.

Now he understood something important and sad about Gentry Cabot. Beneath all her bling and sarcasm, she didn't think she had a single thing that made her desirable or worth the effort. He utterly disagreed. He also knew that no designer label or tattoo or tough attitude would be a substitute for self-esteem.

In addition to caring for Colt, he made a private vow to help her see herself in a better light before he quit.

She laid her head against the back of the chair and started talking to herself. "The tea you know . . . ChariTea you know . . . on the go . . . No. Hm." Silence. "ChariTea on the go." A smile formed, and she looked at him with her first truly happy expression of the evening. "'ChariTea on the go.' That's better than 'ChariTea begins with you.'"

"Maybe, but it still doesn't hammer home the fact that buying your product directly contributes to building a better world."

She frowned. "Maybe that's it."

"What?"

"The better world. That's it." She held up her hand, eyes focused in the distance, and thought for a while longer. "'Thirst for a better world' . . . well, but this satisfies thirst . . . so it isn't quite right. Maybe 'Quenching your thirst for a better world'? Or 'Quench your thirst for a better world'?"

"That works."

"It's longer than 'ChariTea begins with you,' but it has more punch than the current slogan. It doesn't address the convenience element, but I might not win that battle. This is something, though. Something to prove I'm not useless."

"Useless?"

She waved her hand, her expression sealing itself up as tight as a clam. "You know, getting back up to speed and all."

He doubted that was all, but he didn't push. The branding debate seemed like a lot of fuss about iced tea, but she looked so relieved and pleased, like she'd solved the Israeli-Palestinian conflict.

He wished his goals were so easily accomplished. After spending part of Colt's naps today talking to Archer about the single biggest threat to their success—a shortage of suppliers and vehicles—he'd brainstormed ideas to source those items. A daunting task for a guy without wealthy connections.

Suddenly, Gentry snapped her fingers. "Hello? Where'd you go?"

"Sorry. Just thinking about my own plans."

Her green eyes lit up with interest as she leaned forward and rested her chin on her fist. The glass door behind her became a mirror. In its reflection, they looked like a couple on a date. "What plans?"

"My father's friend Archer Cooke and I recently formed an NGO in Haiti to train locals to become EMTs. We have one local, Stanley, on board with us at this point, and we're working with local hospital administrators to structure something that will complement its service. Teaching people basic lifesaving skills will improve lives in communities with little to no access to adequate health care. Our big challenge now is getting vehicles and an ongoing source of supplies."

"Wow." She sat back again. "You want to live there, like . . . full-time? Isn't it dangerous?"

"I'd avoid pockets like Carrefour and Cite Soleil . . . Martissant. We're setting up on the coast, in Jacmel."

"I know zip about Haiti . . . other than that it's hot and poor."

"Very poor. They have a saying about wishing they were lucky enough to be dirt-poor. Deforestation started way back with the French and continued through the mideighties with the clear-cutting of the Haitian-Dominican border, so dirt gets easily washed away during storms, which makes it hard to grow fruit and other food. There've been efforts to cultivate more trees in recent decades. It's having some impact, but poverty is a huge problem."

For a second, he flashed to a memory of some young aides tossing candy at kids in the street. He'd been smiling at their generosity until his father had pointed out the shop vendor sitting outside his empty store, sun glaring off his sweaty face, watching potential sales die. Ironically, many who went to help only made things harder and took resources from those in real need.

"Can't you manage that without living someplace so unsafe and unhappy?"

Safety. Happiness. These were things he hoped to give others, so he would make the sacrifice. It was his privilege to do so, in fact. But he didn't want to preach or talk about his dad—his bittersweet connection to Haiti. The place—grave—where he felt both closest to, and yet most distant from, his dad. "I'll manage."

"But *why*?"

"Unfinished business."

"Cryptic."

He shrugged, hoping to sidestep her probing.

Demonstrating a talent for intuition, she shifted directions. "Do you speak French?"

"A little. Most locals speak Haitian Creole. I know enough to get by, but I'm getting better. Stanley's been teaching me when I'm there."

Her eyes twinkled. "Say something."

"Kote li fè mal?"

"Ooh, kinda sexy." She smiled. Hearing her call him—and the way he sounded—sexy roused him intolerably. "What's it mean?"

"Where does it hurt?" He forced himself to think of an instance where he'd asked that question of a patient in order to move his thoughts away from Gentry's low voice saying the word "sexy."

"Oh." Her smile fell. "I guess most of what you know has to do with sick people."

He nodded. Not sexy at all. Thank God.

She stared at him now, pushing her empty plate aside. "Are there many women who work there?"

"A fair amount. Why?"

"I'm wondering if you get lonely. This life plan of yours won't make finding love very easy. But I guess you already know that, or you wouldn't be homeless now, would you?"

He wasn't ready to discuss Farrah or his love life. The quickest way to shut down that conversation would be to turn it around on Gentry. "Being a single mom must be pretty lonely."

"I'm not lonely," she insisted. "I have my son."

"That's not the kind of love that you're talking about." Before he could stop himself, he added, "In fact, this conversation makes me wonder about Colt's dad."

"Yeah, well . . . get in line." She smirked and finished her wine.

"Still off-limits?" He almost held his breath, then felt stupid for being so curious. A few seconds ticked by, punctuated by a goose honk echoing off the lake below.

"Oh, what the hell. Not like you'll be around long enough to judge me forever." She pulled her knees back up to her chest. "The truth is, I don't know Colt's dad. I met him at a bar while on vacation in Napa. We had a one-night fling, and I only know him as Smith."

"Oh." Ian's thoughts ranged from thinking of how reckless she'd been with her life, on one hand, and almost . . . *almost* . . . envying that sense of freedom. His mother had depended on him for so much in his father's absence that he'd never had much freedom at all.

"Every time you make that face, I'm going to call you McJ."

Her commentary snapped him out of his thoughts. "Mick Jay?"

"Short for McJudgy-Pants." She smirked. "Regardless, I can't regret that night. I love my bugaboo. As for Smith . . . let's just say he was hard to resist."

"Then why didn't you try to find him?" The ludicrous burst of jealousy brought him low.

"I'm not looking for 'love,'" she snorted.

Her words sounded a bit too practiced to be true. And that was beside the point, anyway. "Shouldn't Smith know he has a kid?"

"You can't help yourself, can you, McJ?" Her expression turned from teasing to testy.

It wasn't his business. He knew that, yet he had to be honest. "Speaking as a guy, I'd want to know."

"Trust me on this. Smith's nothing like you."

Her tone didn't sound like a compliment—for either man. "What if Colt has questions about his father one day? Every kid wants to know his parents—even if you and Smith aren't a couple."

She didn't hit him with an immediate comeback, although her viper's gaze warned that she'd thought of one. "For all I know, Smith could be married, or who knows what. My mom says we're better off letting that sleeping dog lie, so to speak."

Yesterday she'd proved how little she cared for her mother's opinions. That comment, however, might cause an explosion.

He watched her gnaw at her thumbnail. She did that when she worried. "I don't often follow my mom's advice, but she's raised enough concern to make me hesitate."

Ian had a definite sense of the right thing to do, but this was not his decision to make. He'd be gone in a matter of weeks and didn't want to be held responsible for the consequences of whatever choice she made. "I guess you'll have to trust your gut to tell you what's right for your son."

"Oh, Ian. Haven't you figured out that trusting my gut almost always leads to trouble?" She passed her remark off as a joke, but she didn't fool him. She looked away, toward the lake, lost in thought. Then, abruptly, she stood and grabbed her plate. "I think it's time I change into something more comfortable."

Suddenly, as if only then noticing her words, she shot him a saucy smile. A cheesy, playful, yet still sexy come-on that he knew she didn't mean seriously.

He should be relieved, he thought, as she sauntered into the house. The woman was trouble. She was reckless. She was, at times, lying to herself and others. Yet she was daring, full of life, and surprisingly vulnerable.

He closed his eyes and turned his thoughts away from Gentry and back to Haiti. To the way he could always feel the sun before he saw it.

To the look of determination on his father's face as he went back into that building to search for a woman's missing child.

Ian had a plan to honor his dad, and no one, not even someone as bewitching as Gentry Cabot, would deter him.

Chapter Six

Foolhardy

According to *Merriam-Webster*: foolishly adventurous and bold : RASH

According to me: searching for Colt's father (also pushing my slogans again on Hunter and Mom)

After yesterday's public debacle, Gentry exercised the benefit of being a Cabot for the first time since taking the job the previous fall. Luckily, Hunter and her parents agreed to a brief, private meeting in her dad's office. A place without interior windows, so gossips and disgruntled coworkers couldn't watch and wonder.

"Hi, Cindy." Gentry waved at her father's personal assistant.

Cindy flashed a polite grin—the kind of smile that didn't give any hint of genuine emotion. "Good morning."

Gentry entered her dad's expansive office, with windows that looked over the adjacent, undeveloped land preserve. Unlike any visit to her mom's ornate office—where the thick, red silk-and-wool Tibetan carpet and handmade live-edge mahogany desk hummed with her mother's tense energy—in here she felt safe.

Her father's space resembled the casual, no-nonsense appeal of the man himself. Standard beige commercial carpet worn from foot traffic. Family photos on the credenza. Traditional but tired office furniture. No attempt to intimidate or impress. Just straightforward functionality that welcomed every guest.

Her parents were seated at the small table in one corner, waiting for her and Hunter. Her dad's Lyme disease symptoms had abated during the past months, although he still had occasional flare-ups. Today he appeared to be having a good day. She kissed him hello before taking a seat across from her mom.

"How's it working out with Ian?" Her dad clasped her hand and squeezed.

The gesture reminded her of when Ian had done the same last night. Her father's touch comforted and settled her. Ian's had stirred up something else. It troubled her, actually, that Ian got her to open up about things she didn't want to discuss. "So far, so good."

"You seem a little more yourself today," her mom added. "On time, too."

Also thanks to Ian. Once she'd gotten over her pity party, she'd appreciated coming home to a clean house and a meal. To an adult who patiently listened and had his own stories to tell. It recharged her. And now, to know her son was in safe hands . . . she couldn't pay Ian enough for that peace of mind. "Miracles happen."

Hunter walked in before the zingers escalated. His presence—confident, proud, handsome—absorbed their attention. Gentry had always tried to emulate his attitude. Her effort rang hollow because, unlike Hunter, she couldn't boast a string of accomplishments.

"Sorry I'm late. I also have to duck out soon, so let's make this quick." He sank onto a chair opposite their dad, removed his glasses to clean a smudge, and looked at her. "What's up?"

Two of the world's most intimidating people were staring at her, so she turned to her father instead. "I'll be quick, but let me finish before interrupting or rejecting my idea."

"Of course," her father said before shooting her mom a pointed glance.

Hunter and Jenna exchanged an impatient look. Anytime those two agreed, Gentry braced for a lightning strike or another natural disaster. Then again, those two *had* laid down their swords in recent months, and yet hell hadn't swallowed the earth.

"I thought more about the slogan—" she began. Her mother's exasperated inhalation—the kind that always made Gentry feel small—interrupted her. Determined to prove her competence, she plowed through. "The name 'Cabot's ChariTea' embodies the USP, so I still think we should add the convenience factor to distinguish it from our regular teas. With that in mind, I thought of 'ChariTea on the go.' But if you don't like that, then how about 'Quench your thirst for a better world.' At least that has some punch."

Gentry sat, fingers interlocked on her lap to keep from chewing her nails, and settled her gaze on Hunter. At the end of the day, ChariTea was his baby. Maybe his approval could trump her mother's rejection.

When he grinned—an uncommon response at work—Gentry broke into a responding smile so big it could almost be mistaken for one of Sara's. Her knee bounced happily beneath the table until she settled it with her hand.

"I like the second one." Hunter looked at their father. "Dad?"

"Me too." Her father patted her shoulder, nodding.

The win sent her floating on air. For a millisecond, Gentry regretted the time she'd wasted in rebellion. Who might she be now if she'd followed in her siblings' footsteps sooner? "Mom?"

Gentry tried not to hold her breath.

"Good to see you getting your head back in the game." Her mother drummed the fingers of her left hand upon the table while staring at the notepad onto which she'd written out both slogans. "They work."

Tepid.

"Do you like them?" Gentry hated the churning in her stomach and the yearning for some praise.

"Let's take them to the marketing team for consensus and go from there." Her mother's refusal to applaud her creativity deflated Gentry more quickly than a pinprick to a balloon.

She fantasized about tossing her pen across the table like a dart aimed at her mother's forehead.

"Great. I've got to run." Hunter pushed back from the table and gave a quick wave. "See you all later."

As Hunter walked out, their dad said, "I gotta say, I'm happy to see us all working together." He leaned back, arms crossed over his chest. "I wasn't convinced you did a good thing when you voted with your brother, but it's working out."

"Let's hope so." Her mom stood to leave. "We'll know in another three months if this gamble was worth it."

Last year, her mother had pushed to sell CTC to an international conglomerate. Hunter had pulled out every stop to prevent the sale, but Gentry held the tie-breaking vote. At the time, Hunter hadn't been speaking to her because of the whole failed adoption. She'd leveraged her vote in exchange for this job, knowing passing up that potential payday might be the only way to mend fences.

"Putting the family to rights is more important than hitting a home run with this product," her dad replied. Ten years ago he wouldn't have said that, but since his illness, her father's priorities had shifted somewhat. Sadly, her mother's hadn't.

"Now you sound like Leslie." Her mother summoned Gentry with one hand while taking a dig at Jed's ex-wife. If Hunter had still been in the office, *he* would've tossed a pen at her mom.

Gentry had never known life without the Cabot interfamily tension. Peace had been a relative term, not a way of life. She'd vowed to do better for her own son. That vow had kept her up the previous night, causing her to mull over Ian's opinions about Smith and family. In a moment of clarity, she now came to another decision. "There's one more thing."

"What?" her mom asked, hugging her notepad and glancing at her watch.

"I'm thinking of finding Smith." Gentry kept her shoulders square even as her body went a bit numb at the thought.

Her mother's eyes rolled up toward the ceiling, but her dad leaned forward, his expression sober but curious. "What's changed your mind?"

"Colt should know who his father is." More than that, he deserved a complete family as opposed to a dysfunctional half of one. Whether Ian or God or a sixth sense toyed with her, she believed Smith would turn out to be a good guy. Not as good of a guy as Ian, most likely. But they'd hit it off before; maybe they would again and, in doing so, could provide Colt the kind of security she'd never known.

"How will you possibly find a man whose name you don't even know?" her mother asked.

"It's a crazy long shot, but I know what he looks like and the hotel we were in." She remembered the outdoor shower of her cottage among the low-lying buildings of Carneros Resort and Spa, and the views across the fields to the distant mountains. "I think I remember his room number, but I'm not positive."

Her father shook his head, hand held high. "That's hard for me to hear, you know. Maybe think a little about your audience."

"Sorry, Dad." She'd never given much thought to her impulsiveness. To the extent it had worried her parents in the past, she'd blamed them for being so neglectful. But as a mother, her perspective had shifted.

"You have no idea whom or what you're inviting into your life," her mother warned.

"If a PI actually finds Smith and learns he's a bad guy, I don't have to contact him." She looked at her father. "I won't do anything to hurt

Colt. But at least I'd have answers so when he's old enough he can make his own decisions."

"I hope you can't find this Smith person. It's easier and cleaner this way." Her mother looked concerned, as opposed to merely irritated about giving up control. "Why borrow trouble when you can simply tell Colt that you got pregnant on a lark and never knew his father's name. It wouldn't be a lie."

"Jenna," her dad said.

"What?" she snapped. "Are we not allowed to call a spade a spade? She likes to boast about her unconventional life. She claims she's not ashamed of that night."

"I'm not!" Gentry insisted. "I don't regret it, either. I didn't troll for the worst guy I could find. Smith was pleasant and friendly and made me feel safe enough to do what I did, so chances are he'll be a decent man who has something to offer his son."

Again, she thought of the kind of influence someone like Ian would offer and wished he weren't running to the other side of the world.

"Given the fact he didn't give his name or want yours, I don't exactly agree with your hunch." Her dad crossed his arms again. He looked tired, which almost made her back down, but this was too important, and she wanted his support.

"We were both having fun on vacation. The nickname thing was my idea, and I didn't ask for, or give, any personal information, either." She wrinkled her nose, because that also wasn't something her dad would want to hear. "But Colt's changed everything, and maybe our son will bring out the best in Smith, too. If I find him."

"You've never asked for our approval before, so nothing's changed." Her mom strode to the door, gripping its handle with unnecessary force. "I hope I won't have to say 'I told you so.'"

If that were true, why did it sound like she *did* hope for the chance to sneer those exact words?

◆ ◆ ◆

Ian descended the stairs at nine thirty in the morning and spied Gentry straddling Colt with a camera in her hands. She hadn't heard him approach, so he paused on the bottom tread to watch. The photographs on the wall beside him proved her talent but didn't quite reveal the tenderness he saw unfolding on the floor in spite of her son's crankiness.

She tickled Colt's belly, her voice soft and low, then adjusted her lens. Colt's tiny body flinched at the burst of rapid-fire snapshots. In response, Gentry bent down to gently rub her nose with her son's and kiss his forehead. "Come on, Boo. Gimme a smile." Gentry made a funny sound with her lips, which momentarily caught his attention, and snapped a few more images before she felt Ian's presence.

She'd pulled her hair into a ponytail, and her cheeks were flushed, presumably from taking Colt on an early-morning run.

"Hey, sleepyhead," Gentry teased as he crossed to the kitchen to brew some coffee. He noticed the faint circles beneath her eyes. She'd been working late at night this week and probably not sleeping well. "What's on your agenda today?"

Saturday: a day off. He couldn't remember the last time he'd slept so late, but watching Colt all week had required more stamina than he'd predicted. The constancy of attention. Colt's shrill cries. His inability to communicate. In hindsight, that all paralleled his humanitarian work pretty well, except here he also had to work in isolation. The lack of adult stimulation layered another dimension of difficulty, giving him a new respect for single parents—and Gentry in particular. "Haven't thought past my first cup of coffee."

"You know you can *never* tell my family I stock coffee. Cabots are tea drinkers—period. My coffee habit is a betrayal of high order." She set the camera on a side table and stretched with a yawn.

Ian pretended to lock his lips and toss the key.

Gentry knelt beside Colt again, wiggling Quackers near Colt to coax her son into reaching for the gross toy. Ian still couldn't believe she chose to give her son that old duck over something new. He sensed a story there, but wouldn't ask.

"Should I make a big pot or small?" he asked.

"I'm all set, thanks." She fiddled with Colt's feet while giving Ian another once-over. "I hate to tell you, but you look like I usually feel."

"You have my sympathy," he joked.

"I warned you this job wouldn't be a cakewalk." She sat back on her heels. "Of course, your help has made a *huge* difference this week. I still could use some sleep, but getting a break from Colt, the laundry, and grocery shopping is such a treat. And having an adult to talk to at night might be the best part. It'll be lonely when you go." She gazed around the clean condo. "And messy."

He chuckled. "Neatness is my way of coping with chaos."

"Commiseration is mine. That's why I love my blog. A whole community of single moms lending a sympathetic ear and offering advice."

"Do you make money from it?" He'd overheard her midnight keyboarding every night, sometimes punctuated by a giggle or by her talking to the screen.

"None. It's a labor of love. I suppose I could monetize it with ads or become an Amazon affiliate and sell stuff online. First, I'd have to build a bigger audience, and even then, it'd be tough to make decent money. Photography is a different story. It'd be amazing to go pro." She shrugged noncommittally. "I can't do either seriously while I've got Colt and CTC taking up most of my time."

"Why not quit CTC and do what you love?"

"Working at CTC is better for my son."

"Because of money?"

"Hell no. Trust me, the old cliché about money not buying happiness . . . that shit is true. Family. Acceptance. Respect. Love. That's what my working for CTC will give my son."

"Colt can get all that from *you* no matter what job you have. When you're happy, he'll be happy."

She shook her head. "My relationship with my family has improved since I started working with them. If I quit to 'take pictures,' I'll revert to being the aimless Cabot, on the outside looking in." She stretched her legs in front of her and rested back on her elbows. "You should know something about family expectations, though, right? It sounds like your family business is charity work."

"But unlike you, I actually love it."

"Sounds nice, but I wonder . . ."

He crossed his arms. "Wonder what?"

"Nothing." She rolled onto her side and kissed Colt's tummy again.

He should get his coffee and get on with his day, but he couldn't let her question go. "Since when have you ever held your tongue?"

Gentry sighed and pushed back up to a sitting position. "I wonder if you've ever tried doing something else. How do you know what you love most if you've only ever tried one thing? I like pepperoni pizza, but if I never try pizza with pineapple or prosciutto or olives, how do I know pepperoni is best?"

That explained a lot about her string of odd jobs and whimsical adventures. "Is that the kind of advice you dole out on your blog?"

"Sometimes."

"Good thing you're sticking with CTC, then," he deadpanned.

Gentry laughed. "It's good to hear you joke. Don't do it too often, though. I don't want to miss you when you go."

He suspected, after another two or three weeks together, he'd miss Colt and Gentry when he left, too. Another thing he hadn't counted on when he took this job. "Thanks, but something tells me you'll be fine by the time I clear out."

"I don't know. I'm pretty dangerous when left to my own devices." She flashed a saucy smile to make him laugh. "Then again, Colt and

I might not be on our own for long. I've decided to hire a PI to track down Smith."

"Really?" All week he'd been studying Colt and imagining what Smith must look like. Good-looking, no doubt, with Colt's shock of black hair and sapphire-blue eyes. It hadn't been pleasant picturing Gentry fawning all over the allegedly "hard to resist" guy, either.

"Yes, really. Why do you sound upset? Remember, you said—"

"I know what I said." He scowled, resisting the urge to fan himself as the airy room turned oddly close and sticky. On Monday, he'd been spouting off judgments like a would-be father who'd been kept in the dark. Six days later, his opinions weren't as clear-cut. Now he had a totally different perspective—a protective one. Jenna's opinion on this matter no longer seemed so selfish. "You'll check Smith out before welcoming him into your lives, though, right? I mean, you don't even know the guy. Based on what you told me, he doesn't seem very responsible—"

Gentry raised her hand and drily remarked, "Neither of us was very responsible." When Colt cooed, she burst into a wide smile before burying her nose in her son's belly to elicit more giggles. In a "mommy voice," she said, "And Mommy couldn't care less, because look at what I got. I'll never be sorry. Never, never."

That right there had become his favorite part of living in this fancy home, where he'd initially felt out of place. Gentry's love for Colt, which she unreservedly showered upon him, filled Ian with the tiniest yearning for something he couldn't even name. An odd ache he'd never had before.

He'd been an only child in a home that focused on others' needs over his. He never questioned his parents' love for him, but watching Gentry and Colt inspired a renewed kind of hope or wish for his future . . . for a family . . . for something more than the satisfaction he got from saving a life or lessening someone's suffering. The exact hope that had caused his final argument with his dad.

A week ago he couldn't wait to return to Haiti. Each day since then, his discomfort with the condo's swanky fixtures and zip code receded in direct proportion with his increased interest in the two Cabots rolling around on the floor.

He admitted none of this to Gentry as he slipped into the kitchen to make the much-needed coffee. Ian reminded himself of his limited role in their lives, and of Smith's claim on both of them.

From the other room, he heard Colt's fussing increase.

"Give me strength," Gentry called out. When Ian returned to the living room with his steaming cup of joe, she was rocking Colt. "Six weeks. That's how long Sara's precious books said colic would last. Well, six weeks came and went three weeks ago. If I had bought those books, I'd demand a refund. It's maddening, getting just little stretches of peace. I pray someday we'll go a whole day with minimal crying." She made a funny face. "Him *and* me."

"At least you can laugh about it."

"What choice is there? Pretty soon he'll be rolling, then crawling, then walking . . ." She rested her cheek against his head. "He won't understand that I'm tired or frustrated or scared. I don't want Colt to remember me as anything other than happy to be his mom. I also want him to be proud of who he is, faults and all."

Her gaze landed on the blue jay perched on the deck railing. Ian detected a tone he hadn't heard before, too. A mixture of regret and resolve. Her unguarded statement focused his own lens and helped him see her more clearly. In truth, what she wanted most of all was to give Colt a kind of security she'd never felt.

"That's exactly why you're a great mom." He knew she didn't quite believe that yet, but he'd keep reminding her.

She snapped her attention back to him. "Keep saying stuff like that and you'll find yourself locked up here forever," she teased. While he drank his coffee, she laid Colt on the floor and stretched his arms out, trying to distract him. "Actually, I had a thought. If my parents are free to babysit and you aren't busy tonight, come with me to A CertainTea. I'll introduce you to my sister, Colby."

"Meet your sister?" He choked on his coffee and pinched his nose to make sure that none dripped down his face.

"Chill. This isn't a *date* date. Colby runs the Maverick Foundation and might be able to help fund your plans. There's no plot to trap you, I promise." Then she playfully twisted her spine to reveal her crossed fingers. "Seriously, though. It's a great restaurant. You've helped me so much this week. Let me try to help you. When you do leave, I'll make a personal donation to your cause, but Colby might be able to be a long-term partner."

"That's very generous." He scratched the back of his head.

"I can't promise anything, but who knows?" Gentry shifted Colt to her lap, with his back against her belly, and jiggled him. Nothing she tried stopped his tears. She closed her eyes, uttering to herself, "Oh, Boo. Please, please . . . You might meet your daddy soon. If you can't stop crying, you'll scare him away."

Ian must've huffed or made some other unintentional sound that drew her attention.

"Got something to say, McJ?"

He shook his head and raised his empty mug. "Time for a refill."

He retreated to the kitchen to regroup. Before pouring himself a second cup, he closed his eyes and rested his forehead against the refrigerator. He should study the Maverick Foundation's website and plan a list of questions, not worry about whether or not Smith would crash into this household and destroy the beautiful world Gentry hoped to create for her son.

◆ ◆ ◆

By seven o'clock, Ian found himself seated in the most elegant restaurant he'd ever visited. If he didn't know better, he'd swear he'd stepped onto a movie set.

Long-range views of the lake eclipsed the ones from Gentry's home, which were partly obscured by the forest. From their table by the floor-to-ceiling open glass doors, he could see some of the waterfront homes and the blue-and-white sails on two Sunfish racing across the lake's choppy surface.

Soft peach light spilled into the restaurant, along with the sweet scent of evening primrose and lilies from the flower beds surrounding the adjacent patio. The celebratory sound of tinkling glasses and silverware should've fostered a festive or romantic mood. If he were a normal man, it would have done both.

Instead of enjoying the setting, he thought of his father and Archer, and what they would think of seeing him idly sitting here.

The Cabots, and everything they owned, embodied the privilege of wealth. Google searches had taught Ian that Jed Cabot was self-made. His older kids hadn't known extreme wealth until their teens. No doubt they earnestly worked hard and brushed up against obstacles from time to time, but they all now enjoyed a life free of worrying about money or security or hunger or anything serious, as far as he could tell.

Ian glanced around the dining room, watching others laughing and leaving fifty- and sixty-dollar meals partly uneaten. Those "scraps" could feed many starving homeless people right here in Oregon, let alone around the world.

"You seem unhappy. What gives?" Gentry sipped her blueberry martini, her long red locks spilling over the straps of the gold dress that looked more like a slip than an outfit.

"Nothing." He scanned the menu again to divert his attention from her figure. Wild Scottish Langoustine, Gulf Shrimp with Fiddlehead Ferns, and an Almond Grilled Wagyu dish for one hundred dollars. Nothing particularly recognizable or affordable.

"If you can't decide, the whole Poached Lobster Tail with Grilled Romaine and Citrus is fabulous." She smiled, oblivious to the fact that the price tag for that dish would feed a Haitian family for weeks. "God, it feels so good to be dressed up. It's my first night out without Colt since his birth."

He set down the menu, self-conscious about his casual cotton shirt. It had a collar, at least, but most of the other men wore jackets. He swiped at the perspiration along his hairline.

Gentry's bracelets jangled as they slid down her arm. She put her menu aside and leaned forward. "I wish you'd say what's on your mind. When people keep their thoughts to themselves, I assume the worst."

He fiddled with his fork, avoiding her gaze. Pride had never stopped him before, but he could barely swallow tonight. "I can't afford to eat here."

"It's my treat, Ian." She waved her hand as if wiping that concern off the table ended the discussion.

"I can't let you do that."

She set her elbows on the table, forearms crossed in front of her body. "You know, all week I've envied your great posture, but now I'm thinking maybe there's a giant stick up your—"

"Hey!"

Gentry laughed. "I'm paying for dinner as a thank-you for the extra hours you put in while I played catch-up at work."

He suspected she'd invent reasons until he gave in, so he stopped arguing. "Thank you."

Her eyes narrowed. "Yet still, you look tense and unhappy."

"It's hard to watch all these people leave their meals unfinished as if there aren't people all over Portland who're hungry." He expected her to slap him with another McJ remark, which he probably deserved.

Instead, Gentry surveyed the room, her gaze following the waiters and busboys clearing tables and pouring refills.

Sighing, she sat back and folded her hands in her lap. "It must be impossible to enjoy normal life if you can't stop making comparisons."

"This is hardly the *normal* life." He gestured around the space with one hand. "This is exceptional wealth."

"You say that like wealth is bad."

"It's not bad, per se." He'd talked himself into a corner. Another reason to hasten back to his own friends, who shared his experiences and sensibilities. "*Waste* is bad. A lack of gratitude is annoying."

"Why is that all you see? *I* see a restaurant that employs more than two dozen people, giving them all livelihoods. Not to mention the many patrons who contribute to the foundation, which donates to places like the Angel House." As she spoke, her spine became more erect. "Cabot Tea employs hundreds of people in multiple states, supporting all those families. And even frivolous little old me . . . every time I spend my money to buy an outfit or pedicure, that's keeping someone else employed. If people like me—like those in this room—stop enjoying some of the privilege of their wealth, then the economy shifts and others suffer, right?"

He'd pissed her off. He should've known not to let her goad him into talking. "I didn't mean to offend you. You asked me to be honest."

"I did and I'm not mad. I don't even deny that I, and others, can sometimes be wasteful and unappreciative. *Everyone* can. You want to talk about that, or how fortunate people could become more aware, compassionate, and helpful, I'm all ears as long as you don't act like all wealthy people are selfish jerks." She drummed her fingers on the table. "And here's something else to think about. Denying yourself the comforts of home by living in places like Haiti might let you *pretend* that you don't have it better than others, but you'll *always* have it better because you're free to come home, where clean water and food and health care aren't scarce." She sat back. "It's good to appreciate what you have and to be generous and giving, Ian, but you shouldn't treat good fortune like a guilty burden, either."

That insight would've shocked him before he knew her better, but Gentry Cabot had a shrewd way of viewing things, and a no-holds-barred rule when it came to opinions. A quick read through her blog proved that much. Before he could respond, an elegant woman approached the table.

Long and lithe, she wore a tailored, sleeveless white silk dress. She looked slightly familiar, but he couldn't place her.

"Colby." Gentry stood to hug her sister. They didn't look alike, but Colby *did* resemble her father, especially in the eyes, which turned upward at their outer edges. "This is Ian."

He stood and shook Colby's hand. "Nice to meet you."

She gestured for him to retake his seat. "It's nice to finally meet you. Sara raves about your mother and the Angel House. And thanks to your help, Gentry's like a new person this week. Colt can be a handful, so you both deserve a little pampering tonight."

Gentry shot Ian a pointed look. "Excellent point and timing, actually." Gentry took her seat and gestured to an open chair. "Can you join us for a second?"

"Sure." Colby settled onto the empty seat.

"Ian and I were discussing his EMT training program in Haiti. He and his partners are looking for more donors or alliances." Gentry shrugged off the details. "He can explain it better than me, but I thought maybe the Maverick Foundation might be interested in helping such a worthy cause."

Colby smiled, but years of watching his parents ask for donations had taught Ian how to spot an "I love the idea, but I can't help" expression.

"I'd love to hear more about your experiences, but unfortunately our foundation's stated mission is to serve the people of Oregon. We don't have the resources to fund international projects." She elbowed Gentry. "Of course, if the ChariTea launch takes off, the foundation could amend that position in the future. Tell me what you need. Maybe I can put you in contact with others who can help now."

"We're in the early stages. My partner, Archer, is a British doctor, but he's been working in Haiti for more than a decade. Haitians have extremely poor access to decent medical care. Unless someone's in imminent danger of death, hospitals won't even fill a prescription from their own stock. Families need to go elsewhere to buy the medication, assuming they can afford it. If the hospital does fill it, then the family has to restock it as soon as possible." Both women's mouths fell open, so he didn't elaborate on the many other ways that medical care was lacking. "Anyhow, we realize we can't fix that systemic problem but hope to improve ambulatory care. Currently, emergency patients walk to the hospital or wait for a ride or come on motorcycles, if at all. If we train locals to be EMTs and provide ambulances and supplies, it'll give more people a fighting chance for a decent prognosis."

"I can't even imagine that." Colby tossed her tawny hair over her shoulder and leaned forward. "What are your biggest obstacles?"

"Haiti's infrastructure, for starters. They're still rebuilding from the earthquake and subsequent hurricanes, and much of the money sent there has been diverted to the wrong people. Another major challenge will be setting up a steady pipeline of supplies." As he spoke to Colby, Gentry's expression shifted to something uncharacteristically somber.

"Have you partnered with anyone specific yet?" Colby asked.

"Not yet. At this point, it's been mostly random donations. We've received enough money to rent an old garage structure and hire one local, Stanley, to start working with us. We still need so much more, including vehicles."

Colby sat back, her expression thoughtful. "I'm sorry I can't commit funding, but let me scroll through my contacts. I've met a lot of philanthropists this past year. Maybe I can make some introductions while you're in town."

"I appreciate any help. Thank you." Ian glanced at Gentry, whose gaze remained fixed on the flickering candle on their table.

"I'm sorry I can't do more." Colby touched her sister's arm. "But I'll get back to you with anything I learn as soon as possible."

"Thanks, Colby. I knew you'd help." Gentry raised her martini glass, but her impish smile didn't reappear.

"Frankly, I'm surprised you're not plotting to keep Ian around."

Gentry's face blanked for the briefest moment, but she snapped right back to reality. "He's been great, but you know me. I never count on anyone for long. No point in planning out the future when it never turns out how you expect."

"My gypsy-spirited sister," Colby teased. "If I didn't know better, I'd swear you were related to *my* mother instead of Jenna."

"Your mom would kill you for saying that." Gentry's left brow shot up.

Colby bumped her sister's shoulder. "I'm sure she likes you much more than she lets on. Your only crime is being Jenna's daughter."

"Who can blame Leslie for disliking my mother? Sometimes even *I* can't stand her."

"You don't mean that." Colby cast Ian a quick glance, as if he'd think less of Gentry for the biting remark. He'd met Jenna, so he understood Gentry just fine.

The waiter arrived, interrupting them. "May I take your orders?"

Colby stood. "I'll let you enjoy your night. The oysters are excellent, by the way. And Ian, I'll get you some helpful information soon."

"Thanks," he said as she waved goodbye. He scanned the menu while Gentry ordered. The cheapest item was some kind of hand-cut pasta and cheese with Australian truffles that he had no idea how to pronounce. When it was his turn, he said, "I'll take the fancy mac and cheese, thanks."

Gentry had been staring at the lake in silence while he'd ordered. It allowed him a chance to appreciate her regal profile. Seeing her expressive face at rest intrigued him.

The waiter returned and refilled their water glasses. Gentry repeatedly tapped a finger on the side of the glass. "I'm sorry for being flip about your life earlier. I don't know you well enough to guess your motives. You must love it there . . . and love your dad to want to honor him this way."

His father's face surfaced in his mind, followed closely by the two-story flamingo-pink building that had been damaged by the earthquake, and then the aftershock that brought down what had remained while his father was inside.

"You look haunted." Gentry's eyes went round.

"That's about right," he muttered aloud.

"Sorry. I'm not good at respecting 'normal' boundaries . . . in case you hadn't noticed." She allowed him a chance to decide whether to share more. When he remained tongue-tied, she said, "I admire your work ethic, but you need some joy, too. Before you leave, I'm determined to make a few fun memories with you, Ian Crawford." She raised the martini glass to her lips and enjoyed a long swallow. "Promise me, once you go, you'll remember to make yourself happy now and then. Not to be clichéd, but you do only live once."

Chapter Seven

Merriment

According to *Merriam-Webster*: lighthearted gaiety or fun-making : HILARITY

According to me: my mission for Colt (and Ian)

"You might as well come inside." Gentry turned off the engine and stared at her parents' home. "I need to visit for at least ten minutes or my mom will find some new way to torment me at work."

Ian shifted in the passenger seat, rubbing his palms along his thighs. "They probably prefer to spend those few minutes without me."

"Oh, trust me. My mother wants a chance to get a clearer read on you, and *that* will take the pressure off me." Gentry winked, although she was dead serious.

"Great," came his dry response.

Gentry patted his hand, then withdrew, resisting the urge to turn his palm over and trace its lines to discover new things about him. "If I can put up with her judgment for twenty-six years and counting, you can do it for a few minutes. It'll be fun. A 'judgy' standoff. Maybe I should sell tickets."

"You're hilarious," he mocked, tugging on her hair. For a second, they sat there, her hair wound around his finger; then he released it.

She covered her breathlessness with a joke. "Now, now. Don't envy my sense of humor. I can teach you to have one, too."

"Keep it up, wiseass." He twisted in his seat. "But here's my question. Why do you two argue so much?"

Resentment. Disappointment. Attention. "Habit."

She flung the door open and exited the car, eager to walk away from that discussion. Rounding the hood, she observed her parents' home from the perspective of an outsider like Ian.

Not a pebble littered the intricately designed granite walkway. No weed dared blemish the massive flower beds. Everything was perfectly manicured and tended to, exactly like her mother. And just like with her mother, most of that tending came from someone else's effort—the stylist, the decorator, the gardener, and so on.

To meet Jenna Cabot now, one would never believe she'd been Jenna Buchanan from Danbury, Connecticut. Daughter of a single, working mom who'd worked at Ruby's Dry Cleaner by day and waited the counter at the Silver Star Diner by night. She and her sister had been raised in a tiny but clean apartment. Gentry's mom had studied endlessly, knowing her only shot at attending college required a full scholarship.

When Jenna was eleven, her father, a mall cop with a gambling habit, had taken off for parts unknown. If Gentry's mom had any sorrow about that, she never showed it. But that history made Jenna leery of most men.

Gentry had met that grandfather once, when she was around ten years old and too young to understand the truth. Having had no other living grandfather, and being from a dysfunctional family, she'd been thrilled when Grandpa John had appeared. Finally, someone who might like *her* best.

She remembered dragging him by the hand up to her room to show him her drawings. She'd even performed a little of her ballet recital to win his love. To become his someone special. Grandparents loved their grandchildren, after all. They bragged endlessly, especially Shelly Smythe's grandmother.

Of course, Grandpa John had only come to Oregon in search of a handout. He'd been there less than forty-eight hours when her mom had handed him five grand and told him to leave. He took the money without looking back or contacting Gentry again.

"What's wrong?" Ian touched her shoulder.

She emerged from that memory slightly shaken. Back then she'd been livid with her mom for sending Grandpa John away. Now she understood that keeping that man out of her life had been a giant favor. "Sorry. Zoned out. Must be the martini."

"Maybe I ought to be driving."

"I'll be fine." She opened the door and watched Ian struggle not to react to the marble floors, bronze banister, and soaring ceiling. "Okay, McJ. Take stock and then bury that indignation before my mom sees it."

He raised his hands. "I didn't say a word."

"You didn't have to. You'd suck at poker." Their conversation got cut short by Colt's wail echoing through the cavernous home. She clapped her hands together. "My little bugaboo knows I'm here."

Ian grinned. "He's clairvoyant."

She gestured for him to follow her back to the family room. In the past, she'd proudly brought friends home. Tonight her stomach twisted uncomfortably with each step they took through the rambling home. She didn't dare look back at Ian, who no doubt would turn it into a shelter for as many people as he and his mother could squeeze under its roof.

Her mother stood over Gentry's nearly naked son in the corner of the family room, dabbing at her shirt. Gentry covered a smile, knowing

Colt had just peed on her mom. Not a surprise, when she thought about it. After all, changing diapers had always been the nanny's job. "Everything okay?"

"Everything's perfect." Her mom dropped the towel and cradled Colt. He wriggled and fussed, but Jenna didn't give up easily. She continued to nuzzle him against her bony shoulder.

Gentry hugged her dad after he and Ian shook hands. "I bet you're ready for a little peace and quiet."

"No, no. We love having Colt to ourselves. I'm thinking he'll be a terrific singer with all the practice his lungs are getting." Her dad beamed at Ian. "I can't get enough of my grandkids. Two in less than six months. I'm blessed!"

Her mother raised Colt in the air. Staring into his eyes, she affected a gooey grandmother voice. "But you're my favorite, Colton Cabot. Yes, you are. Yes, you are!"

Her mom seemed doomed to repeat history with her "us versus them" mentality when it came to Gentry's siblings.

Ian's brows rose right before he looked away.

"We don't have favorites," her dad hurried to add. "Both boys are adorable Cabots."

Her mother finished dressing Colt, continuing to speak her mind through a false conversation with Colt. "Right now you're a Cabot. But what if your mommy finds Smith and he wants to change your last name? We don't even know what that could be, do we? Has she thought of that?"

"I'm standing right here," Gentry sighed.

"I know." Her mother held Colt tight again, brushing his wispy dark hair with her hand. "I'm hoping you'll reconsider this idea of hunting down Colt's father."

Gentry considered her options. A: make like normal with a sarcastic remark. B: tell her mom it wasn't any of her business. Or C: show empathy. "I get it, Mom. You worry that Colt's dad will be like *your* father. But what if he's like mine?"

She smiled at her dad, who threw his arm around her shoulders and hugged her.

"There aren't many fathers like yours." Her mom said it in a way that sounded like a compliment about herself for snagging him—or stealing him, if you looked at it from Leslie Cabot's perspective.

Either way, Gentry's patience had run out. "I've made up my mind, Mother."

"How was dinner?" Her dad changed the subject.

"Fine." Gentry turned to Ian, who, despite her best efforts, hadn't quite removed that stick from his behind. "I'd hoped Colby could kick some foundation money Ian's way, but it's against the charter or something."

"She offered other help that will likely be as valuable," Ian said. Mr. Manners. No wonder Sara liked him so well.

"I'm sure she'll make good on her promise," her father said. "Did you like the food?"

"Of course," Ian said.

Her father shook his head, chuckling. "I know it's top-notch stuff, but I prefer food I can pronounce."

Ian grinned. "I was skeptical at first, but my meal was delicious."

"Well, that's good. I'm grateful the place is doing well. Colby and Alec needed a win after everything they've been through," her dad said.

Gentry reached for her son, eager to leave. Nothing had gone quite according to plan tonight. While she didn't know how to salvage it all, she knew more time with her mom wasn't the answer. "We'd better get Boo to bed. Thanks for watching him."

"Anytime." Her mother hovered, stroking Colt's head, her face soft and full of adoration. "I love this little fusspot."

Gentry couldn't recall her mom ever being so gentle with her. Instead of hugs, praise, and tenderness, Gentry had been dealt rules, lectures, and consequences. That bitter memory caused her to flinch when her mother tried to kiss her goodbye.

She allowed her mom to love on Colt because she wanted everyone to love on her son, but she couldn't pretend that she and her mom enjoyed a warm rapport. For Pete's sake, they were still working on cordial.

"See you on Monday," Gentry said as she and Ian left.

Colt was unusually quiet during the ride home. She should be doing cartwheels that he'd settled down, but she couldn't quite trust it.

"What did your dad mean about Colby and Alec?" Ian asked after a minute, referring to her dad's slip about them needing a win.

She supposed their history wasn't much of a secret anymore, and Ian didn't appear to have an agenda.

"Here's the short version. Colby's late husband, Mark, committed suicide in front of her by jumping off their condo balcony several weeks after he'd dared their friend—Alec's brother, Joe—to jump off the cliff above Punch Bowl Falls. That dare killed Joe. Everyone grieved for a long time . . ." She thought of Alec's other secrets but decided not to share all the details. "Until recently, no one but Colby knew Mark was bipolar, because he wanted that kept secret. So, basically, it took a long time for the families to heal, forgive each other, and put their lives back together."

"Wow." Ian stared ahead, eyes wide and fixed on the road. "I'd never suspect so much turmoil and loss—"

"Because people with money never suffer real pain and loss, right?" She probably shouldn't have been so sarcastic, but she wanted him to stop making assumptions about people like her.

He didn't reply, so she kept quiet for the remainder of the drive home.

The silence gave her time to think. Think about her mom's past and the present. Think about her sister's change of circumstance. Think about her life and her choices. About the things she wanted for her son but didn't know how to provide.

And then she thought about Ian.

She didn't want to interfere with his plans to save the world, but it seemed a shame he couldn't do it from Oregon. If they had more time together, she'd probably learn a lot from him. And she could teach him a thing or two, like how to enjoy himself now and then. Everyone needs good memories to get them through the days when life slams into them like a tsunami.

But even when the worst happens, beauty can come from destruction—like Colby and Alec's love, or Ty becoming a Cabot because of his mother's overdose.

"You look like you're plotting," Ian said when they pulled into the garage.

Gentry unfastened Colt from his car seat and laid his sleepy body on her shoulder. In a quiet voice, she said, "I'm sure you caught my mom's little dig against Ty. I don't want Colt to think of Ty as anything less than a cousin. Honestly, I wonder if my mom ever hears herself."

"Colt will take his cues from you. If you accept Ty as family, he will, too."

Could it be that simple? "I hope so. The truth is, I haven't spent much time with Ty lately because I've been struggling to handle Colt."

Ian held open the door for her. They stopped in the entry, which was lit by a small lamp.

She didn't turn on the overhead lights, hoping to keep Colt lulled in his half slumber long enough to transfer him to his bassinet.

Ian locked the front door, then raked a hand through those mahogany waves of hair. "Invite Ty over tomorrow. I'll lend a hand. Your brother and Sara might like a little Sunday break, and you can spend time with your nephew."

"You'd help?" She stopped and stared at him. Most men she'd known wanted her for her body or her money. None had ever gone out of their way to be kind without some other agenda. "I mean, I'll pay you for working."

"No need. I'm not busy, and I want to help . . ." Ian's eyes looked darker than normal. His pupils were almost as big as his irises in the dimly lit space. All week they'd exchanged these little moments—the kind riddled with delicious tingles.

At another time in her life, she would've taken advantage of it and kissed him. The mere thought made her gaze at his mouth, which sent a rousing shiver down her back. But Ian Crawford wouldn't be impressed by a bold sexual move. And anyway, she still had Colt in her arms.

"Let's make it fun. I'll plan a picnic by the lake." Gentry's imagination kicked into gear, coming up with a plan to ensure both Ty and Ian had a memorable day.

"Sounds nice."

He stood so very close yet remained impossibly far away. She did *not* want to like him. Or be curious about how his coarse hair would feel in her fingers. Or fantasize that he could soothe her the way he did her son. Those thoughts only set her up for rejection, like with Grandpa John and everyone else who so easily left her behind.

As Ian would when he left for Haiti.

And still, whenever Ian did go, she wanted him to remember her fondly . . . at least for a little while. "I'll make it perfect."

◆ ◆ ◆

Ian sprawled out on the gray-and-lime-green plaid blanket, feeding Colt from a bottle, while Gentry chased Ty around the edge of the lake with her camera. In a pile beside Ian lay a giant bubble wand, water guns, and a beach ball, all of which Gentry had purchased that morning.

Hunter and Sara had hesitated to leave Ty with them. Born to a drug addict hadn't been the easiest start in the kid's young life, so Ian didn't take offense to their protectiveness. Gentry had worn her brother down, though, as Ian suspected she did often. Sara had dropped off Ty an hour ago, along with a list of instructions and rules, which Gentry conveniently "forgot" on the kitchen counter.

Now she chased the toddler along the water's edge, snapping photos as they went. Ty's delighted screeches echoed across the lake as he splashed in the water, sandy mud oozing between his toes. Within twenty minutes, his mud-soaked shirt and pants clung to him. His overstimulated smile would melt even Jenna's heart.

Ian couldn't remember spending idle time with his own parents. Picnics he'd attended had been church affairs where they'd also collected money, or clothing for shelters. He hadn't a single memory of his mother chasing him with a camera, her hair flying in the breeze, creating a scene for the sole purpose of making him laugh.

He'd never thought he'd missed out on anything until the joyful sounds of Ty's rare giggle, and the rustling leaves overhead, caused a slight pang.

Eventually Gentry and Ty returned to the blanket to eat. Ian placed Colt in the car seat so he'd be safe but upright and able to observe. He stretched a bit, savoring the sunny afternoon and mood. A mood he attributed to the complicated, playful woman who'd been consuming more of his thoughts each day.

"I got Ty to laugh, now I need to work my magic on you." Gentry smiled at Ian, her cheeks pink from exertion.

As if that magic hadn't already taken root. "Planning to chase me with the camera?"

"No. Getting you to loosen up will take a bit of creativity—possibly even something mildly shocking," Gentry teased.

Her warning made his body hum and the hairs on his neck come alive. She excited him with very little effort. A dangerous reality for both of them.

She looped her hair up into some kind of knot on her head and then fixed Ty a plate with a crust-free ham sandwich, orange slices, and a vanilla cupcake. "Ty, this is our secret, okay?"

"'Kay." He immediately stuffed the cupcake into his mouth, eyes wide with sugar fever.

"Eat the other stuff first, honey." She grimaced at Ian as she handed him a ham-and-turkey sandwich loaded with extras, muttering, "Now I get Hunter's no-sugar rule."

"You know you'll get busted." Ian had no doubt Hunter would not find it cute that Gentry had broken his rule. "I'm surprised by you, too, considering how you insisted that I follow *your* rules."

"Not letting my son cry himself to sleep is not the same as giving a kid a treat. Jeesh, you, my brother, and Sara could benefit from a little rule breaking now and then. Moderation in all things, I think." She leaned forward and drolly added, "No one ever died from a cupcake."

"This *is* the first time you've used your oven, so these cupcakes might actually be lethal," he said, straight-faced, bracing for a whack to the thigh.

"Even I can't mess up box-brand cupcakes and canned icing."

"Let's test that." He gestured for a cupcake.

She stretched across the blanket to reach the Tupperware container. Seeing her on her hands and knees in those microshorts and tank top did strange things to his heart. Fortunately—or unfortunately—she was quick to sit back on her haunches.

He reached out for the cupcake, still buzzing from his physical response, so he didn't pay much attention to her funny expression. Before he understood what was happening, she lunged forward and smashed that cupcake in his face. She then scrambled backward, laughing nervously at his stunned response.

Both of them ignored Colt's startled cry as Ian jumped to his feet to chase after her. Once he caught her from behind, he lifted her off the ground and swung her around while she laughed. A burst of joy shocked his heart.

Gentry wriggled in his arms, all laughter and soft curves and perfumed hair. His senses lit up, setting him on fire. Everything in him longed to lay her down on the soft grass and kiss her senseless. Instead, he rubbed his sugared face against her neck and shoulder. Torture for him, because her soft skin tempted him beyond control.

He released her before he acted on his urges, then swiped the icing off her neck with his fingers, licking one.

"Look at you, Ian Crawford." Her eyes twinkled as she fell to the ground beside Ty, then she carefully avoided Ian's gaze while fixing the hairs that had fallen loose. "Now I finally know what you look like when you're truly happy."

Ian didn't know what to say to that, so he brushed off the last of the crumbs from his shirt before taking a seat on the blanket. He rocked Colt's car seat, buying himself a few seconds for his heart to settle.

Thankfully, Gentry didn't bombard him with questions or commentary. She tended to Ty, encouraging him to eat the healthy food he'd ignored. Once Ty had cleaned his plate, Gentry filled the large plastic dish with the liquid soap and tested the bubble wand.

Ty's eyes grew three sizes rounder as she created a massive oblong bubble that glistened in the sunlight. He tried to catch it, popping it in the process. Before the kid's tears spilled over, Gentry formed another and then popped it herself.

"Your turn!" She knelt down to hand Ty the wand, but Colt started crying again, as if he sensed losing his mother's attention to a rival. Definitely his mother's son, Ian thought with a smile.

"I've got him," Ian said, enjoying watching Gentry play with her nephew. What a gift she was to these two boys—so wild and free and full of humor.

"Thanks." Gentry patiently showed Ty how to manipulate the wand to create the enormous bubbles that glistened with misshapen rainbows.

Once he got the hang of it, she picked up her camera and shot photos from every angle.

Sunlight filtered through the trees while Ian jostled Colt on his lap and continued snacking on his lunch. In the distance, a pair of sixty-something women was walking toward them on the nearby path. As they passed by, the chubbier lady waved at them, exclaiming, "You have a beautiful family."

"Thank you!" Gentry hollered back without correcting them, her face lit up with a giant smile.

Funny how five words altered everything.

Minutes earlier, Ian was simply helping Gentry create memories for son, her nephew, and herself. Now the ten-pound weight on his lap felt like more than just his charge. Gentry's easy laugh and Ty's curious face also took on a different—if illusory—meaning. For those few seconds, Ian imagined himself a father, a husband, an uncle.

It didn't feel quite right, but it didn't feel all wrong, either.

Gentry broke his train of thought when she ran through Ty's large bubble while singing out, "Ta-da!"

Ty's dimples deepened as he struggled with the wand to make another.

"Why didn't you correct her?" Ian finally asked.

Gentry shrugged. "I liked being a family, even if it only lasted four seconds."

She turned away, redirecting her attention to Ty.

A study in contradiction, this woman whose only consistent behavior was an attempt to build a family for her son, even as she held *her* mother at bay.

Colt fussed in his lap, so Ian nicked his finger across some frosting and stuck it in the baby's mouth. Within three seconds, Colt's mouth clamped around Ian's index finger and sucked it dry.

For the past ninety minutes, Ian hadn't once thought about his future, Haiti, or any of the other things that usually preoccupied him.

He'd been swept up in the idyll of a summer day, happy kids, and a beautiful woman.

Now, with Colt snuggling against him, he knew a moment of panic. A few more weeks spent this way might make him soft. Leaving this baby would test his heart. And Gentry—saying goodbye to her and the different kind of future she dangled before him—might mess with him the most.

Chapter Eight

Flutter

According to *Merriam-Webster*: **a :** to move with quick wavering or flapping motions; **b :** to vibrate in irregular spasms

According to me: my insides when Ian is close

Ian conveniently avoided Gentry's gaze while helping buckle the kids into their seats. For a little while today, she'd thought he'd let himself relax. He'd even frolicked! Then she'd spooked him with that family remark. Like a groundhog, he'd burrowed underground.

Ian closed her car's back door. "I'll grab an Uber."

"Don't be ridiculous. It's five minutes out of my way, tops." Okay, fifteen. But Gentry wanted to see the infamous Angel House and meet his mother. She could learn a thing or two about mothering from the woman who'd raised a man with so much compassion. "I've got a little time before Hunter and Sara expect Ty back home. Plus, I bet your mom would enjoy seeing him."

Ian slunk into the passenger seat. "She probably would."

Gentry rolled down all the windows and cranked up the radio, forcing all three passengers to listen to her not-too-awful rendition of

Rachel Platten's "A Better Place." She hadn't chosen the sweet love song, but her heart raced to match its peppy tempo. The lyrics sounded like they'd been ripped from her thoughts and, as such, pumped hope and happiness and a little sorrow into her chest.

Ian sat unnaturally still until he turned and stared out the side window. That only made Gentry want to sing louder, to do anything she could think of to provoke him into revealing something that proved maybe she wasn't imagining the earlier signs of interest. Of desire. Of more than that, though, because, for her, Ian Crawford was the first man who could tempt her into thinking beyond a fling, even *with* that stick of his still making an occasional appearance.

He didn't use her. He wasn't phony or fickle. Ian's past showed that he knew how to love and commit. He challenged and encouraged her, giving her confidence in her ability to mother Colt. And today, when those women thought Ian was her husband, well, that'd shot her daydreams to a whole new level.

She told herself that harmless fantasies were safe because Ian came with a built-in expiration date. His prior commitment wasn't the same as rejection. Either way, she couldn't have him pity her or think that she'd be pining away for him.

"I can help you raise money," she blurted out, surprising them both.

"What?"

She couldn't blame him for failing to follow her train of thought, which changed tracks so often even she had a hard time keeping up.

"We struck out with Colby, but maybe I could help set up a kick-ass crowdfunding page."

"There might be restrictions on NGOs."

"So I'll figure that out. I could promote it on my blog. Do you have photos of the people and kids you've helped?"

"Not really. I used to take pictures in the beginning because I wanted to capture everything. Now I'm too focused on the work to think about that." Ian rubbed his jaw while mulling over her plan, eyes bright with interest. "Crowdfunding, though. It's not a bad idea."

"How come every time I have a good idea, people act so surprised?" She tightened her grip on the steering wheel. "Do I seem like an idiot?"

"You're definitely *not* an idiot." Ian took his phone out of his back pocket and started scrolling through his contacts. "I'll shoot Archer an e-mail to see if he knows of any restrictions on crowdfunding."

"Archer?"

"My dad's doctor friend. The one who teaches me French."

"I know who he is. Why would he know about crowdfunding?"

"He's got more experience with NGOs and donors than I do. Until recently, I'd run around the world volunteering wherever needed. Archer's stayed in Haiti. He knows all the players and can get quick answers."

Although Gentry couldn't imagine living under the conditions and with the risks Ian had described since they'd met, part of her envied the adventure of his unusual life. The contrast made her realize how empty her attempts—or *mis*adventures—had been.

They pulled up to the curb in front of a rather unattractive, mustard-yellow, brick-and-siding split-level home on a quiet tree-lined street. "Did you grow up here?"

"No. My mom took this position after my father died." Ian opened the door. He always avoided eye contact whenever his father came up. Gentry smelled a story there.

She squelched her questions for now. "Should I wait here?"

He finally met her gaze. "Yeah. Let me grab her."

Gentry spent a second checking on Colt, who'd fallen asleep in the car seat, as had Ty. She walked around to the other side of the car to wake her nephew. Her shorts rode up her butt as she bent over to unbuckle him, causing her to tug at them with one hand while finger-fluffing Ty's hair with the other, hoping to make a good impression on Ian's mother.

"Ahem." Ian cleared his throat from a few feet away.

Gentry turned around before he cleared the smirk off his face and his mother finished her head-to-toe assessment. The woman's gaze lingered on Gentry's ankle tattoo for a moment. Gentry knew Mrs. Crawford had probably seen it all, but she probably preferred her son to hang out with more wholesome women.

The older woman's matronly face was surrounded by silver hair. Given Ian's height and more angular features, he had to resemble his father, because his mom was round everywhere.

As an afterthought, Gentry stuck her hand out. "Hi, I'm Gentry Cabot. Sara's sister-in-law."

"Hi, Gentry. I'm Gloria." Gloria's gaze now darted between her son and Gentry. "Thank you for giving Ian a place to hang his hat while he's in town."

"It's been my pleasure," Gentry admitted, blabbing, "I'll be lost when he goes."

Ian blinked at the sentiment. "You'll be perfectly fine."

"He thinks if he repeats that enough I'll eventually believe him," Gentry admitted to his mom, whose gaze studied her son. "The daily chaos *before* he showed up proves otherwise. But he's got his plans, so I'll have to manage on my own."

"You won't be on your own for long." He caught her eye, then looked away. A hint that maybe Ian didn't look forward to Smith taking his place. Too bad she couldn't dig into all that right now.

"Being a single mom can be scary," Gloria said. "But you look like you can handle it."

Gentry had heard that kind of remark her whole life. At first it sounded like a compliment, but beneath the shiny top layer was the ugly stuff. The snap judgment. Gloria had taken one look at Gentry's tattoos, snug clothes, and ring-free finger, and dubbed Gentry trashy, hard, or smutty. None of those labels were a compliment.

"I'll do my best." Gentry smiled, burying the pain of such dismissal. "Before I go, I thought you might like to say hello to Ty." She stepped aside so Ty could exit the car.

Gloria crouched and opened her arms for a hug. "Oh my, Ty. Look at what a big boy you are now!"

Ty had never been demonstrative, and only recently had become affectionate with Sara and Hunter, so it didn't surprise Gentry when he didn't run into Gloria's arms. It *did* surprise her when he took off for the house, calling out, "Mama."

Gentry clutched her chest like she could somehow block the dagger those cries jabbed into her heart.

"Oh dear," Gloria said. "He must associate the house with Pam."

"Crap!" Gentry took off after Ty and scooped him up. He struggled, reaching over her shoulder.

"Mama's not there, Ty. Let's get you home to your mommy." All she could think to do now was distract him, compounding one mistake with another. "How about another cupcake?"

She asked Ian to buckle him back in the car seat while she fished around the trunk for another cupcake. The icing had melted a bit, but the treat might keep him occupied long enough to let her get away from this place and those memories.

"It's okay, Gentry." Ian rubbed her arm.

Her body flushed with waves of heat as tears threatened to spill. *Idiot. Idiot. Idiot.*

After handing Ty the cupcake, she closed the door and faced Ian and his mom. "I'm so sorry. It never occurred to me that coming here could upset him. Sara's gonna kill me."

"Sara is a lovely woman. I'm sure she'll understand," Gloria said. Gentry's gaffe had softened the woman's condescension. In this case, Gentry would make an exception and accept her pity.

"We all make mistakes," Ian assured her.

"Sara *never* makes mistakes!" Gentry kept running her hands over her hair as if that would get her out of the jam with Hunter. "I'd better go. Sorry to be rude. Nice to meet you, Gloria." Gentry scooted around to the driver's side with a quick wave.

At least the cupcake-palooza distracted Ty, who'd stopped calling for his mother. She'd have to remember to remove the icing from his cheeks before Sara and Hunter saw it.

In her rearview mirror, Gentry watched Ian and his mom pile into a run-down Honda. If she had to guess, they were on their way to a soup kitchen or something similar. Definitely *not* going to Pioneer Place for a shopping spree. She made a mental note to herself to be sure to expose Colt to *both* types of mother-son outings when he got older.

She arrived at Hunter's ten minutes later, grabbed a fistful of baby wipes from Colt's diaper bag, and cleaned Ty's face and fingers. She kissed his head, eyes closed, thinking her hundredth silent apology. "Okay, let's go see your mommy and daddy."

She detached Colt's car seat from its base and carried him to Hunter's front door, with Ty in tow.

Sara greeted them and immediately crouched to hug her son. "Did you have the best time? I missed you!"

Ty accepted the hug before pushing away to run through the house, presumably on a hunt for his toys.

"Wow, he's wired!" Sara stood with a puzzled expression. Shrugging, she then offered Colt her best smile while asking, "Is Ian in the car?"

"No." Gentry couldn't have this conversation on the porch. "Can I come in?"

"Of course. I want to hear all about your day with the boys." Sara waved her inside. "Hunter's in the kitchen."

Gentry hadn't spent much time here since those early weeks of pregnancy, when she'd moved in to escape her mom. Every time she remembered the adoption promise she'd broken, an uneasy feeling—like the one experienced when cresting the high point of a roller coaster—grabbed hold. After today's incident, Gentry's doubts about whether keeping Colt had been in his best interests soared. Hunter and Sara might be uptight and too structured, but they'd never be as thoughtless as she'd been today. What kind of emotional damage had Gentry caused Ty, and how might she hurt Colt in the coming years?

Gentry set Colt's car seat on the island and kissed her brother hello. Hopefully, he wouldn't notice her clammy skin. The near-spotless kitchen smelled like sautéed onions. A quick glance at the plate beside the stove revealed a cheeseburger waiting for its topping.

She aimed for a joke. "You have the worst eating habits."

"I've cut back." He shrugged. "Ask Sara."

"You have an interesting way of making things sound better than they are," Sara teased, then cocked a brow at Gentry. "Sure, he's cut back . . . a little. Now, here's an important question. Can I cuddle Colt?"

"Sure." If Sara had Colt in her arms, it'd be harder for her to strangle Gentry when she learned about Ty's visit to the Angel House. She removed Colt from his car seat and handed him over, waiting until Sara seemed blissfully distracted. "So I have a confession."

"Let me guess. You broke our rules." Hunter lowered the wooden spoon, shaking his head and smiling as if he expected it. "Which one?"

He didn't seem too upset, but only because he had no clue she'd gone beyond breaking his silly rules and done something truly stupid.

"I drove Ian to the Angel House with the kids in the car. I thought maybe Ty would like to see Gloria, but as soon as he did, it triggered memories of Pam."

All the blood that drained from Sara's face magically appeared in Hunter's cheeks. "What's the matter with you? You know I don't even like *Sara* going there since that violent husband attacked her."

"I'm sorry. I think of Ty as yours, so Pam never crossed my mind. I was stunned when he ran toward the house, calling out, 'Mama.'"

Gentry closed her eyes to avoid seeing Sara's face.

"For God's sake, Gentry. When will you learn to think before you act?" Hunter banged the spoon on the side of the pan, all traces of humor erased.

"I'm sorry." Her spine curved like a shrimp, and she looked at the ground.

"He seems okay now." Sara put Colt back into his car seat, her voice slightly strained. "How'd you calm him down?"

Gentry closed her eyes again, mumbling, "I gave him a cupcake."

She heard the spoon clatter in the stainless steel sink right before Hunter muttered in dismay, "How the hell can I trust you with our son when you show such poor judgment *and* disrespect our rules? He looks like you tried to drown him in muddy water, too."

"I'm sorry. But we had *fun*, Hunter. We played by the lake with giant bubbles and squirt guns. I took some amazing photos of him and Colt. Wait until you see them." She hugged herself. "I loved spending time with him. We had a perfect morning, and he was so happy, giggles spilled out of him."

"Until confronted by memories of his dead mother, you mean?" Her brother spoke low enough not to be heard by his son, his owlish gaze tearing through her like claws. "Let's just hope he doesn't have nightmares about Pam tonight."

Ty was playing quietly in the family room by himself. He didn't appear to be suffering. Did the memories of sitting beside Pam's dead body for hours lurk in his memory? Would those be his nightmares?

Tears formed behind Gentry's eyes. Even when she had the best intentions, she screwed up. At this rate, she might as well give up trying to be one big happy family. For every step forward, she stumbled ten steps backward.

"It was an honest mistake, Hunter. She obviously feels bad about it, so let's not make it worse. That won't help anyone." Sara crossed to her husband and stroked his back. "I'll take Ty upstairs and read to him. He needs a nap, anyway. No fighting while I'm gone."

On her way out of the kitchen, Sara squeezed Gentry's shoulder. After she disappeared, Gentry faced her brother.

"I'm sorry," Gentry reiterated, her voice tight with desperation. "Really, really sorry."

Hunter shoved his burger into his mouth. Perspiration dribbled down her spine during the endless seconds she waited for him to finish chewing. He sighed, his tone shifting from anger to frustration. "You're a mom now, Gentry. You've got to start thinking like one."

"I do."

"Do you? Have you figured out Colt's childcare? How will Colt feel when Ian disappears from his life? Last year you swore there'd be no way to find Smith. Now suddenly we're hiring a PI. Seems to me like you still jump into decisions without considering the consequences."

Being thrust on the defensive brought her armor up and, with it, her chin. "Hiring the PI *is* me thinking like a mom. Colt will want to know who his father is."

"Colt's your business. But when it comes to Ty, you've got to respect Sara's and my wishes." Hunter sighed, slapping the crumbs off his hands after he finished the burger—in record time, she thought. He set his plate in the sink, then surprised Gentry by slinging an arm over her shoulders. "We'll let today's slip-ups go since Ty seemed calm enough."

"I swear, I swept him away as soon as he reacted. I know the cupcake thing wasn't the best solution, but I panicked."

"I understand. But be honest with me. Exactly how many cupcakes did you give my son today?"

Gentry stared into his intense hazel eyes. "Not near enough."

◆ ◆ ◆

Ian's plan to slip up to his room unnoticed fell apart the moment he entered the condo. Gentry lounged on her sofa in pajama shorts and a tank top, a MacBook resting on her thighs, with a glass of red wine keeping her company.

"I thought you'd never come back." She set the laptop to one side and crossed her legs. Raising her hands in a "hold the phone" manner, she launched into a recitation of her afternoon. "I have good, bad, and frustrating news. The good—Hunter didn't kill me, and Colt went down easily tonight, thus the celebratory glass of pinot noir." She pointed at the wineglass, then huffed, moving on. "The bad news? Hunter and Sara probably won't let me be alone with Ty for months—maybe years. I've been crossing my fingers and toes that he has sweet dreams tonight instead of nightmares. Our whole beautiful morning ruined by one snap decision." Gentry took a break to sip some wine.

"Gentry—" Ian began, but she cut him off without sparing him more than a passing glance, eager to finish her diatribe. She must've been storing up all afternoon, waiting for his arrival.

"And finally, the frustration. There are a lot of options for the crowdfunding, but I need your input. Different platforms require different things, like photos versus videos, details about the purpose, and so on. I couldn't get very far on the scant information I have. Of course, I can make suggestions if you'd like, based on what I *did* learn."

"Stop, please." Ian held up his hand. "This can all wait."

Her brows rose high on her forehead in surprise, as if he'd slapped her across her cheek. Only then did she take a breath and actually examine him.

"Sorry," he mumbled, tossing the key on the entry table.

She set her feet on the floor, then narrowed her eyes. "What's wrong?"

"Nothing you need to worry about. I appreciate that you're trying to help. I just . . . can't . . . do this now."

He started for the stairs, but in a few hurried strides, she beat him there.

"Hold up." She rested one hand on the iron banister, turning her body into a tollgate, the price of which—information—he didn't want to pay. "Tell me what happened."

Another night, he might. But the last thing he needed just then was Gentry Cabot standing so close. "I know you're used to getting your way, but not tonight. I want to be alone."

"Whoa! Insults? Okay, Ian, what's got you this upset?" She displayed uncommon patience as she reached for his hands, but he pulled away, making her frown. "I don't understand. I thought we were—"

"What?" he snapped, head pounding so hard he thought his temples might explode. "Thought we were what?"

"Friends," she finished, blinking twice.

Friends? Whatever they were or might ever have become, he doubted it was that. And while he'd been playing make-believe family today on a grassy knoll, his actual friends were in trouble.

"I'm off the clock now, so if you don't mind, I'd like to go upstairs." He immediately regretted that remark.

Her green eyes flickered from hurt to anger.

"I see." Crossing her arms, she argued, "In that case, as your *boss*, I need to know if whatever hijacked your manners will affect your ability to take care of Colt tomorrow."

"It won't." They stood at the base of the stairs, locked in a game of chicken. The night-blackened windows behind her reflected the pristine interior of this home. A home that wasn't his and was as opposite of where he should be as possible.

She stepped aside and waved him on. "Fine."

He brushed past her and took the steps two at a time, but not fast enough to avoid catching her staring at him from below. He'd apologize in the morning. Right now he needed to close his eyes and think.

He shut his bedroom door and flopped onto the mattress. The pillow-top support and snowy-white linens surrounded him in lavender-scented luxury. His skin itched from the sin of it; his hands balled into fists.

Marie Ormont's friendly smile surfaced in his memory. A Kansas native and middle-aged mission worker, she'd spent the past four years running a home in Port-au-Prince that fed children two meals per day. Or she had, until this week. Some gang members had shot her in her car and had taken her ten-year-old son, Timmy.

Missing. Kidnapped. Disappeared. Whatever the word, the result was the same. Two more victims of the poverty and corruption that would never end if people like Ian got distracted and failed to make a difference. He punched the down comforter, as if flattening it would change a thing. Not that his being in Haiti would've made much difference for Marie.

Ian flung an arm over his eyes to relax. He remembered his father's advice when, a decade earlier, a native they'd worked with had also "disappeared." *We do what we can, when we can, but we can't save everyone. All we can do is honor their lives by continuing to serve those in need.*

When that didn't make him feel better, he rose from the bed and stalked into the bathroom.

He stripped out of his clothes, tossing them in the corner, and stepped into the enormous slate-and-glass shower stall. Four people could comfortably shower together here. Last week it had taken him several minutes to figure out all of its nozzles. Now he set them all to ninety-four degrees.

Any other day, he'd never stand there watching gallons of water flush down the drain for an unnecessary shower. Had he convinced himself that the citrus-scented shampoo and soap might wash away his angst or his worry for other friends who might become targets? More the fool.

The hot water didn't even ease the tension in his shoulders.

He toweled off and then rummaged in his drawer for clean boxers. Pacing the room, he shook out his arms. Eventually, he pulled back the gauzy drapes and peered into the darkness, catching sight of his own reflection. He ran his hand through his hair and rubbed his jaw. Clean-shaven, another rare circumstance that he didn't want to grow accustomed to.

Below him, a golden glow shone onto the lower deck from the living room. He heard nothing, though. Perhaps Gentry had fallen asleep on the sofa, like she'd done twice this past week.

Gentry. He hadn't meant to snipe at her, but she kept pushing. Always seeking a way in. She didn't respect boundaries—not her brother's, not his. Infuriating.

And yet she was generous and playful. He'd been mesmerized today, brightened by his proximity to all of her sparkle and youthful exuberance. He couldn't recall the last time he'd felt so free. She'd also spent her evening reading up on NGOs. For him.

He'd repaid her interest and efforts with insults. He'd been an ass, mostly out of fear of his own confused emotions.

His father wouldn't understand. Not even a duty to his own wife and child had kept *him* from putting himself on the line for others. Yet here Ian sat, in this safe, lavish home, while others fought on in his absence—some losing their lives in the process. In the quiet, he wondered with a shudder whether his dead father could see into his heart, to the most unwelcome truth. To the part of him that wanted to stay put. That wanted the kind of happy moments and memories Gentry promised.

He laughed aloud at the ludicrous reality. Eight days. Eight days since meeting Gentry Cabot, and his life had run amok. She was a different kind of natural disaster, he supposed, but none of his skills could save him from the danger she posed.

Tap, tap, tap.

He glanced over his shoulder toward the bedroom door.

"Ian? I see your light on." Beneath the slight space at the bottom of the door, a shadow fell from where her bare feet stood.

Relentless woman. Had she marched up here to punish him? He certainly deserved that.

He crossed the room and stood—hand on the doorknob, forehead pressed to the door—not knowing what he wanted, or what to say.

"Ian," she said, her voice low. "Please."

Closing his eyes briefly, he opened the door. She stood in the hallway, arms at her sides, chin raised, proud as ever. When her gaze dipped to his bare chest, she pressed her lips together and raised her eyes to meet his.

"I'm sorry I snapped at you," he said.

She strode past him like she owned the place, which she did. When she reached the middle of the room, she stopped to stare at the indent that remained in the comforter. She pivoted toward him and drew a deep breath. "If anyone understands pushing people away on purpose, it's me."

He leaned against the wall by the door, tucking his hands behind his back. To discourage a long conversation, he kept quiet.

Gentry didn't take the hint.

"Please tell me what's wrong. You need to talk to someone so it doesn't eat you up. Unfortunately for you, I'm all you've got right now, even if you don't consider me a friend." She sat on the bed, then stretched out on one side, supporting her head with her hand. "Believe it or not, I'm a good listener. So go on. Share."

He caught himself gawking at her long form sprawled across his bed, before his brain circled back to the conversation. No way would he risk moving from his safe spot by the door.

Knowing Gentry wouldn't stop until he satisfied her demand, he said, "Archer finally replied to my e-mail . . . with terrible news."

He paused, expecting a barrage of questions and guesses. When she remained quiet, he shifted his weight to his other leg. "A friend of ours was shot, and her young son kidnapped."

Gentry pushed herself upright, her forehead wrinkling above a frown. "Oh my God. That's awful."

"Yes." There wasn't more to say. Gentry didn't know Marie. She didn't know Haiti. She didn't know a lot of things, and he had to remember that.

"Is she . . . Did she die?"

"Yes." He nodded, trying not to picture Marie's gentle face warped by fear and panic. "She was killed."

Gentry flattened her hand against her chest. "How old is her son?"

"Ten."

"Oh no!" Both hands covered her mouth. She shook her head as if that could change the story. "I'm so sorry. What happens now?"

"I don't know. There will probably be a ransom demand, but sometimes people are taken and you never learn what happened."

"Wait a second." She scrambled to her feet, eyes filling with a different kind of alarm. "You mean this kind of thing is common?"

"Not as common as it was six or seven years ago, but it still happens. Especially in certain areas of the country."

She raised her hands out from her sides. "Then you should *not* go back there, Ian."

"No? Should I hide here, in obscene luxury, and let it be someone else's problem?"

"Absolutely. Yes, you should. You've done more than most already. It's okay to retire from that life now." Her red hair seemed to vibrate with the vehemence of her voice.

"No."

"Well, don't count on me to help raise money so you can return to a place where you could get killed or kidnapped. And I won't let my sister help you, either."

"This isn't about you, or what you will or won't do to stop me." He waved her off. "And you think you're a good listener."

"I did listen. I heard what you said, and what you didn't say. What you never say. There's something you're not telling me. Something about why you're determined to risk your life." She crossed her arms. "Was Marie someone *special*?"

He rolled his eyes. "Who knew *you* were prone to romantic fancies?"

"Fine, if it isn't love, then what's driving you? You're relentless. You've let it destroy your last relationship. Worse, you're so fixated on it you punish yourself for enjoying anything normal."

"I don't punish myself." He pushed off the wall and paced. "This conversation is over. I'm going back, with or without your help. If I were you, I'd use the next couple of weeks to figure out your situation with Colt, because I won't be here much longer."

"I never expected you would be. But am I supposed to let you fly off and never know what happens to you?"

"You didn't even know me eight days ago."

"But I know you now."

"You'll forget about me just as quickly, especially once Smith shows up." He might be throwing wild jabs at her, but he just clocked himself with that one.

Gentry caught his arm and gently pushed him against the wall, crowding him with her heat and perfume and all that loose hair. "How can you be so brave about some things yet such a coward now?"

"How am I a coward?"

"Pretending we're not friends. Pretending you don't watch me when you think I'm not paying attention." Gentry flexed the power of her physical appeal, which made her particularly lethal. She placed her hands on the wall on either side of him, pressing forward until they were nose to nose. "I don't run into disaster areas, but at least I'm not afraid to admit that I won't be forgetting you any faster than you'll forget me."

Her voice had gone husky at the end of her rant, and her gaze dipped to his mouth. "If you're hurting, let me help you feel better. If you want to make something good of the life you've been given, follow your heart, Ian."

He might be standing there, nearly naked, practically skin to skin with a scantily dressed goddess, but he still had willpower. Or so he thought until she pressed her lips to his clavicle.

God help him, his hands shot to her hips. He gripped the flimsy cotton fabric in his palms and then let it go, skimming his hands around the curve of her ass. She held still, letting him touch her. Eyes wide-open, her gaze locked with his, she held herself mere inches away from him.

Her breath heated his skin. The bedroom turned hotter than Haiti, with his heart beating like a boula drum.

Gentry's hands remained planted on the wall as he traced his fingers along the outline of her waist and up her spine. He hesitated when his hands reached the underside of her breasts. Three heavy breaths later, he tenderly cupped the weight of her in his palms. The thinnest cotton separated their skin, yet somehow touching her like this seemed infinitely more intimate than if he'd removed her clothes.

When his thumbs brushed against the buds of her nipples, her eyelids fluttered. Her response unlocked the last bit of his resistance, so he kissed her.

She fell against him, her fingers threading through his hair. Thankfully, the wall supported them, because his knees were giving out.

Chapter Nine

Risk

According to *Merriam-Webster*: possibility of loss or injury : PERIL

According to me: kissing Ian

A year of celibacy urged Gentry to climb Ian's body like a tree. She would've if her arms and legs weren't laden with want. Whether her long dry spell or Ian's magic touch caused her full-body inferno almost didn't matter. Except it did, because she suspected that making love with Ian would be a singular experience—figuratively and literally.

In almost any other case, that result would fall somewhere between "fine with her" and "perfect." With Ian, she grudgingly admitted that a one-and-done would not, in fact, be enough. Right now her heart and head were too steeped in happiness hormones to care about self-preservation.

His firm chest and shoulder muscles flexed with each pass of her hand. The growly sound at the back of his throat made her wet with longing.

"Ian," she panted, now running her hands down his waist. Her body trembled with eager anticipation, and that rarely happened.

Gentry reached between his legs to discover that every part of his body was long and hard.

"Wait." He grabbed her wrist, prying her hand away. "Stop."

Ian shook his head as if awakening from a dream—or possibly a nightmare.

"Why?" She leaned closer, hoping another kiss would clear whatever imaginary hurdle he'd hit.

For a second, she thought she'd won the little contest, but he pushed back again, this time breaking free and stepping away.

"We shouldn't do this." His hungry gaze roamed her body. He pressed the heels of his palms to his eyes. "Go downstairs now, please."

"I don't understand."

"I think you do. I'm gone as soon as I can afford to go. You're hunting for Colt's dad. This"—he gestured between them—"can't lead anywhere good."

"Oh, I beg to differ. I think it's pretty obvious we could both benefit from a good f—"

"Don't say it, Gentry." He cut her off. "Don't reduce all this to that."

"So you admit that 'this' is *something*?"

Ian crossed his arms and looked at his feet. She supposed that was as much of an answer as she would get tonight.

Options came to mind. A: strip and seduce. B: throw that stupid baseball on his dresser at him. Or C: sarcasm. Any of those things would get his attention and give her a chance to wear him down. But Ian was unlike any man she'd ever met, and although she didn't always understand him, she suspected those antics would push him further away.

She stood there, waiting for him to do or say something. When he refused to even meet her gaze, she walked from the room. Closing his door behind her, she left him with his precious solitude.

That might be the most perplexing thing of all. She'd been alone for much of her life—granted, some of it self-imposed in a twisted kind of rebellion. Still, she couldn't imagine choosing it now, when faced with the possibility of something genuine. Not that she had much practice with genuine relationships. Could "this" be one if neither of them ran or pushed the other away?

Ian swore he wouldn't be anything more than a cameo appearance in her life.

A vivid, memorable one—like Smith—but still merely temporary. Temporary had always been enough before. But despite his behavior tonight, Ian had swept into her world and opened her heart.

She couldn't pretend that loneliness didn't hurt anymore. Her siblings' loving relationships glittered like another medal for an achievement that eluded her. Her only solace now was Colt. With him around, she'd never be totally alone again.

◆ ◆ ◆

Gentry snuggled Colt to her chest for comfort after her restless night. She'd role-played cool detachment in her head at least twenty times since waking at five thirty. The clock now read eight forty. She'd put off facing Ian as long as possible. Time to be a grown-up.

When she emerged from her room, she saw him sitting on the tufted leather ottoman, elbows on his knees, head down, surrounded by strangely gloomy dove-gray walls. She could blame that flatness on the cloudy Oregon weather or admit that it had a lot to do with her mood.

Ian stood when she and Colt entered the room.

"Good morning." The circles under his eyes were darker than hers. She would be sympathetic if their shitty night hadn't been his decision.

"Maybe for some." She immediately regretted revealing that his rejection had hurt her. Turning her back to Ian, she kissed Colt's face several times before putting him in the baby swing. Colt treated her to a smile. A real smile! He hadn't smiled often in his young life, but the big, toothless thing of beauty made her missteps with Ian irrelevant. She lightly brushed Colt's silky hair and tickled under his chin, wishing she could play hooky and spend the whole day with him. "Mommy will see you later, Boo. I love you."

Sparing Ian a brief glance after grabbing her laptop bag, she said, "I'll be home by six."

"Gentry, wait," he began.

She waved him off, keeping her chin up even as her gaze fell to a distant spot on the floor. "I can't be late when Hunter's already angry about Ty. No need to rehash last night, either. I got the message. When you're set to leave, I'd appreciate a few days' notice."

With a sharp nod, she marched into the garage without looking back, so she didn't see his reaction. All she did know was that he didn't burst into the garage to apologize before she drove away.

Fortunately, a lengthy to-do list at work forced her thoughts away from Ian. She worked with the graphic designer all morning to generate messaging and memes for their social media platforms now that the marketing team had voted, unanimously, for her "Quench your thirst for a better world" slogan. That win took the sting out of her personal situation, although it also reminded her of time spent on the deck with Ian.

Enough pining. Time to capitalize on the wave of her success. She stopped by Becky's workstation on her way to lunch. "Want to grab a quick bite at Coco's?"

Becky held up her brown bag. "I'm all set, thanks."

"I'll order takeout so we can eat out here," Gentry offered, referring to the café tables on the covered patio that gave the employees an alfresco dining option, rain or shine.

"Maybe another time, Gentry." Becky glanced around as if worried someone else was listening.

Gentry became acutely aware that her coworkers' stations were suddenly buzzing with busywork. "Did I do something to offend you?"

"No."

"Really? Because it seems like, since I've returned from maternity leave, you've kept your distance."

Becky cleared her throat, but no one around them came to her rescue. "It's not personal. I've been super busy. If this product launch flops, heads will roll."

"You still should take a break now and then so you don't burn out."

"Of course *you'd* say that. You have nothing to lose. The rest of us have our jobs at stake."

Hunter's warnings raced through Gentry's mind, but she wasn't like him. She could do only so much pandering and proving herself before reaching the end of her admittedly short rope. "That's some seriously flawed logic."

"Excuse me?" Becky's left brow rose.

"You heard me. In case you forgot, as an *owner*, I took a big gamble when I voted to give Hunter's idea the green light instead of selling the company, so, in fact, *I* have more to lose than any of you if this launch goes south. In fact, thanks to my vote, you all still have jobs. Remember that the next time you snub me."

"Gentry!" Her mother's voice squashed Gentry's sense of victory.

Everything fell silent for about five seconds; then the frantic typing resumed, surrounding her with a keyboard symphony. The perfect soundtrack for a workplace scolding.

Ignoring the inevitable, Gentry kept her gaze locked on Becky.

Her mother cleared her throat. "I'd like to speak with you . . . in my office."

Gentry affected a bright smile before facing her mom. "Certainly, Mother. Lead the way."

Once they were in her mom's office with the door closed, Gentry dropped onto the silk-covered Charlemagne armchair across from her mother's desk. Her heels sank into the crimson Tibetan rug. Today its thick pile would serve an important secondary service: absorbing the sound of raised voices.

She crossed her legs, letting one swing back and forth, knowing Ian's rejection had contributed to her taunting Becky. Maybe she'd apologize later . . . if Becky also apologized. "I don't suppose you're about to congratulate me."

"Don't be smart." Her mother folded her hands on her desk. "You look like hell. Did Colt have a bad night?"

He'd slept for almost five straight hours for the first time. More sleep than *she'd* gotten last night, in fact.

"Colt's fine. I'm fine." Gentry set her hands on the chair's arms, preparing to run. "Is that all?"

"Hardly," her mother sighed. "You can't threaten employees, Gentry. We don't need HR trouble. Especially not now."

"What are you talking about? I report to Becky, not the other way around. If anything, I should be the one filing complaints. Everyone here treats me like I don't belong."

Her mother quickly checked something on her computer screen while saying, "Will lording your ownership over everybody make them treat you better?"

"At this point, I don't care. I'm sick of not getting credit for the work I've done. You certainly haven't helped matters, either."

"Why does every mistake you make end up being my fault? Your favorite pastime is recounting all the ways I've failed you." Her mother shook her head. "Yet now *your* son's at home with a nanny."

"He won't be with a nanny for long." The look on Ian's face last night resurfaced, making her heart skip. Not that her mom's response was on point. Gentry's childhood complaints weren't only about having a nanny. They were about the scraps of attention she'd gotten from her absentee family most of her life. "Let's not get sidetracked. What I'm saying now is that you go so far out of your way to make sure that there's no whiff of favoritism here, you never give me credit for my contributions. If *you* don't believe I deserve to be here, why would *they* give me a chance?"

"No one *deserves* anything, Gentry. Your father built this company from nothing. For almost three decades, I've helped him, and Hunter has, too. But believe me, we paid our dues, and you have to pay yours. You've been handed an opportunity, but it's up to you to have the grit to see it through. My job isn't to make that easier for you, and if I did, it would actually make things worse."

Gentry stood, suddenly sick of herself and her need for acceptance. It never worked out. What she wanted remained visible but out of reach, locked behind an impenetrable glass wall.

"Sit." Her mother pointed at the empty chair.

"No." Gentry gripped the wooden frame of its back. "If you want to discuss one of my projects, fire away. I'll fill you in on the awesome ideas we came up with this morning. But I won't sit through a lecture when I only defended myself after Becky insulted me."

"She did?" Her mother's gaze sharpened.

"Oh, now you want the whole story?"

"Yes, please. I'd like to be well informed in case this lands on Ross Hardy's desk."

Ross Hardy was the head of HR. A decent, if conservative, guy. Gentry recapped the entire exchange, starting with her lunch invitation. If she'd thought her mother would side with her after hearing all the facts, she'd been high.

"Let's be honest. You have a reputation of your own making to overcome around here. From everyone's perspective but yours, you've carried a humongous chip on your shoulder while leading a decadent life. If you want respect, my advice is to keep your head down and do your job. It takes more than a few months and a handful of good ideas to prove your worth."

If Gentry's eyes weren't already black-and-blue from the lack of sleep, that one-two punch would've done the trick. Why did she bother? She could so easily stay at home, blog, take photographs, and be with her son.

The past twelve hours had drained Gentry of her fight. "Are we done? I'd like to grab lunch and get back to work."

"Fine."

Some mothers might offer to join their child for lunch in a show of solidarity or, at least, compassion. Hers waved Gentry away and returned her attention to her computer.

Gentry closed her mother's door and strolled past the workstations with her eyes fixed on the EXIT sign. On her way out of the building, she passed a group of three coworkers. They stopped talking as she approached. She strode past them, flashing a tight smile.

Any other time, she might've made a flip remark, but she didn't need Ross or Hunter on her case. Now she had no one to turn to. Even Colby, who might try to be helpful, would probably still agree with her mother's advice.

All the changes she'd undergone for Colt had left her vulnerable and weak—and no better off.

When she reached the parking lot, she trotted toward her car. Sitting in her front seat, she gripped the steering wheel. It started raining, which suited her perfectly. She stared at the black Acura parked in front of her car, tears burning in her eyes. When someone else approached a nearby car, she pretended to be looking at herself in her rearview mirror rather than look like a lunatic.

Screw it. She fired up the engine even though she wasn't hungry. She knew she should eat something. Most of all, she needed to get away from Cabot Tea and think.

◆ ◆ ◆

While Ian taped his and Colt's artwork to the refrigerator, an unexpected knock at the door startled him. At first he thought Gentry had decided to drop by for lunch, as she'd done once last week, but Gentry wouldn't knock at her own door.

Through the peephole, he watched Colby shake out her umbrella. Before she rang the bell and woke Colt from his morning nap, he opened the door. "Hey, Colby. What's up?"

Colby set her wet umbrella outside before stepping into the entry. "I'm on my way to the restaurant, but I wanted to drop off some information. Is this a bad time?"

"It's a good time, actually. Colt's still asleep."

"So we have five minutes . . . maybe ten?" She laughed, which made her eyes curl more at the outer edges.

"Something like that." He smiled.

Colby set her leather bag on the table and opened it to retrieve whatever she'd brought him. She reminded him a bit of a modern-day Audrey Hepburn. Simple hairstyle, light makeup, a conservative but feminine navy-blue dress. He crossed his arms, suddenly self-conscious of his uncombed hair, aging U2 T-shirt, and bare feet.

She turned and handed him a manila envelope. It seemed Gentry had not yet forbidden Colby from helping. "I've made a short list of contacts. If you'd like, I'll reach out to them first, or you can reference me when you contact them. One, in particular, might be of interest. Marcus Fairfax, of Fairfax Auto Palace."

"The luxury car dealer?"

"Yes. He has a history of philanthropy. Better yet, his twenty-three-year-old son is an EMT who does a lot of local charitable work. I think your project could interest them. Given their multiple dealerships, they may be able to get vehicles at a good price."

"That's an amazing lead, thank you."

"Happy to help. Have you contacted the World Health Organization yet? Based upon your plans, it might be an important ally."

"Archer is dealing with them and other health-care groups." He looked at the envelope. "I wish I could repay this favor. Gentry jumped in and asked for your help so fast I wasn't prepared."

Colby's quick smile appeared. "She can be excitable and impulsive, but that's part of her charm, I think."

"She's unpredictable." He felt a tug at the corners of his mouth.

"I don't know where she got that gene. None of the rest of us do much without a plan. She'd say we 'overthink.' I suppose there's some truth in that." Colby grinned. "Anyway, if you have questions about any of that information, call me."

"Thanks." He waved the envelope in the air. "I appreciate your time."

"You're welcome." She grimaced, hesitating. "Would you mind if I use the restroom before I go?"

"Of course." After she dashed down the hall, Ian opened the envelope and pulled out the memo. If he hadn't known Colby had been a lawyer, he'd guess it from the organized outline of information: names, addresses, e-mails and phone numbers, bios, donor histories. Everything arranged alphabetically. His gaze homed in on Marcus Fairfax's bio.

When Colby returned to the living area, her attention snagged on Quackers, who'd been discarded on the ottoman. She came to a complete stop, eyes wide. "Oh God. I can't believe she still has that thing."

She wandered across the room in a trance and picked up the raggedy stuffed toy, gently wiggling it. A sentimental smile appeared. "Hello, Quackers."

"You know this duck?"

"Of course." Colby stared at the ratty toy and shook her head. "She wouldn't let anyone touch him for years. She'd even carry him like this"—Colby stuffed Quackers under her armpit—"when she needed to use both hands."

"Wow." He'd been watching Gentry force that old thing on Colt every day. "What made it so special?"

"Hunter gave it to her. She must've only been five or six at the time. He was around fourteen and had his first 'paying' job at CTC that summer—less than minimum wage and straight from our dad's pocket, no doubt." She removed the toy from her underarm and petted it. "Anyway, he bought it for her birthday."

"Didn't she get other gifts that year?"

"You've met Jenna and seen that house, right?" Her sarcastic tone matched her smirk. "Getting enough toys was never the problem."

"Then why was this duck a big deal?"

Colby grew quiet, as if searching her thoughts for the right words. She set Quackers back on the ottoman and hugged herself.

"Hunter and I were always close, while Gentry was younger and lived with my dad. We didn't mean to exclude her, but we were adolescents still learning to handle our new family dynamic. We were probably a little jealous, too, because she had our dad . . . and a pool!" Colby laughed at how foolish kids' priorities could be. Then she settled her hand across her heart. "If you had seen her face when Hunter handed her a present that he'd bought with his own money. It wouldn't have mattered what was in that box. To her it meant everything—meant she mattered—though I doubt Hunter remembers." She let her hand fall and sighed. "We should've paid more attention to her when we were younger. It's one of my big regrets."

Ian hadn't any siblings or sense of a normal family, and that had never bothered him much in the past. "You've got time now."

"I know. But years of not being close have made her prickly and defensive even when, deep, *deep* down, I think she's still yearning for her place. Maybe that's why she's tried on so many different hats. Now she has Colt, though. The romantic in me keeps hoping she'll let herself fall in love and create her own little family. Who knows? Maybe Colt's dad could turn out to be her prince, after all."

"You think?" His hands balled at his sides until he flexed them.

"More like a wish, I suppose. I know something about feeling alone even when surrounded by family, and I also know how love can grow in the most unexpected ways." Colby pressed her lips into a tight line.

"It's a nice dream, anyway." He'd officially gotten in over his head in this conversation.

"A cynic, I see. I suppose your experiences haven't left much room for romance." She tipped her head, and he saw a light flicker in her hazel eyes. He could tell she'd formed a thought she chose not to share. "I'd better let you relax before the little rug rat wakes up. Give Colt a kiss from me."

"Will do." He followed her to the door. "Thanks again for the notes."

"You're welcome."

Ian closed the door after Colby left. He padded through the house and picked up Quackers. Love-worn, not ratty. That designation improved Quacker's appeal. On the other hand, his chest ached a little as he imagined Gentry clutching this toy as some kind of lifeline to love. To a family that was too busy to notice that she needed more from them.

Gentry's wounds weren't life threatening in a traditional sense, yet they were real and painful.

He'd been struggling all night and morning to make sense of his choices. Worrying about Marie's son, Timmy. Worrying about his father's legacy and wishes. Questioning his life in the face of Gentry's accusations.

When he'd taken this job, he'd planned to leave Gentry better off than when he arrived. Last night proved how far short he'd fallen on that goal. He had a couple of weeks to do better so he could leave here with some peace of mind. To show her that she didn't need to cling to an old toy to feel loved.

◆ ◆ ◆

Ian was peeling an orange in the kitchen when he heard Gentry drop her bag in the hall near her bedroom. From his spot by the refrigerator, he saw her stride past the kitchen, straight to the playpen, where Colt restlessly wriggled his arms and legs. She lifted him out of his prison and kissed him, whispering things too quietly for Ian to make out the words.

With her back still turned to him, she asked, "Any trouble today?"

"No. I think the infection is definitely gone. He ate well. Napped." Then, because she refused to look at him, Ian added, "Colby stopped by."

She swiveled. "Why?"

"She dropped off some information—fund-raising leads—for me." He approached Gentry as one might approach a grenade and nodded toward Quackers. "She also gave me the scoop on him."

Gentry scowled. "I have no idea what you're talking about. There's no scoop."

"I asked why you were so attached to that mangy thing—"

"He's not mangy," she interrupted.

"Your sister said Hunter gave it to you when you were little."

Gentry's nostrils flared a touch, but she shuttered all emotion and shrugged. "Who remembers?"

"Apparently Colby does." He could stop . . . or not. "In fact, it opened up a bunch of memories for her, not all of them good."

Gentry's frown returned. With an acerbic lilt, she said, "Who knew Quackers was such a gateway to the past."

"There's more."

"Do tell." She swayed, with her son gripped tightly in her arms.

"She has regrets about the way she behaved back then."

"Why are we talking about this?" Gentry abruptly ended the conversation by kissing Colt and turning away, but not before Ian noticed the flush rising up her neck and cheeks. "So much nonsense over a toy."

He raised his hands, stepping back. Now who was being the coward? he thought. "Sorry. Just making small talk."

"No need. You're off the clock and free to do whatever it is you need to do to secure your exit strategy." She turned on her heel and marched toward her room with Colt.

Message received. She was still pissed about last night. Her arrival hadn't gone at all as he'd planned.

She'd have to come to the kitchen sooner or later, if only to eat . . . or drink. Probably both. Then she'd see what he'd left for her on the refrigerator. For now, he'd wait on the deck and finish his orange.

The rain had stopped hours ago. Few things soothed him like the scent of a loamy Oregon forest. Pretty much the opposite of the burned wood and trash odors of Haiti's many and continual bonfires.

As predicted, Gentry wandered back to the kitchen about thirty minutes later. She must've settled Colt, or maybe she was fixing him a bottle. He watched through the plate glass as she stopped at the refrigerator and fingered his peace offering.

He'd dipped Colt's feet in washable blue paint and pressed them to a sheet of computer paper, turning those footprints into the wings of a badly drawn butterfly. Across the top of the page, he'd typed a quote he'd heard before: "A mom's hug lasts long after she lets go," in the hope that it might alleviate some of the guilt she battled every day when she left for work.

He slid the glass door open and stepped inside. She looked up as he closed it.

"Look at this. A humanitarian and an artist." Her expression remained closed, but her voice had mellowed.

Ian remembered Colby's observation about Gentry's defensive mechanisms, so he wasn't offended by her lack of gratitude.

"Picasso's got nothing on me." He hesitated. "I thought you might like to take that to work."

"Thank you." She opened the refrigerator door and pulled out the pink box of cheesecake she'd bought earlier in the week. "Although maybe I won't be working there much longer."

He stopped his approach, stunned. He knew she'd been struggling to juggle the demands of the launch with her general lack of sleep, but had she been fired? "Why not?"

"My reasons for working there aren't really paying off. Or, at least, not enough to make the humiliation worth it." She waved that thought away and grabbed a fork. Without bothering to plate a slice, she opened the lid and ate directly from the box. "Maybe Colt's better off if I stay home. I could pursue photography. We'd be free to travel, which might come in handy if we find Smith." She looked right at him. "Might as well be the cliché everyone already thinks I am. At least it'd be fun."

"You're a lot of things, but clichéd isn't one of them."

"Ha!" A disbelieving grin popped into place. "You've been making assumptions about me from the minute you walked through my door."

"Everyone has first impressions." He shrugged unapologetically. "They change when people learn more about each other. One thing I hadn't thought about you until right now was that you were a quitter."

"And here I'd thought McJ had retired on Saturday. Guess you can't help yourself." She stared at him while shoving a huge chunk of cheesecake into her mouth.

He should walk away now because it'd be easier for both of them if they maintained a barely cordial relationship until he left. He turned to go but then whirled around and crossed to her, pulling the remains of the cheesecake away. "Stop it."

She reached for the cheesecake. "Are you judging my diet now, too?"

He clasped her wrist. "Stop pretending you don't care about anything. We both know that's a lie. Let's deal with last night like grown-ups."

She pulled free from his grasp. "This is me being grown-up. What happened—or didn't happen—last night is no big deal, so get over yourself."

"Now who's the coward?"

Instead of another dig, she ducked to get around him in an effort to flee the kitchen. He caught her by the waist and tugged her against his stomach, keeping his arms wrapped around her waist. "You think I put on the brakes last night because I don't care, but that's not true. I stopped because I do care."

"Let go!" She broke free. "I don't know what Colby said today that has you feeling sorry for me and making art to cheer me up, but I'm fine. I don't need pity."

"That's not what this is."

"What *is* it?"

"Honesty. I'm clearing the air so we can go back to being friends."

"From not friends to make-out buddies to hands off . . . now we're friends again? Well, thanks for clearing that up."

He wilted against the countertop. "You don't make anything easy."

"So I'm told. Fortunately, you won't have to deal with me for much longer."

"What don't you get, Gentry? I can't afford to care more. I tried that once, with my ex, Farrah, and it didn't turn out well. I try to learn from my mistakes. My life's not compatible with relationships." He gripped the countertop behind him, forcing the next thought out despite some regret. "You need a guy—Smith or someone else—who can help you build a family for your son."

Tapping her foot, she crossed her arms. "On that last part we mostly agree."

"Finally." He nodded, thinking she'd beat a hasty exit now. Instead, she closed the gap between them and put her hands on his chest.

"But in case you're wrong about all the rest." She kissed him.

The sensual kiss tasted like sweetened almond. Instinct forced his arms around her before he thought better of it. Her body, soft in all the right places, made his hot and hard. But as much as he wanted her, the last thing Gentry Cabot needed was to get close to another person who would walk out of her life.

"Gentry." He broke the kiss but hugged her tight. "We both know the timing is wrong."

"The story of my life." She cupped his face, a sad smile on her own, then let her hands drop. With a half shrug, she said, "Guess we'll settle for friendship, but don't expect much. I don't have a lot of practice with that, either."

Chapter Ten

Matchmake

According to *Merriam-Webster*: to bring about a marriage especially by scheming

According to me: one thing I do better than Colby

A stiff breeze carried the scent of wisteria, which wrapped its way around the stone columns of CTC's covered patio, while the sun played hide-and-seek with cumulus clouds. Staff members occupied about half the teak-and-aluminum café tables, leaving few options for privacy. Privacy from others was something Gentry now chose for herself despite her decision to tough it out at CTC.

"I forgot how cozy this patio is." Colby set a white paper bag on the corner table Gentry selected and unpacked the to-go containers Alec had prepared for them. "Hunter and Dad couldn't join us for lunch?"

"Actually, I wanted to talk to you alone." For three days, Gentry had been mulling over Colby and Ian's private chat about Quackers.

"Super, because I also have something personal to discuss, too." Colby took a seat. Her sister's glowing face and broad smile tipped Gentry off to big news. "May I go first, please?"

"Are you pregnant?" Gentry clapped, delighted by the idea of Colt gaining another cousin.

"No!" She laughed, poking Gentry's arm. "I'm a *bit* more traditional than you, so we're waiting until after the wedding. But what a perfect segue."

"Ah, you finally set a date." Gentry opened the calendar on her phone and waited for the information.

"Yes, we did. September thirtieth."

Gentry set the phone down. "That's not even three full months from now. How will you arrange everything in time?"

"It'll be small—thirty or so guests." Colby creased the napkin on her lap, eyes glued to her hands. "Given all the history, we don't want a lavish production, but I also don't want to elope . . ."

She left "like I did with Mark" unsaid.

Gentry patted her sister's shoulder. "Dad will be thrilled. Leslie, too. Will it be at A CertainTea?"

"Yes. If the weather cooperates, we'll have the ceremony in the lakeside gazebo, then have the reception on the patio. Otherwise, we'll do everything inside."

"And the honeymoon?" Gentry wiggled her brows.

"Alec wants to take me to Mougins and then tour the French wine regions along the coast." Her sister's smile returned in full force. "I can't wait to see where he lived and worked all those years."

"Sounds like heaven. I'm so happy for you." Gentry remembered the first time she saw Alec walk into A CertainTea after he'd disappeared for a year. The way he'd looked at Colby had told Gentry everything she needed to know, so she'd done whatever she could—including flirt with him—to prod her sister into action. It hadn't been easy, but now Gentry could tease her. "You owe me big for stepping aside last fall . . ."

"Ha-ha." Colby chuckled before sampling the burrata with pesto, pine nuts, and some kind of yellow flower. "But with that in mind, I'd love it if you'd be my maid of honor."

"Me?" Gentry pointed at herself with surprise.

"Yes, you." Colby's expression pinched in confusion.

"Not Sara or your mom?"

"My mother will revel in her mother-of-the-bride role. Sara will be a bridesmaid, of course, but you're my sister. I want you beside me."

Gentry leaned on her elbows, bracelets hitting against the metal edge of the table. "You trust me to plan the bachelorette party?"

"No tattoos or strippers." Colby raised her index finger, then took another bite of the burrata.

"You're no fun," Gentry teased.

"It's pretty well established that you got all the 'fun' genes." Colby winked and set her fork down. "So is that a yes?"

Gentry didn't know why she could never accept any show of affection without suspicion, but she replied, "Are you asking because you think my feelings would be hurt if you chose Sara?"

Colby flinched, her voice thin. "Why would you think that?"

"Because Ian was full of theories about Quackers after your recent visit. It sounded like you've come to a bunch of conclusions about me and about our past." Gentry stared at the shrimp salad she'd been picking at. "I don't want you or him, or anyone else, being nice to me out of some kind of guilt complex."

Colby raked her hand through her hair, sighing. "I'm sorry if I upset you. You know I've been trying to be closer, but not out of pity. I was too young, and then too preoccupied, to notice sooner. Now I know that *I* missed out on having a relationship with my sister, and I'm trying to fix it. Is that so wrong?"

"No." Inside, Gentry battled the discomfort of being vulnerable. "I wouldn't be working here"—she gestured around CTC—"if I didn't want Colt to grow up surrounded by family."

"*Colt*, huh?"

"Yes, Colt. I'm already grown. The past can't change my future. Frankly, I'm not sure working here will, either."

"Hold that thought for a sec, but"—Colby grabbed her hand—"relationships are always changing. Everything we do and say brings us closer or pulls us apart. But it takes two people who are willing to be vulnerable. Most of the time, you're guarded."

Conditioning, she thought, but didn't say. "Sorry."

"No apologies needed. Just say you'll be my maid of honor." Her hopeful smile unlocked something soft and tender in Gentry's hardened heart.

"Do I get to pick my own dress? Or maybe my Gaultier pantsuit with the bra top?" The hesitant look on her sister's face made Gentry laugh. "I'm kidding. I fully expect to look like a cross between a nun and a librarian."

Colby snorted, shooting a little water through her nose. After dabbing her face, she said, "I found a short navy-blue belted Vera Wang dress for Sara and you. Classic but a touch flirty."

"Short?" Gentry smiled in surprise. "It'll go great with my thigh-high gray snakeskin boots."

"Then no one will see the ankle tattoo," Colby teased.

"That *would* be a loss." Gentry stretched out her leg and turned her ankle to admire the vine on her leg.

"So it's a yes?" Colby squeezed Gentry's hand again.

"I'd love to be your maid of honor." Gentry leaned over for a side hug with her sister. "Too bad Colt's too young to be a ring bearer. Is Ty?"

"Not sure. Alec is asking Hunter to be his best man. Maybe Ty could come down the aisle with Sara."

Gentry imagined Colby in a wedding gown. Something simple and elegant—silk organza with a hint of lace or crystal. Elie Saab, perhaps? Whatever Colby chose to wear, she would glow even more with Alec at the altar than she did now. "Dad will be sobbing when he gives you away."

"I know I hurt him when I eloped." Colby's smiled faded as Mark's ghost drifted into their conversation. "I want to do this wedding—this *marriage*—right."

Alec was the perfect guy for Colby. They'd known each other since childhood, and they were both quiet, gentle people who'd suffered tremendous losses and had come through it together. Was that the key . . . finding someone like oneself instead of one's opposite? That theory pretty much knocked Ian off her list. "It'll be perfect, I'm sure. Everything you do usually is."

"Hardly, but thanks." Colby tossed her long, tawny locks over her shoulder. "So what's making you second-guess working here? Is it Hunter? I know he's hyperfocused on the launch."

"He's actually been better than my mom and the people in my department."

"Really? I would've thought Jenna would bend over backwards to keep you happy here."

"Have you *met* my mother?" Gentry mocked, staring at her iced tea, wishing it would magically transform into a robust cabernet. "She thinks if she's nice to me, others will dislike me. But when she's dismissive, no one takes me seriously."

"I remember her relationship with Hunter taking its nosedive once he started working here." Colby wrinkled her nose. "Could Jenna be a little jealous? Maybe she preferred working here alone with Dad. But Hunter hung in and earned everyone's respect, so you can, too."

"Unlike Hunter, I'm not sure it's worth it."

"I thought you liked social media marketing? You've been so helpful with A Certain Tea."

"I like it fine, but it's not a real passion. Not like photography." She risked opening up to her sister. "I was willing to leave Colt in someone else's care because I thought I'd gain some respect working here. But the last thing I want is to be like *my* mom, putting my job ahead of my child. I want to be a good mom, like Sara."

"You are a good mom."

"Not like Sara. She's made Ty the focus of her life."

Colby sat back, tilting her head. "Given Ty's past and special needs, she felt that he needed her full-time for a while. But most women keep full-time jobs and raise families. I think the best moms are women who learn to balance their kids' needs with their own. Colt will feel loved by the way you use your time together. Don't compare yourself to anyone, most especially not to Jenna. She's an extreme example of ambition."

"Always diplomatic," Gentry sighed. "But let's change the subject."

"Okay, then tell me this. Is there something between you and Ian? I know he's coming off a broken engagement, but he seemed very interested in hearing about you. I also sensed a little tension—the good kind—when you two came to the restaurant."

Gentry gulped some iced tea to douse the heat rising from the memory of Ian's bare chest and kiss. "He's itching to get back to Haiti."

"There's a nonanswer." Colby rolled her eyes, but Gentry kept quiet. "Couldn't he travel back and forth?"

"Colt needs stability, not part-time interest." Gentry drained the rest of her iced tea. Time to wrap up this lunch.

"*Colt* again, huh?" Colby toyed with her fork. "What about Smith? Any news there?"

"No, but Hunter hired an investigator at the end of last week."

"Given how little you have to go on, are you holding out hope? What can the PI work with? You don't even have a photo."

"I have the date, a description, and the fact he was a guest there. He also knew a lot about wine. Maybe he's a regular, and someone on the staff will recognize him. If not, at least I can tell Colt I tried. If we find him . . ." Gentry placed her hand on her stomach to quell the queasiness that gurgled whenever she thought about finding him.

"What are you hoping for if that happens?"

"It'd be nice if he took an interest in Colt."

"Are you prepared for less?"

"Of course. But everyone should stop assuming he's a jerk. We were both having fun with the whole 'sexy stranger' element. He didn't lie or anything. Neither of us thought past the next morning."

Colby ate her last bite of burrata. "Let's hope he's not angry when he finds out about Colt."

"If he's gotten married or something, it could be a rough conversation." Gentry thought about that for a second. Colt would be exposed to whomever Smith did date or marry. He could have a stepmom, for all she knew.

"Are you *sure* you want to open that door?" Colby reached out to stop Gentry from gnawing on her thumbnail. "It's not too late to call off the search."

"No. I think it'll turn out fine. Better than fine."

Her sister hesitated. "Do you think there could be something between you and Smith?"

Gentry's pity meter registered red-hot territory. She huffed. "I don't expect a proposal, for God's sake. But I wouldn't rule anything out at this point."

The truth was, Smith couldn't compete with Ian. At least not until Ian faded from her thoughts. If Ian was like every other man, that would happen the minute he moved out. But he wasn't like any other man, and she knew it could take a long time to forget him.

"Hm." Colby began gathering her empty containers.

"Why the frown?"

"I'm being selfish." Colby waved, shaking her head. "I doubt Smith's from Portland. If you two get serious, you might move just when we're all starting families."

"You're jumping *way* ahead. All I'm saying is that my future is uncertain and wide-open."

"Too bad Ian's so set on leaving. He seems like a solid guy."

Solid muscle. Solid heart. Solid gold—minus the judgment. "He'll never settle for a normal life. Besides, I cause disasters, not fix them!"

"Then he should stay and give you 'aid,'" Colby teased.

Gentry sighed. "Colt comes first. His needs should guide my decisions."

Colby grabbed both of Gentry's hands. "You probably won't take this as a compliment, but you've grown up a lot since becoming a mom. I hope you find someone who can appreciate and love you like you deserve."

"So do I." Gentry pretended that something had flown into her eye so she could hide any tears forming. "Now let's get back to the bachelorette party . . ."

◆ ◆ ◆

The skies had begun to sprinkle rain, and given the heavy cloud cover, Ian doubted it'd stop anytime soon. He came inside from the deck and tucked his phone in his pocket.

"Where are you off to today?" Gentry asked from her spot on the floor, where she'd laid Colt on a blanket for tummy time. In the days since their stolen kiss, she'd relegated him to the friend zone with ease.

Him? Not so much. Even now—with her sitting on the floor, bare legs spread on either side of Colt's blanket, her hair in a knot on her head—he longed to untie that knot and run his fingers through her hair.

She snapped her fingers twice, impatient for his answer.

"I promised my mom I'd help with the blessing-bag assembly at our church today."

"What's a blessing bag? Rosaries and Bibles and stuff?"

"No." He noticed her absently stroking Colt's arm. No one would call Gentry sweet, but if they saw her interact with her son every day, they might. "We pack bags with basics like toiletries and snacks, and then distribute them to the homeless."

"I thought shelters bought their own food. Isn't that why Colby's foundation sends them money?"

"This is for the folks who can't get into the shelters. Today I'll be taking things up to the Springwater Corridor." He rubbed the back of his neck with his hand. Between nightmares about Timmy, stress from Archer, and fantasies about Gentry, he hadn't been sleeping well.

She raised one brow. "You don't look too happy about that."

"What?"

Gesturing toward his face with her hand, she said, "You walked in from the deck like a man headed to the gallows."

"Archer called with more bad news."

"About Timmy?" Gentry held her breath.

"No. Nothing new on that front." As with any time he thought of Timmy, he said a prayer and forced his thoughts away from images of the small child huddled in some tent, terrified and alone.

Her gaze fell to Colt. She leaned forward to kiss his head, muttering, "Listen up, Boo. You're never going to Haiti."

Ian blamed himself for her fear. Haiti and its people *were* worth saving, if corruption could only be dismantled and natural disasters kept at bay. "It's not all cholera, kidnappings, and natural disasters. The majority of Haitian people are resilient and generous. They have a rich culture, exotic music, and great food. There are miles of unspoiled beaches in places like Jacmel, desperately awaiting tourists."

"So what's got you so defeated?"

No point in lying.

"Nurses and hospital staff are striking. It's crippling the already-poor health-care system. But I can't blame them. Poverty wages. Horrible conditions—I've seen rats in 'hospital' hallways." He shook his head and sank onto the sofa, shamefully admitting to himself that he'd miss the clean lines of Gentry's home and the pervasive citrus scent from the candles and cleaning products. "Every time we catch one break—like my meeting with Marcus Fairfax next week—something else blows up."

Gentry chewed on her thumbnail while moving Quackers slightly farther from Colt's reach. "I'm sorry."

Ian had expected a rant or sarcasm or something more Gentryesque. The calm support threw him. "Thanks."

"Can I ask you something?" Her pretty eyes crinkled above a tentative smile, capturing him in their thrall.

"Sure." He blinked to break the spell.

"Why must it be Haiti? Aren't there other, less unstable communities that could benefit from your idea?"

"We'll have the biggest impact in the place that needs the most help."

"I don't buy that." When Ian didn't respond, she kept talking. "You're fixated on Haiti. It's personal."

"I've spent the most time there, I suppose."

"It's more than that." After spending two weeks with Gentry, he should know better than to underestimate her intuition. In the face of more silence, she said, "I thought we were friends. Don't friends share this stuff?"

Colt whimpered, so her attention reverted to him. She lifted him into her arms and repositioned herself so she sat cross-legged, jiggling him. When she got him settled, she glanced up at Ian and flashed a resigned smile. "People think *I'm* guarded, but you're the Fort Knox of personal information."

He snickered. "Heart of gold, you mean?"

"That too." She smiled. Then, as if catching herself doing something wrong, she reined in her emotions. "In the time you've spent here, you've learned all about my family and me, most of which is hardly flattering. Yet I know almost nothing about your life, other than the Mr. Perfect thing you project."

"Why tarnish my perfect image with the truth?" He found himself smiling, despite the crappy weather and his disheartening conversation with Archer.

"Wheeee!" Gentry rolled onto her back, balancing Colt on her shins while holding him in place. Her son squealed and stiffened with surprise, causing her to giggle. Their play brightened the room like a sunrise. In her baby-talking voice, she spoke to Colt. "I finally met someone more emotionally blocked than me, Boo. It's a miracle!"

"I'm not blocked." Ian crossed, then uncrossed, his arms.

She raised Colt up like an airplane, stretching his arms wide. "Prove it. Tell me something about your father. Something you've never told anyone."

Ian said what always came to mind first. "Everyone in our community loved him."

"That's not personal." She frowned, rolling forward and laying Colt on his back. "What's your favorite memory of him? Did he tell good bedtime stories, or play the guitar around the campfire, or teach you how to ride a bike? Help with homework, talk about girls? Give me something that tells me about your relationship."

Sadly, Ian didn't have those memories. Not with his father, anyway. Brian Crawford hadn't been that kind of dad. He'd traveled and, when at home, busied himself with plans for some event or other. If Ian's family had been a cake, his mom had been the batter; his dad, the icing. Everyone saw the icing, and his dad had liked it that way.

Unable to honestly answer the question, he said, "He treated everyone with compassion. He deeply cared about humanity. He gave everything, including his life, to improve the welfare of others."

Gentry sat up, having seized on the key detail he'd let slip. "He died while helping someone?"

Ian sighed. "Yes."

"How?"

Ian looked away, instantly transported back to the dusty streets of Port-au-Prince in 2010, choking on the smoke-filled air, surrounded by debris and despair and pain.

Ian stabilized the tenth fracture of the morning, waiting for more doctors to arrive. The city, an inferno and wasteland at once, reaffirmed his decision that this would be his last such journey. He had to accept he couldn't live like his father, always mired in chaos and sorrow. If he did, it would consume him, and he'd never be free.

Ten yards away, his father continued barking orders at others as he helped coordinate the rescue and aid effort. His clear, bright eyes remained full of vigor despite the evidence of aging revealed by his salt-and-pepper hair and weathered skin.

His father caught Ian staring at him, but looked away. They hadn't spoken much all morning. Their disagreement from last night's flight still sat between them like the Great Wall of China. But Ian had made up his mind. He wouldn't keep up with his father's punishing schedule anymore, or spearhead his father's dream of starting a foundation to improve emergency care. Ian would still serve the community, but in Oregon, with his mother. He'd finally have time for a girlfriend, some joy, and a life of his own.

"Ti bebe mwen an!" a severely wounded young mother cried, pointing toward the half-collapsed building behind Ian. "Tanpri konsève pou ti bebe mwen an!"

Ian couldn't fully understand her hysterical words, but she seemed to think her child was trapped in that building. His father hustled to Ian's side, speaking to the woman in his broken Creole. Calming her. Assuring her.

"What's going on, Dad?"

"She thinks her infant son is still in there." He whipped his head around, looking for other emergency workers. The area where he and Ian now worked teemed with sick and injured Haitians and medical workers, but other first responders weren't in the immediate vicinity. "I'm going in."

Ian gripped his arm. "No, Dad. That's not your job."

"Should we wait on the sidelines and let the child die in there? Let this woman's suffering go on?"

"That building looks unstable. You could get hurt or make things worse."

"I'm not like you, Ian. I can't turn my back on her, or live with myself if that kid dies because no one tried to help."

The blow of his father's disappointment caused Ian to loosen his grip. "Insult me all you want—you know I'm right. If you barge in there and get hurt, what good will that do? You've always taught me not to make things worse or divert resources. There are too many critical patients to save out here for me to risk going in there for one person who may or may not be there, or be alive."

They stared at each other, the voices around them blurring together like the roar of an airplane engine. "You don't understand, son. This work . . . this is my destiny. It isn't something I can hang up in a closet because it's inconvenient or I'm tired or afraid. You help these people. I'll get the baby."

Ian watched his dad march toward the building, panic gripping his muscles. "Dad!"

His father disappeared behind a broken wall. Ian's heart climbed into his throat. He stood alone amid so much agony that he wanted to fall to his knees and cry. Wanted to run as far away as possible.

The ground rumbled as if unable to bear the weight of so much suffering. An aftershock, perhaps, or had he imagined that? Then an exploding sound caused him to look up. Pop! Crack! Then a thunderous crash as the remains of the flamingo-pink building collapsed to the ground.

The young mother's wail pierced the sky, while Ian stood, mouth open in a silent scream.

"Ian?" Gentry's voice filled with concern.

He brushed aside the tear that rolled down his cheek. "My father died in Haiti."

"Did he disappear, too?" she asked, her voice thin, like that of a child listening to a ghost story.

"No." He looked up at her open, sympathetic expression. Her cool green eyes begged for him to share more. "I was with him in Haiti after the big earthquake. My dad charged into a half-destroyed building, searching for a woman's child. He wasn't a first responder. I told him not to go, but I didn't go in myself because I was tending to so many critically injured people. Then I watched what remained of the building collapse on top of him."

His chest hurt now, like anytime he thought about that day. It was as if his body had recorded, with perfect recall, the horrific helplessness he'd experienced. Like then, his vision got dark around the edges, his mouth filled with the tang of adrenaline.

"I'm so sorry." She jumped to her feet and hugged him as if he were so fragile he might disintegrate in her arms. She stroked the back of his head. "Now I see."

He pulled free. "See what?"

"Your obsession with Haiti. Survivor's guilt. Maybe you should talk to someone—a professional—so you can move on from mourning."

"It's been years." He kept his arms at his sides, refusing to embrace her again because he didn't trust himself to let go. "I've mourned."

"After watching Colby grieve Mark's suicide—a death she, like you, witnessed—I know that kind of pain lives on right under the surface."

Ian shrugged. True or not, it didn't change anything. Nor did that truth make it easier to discuss.

"One more question," she said. He braced himself, unsure if he wanted to discuss this further. "Is this misplaced guilt why you won't live a normal life?"

"It's my normal, Gentry. I'm founding this project to honor my dad and his work. It's that simple."

"I doubt that." She sank to the floor and snuggled Colt, talking to herself as much as to him now. "Nothing about family is ever simple."

"For some of us it is."

She narrowed her eyes, which always warned of a shrewd, and often pointed, observation. "As wonderful as your dad was to strangers, it doesn't sound like he had much time for your mom or you. I know a little bit about how it feels when something—or someone—else always comes first."

His hands balled on his hips, his body flushed in the heat of denial. "I don't resent my father."

"I guess that makes you a better person than me . . . not that that's a shock to anyone."

"Why *do* you resent your parents?" Ian gestured around the condo. "Isn't all of this—all the freedom you have—thanks to them?"

Gentry's shoulders drooped. He'd expected her to get mad, not disappointed. "Now you sound like *her*."

"Your mother?"

"Yes. She thinks I'm an ingrate, and, apparently, so do you."

He stood at the edge of a minefield now, but he'd have to cross it if he ever wanted to understand her. "I think you have at least as much to be thankful for as you do to be angry about."

"I don't expect you to understand. I wasn't abused or homeless or sickly. No easy-to-identify reason for my tenuous relationships."

"Make me understand."

"Why? So you can judge my hurt on some scale of suffering? I'm pretty sure loneliness won't rank too well against death and disease. If I complain about seeing other moms playing with their kids at the park while my nanny sat on the bench reading a book, you'll say I was lucky to be in a neighborhood with a nice park. If I bitch about how my mom drove a subtle wedge between Hunter and Colby and me even though I would've loved their company, you'll say at least I have siblings. If I confess to envy about their adventures with their mom, wishing Leslie would adopt me so I could be part of it, too, you'll shake your head.

"I've never pretended to be perfect or mature. I admit a lot of my past behavior was about getting *any* kind of attention. My mom cared more about how I reflected on her than she ever cared about me. Sure, she'd claim she worked hard so I could have everything. But all I ever wanted . . ." She stopped short of finishing the thought, but Ian could guess. All she ever wanted was to feel loved.

"You're an adult woman now. When you look back, don't you have more perspective? Can't you forgive mistakes?"

"I try, Ian. I really do. But all the criticism . . . and look at the hypocrisy. My mom didn't work hard for *me*. Look at her house, her clothes, her newspaper clippings. She did it for herself at *least* as much as for me. If she'd acknowledge that fact, then maybe we could get past it. Instead, she dumps all of our problems on me. On my behavior." Gentry looked at Colt. "I'd never do that to my son. When *I* go to work at CTC, it's for his benefit. So *he* can be part of a family that's, hopefully, less dysfunctional."

Her rapid-fire reply left Ian a little bruised. "I'm sorry you felt neglected."

She shrugged. "Do you still deny how similar we are, despite our different bank balances?"

"Similar?" He couldn't think of two less similar people in the city.

"Your dad's goals may have been loftier than my mother's, but they still left you behind." She said that with no judgment whatsoever. "If you hadn't followed him around the globe, how much of his time would he have given you? How much of his love?"

Her words cut a little too close to emotions Ian didn't want to acknowledge. "Why are you trying to hurt me?"

"I'm sorry. I don't mean to." She stood and grabbed his hands, squeezing them. "But I hate to see you spend the rest of your life chasing a ghost instead of following your own dreams."

"This is my dream, and I'm happy with it."

"You rarely look happy." Her eyes flickered with sympathy.

"It's called reserve." He pulled free from her grip.

"Oh, McJ, now you're being touchy." She sank back to the floor to pump Colt's little legs. "I'm only trying to help."

Help? How did probing questions and unflattering conclusions help?

"I have a request," she said, undaunted by his increasingly dark mood. "If someone in my family can watch Colt this afternoon, can I come with you today?"

"Why?" He'd become a mouse circled by a hawk.

"I told you before. I want to make some fun memories before you leave. Plus, I want to get in on this good feeling from helping others. Let me come. I promise I'll be good, *and* I won't ask any more personal questions."

He doubted she'd find it much fun, but if it would get her to stop questioning him about Haiti, his father, and his personal life, it would be worth it.

"You know it's raining." He pointed at the gray clouds and huge windows dotted with water drops. "We'll probably get wet."

A bright grin stretched across her face. "We'll make like Gene Kelly, then."

Chapter Eleven

Revelation

According to *Merriam-Webster*: a pleasant often enlightening surprise

According to me: a spontaneous side of Ian

Gentry popped her bubble gum and hummed along to the radio during the drive to the church, unaware of the battle raging in Ian's head. He hadn't fully processed her thoughts about his dad. Hell, he still couldn't believe what he'd shared with her, or understand why he'd blabbered.

"Cool building." Gentry peered up at the funky church spire, then smirked. "Watch it burst into flames when I walk through the doors."

He couldn't help himself. He chuckled.

She exited the car, dashing through the raindrops and through the back door that led to the basement. Ian caught up to her right before they entered the reception room, where a dozen volunteers were beginning to separate the donated items into piles.

His mother looked up and froze. He didn't understand the apprehension on her face until he saw Farrah standing beside her.

Dressed exactly like one might expect of a first-grade teacher during the summer, she wore chino shorts and a navy crewneck T-shirt and had braided her blonde hair. She'd always been petite, but she'd lost weight in the weeks since he'd moved out. He remembered the mixture of sorrow and determination she'd shown that day. The disappointment and tears she'd tried to hide. He surveyed her skinny legs and let the guilt take him under. While he'd been lusting after Gentry, Farrah hadn't been eating. It'd been Farrah's choice to end it, but what kind of man moves on without looking back at all? One who shouldn't have been engaged, for starters.

"Ian," Farrah said, her eyes roving from him to Gentry and back again.

If he'd had trepidation about introducing Gentry to his mom's circle of friends, it just doubled. "Hey, Farrah. How are you?"

Farrah's eyes darted to Gentry again before she softly said, "Been better."

Ian held his breath, unsure of an appropriate reply; then Gentry stuck her hand out to Farrah. "Hi, I'm Gentry."

Farrah reluctantly shook Gentry's hand. He noticed Farrah's face go pale and her chin wobble. He hesitated, unable to promise it wasn't what she thought yet unable to put any clear label on his relationship to Gentry, either. Luckily, his mother stepped in.

"Gentry hired Ian to take care of her baby until he heads back to Haiti. She couldn't put the child in day care because he was sick."

"Oh, that's nice." Some color returned to Farrah's cheeks, along with a relieved smile. "Congratulations . . . on the baby, I mean. I hope he's okay."

"Thanks," Gentry said. "He's much better now."

His mom then asked Gentry, "Is Ty okay after the little incident?"

Ian winced at the reminder he suspected Gentry didn't appreciate.

"Fully recovered." Gentry pasted a polite smile on her face. "Apparently, cupcakes are the antidote to nightmares." She ended that conversation with a sharp nod of her head. "So what's the deal here? How can I help?"

Ian's mom cleared her throat. "We're gathering all the items into piles, and then we'll stuff all those cinch sacks over there. Once that's done, we'll spread out to different areas of the city to deliver them."

"Sounds easy enough." Gentry tugged at Ian's arm, pointing at an empty rectangular folding table in the far corner. "No one's started on that pile of boxes. Let's go over there."

"Sure." He nodded at his mom and Farrah, their blistering gazes like a thousand suns burning his skin. When he and Gentry moved far enough away to speak without being overheard, he expected to be grilled. Instead, Gentry began picking through the items, her face wrinkling with dismay. He scanned the dental products, deodorant, socks, Band-Aids, wet wipes, lip balm, sunscreen, vitamins, tissue packs, plastic combs, mints, water bottles, and cereal bars. "What's wrong? Not your favorite brands?"

"It's hard for me to imagine not having these simple things." She gazed up at him, clearly disturbed.

"Few can. Homelessness is a real crisis. They need basics, like food"—he held up a granola bar—"and toiletries. In the winter, we'll need to find blankets, socks, and coats."

"There are kids, aren't there?"

"Yes, unfortunately."

She stared at the pile and frowned. "Would it be okay to add something else? Something to make them smile?"

"Smile?"

"Well, I get that this stuff is most important. But something unexpected can really lift the spirit. Make a person feel hopeful." She tapped her fingers on her lips while thinking. "There's a Walmart we passed on our way here. If it's okay, I'd like to add some things to these bags."

He supposed it didn't hurt anything, so he nodded.

"Great. I'll be back in twenty minutes."

"Hey!" he called, but she'd run out the door without looking back. He had no idea what to expect when she returned.

Smiles and hope. Two things Gentry seemed determined to give him, her son . . . almost everyone except her own mother.

He shook his head, vaguely aware of *his* mother approaching.

"Thanks for coming, honey. I didn't know Farrah would show up." She looked toward the door Gentry had recently run through. "Or Gentry."

"Neither did I."

"I suspect Farrah's here to try to patch things up with you." His mom spoke quietly while helping him sort.

He cast a quick glance at Farrah, who kept her head down at the moment. "She didn't know I'd be here."

"Hmph," his mom clucked. "A good guess, then."

"Did Farrah say something to you, or is this wishful thinking on your part? She's always supported the church."

"She has, but I think she'd be open to reconciliation. This could be your chance to patch things up and start a family of your own."

"It's too late for that."

His mother's brows rose, but she kept quiet.

He could feed her a line about how unfair it would be to marry Farrah and then take off for a year or more in Haiti. Truth was, his infatuation with Gentry proved his feelings for Farrah had dwindled long before she'd ended things.

Ian blocked all that out, working methodically, grouping items together for bagging. At one point he looked up and caught Farrah staring at him. Eventually, she came over to his table. "Need help here?"

"I've got it covered, thanks."

"Where'd your boss go?" Farrah linked her hands behind her back.

Ian didn't want to two-step with Farrah today, but his mother hovered nearby, so he had no escape. "Walmart."

"Why?"

"I try not to predict anything where Gentry's concerned." He felt the corners of his mouth lift, then erased his smile as soon as Farrah noticed it.

"She's pretty." Farrah searched his gaze for an answer to the question she wouldn't dare ask.

Sweat broke out on his scalp. He wouldn't say anything that might hurt Farrah more than he already had, so he cast about for neutral territory. "How's summer school?"

She shrugged. "I have Jimmy Eldrige in my class again."

Jimmy Eldrige, a kid with severe ADHD, terrorized most teachers, but he had a little crush on Farrah. Ian figured Farrah gave him something he didn't get at home: compassion. Her name in Arabic meant "joy," and that's pretty much what she gave her students. He tipped his head and smiled. "Guess *he's* thrilled."

Farrah smiled, too. "Ian, it's good to see you. I was thinking . . . well, wondering if maybe we could grab a coffee before you go?"

"Oh, I don't know. My schedule's pretty full." Before he could elaborate, Gentry reappeared, like some kind of Sherpa, carrying dozens of shopping bags on her arms and back. When she reached their table, she spun around and let the bags drop.

"What's all this?" Ian caught one bag before it fell to the ground.

"Don't be mad. I just couldn't decide, so I picked up a bunch of things that would be useful and a little fun." Gentry beamed at him and Farrah and then began emptying the bags. An array of things tumbled onto the table: inspirational notecards, paperback novels and magazines, tiny bottles of perfume and toys, and a ton of McDonald's gift certificates. "There's not enough of any one item to stuff every bag, but I tried to get a mix of things, especially the toys for kids. The novels will help people pass the time. The perfume is probably stupid, but it might make some feel pretty."

"McDonald's?" Ian flipped through a booklet that contained McDonald's "money" that could be spent on any menu item.

"I thought everyone could use a hot meal." Gentry shrugged, stuffing the receipts in her pocket before anyone could see what she'd spent.

"It's very thoughtful, although I wonder if we might've been better off getting more socks or other practical items?" Ian's mom placed her hand on her cheek while reading the back of some romance novel.

"You're probably right, but I really wanted to give something unexpected." Gentry began organizing her loot. "Maybe we use a Sharpie to mark the cinch sacks with toys with a *T*. Then we can make sure those go to parents with young kids."

Ian grinned, appreciative of the beauty in her crazy idea. "Sounds like a plan."

"I'll let you two finish up here," Farrah said, backing away without forcing an answer to her earlier invitation.

"Nice to meet you." Gentry smiled at Farrah but didn't invite her to stay.

Farrah hesitated, looking at Ian.

"Good to see you, Farrah. Take care." For a second, his heart stopped. He'd hurt her again. He could see it on her face.

She nodded and retreated. He tucked his chin, closing his eyes to shake off the guilt. Gentry elbowed him, holding out a book with a man's abs on the cover. "You never told me you were a cover model, Ian."

He chuckled, grateful that she'd come along. He'd never had much fun doing these runs, but she made him laugh.

Forty minutes later, Ian and Gentry loaded her trunk with forty of the blessing bags. Gentry redid her ponytail, sweeping the damp tendrils around her face back into place, then started the engine.

On the drive up to the Springwater Corridor, she said, "Farrah reminds me of Sara. Blonde, sweet, classy. I guess I shouldn't be surprised."

Farrah had all those qualities, but he recognized a booby trap when he heard one. Knowing Gentry saw herself as the antithesis of those women, he kept his mouth shut.

"What kinds of things did you two do for fun?" Gentry prodded, signaling left and then slowing down to look for parking.

If he refused to answer her simple question, she'd read way more into it than necessary. He didn't want to talk about Farrah, but soon enough the conversation would end because they'd be busy handing out the bags. "Normal couple things. Movies. Meals."

Sex, he thought, but didn't say. It didn't speak well of him that, when he said it, he'd pictured sex with Gentry instead of Farrah.

"Do you miss her?"

Not like he should. "I miss some things."

"Sex?"

Seems they both had that on their minds. Ian crossed his arms. "Farrah's sweet. A nurturer. She teaches first grade and Sunday school. She's patient with kids. She'll be a great mother someday." For some reason, that comment made Gentry frown. "She likes to bake."

"Sounds like a peach." Gentry's slightly sour tone smacked of possessive envy, making him grin. "But that's all generic stuff. What made her special? What made you think she was 'the one'?"

He wouldn't disrespect Farrah by admitting the unflattering truth—he'd never been struck by that certainty. "I guess she reminded me of my mom."

"Ew!" Gentry's nose wrinkled before she laughed. "TMI."

"Not like that, sicko." He pinched her arm in jest. "She had a big group of friends and family. She kept herself busy while I was away. Trouble started when her friends got married one by one. Then her closest sister moved to Seattle. Turns out she wasn't as independent as my mom." He looked out the window, recalling his young life with his mother, who'd dragged him around to all her organizations.

"That's unfair." Gentry rolled her eyes before cutting him an annoyed glance.

"How so?"

"Farrah's not codependent just because she wants a partner who's present. That's called normal. What's the point of a boyfriend or husband if he isn't going to be around?" Before he could defend against that blow, she added, "Your mom had *you* to keep her busy and keep her company. Maybe she played it cool with your dad because she didn't have a choice if she wanted to keep her family together. You can't know what she thought or felt—you were a kid. You remember things the way you want them to have been."

"That's not true." But an unpleasant memory struck. A Thanksgiving when his father hadn't made it home. Ian had been watching a Seahawks game after dinner. When he'd gone back to the kitchen to get more pumpkin pie, he'd overheard the tail end of his mother complaining to her sister about being tired and lonely. His aunt Sally had made some sarcastic quip about the Crawford way, but his mom slapped her hand to shut her up when she noticed Ian.

Ian now stared at the road ahead, watching the wipers clear raindrops from the windshield. His head hurt from being bombarded all day with probing questions about his past.

Gentry found a spot near the wildlife refuge on SE 111th.

"Too bad we don't have a wagon," she mused. "Where should we start?"

"We'll head out along the path there." He helped her string the bags on her arms. "They say there are about two hundred homeless people living in tents between here and Southeast Eighty-Second. We don't have enough for everyone, so we'll do what we can, then turn back. Will you be okay with that?"

"Yes. I've actually been here before. My last boyfriend, Jake, had a hot dog cart, which he would set up all over the place." She began walking toward the trailhead. “One time he came up here to feed a bunch of people for free and brought me along.”

“Oh.” It struck him as unlikely that Gentry would date a street vendor or feed the homeless, but then again, she thrived on shattering expectations.

Looking down the pathway, Ian saw a veritable village of homeless people, including a few unfortunate children. Tents, shopping carts with worn belongings, folding chairs, old bikes, and assorted items were strewn along the edges of the path, beneath the trees. Shortly after starting along the paved walking trail, they promptly came upon the first hovel.

Gentry crouched to speak with a middle-aged woman with graying hair and weathered skin. Her clothes were stained; her hair, matted.

“Hello.” Gentry stayed back several feet, but it seemed to Ian that she did so out of respect for the woman’s personal space rather than fear or disgust. “Sorry to intrude, but I’m wondering if you might like a little gift?”

The woman’s brows drew together, and she briefly glanced up at Ian, then skeptically answered, “Sure.”

“Here you go.” Gentry handed her a green-and-black cinch sack.

The older woman scanned the vicinity as if checking to see if anyone might come steal it from her, before eagerly dumping its contents onto her torn blanket. She promptly opened a cereal bar and took a bite. Then her gaze fell on the book. It had a dashing couple from a bygone era on its cover and a title about some scandalous duke. The woman flashed a surprised smile. “Thank you.”

“You’re welcome.” Gentry stood, motioning to Ian to keep walking.

Ian fell in beside her as they continued their journey. “You’re efficient.”

“I won’t patronize anyone. And how can I honestly say ‘Have a nice day’ when the rain’s picking up and she didn’t even have a real tent?”

If Ian had thought he'd be taking the lead, he'd been wrong. Gentry walked ahead, crouching by another woman. She repeated this abbreviated routine several times.

He watched her work the corridor, noting the way her red hair turned dark when wet. She'd shucked the designer clothes in favor of jean shorts full of holes, although he'd bet they were still expensive. Gentry offered a compassionate smile to everyone they encountered. She braved the corridor without too much discomfort, except when they came across children. That's when trouble clouded her eyes, even though she did her best to hide it.

Thirty minutes later they'd run out of bags. The drizzle had turned into a light rain while they made their way back to the car. Gentry didn't complain or pull a fuss about her hair or clothes getting wet.

"Should we jog?" he asked, wiping back his bangs.

"We're already wet. If I turn something unpleasant into a game, it's usually not as bad." She started to whistle the melody to "Singin' in the Rain" as they journeyed toward the car.

It reminded him of her Gene Kelly remark from earlier in the day. "Is there a reason you like that old movie so much?"

"Sixth-grade dance recital." She dipped into an exaggerated bow, then began skipping ahead, whistling louder.

"You liked being onstage, I bet." He trotted beside her, trying to picture her at eleven years old, all coltish legs and giant eyes.

She slowed to a walk, shrugging. "Not really. But my dad made it to that show." Then she skipped ahead again.

He let her go, knowing she'd need a bit of distance after that admission. She spun, arms flung outward, face up and welcoming the rain.

He caught up to her at the car, where they huddled in the front seat in their wet clothes.

"Thanks for coming with me." He touched her hand, wishing he had better words to express his feelings.

She sighed. "Hate to admit this, but I would've been a little nervous to do that by myself."

"Don't *ever* do that alone." Some of the men had leered at her shapely legs and chest even with Ian standing beside her. "You could be attacked."

"Ha! That's rich, coming from you."

"That's different. I know what I'm doing and how to avoid danger."

"Well, we just helped a bunch of people without risking cholera or kidnapping. I know it isn't lifesaving work, but if you worked with Colby or other groups, you could make a huge impact right here in Portland." She cast a quick glance at him before pulling onto the street. "But no more lectures from me. Today should be about fun. That's another thing you probably don't experience too often in Haiti."

"There's fun to be had in Haiti. Waterfalls and beaches."

She wrinkled her nose, replying wryly, "I'm betting *you* don't allow yourself much leisure time."

He didn't like her impression, although he also couldn't pretend that he took much time to sightsee or relax. Truth was, maybe he did have a stick up his ass like she claimed. Then he got an idea. A bizarre idea, but one he thought she'd enjoy. "I can be fun, Gentry. In fact, let's go play mini golf."

His matter-of-fact yet absurd pronouncement drew a disbelieving glance. "Mini golf . . . in the rain?"

"Glowing Greens." The indoor mini golf course boasted neon-and-black lights and crazy 3-D decor.

Her eyes went wide. "I haven't been there in ages . . . and when I went, I was drunk. Do you plan to get drunk today, too, Ian?"

"No. I've never been there, so I want to see it sober."

"You've *never* been?"

"Nope."

"Then let's go!" She shifted the car into reverse and backed out of the lot, smiling as if he'd given her a diamond ring.

He'd put that smile on her face, which made his chest fill with the heady fizz of joy.

◆ ◆ ◆

Four Voodoo doughnuts and two legitimate belly laughs into the afternoon, Ian stared at Gentry as she lined up her putt. Her white shirt glowed under the black lights of the indoor miniature golf facility—a 3-D neon extravaganza that must've been designed by someone in the middle of a psychedelic hallucination.

"Were you ever that wild, Ian?"

"Hm?" He picked up his ball and followed her to the next hole.

"Those boys, running and laughing." She pointed in the direction of a birthday party of energetic ten-year-olds circling one another on a nearby hole, where a few mothers failed to keep them organized. "I'm trying to picture you that way but can't. I can only see you like you are now."

"In other words, boring?"

She chuckled. "Well, we wouldn't have been coconspirators. That's for sure." She lined up a shot and took it.

He looked at the eager boys, joking with each other. Some vying for a sort of leadership role, others more interested in unwrapping candy than playing golf. "I was pretty quiet. An only child. Spent a lot of time with adults."

"I hated grown-ups." She paused to putt. "And I wasn't quiet."

"You weren't an only kid, either."

"Kind of was." She picked up her ball after sinking it in the cup. "At least I got to run around with neighborhood kids instead of being dragged to my parents' work like you were."

"You probably had big birthday bashes like that boy, too." He lined up his shot, but it hit the purple fin obstacles and went sideways.

"You didn't?"

"Not in our budget. I'd have a few neighborhood kids over. Duncan Hines cake. No gifts."

Gentry's eyes grew as round as the doughnuts they'd devoured. "Why no gifts?"

"My birthday is December sixteenth. I think my parents worried I'd get something that Santa had already bought, so they'd tell parents to have their kids make something or bring candy."

Gentry tossed up her orange ball and caught it. "I had huge birthday parties with all the bells and whistles—petting zoos, bounce houses, kids from the whole grade. My mom would busy herself with the parents. My dad manned the grill. Colby and Alec would sit off to the side, counting the minutes until they could go join their friends somewhere else. Half the kids in my grade weren't my friends. They only came for the pool and the cool goody bags my mom gave out." Her gaze wandered to the group of boys behind them. "I would've rather spent the day with Hunter and Colby."

Ian looked at the harried mothers shuttling those boys to the next hole. "Parenting is an impossible job, isn't it? You can't control the way your kids interpret your choices, or what they remember. You think you're doing something great, but they wish you did something different."

He could only assume she'd heard him, because she kept staring into space without offering her two cents. Was she thinking about her own parents, or about her son?

Time to lighten the mood. When he teed up on the eighteenth hole, he exaggeratedly wiggled his hips, making her giggle. "What's the score?"

She dragged her eyes away from the curve of his behind. "I'm winning."

By one stroke, if he'd been keeping correct count.

"Not for long." He knocked the ball, which rolled right up the ramp, to the alien monster with an orange hat, and into the hole. "Good luck beating that!"

She set her ball down and took her shot, which backfired and rolled back to her feet. "Well, dang." She picked up the ball, but instead of swinging again, she walked up the putting green and placed the ball in the hole she liked best. "Tie!"

He laughed, letting that airy sensation take over again. The frustration that began his day had all but dissolved, thanks to her.

Gentry's gaze wandered back to the young boys. Her peculiar smile piqued his curiosity.

"You picturing Colt a decade from now?" It dawned on him then that he wouldn't know Colt at ten. Hell, he wouldn't even know the kid at one.

Gentry's palm cupped her cheek. "Right now he needs me for everything. When he grows up, he won't need me at all. I'm eager to see who he'll become, but I also don't want it to go too fast."

A surge of emotion roughened his voice. "I don't know who he'll become, either, but with you as his mom, I'm pretty sure he'll be interesting."

"I'll take that as a compliment." Her green eyes shone in the black lights.

"I meant it as one."

Chapter Twelve

Orgasm

According to *Merriam-Webster*: intense or paroxysmal excitement; *especially* **:** the rapid pleasurable release of neuromuscular tensions at the height of sexual arousal that is usually accompanied by the ejaculation of semen in the male and by vaginal contractions in the female

According to me: something long overdue, and so much better than I remember

Gentry couldn't read Ian. Perhaps that accounted for some of his appeal.

Reading men had never before presented a challenge. Pretty much all of them wanted sex, however, and whenever they could get it and with whoever was willing.

They didn't have to like you or even find you pretty, a fact that had been underscored when she'd overheard high school boys' crude jokes about how "all girls look the same between their legs." In her experience, guys rarely cared if you liked *them* much, either. In fact, given how often guys complained about girls becoming clingy, she guessed some men preferred to have sex with women who had no real interest in them whatsoever—as long as they could fake an orgasm well.

By the age of eighteen, she'd adapted to these realities by keeping her heart on lockdown while enjoying the powerful pleasures of flirtation and sex. That way of life worked for her until Colt came along. Until her heart had been thunderstruck with a love so vast and protective that she couldn't be bothered with lusty games and stupid men.

But Ian wasn't stupid. Stubborn, perhaps, but not stupid. Not heartless. Not cocky. Not governed by the head between his legs.

She wanted his affection, respect, and belonging. A terrifying reality, because, until recently, she'd successfully avoided the pain of dashed hope where men were concerned.

Romantic hope, the great destroyer of rational women. There should be a T-shirt or a mug.

When they returned to her house after picking up Colt, she transferred her sleepy son to his bassinet. Sara and Ty must've worn him out. Not that *Sara* had seemed the least bit tired. Even her blouse still looked freshly pressed when handing over Colt, who'd been recently fed and changed into a clean diaper.

Gratitude and annoyance wrestled in her chest like pigs in a trough. Sara never even complained about Colt's colic. Did she have special ears that didn't hear it? Or was Sara's heart that pure, and her patience that remarkable?

One benefit of her son's colic was that it stopped Hunter from keeping her there to discuss work. He'd practically shoved her out the door, wincing as Colt wailed.

Last night she'd started to work on the Snapchat campaign but then gotten invested in replying to one young single mom's blog comment where she'd lamented her choice to be a single parent, worrying it would scar her child. Gentry identified with that fear, especially because she'd heard nothing on the search for Smith. But Ian almost had her convinced that Colt could thrive as long as he had her unconditional love, and as long as she didn't let herself get so overwhelmed that she'd wear down. She knew she'd been handling motherhood better these past weeks because of his help.

Tonight she'd have to focus on CTC. Absolutely. No excuses.

For now she closed her bedroom door after settling Colt into a nap and shuffled down the hallway toward the living room. Ian stood at the wall of windows, watching the rain. The droplets sprinkled across the plate glass. Dim lighting from gray skies shrouded them in a melancholy kind of peace.

She stopped to admire the lean lines of his body. No one would complain about any of his physical attributes. Sometimes his moods were black as night, but when he smiled, it was as welcome and radiant as the sun bursting through a cloud.

Soon he'd be gone. She wanted to memorize each detail, like the curls of his hair against the back of his neck, or the slight bump on the bridge of his nose, or the dark hair on his calves. His tight butt was already unforgettable. She pressed her lips together to keep herself from making a wisecrack.

"Thank you," she finally said.

He flinched, then turned. "For what?"

"For today. For the spontaneity." She stood still, hesitating to approach him. All afternoon she'd been at war with herself over this man. "I liked seeing you kick back for a while."

"It turned into a good day." He smiled, his eyes crinkling in the corners. Even his posture relaxed.

It seemed as if he'd let go of his early discussion with Archer, for which Gentry was both proud and grateful. "You look peaceful now. Can I ask one last favor?"

He shoved his hands in his pockets. "Shoot."

"Can I snap some photos? Not for my blog. For memories . . ."

Memories. The word was a bitter reminder that, while she enjoyed his company, he was busy making plans for a life far away from here. If she'd hoped their single day of adventure would persuade him to change his mind, she must have been losing her own.

Ian shrugged self-consciously. "As long as I don't have to pose."

"Hang on!" She dashed to the hall closet for her Nikon D7500 and tiptoed back to the room, hoping to catch him unaware again. She spied on him, using the large window as a mirror, while he finger-combed his wavy hair. Before he noticed her reflection, she zoomed her lens and snapped a few candids.

He spun around, laughing at himself. "No fair!"

"Oh, Ian. Surely you've figured out by now that I don't play fair," she teased, continuing to snap photos even as he approached her, his arms thrust forward in an attempt to block the shots and grab her camera. When he came close enough to snatch it from her, she held it high and away. "Okay, okay. I'll stop."

He narrowed his gaze, lowering his arms like a gunman being forced to drop his weapon. "Can I trust you?"

"At your own risk," she joked, pointing to the part of the sofa bathed in a bit of remaining daylight. "Sit in that corner of the couch, please."

While he got comfortable, she returned to the closet for her tripod and then set up her camera, focusing its lens. "Leave room for me on your left."

She hit the self-timer and scooted across the small carpet, plopping herself beside him and leaning in. Willing the timer to slow down, she savored the warmth of Ian's body as she pressed against him under the guise of staying within the frame. "Say 'cheese.'"

The flash went off, leaving her no choice but to separate.

"Don't move. Let me see how that came out." When she viewed the photo, his face looked distorted, as if he'd been looking at her, then turned toward the camera as it shot the photo. "Oh no. That's blurry. Try again and don't move."

She reset the timer and resumed her cozy spot beside him, this time inhaling the scent of his cotton shirt and her citrus bath soap. When she checked on that photo, she laughed. "Can't you smile like a normal person?"

"Let me see." He motioned for the camera with his hands. "I can smile."

Naturally, she welcomed yet another chance at body contact. When she showed him the two photos, he chuckled. "Maybe that's appropriate. Despite your earlier joke, I'm no cover model."

"You've got potential, Ian Crawford. Let's try something else." Gentry would need to engage him to get some candid close-ups. She twisted on the cushion while quietly adjusting the camera, preparing to aim and shoot. She couldn't help but notice his full lips through the lens. Those lips were meant for kissing, and he did that well. The memory gave her an idea. Just before snapping the photos, she asked, "Do you ever regret stopping our kiss?"

Snap. Snap. Snap.

When she looked at the pictures, she burst into giggles. "Oh my God, your face! Priceless."

Flushed, he reached for the camera, but she pulled it away, teasing. Suddenly she was on her back, pinned down, both of them laughing and breathing a bit heavier from wrestling.

Then his smile changed—softened—until a sober expression replaced the last hint of a grin. Heat lit up his eyes, but they also looked sad as he hovered over her, his weight suspended by his elbows.

Her heart beat erratically, battling a rising tide of new and terrifying truths. This man might be her first genuine friend. Such a gift, yet friendship alone wouldn't satisfy the pull—the need—for more. What if this could be more? What if it could be *everything*?

Desperation pushed her to be more honest than she had ever been with any man. She let the camera slide to the ground before reaching up and touching his hair. "I know you think we're a disaster in the making, but I . . . I really like you."

He clasped her wrist and brought it to his chest, flattening her palm so that she could feel his pounding heart.

"I really like you, too" came his hoarse reply. Without taking his eyes off hers, he raised her hand and kissed her wrist.

The heat from his mouth sank beneath her skin and slid through her entire body. Last time they'd been on the brink of crossing lines, she'd scared him off. Now she willed her impulses into submission, praying that, by letting him set the pace, he wouldn't stop.

The steady patter of rain against the windows created a sensual cocoon. Gentry held her breath, barely blinking for fear of missing out on the array of emotions crossing Ian's face.

"Ian," she whispered. She knew he'd lost the battle with his conscience once he slid his arms beneath her shoulders and cupped her head, his thumbs gently tracing her jawline. When she wet her lips, his gaze fell to her mouth. Like a magnet, her moistened lips pulled him closer. In the moment where they shared one breath, she closed her eyes, and then he kissed her.

A warm, tender kiss that gradually roughened with the edge of desire. Still, she waited, afraid to make a move that might send him running. *I really like you, too,* he'd said.

Instinct caused her to wrap her legs around his hips. He tightened his hold and deepened their kiss, a low moan filling in his chest. She skimmed her hands along his back and over his butt, wanting him close. Wanting some part of his kindness and virtue.

Her hands itched to touch his skin, but she didn't dare. She restrained every urge except the one that made her hips undulate. Fortunately, Ian suffered from the same restlessness. The friction set off an explosion of tingles that fanned through her core and to her limbs, over and over, each time coming a little quicker and stronger.

Finally, Ian tucked his hand beneath her shirt and cupped her breast, his thumb feverishly circling her nipple.

"God," he uttered before his mouth descended on her neck, leaving a warm, wet trail of kisses along the sensitive skin. His muscles were hard, his hips impatient. "I can't stop myself."

"Don't." Seizing the moment, Gentry raised the hem of his shirt and gently scratched his back with her fingernails. She could feel the goose bumps rising on his skin. She nipped at his earlobe and whispered in his ear, her heart racing from the pleasure-laden sound of his heavy breath.

He levered himself up long enough to remove his shirt, treating her to a close-up view of his abs and bare chest. She stroked his chest while he stared down at her, his pupils fully dilated so that his eyes no longer appeared green. Joy and panic tussled for control of her needy heart.

She couldn't catch her breath. The rain now came down in sheets, pounding loud like her heart. The moment stretched until his gaze dropped to her cleavage. Then the pace of everything shifted into high gear.

Within seconds, their clothes lay abandoned on the floor, their bodies fumbling around, a tangle of arms and legs, rough kisses, mumbled affections.

"Condoms . . . ," she managed, having barely enough presence of mind to remember. But unlike with Smith, she was sober and clear-eyed today.

He kissed her quickly and then reached for his wallet, leaving her squirming on the sofa, wet, needy, and eager. Exposed—the one thing she swore she'd never let herself be with any man. *I really like you, too.*

He tore the packet open with his teeth, fitted himself, and then tugged her hand.

"You on top," he commanded, removing the loosened ponytail holder from her hair so that her curls cascaded over her shoulders. "I want to see you."

His husky tone conveyed deeper meaning in those words. For the first time ever, she wanted to be seen—truly seen—by a man.

His hands clamped on her hips and then rose along her waist to cup her breasts. They sat, face-to-face, kissing and fondling with the slow rise and fall of her body.

In the past, she'd enjoyed games, dirty talk, props—anything to distance herself from the person. From emotion. She'd trained herself to focus squarely on physical sensations.

Today she kept her eyes open and her big mouth shut. She exposed her heart entirely, even if he didn't know it. But he might figure it out, given the tears stinging her eyes.

◆ ◆ ◆

If it were possible for Ian to be in heaven and hell at the same time, that's where he was. Gentry Cabot might be the singular most breathtaking woman he'd ever known, let alone so intimately. He strained not to spill too early, but her dropping all pretense proved overwhelming in every way.

She had a body and mouth meant for hours and hours of pleasure. He noted each curve and freckle, the sweet floral scent of perfume, the humidity-coarsened texture of her hair. He even noted the moments of candor and surprise in her eyes, which might've been the most amazing gift of all.

More. The word repeated in his head over and over with each kiss, stroke, nip, and grind. *More. More. More.*

He'd lost control of himself and could hardly care less as he laid her back against the cushions, bodies now sweat soaked, and gave over to the orgasm he could no longer hold back.

Tiny aftershocks seized him while he remained buried inside her, but Gentry didn't complain about his weight or push him aside. She became uncommonly quiet, especially for her, and he wondered if she was as disoriented by what had happened as he was.

The downpour outside, reminiscent of the heavy rains of springtime in Haiti, served as an unwelcome reminder of his plans. Of the fact he would be leaving soon. It seemed unjust that they, two different people with very different lives, could share this kind of connection.

He didn't want to give it up too soon, not when he'd finally tapped into something so exciting and unpredictable. Something unlike anything he'd shared with other women.

Then a thin layer of guilt tinged the tenderness rising within him as he recalled Farrah's face today. She'd broken their engagement, so he hadn't exactly betrayed her. But what of his emotions? How had he moved on so quickly to another woman? Not only by having sex, but also by caring. By being so intrigued and infatuated that he hadn't, until now, given Farrah a thought.

Who the hell was he becoming, and was this a better or worse version of himself?

He kept his head tucked in the crook of Gentry's shoulder while he fumbled for the right thing to say. No doubt she'd been perfectly comfortable with the spontaneous sex. For him, it struck a new chord. He basked in the pleasant hum of contentment, which would be hard to surrender.

The unexpected bark of Colt's fussing through the baby monitor spared them both a clumsy conversation.

"Gotta work on the kid's timing," Gentry teased, and Ian both felt and saw the mask of detachment fall into place.

He could kick himself. If he'd said something—anything—kind or heartfelt, she wouldn't have retreated. After everything she'd revealed today about a lifelong sense of loneliness, she deserved more. She deserved the truth.

It seemed that he, too, had a mask of sorts—silence—that he used to keep his distance. The kind of emotional distance that enabled him to keep moving from country to country, crisis to crisis.

"I'll get him," Ian offered. He pulled his boxers on while enjoying the view of her naked body sprawled out on the sofa, and then trotted into her room to check on Colt and collect his thoughts.

As soon as he entered the room, he choked on the odor of the dirty diaper that must've awakened Colt from his nap.

"Hey, little stinker. Your mommy dodged a bullet. I think she knew it, too." When he went to lift Colt from the bassinet, he discovered the full extent of the problem. "Good God, man, you need new clothes, too."

He gingerly transported the poop bomb to the makeshift changing station and peeled the soiled clothes away, grabbing about a hundred baby wipes. After cleaning the majority of the mess, he filled the blue plastic baby bath with warm water and gave him a quick cleaning, making sure to wash up to his neck and the back of his head.

Having done this more than once, he completed the task in less than five minutes, which made him oddly proud. Given Ian's lifestyle, it'd be unlikely that he'd have kids—at least not for some time. Caring for Colt had given him a taste of fatherhood, and more empathy for all parents.

He swaddled Colt in a towel, then brought him up to his chest and inhaled the scent of his skin. Ian would miss the mad pooper when he left. He'd miss Gentry, too. He laid Colt on the changing station again to put him in a clean diaper and pajamas.

The baby monitor camera was on, though pointed at the bassinet. Gentry couldn't see him, but she'd hear anything he said.

"Okay, buddy. You're good to go. Promise me you won't do this to your mom once I leave. She's got a lot on her plate, so you have to be the man of the house and help her out however you can." He let Colt clasp his index fingers and then moved Colt's arms like one might play with a doll. He glanced at the monitor, then cleared his throat. "Your mom will give you an amazing adventure and a life filled with love, so you'd better appreciate her and love her back." Ian avoided looking at the video monitor. Who knew what his expression might reveal? Regardless of how happy he was here with Gentry and Colt, his path had been forged already and would take him away from this home.

Colt wriggled, so Ian cradled him to his chest. The kid grew a pinch every single day. Showed more spark of personality, too, exactly like his mom. He'd be a handful, but whether she knew it or not, Gentry could handle it on her own.

Then again, she probably wouldn't be alone forever. Not many guys would turn her away, and if she found Smith, she could put together the family she'd always wanted. Ian would never burden her with the truth, but the idea of Colt's father taking Ian's place sent a painful jolt to his heart.

"Everything okay in here?" Gentry stood by the door to her room, fully dressed. A pity about that.

"He's good to go." He handed Colt to her and then bunched the soiled clothes and towel, guessing she wouldn't mention what she'd overheard. "Straight to the wash with this."

"Thanks." She averted his gaze and nuzzled Colt.

She'd never been stupid. She understood their situation and would make the best of it, as would he, without asking questions. Just as well, because he didn't have any answers.

He began his escape, then she said, "Ian?"

"Hm?" The bundle of soiled, wet clothes in his hand still stank to high heaven.

She rocked her son while smiling at Ian, and a part of him wanted to walk over and hug them both. "It's okay, you know."

"What's okay?"

"What happened with us. I know it doesn't mean everything or change anything, and that's okay. The fact that it meant *something* is enough." She kissed her son and murmured in his ear.

Her courage forced him to find a little of his own. "It definitely means something. And, in fact, kinda does change everything . . . except my plans."

"Don't worry. I don't expect any promises." She kissed Colt's slobbery cheek again. "But who knows? Maybe one day a shadow will fall across the hot dirt path you're on, and you'll find yourself staring up at me."

"In a skimpy dress and high heels, I hope." He winked, pretending this conversation wasn't tearing little pieces from his heart.

"And a jug of clean water." She hiked her thumb toward the window. "Fresh from Oregon."

He chuckled softly, thinking that she could well be as life sustaining as a jug of water under the right circumstances. He could have stood there and stared at her forever but for the shit-stained bunch of clothes in his hand. "I'd better deal with this or we'll need ten cans of Febreze."

"I'll order something for dinner." And in a snap, it was as if the past hour hadn't happened.

Instead of skipping away with relief, he felt his first step was clumsy. The second one, too. His body seemed heavy, like he'd been filled with sand. Before he became mired in self-pity, Gentry called to him. "One last thing. While you're still here, it'd be fine with me if you wanted to sleep in my room."

Chapter Thirteen

Ill-timed

According to *Merriam-Webster*: done or happening at a time that is not good or suitable

According to me: finding Smith

Ian's surprise drained him of color.

"Don't faint. I'm not proposing or anything. But why spend the next week or two—or three?—denying everything we feel? I say we roll with it."

"Of course you do." His mouth twitched as if fighting a smile.

"Come on, McJ. We had a banner day." His blush set off a shower of tingles, but she feigned nonchalance. "Let this run its course. What can a few more good memories hurt?"

He scratched his jaw, hesitant.

Gentry had never begged a man for anything, but Ian was worth it. "I promise, I don't snore."

"I bet you hog the bed, though." His eyes twinkled, suggesting she was close to winning him over.

She cocked her hip, telling herself that she looked sexy despite the fussy baby in her arms. "You'll be so worn out you won't even notice."

He barked a laugh. "True enough. First things first." Ian raised the bundle in his hand. "I need to burn these."

He trotted to the laundry room without giving her an answer, but the gambler in her bet he'd acquiesce.

She squeezed Colt and laid her cheek on his head. "You like Ian, right?"

She remembered the live baby monitor too late. Shrugging, she made a smug but silly face in its camera in case Ian was watching. When she didn't hear him snicker from the other room, she assumed the washing machine had his full attention.

"Let's get you a bottle, Boo." She kissed him and went to the kitchen, amazed at how bright it was now, despite the storm outside. Her house felt more like a home. A place where Colt could thrive.

Ian met her in the kitchen while she mixed Colt's formula. She debated whether to press him, but her phone went off before she got up the nerve.

Hunter. *Shoot.* If he asked for the new campaign summary, he'd be mighty unhappy.

Time to own up, she supposed.

She handed Colt to Ian and then walked into the living room for a bit of privacy. No need for Ian to hear how she'd been falling behind at work.

"Hey, what's up?" She aimed for brightness.

"Are you free?"

His wary tone opened a pit in her stomach. "Now?"

"Yes."

"Why do you sound so weird?"

Hunter paused. "We found Smith."

"Oh!" The unexpected reply sent her stumbling into the ottoman.

Shaken, she surrendered to her adrenaline rush and sank to the ground to pull herself together.

"Sis, you okay?"

"Uh-huh." She blinked, still somewhat stunned. "I'll be there soon."

She hung up and flung her phone onto the couch. Covering her mouth with both hands, she gazed at a photograph of her son. Their son—hers and Smith's.

Ian came into the room and stopped short upon seeing her on the ground. She must have appeared half-catatonic. He rushed to her and knelt, laying Colt on the carpet. "What happened?"

Gentry clamped down on the silent scream building in her chest. "They found Smith. Hunter wants me to come over."

Ian's face gave nothing away. She supposed he'd seen and handled much worse chaos than the events unfolding in this living room. "Are you okay?"

Why today, of all days? If Ian hadn't already been contemplating his retreat, the specter of Smith would surely push him away.

Defeated, she admitted, "I'm afraid."

He didn't wrap his arms around her or make promises. Instead, he reverted to typical EMT behavior, questioning her like a patient and assessing the damage. "Isn't this what you wanted?"

"Isn't it pretty clear that I never know what I want?" She smirked.

He cleared his throat and looked at his feet before rising.

"I wasn't talking about you." She stood and reached for his hand. "Don't use Smith as a reason to backpedal from what happened today. Finding him has never been for or about *me*."

His eyes strayed to Colt. "You obviously liked him."

"As everyone likes to point out, I barely knew him. *You're* the one who encouraged me to find him." When he sighed, she added, "I know you were right to nudge me, but it doesn't make it easier. I'm not ready. I thought I'd have more time to prepare."

He gently pulled her thumbnail from her mouth and then brushed aside some of her hair. Holding her chin, he looked into her eyes, and she wished the two of them could grab Colt and run away. "Don't panic. Finding Smith might end up being a good thing. Stay positive."

How could she stay positive if Smith's arrival hastened Ian's return to Haiti? She almost shoved at Ian's chest in a pique of misplaced anger. How the hell had he destroyed decades of her keeping her distance in less than three weeks' time?

"I'll stay here with Colt," Ian offered, unaware of his precarious position.

She glanced out the windows. Normally she could walk to Hunter's, but not in this downpour. "I'm still shaky. Can you drive me?"

"Sure."

When she released his hand, he reached for her waist and wrapped her in a reassuring hug. She waited for him to say something wise to make them both feel better, but he held her only for several silent seconds. He finally let go with a quick kiss to the forehead and then bent to lift Colt off the floor. "Let's go."

Within two minutes, they were parked in Hunter's driveway.

"I feel sick." She placed her hands on her stomach and looked over her shoulder at the car seat behind Ian. Her son's life was about to undergo a monumental change. One she couldn't predict or manage. "I've no idea how to tell Smith about Colt."

Ian turned off the engine, staring at Hunter's home. "You've never had trouble being blunt. That should help you now."

His tone stung. "Are you angry?"

"No. Sorry. The timing . . ." He shrugged and glanced at her, then reached across the seat to squeeze her hand. "Actually, maybe it's perfect timing. *Before* things get more blurred . . ."

"Ian." Any hope that Smith wouldn't affect whatever they felt for each other died when she looked at his wan smile.

"This is good for Colt." He released her hand. "He's the priority, as he should be."

She couldn't argue, although she wouldn't roll over and let Ian waltz off without a fight. That fight would have to wait until later, however, because a hundred yards away was a file with Smith's name on it.

Together she and Ian walked through the rain like mourners at a funeral, with her clutching Colt as if monsters might pry him away. They climbed the two porch steps of Hunter and Sara's Craftsman-style home, which hung on the edge of the cliff above the lake. While they waited for someone to answer the door, Ian stroked Colt's head and awkwardly planted a kiss on her cheek. "I hope he's a good guy."

He could never be as good as you. "Me too."

Sara answered the door, wearing her cheerleader smile. Gentry knew her sister-in-law meant well, but just once she'd like to see Sara make a mistake or be in a bad mood. Well, she'd seen that once, but only because she'd caused it by breaking her promise about the adoption. And even then, Sara hadn't lashed out. She'd simply buried her face in Hunter's shoulder and cried until he whisked her away.

Gentry brushed off that bad memory as Sara welcomed Ian. Sara then turned to Gentry. "By the way, thanks for those gorgeous photos of Ty that you took by the lake. You have a true talent."

"Thanks." Of course, that also reminded her of her gaffe with Ty and the Angel House, although thankfully her nephew hadn't had nightmares. Or none she'd been told of, anyway.

Sara then caught her lower lip beneath her front teeth. "Hunter's waiting for you in his office."

"Yippee!" Gentry handed Colt to Ian.

Sara patted Gentry's arm, then turned to Ian, reaching for Colt. "Join me for coffee and a brownie?"

"Sounds good," he said, keeping Colt to himself. Seeing him hold Colt that way made Gentry wish *he* were her son's father. He cast a quick glance at Gentry, but she couldn't read his sober expression.

Along the route to Hunter's office, she passed through a hallway of photographs and memorabilia. A framed finger painting by Ty. Hunter and Sara at their UC Berkeley graduation ceremony. A gorgeous wedding photo from the Sonoma vineyard where they'd been married. Her brother and his wife had a real grown-up life and family, while she straggled behind, trying to catch up after years of misspent youth, an unplanned pregnancy, and little example of how to be a good mom.

She stood in the hall outside Hunter's office, hand on the wall, drawing deep breaths.

"Gentry, is that you?" he called out, having probably heard her footsteps.

"Yep." She found her brother seated behind his massive, neat mahogany desk. A manila envelope lay on its edge, close to the leather chair to which he gestured for her to sit. "Would you like me to stay or go?"

She pressed her body deep into the back of the chair, her hands gripping the arms like she'd done whenever she'd been sent to the headmaster's office. "Just tell me . . . good news or bad?"

He removed his glasses and set them on the desktop and then rubbed his eyes. "I didn't look. This is *your* life, Gentry. You should be the first to read this. You can take it home to review privately, or open it now if you want to lean on me."

Given what had transpired with Ian, it might be more considerate to lean on Hunter.

"Thanks." She set the paper land mine on her lap, breath held and body still as if that would prevent its detonation. Hunter pushed back from his desk and started to rise, but she gestured for him to sit. "Stay, please."

"Of course." His chair creaked as he leaned forward, hands clasped together, a study in discipline. Something she should try to learn before too long.

Gentry swallowed the hard lump in her throat as she slid her finger along the envelope's edge. Inside, she retrieved a one-page, single-spaced fact sheet and two photographs. She squinted at the man in the picture first, noting his glossy black hair and square jaw. A memory of Smith played: him handing her another drink and pushing a room key across the fire pit table. The smell of his cologne—suddenly sharp and vivid—filled her nostrils.

She glanced at the memo, her mouth pasty and sour. Peter Smith.

Peter. A prim name for a man who'd been anything but. And now she could choose to tell him he was a father. She kept her eyes on the photo, partly to avoid her brother's gaze.

Her heart swelled with fear, pushing against her lungs to the point where it almost hurt to catch her breath. She looked up, gaze fixed on nothing in particular, unable to collect the thoughts that were buzzing around like flies at a picnic. Then she noticed the photograph of Hunter and his son, Ty, on his credenza. Father and son.

Her son deserved that, too, didn't he? Wasn't that the whole point of this search?

She forced her eyes back to the memo and tried to concentrate on key bits of information. San Francisco. Master sommelier. Thirty-three. Unmarried. One sister. Two nieces. Widower father. No bankruptcy. No criminal record.

"Gentry?" Hunter's disembodied voice made her look up. "Well?"

"It's definitely him." She studied the photo again. Handsome as she recalled. A Justin Timberlake smile that matched the playful personality she remembered. Smith—Peter—had been like her. Laughed easily. Poked fun. Played. On the surface, she and Smith appeared to be as well matched as Colby and Alec. Then Gentry thought of Ian, and her chest ached.

But Ian was leaving. He'd never pretended, not for one second, that he wouldn't complete his mission in Haiti. Honestly, McJ didn't seem to want the kind of life Gentry hoped to create for herself and her son. Although Ian's influence encouraged Gentry to develop a bigger social conscience, she still wanted to enjoy her lucky accident of birth without constant guilt and disdain.

She pushed the photograph and paper toward her brother. "There aren't any red flags."

Hunter scanned the memo. "He might know Alec!"

"What?"

"They attended the same culinary institute in New York. He's a bit younger, but they might've crossed paths." Hunter's intense gaze switched to the photographs. "God, he looks like Colt, doesn't he?"

Gentry nodded. *That* had not been a surprise.

"Guess we know why he was in Napa." Hunter continued talking, but Gentry wasn't listening.

Peter Smith, the sommelier from San Francisco. Her mind went back to that sultry late-summer evening in Napa. Her friend, Erica, had been struck by a migraine and gone back to their room at the Carneros Resort, but Gentry had wanted to enjoy the night and another Lavender Lemonade cocktail at its FARM restaurant.

She'd taken a seat by the large fire pit in the covered outdoor area when she'd locked eyes with one of the most classically handsome men she'd ever seen. Usually she went for guys with a little more artsy flair. More hair. Tattoos. Rebels with odd taste in clothes. But fresh off a brief relationship with a cynical hipster, something about Smith's tailored clothing and cropped hair had appealed.

"You look like you need some company." He smiled, standing by the empty chair to her left.

"Only if that company is fun." She sipped her second cocktail, noting the vodka buzz starting to hum in her legs. "Are you fun?"

He gestured to the empty seat, a question in his bright blue eyes. When she nodded, he sat beside her. "My friends think so."

"Are they here to vouch for you?"

"Not at the moment, no." He pushed back the cuffs of his sleeves, revealing toned forearms. "Give me a few minutes to prove myself. I can't be worse company than none at all."

"I don't know. I'm usually fine on my own."

"Humor me and play along." He raised his hand to call a waiter. "I'll have a Smoked Cherry Manhattan, and she'll have another . . ."

"Lavender Lemonade," she supplied. The waiter nodded and left them alone.

"You like it sweet." When he stretched his arms along his chair's arms, she noticed his elegant hands. Long fingers. Not hairy. One silver ring on his right pinkie finger. A sign of individuality amid an otherwise strictly Brooks Brothers look.

"I like all kinds of things." A sexual buzz now mingled with the alcohol.

He chuckled. "What's your name, beautiful?"

Beautiful. Good start. "Let's play a game. No real names. Call me Artemis."

"Goddess of the hunt?" He shook her hand, winking. He had really nice hands. "Call me Smith."

"So, Smith, do you like other games?"

"Depends on what kind you have in mind."

Gentry leaned closer, like an old friend sharing a secret. "How about the role-playing kind?"

His brows rose, and he glanced around with a nervous chuckle. He looked at her, eyes narrowed. "Am I about to be the butt of a joke?"

"Nope." She raised her right hand. "I swear."

His gaze roamed her bare legs and low-cut silver shimmer dress. "Who do you want me to be?"

"I'm not sure yet. Any suggestions?"

That night, Gentry had laughed at the absurdity of him picking such a bland nickname, having had no idea it was, in fact, his name—or part of it, anyway.

"Gentry," Hunter said, his tone making clear it was at least the second time he'd tried to get her attention.

"Sorry, I was just remembering." Her cheeks warmed.

"Good memories?" He seemed to be holding his breath, and she suspected he didn't want details.

She couldn't lie. "Yes, actually."

"Well, based on this, I don't see any reason not to contact him." He pushed the papers aside. "When will you call him?"

The reality set in . . .

"I don't know. Maybe I'll e-mail." Bile surged up her throat. "God, he's going to be pretty freaked out. What if he doesn't remember me?"

Hunter grimaced. "I'm sure he will. Wild one-night stands with strangers and fake names aren't exactly the kind of thing guys forget."

"Because you have so much experience," she replied, knowing Hunter had fallen for Sara at twenty and never once strayed.

"I know a lot of guys and hear my fair share of locker-room talk. Trust me, he'll remember you." Censure colored his tone.

She thought about the afternoon and Ian's kiss. She wished this news about Smith had come tomorrow, or next week, or next month.

"What's wrong?" Hunter came around his desk and took the chair beside her, holding her hand. He also had rather elegant hands. Maybe Smith would be reliable and strong, like her brother. "I thought you wanted this for Colt."

"I do." Despite the attraction she and Ian shared, she was the last person who'd convince him that a life here in Oregon could be as rewarding as his plans for Haiti. Hell, she hadn't even convinced him to share her bedroom. Talk about humbling truths. At the end of the day, she had nothing that Ian truly needed to be happy. "This *is* good news for Colt."

"It's still scary, uncharted territory." He released her hands. "How can I help?"

"You can't. It's all on me. I'll figure it out . . . soon."

He rubbed her back. "It'll be okay. You don't need this guy for anything, so that's a plus. If he wants a relationship with his son, you'll be in the driver's seat. He's not on the birth certificate, and he lives hundreds of miles away."

"You know it's not that simple." A moment of panic fired off another round of stomach acid. "What if I have to share custody?"

Hunter's protectiveness surged, lighting his intense hazel eyes. "We can throw this folder in the trash right now, Gentry. I haven't told Dad or anyone, other than Sara."

She had an out. If Hunter promised, she knew he'd take the secret to his grave. But this kind of secret would corrode her relationship with Colt over time, even if he never knew why.

"I can't do that to Colt." She'd spent a lifetime picking on every one of her mother's failings, but even Jenna had never lied to her. "I started this. Now I have to see it through."

"Okay." He scratched his forehead, looking almost sheepish, which was never something she saw before. "You know, I still worry that some distant family member of Ty's will show up on our doorstep. But when you do what's right, you have to trust that love wins the day. Loving Colt—putting his needs over yours—will never steer you wrong."

"Thanks." She stood, taking the papers from his desk. "Guess I'd better get home and draft a message."

"Photos will help." Hunter stood, too. "Smith won't have any doubts when he sees Colt's face."

"Good point." She certainly had hundreds to choose from. Ever since the photography classes she'd taken in college, the camera had been her refuge. A way of seeing people from a different vantage point. Of capturing the scraps of joy and contemplation, of sorrow and even anger, which all looked so similar despite everyone's differences.

Hunter followed her to the family room, where Sara was with the boys: Colt in her arms, Ty on the floor with a wooden toy truck. Through the room's windows, Gentry saw Ian on his phone, one finger in his ear, face pinched with the strain of hearing the caller.

"So?" Sara asked. "Are we happy with what we've learned?"

Hunter put his arm around Gentry's shoulder. "He seems like a decent guy."

"Then why does Gentry look like she's going to be sick?" Sara asked her husband, but kept her eyes locked with Gentry's.

"It's a lot to process." Gentry sneaked another peek at Ian, whose worried frown temporarily distracted her from her own concerns. She sighed, suddenly exhausted from the day's events. All she wanted to do was snuggle with her son. "Why is doing the right thing always so much harder than being selfish?"

Sara and Hunter both laughed, and her brother hugged her harder while saying, "On the upside, you feel good after doing the right thing, even when it's hard."

"We'll see." Gentry grimaced. "My old way of life felt pretty good compared with now."

Sara's tight smile proved she doubted the truth of that statement. In any case, it seemed that she picked up on a need to change the subject. "Colt's colic is still pretty bad. I wonder if he has reflux? Maybe you should ask the doctor."

Gentry didn't have the energy to fend off Sara's advice. Last time, Sara's concerns had been validated, which also made Gentry a little gun-shy about arguing. But surely Dr. Evans would've thought to test for that by now if it were a real possibility. "Maybe."

Sara kissed Colt's head and then handed him to Hunter for a good-bye hug. She turned to Gentry, face glowing. "I let Ty hold him for a minute. Don't worry, though. They were safe on that chair while I knelt in front of them. They're adorable together. Ian snapped a picture with his phone."

Gentry crouched beside Ty to give him a hug, grateful that her son would have this bond throughout his life. Love wouldn't steer her wrong, she told herself again. "You're such a good big cousin."

He squirmed until she released him, which made her smile. He might not be of Hunter's blood, but he was just as stiff. And with all of Sara's rules, his only chance of freedom would be sleepovers at Aunt Gentry's house.

"Pumpkin, go color for a minute." Sara pointed Ty toward a coloring book left open on the coffee table. When he wandered off, she resumed her conversation with Gentry. "Ian was telling me about your day. Sounds helpful and . . . inventive."

Gentry failed to catch Ian's attention. He'd stopped pacing but remained on the phone.

"It was a great day until Hunter called," Gentry admitted.

"Ian said something along those lines, too." Sara bumped shoulders with Gentry. "Maybe my matchmaking wasn't so far off base after all."

Gentry had risked as much vulnerability as she could stomach in one day. She couldn't let anyone think she'd be pining for Ian once he left, either. "He's moving to Haiti soon. Not exactly an ideal boyfriend."

"You never know what might happen in the future. He won't live there forever."

Given how difficult it had been for Ian to share the story of his father's death, Gentry didn't think she should tell Sara about the guilt Ian felt, however absurd. That left her unable to explain why Ian could be there for quite some time. Even if he didn't spend his life in Haiti, there'd always be another crisis somewhere in the world.

"I won't pin my hopes on a maybe. Besides, Smith might come to town, and who knows what that'll mean for all of us." She felt a frown form; then Ian came inside. He nodded at Hunter and stood by the sofa, hands restlessly tapping against its back, gaze darting around as if searching for an answer he couldn't find.

Gentry reached for Colt, who'd been surprisingly calm in her brother's arms. "We'll get out of your hair now."

"Okay." Hunter handed him over like he was made of fine porcelain. He gave her a kiss. "Call me if you need anything."

He then shook Ian's hand, and the two of them exchanged pleasantries for a moment while Sara retrieved Colt's diaper bag.

Outside, Ian helped Gentry reload the car. She waited for him to ask her questions, but he didn't. Whatever his call had been about consumed him. She decided not to push for information, but his lack of interest in Smith simmered. They drove the mile to her condo in silence, and unpacked the car without a word, too.

Inside, she dropped the diaper bag on the floor and laid Colt in his playpen.

"I'll leave you alone for a while," Ian said, starting up the stairs, barely looking at her.

Gentry called out, "Are you mad at me, or is there some other reason for the silent treatment?"

◆ ◆ ◆

He stopped on the third tread and glanced at the photos on the wall. Reminders of the direction Gentry's life was taking, which in no way fit in with his plans. Plans that foundered while he lived here in luxury. The fact he'd so quickly succumbed to comfort clawed at him, especially after speaking with Archer. Looking over his shoulder, he said, "You've got a lot to sort through. I don't want to pry."

"A *lot* has happened today." She nodded to the sofa, where they'd made love not long ago. "I know we both suck at this, but maybe we should talk about how we feel."

Weeks ago the idea of suburban life had seemed ill-suited to him, but his feelings had softened. He might've dragged out his return to Haiti for a few more weeks absent the discovery of Smith or the phone call he'd just received.

Caring for Colt had given him a special purpose and, together with Gentry, lulled him into a sense of belonging. A glimpse at the kind of family life he'd never known.

But this wasn't his family. Another man fathered the beautiful boy staring at Ian from the photo gallery. One who'd be arriving all too soon.

"Gentry . . . ," he sighed. "I'm sorry, but I'm not in the mood right now."

"What was that call you got at my brother's?" Gentry's hands were now on her hips.

"Nothing that involves you."

"Fine." She marched across the entry to the bottom of the stairwell, her cheeks as red as if he'd slapped her. "Don't you want to know *anything* about Smith . . . Peter?"

Peter Smith. Gentry and Peter. Colton Cabot Smith. Each iteration turned his stomach. "Not particularly."

"I thought you cared about Colt and me." Her words came at him like darts.

"I do." Hadn't he made that rather obvious this afternoon? He'd never look at her or the sofa the same way. "That's why I don't want to think about Peter Smith." They stared at each other. "You'll do what's best for Colt. My opinions about his father are irrelevant."

"They're relevant to me. And I could use someone to talk to right now. I've got a lot to process, you know."

He had to put distance between them for both their sakes. "Call a friend."

"I thought you were a friend."

"A *girl*friend." He didn't want to discuss another man she'd slept with. Not here and not now, anyway.

"My girlfriends bailed when I dropped out of the party scene."

"So call your sister."

Her green eyes narrowed to slits. She didn't say a word, although he knew at least three snide remarks had passed through her quick mind. Then she closed her eyes. When she opened them, she sighed, circling her index finger between them. "I know this move, you know. You're pushing me away to protect yourself, but you've met your match, Ian Crawford. I'm not going to take the bait. Make no mistake. We're going to hash this out."

"There's nothing to hash out."

When he didn't elaborate, she asked, "Do you regret today?"

He wished it were that simple. "We were impulsive. In light of all the circumstances, doesn't it seem like a mistake?"

"A mistake?"

"You know what I mean. Being a nanny was supposed to be a temporary job. I never planned to get involved with you and your family. Meanwhile, there are ransom notes and other crises going on while I'm here changing diapers and indulging . . ." He let that thought die. "The best thing I can do for both of us is pack up and move out."

Those final words hung there between them, a challenge and an insult rolled into one. Disgusted with himself, he would've welcomed a kick in the groin. He braced for a rant, but her eyes were now wide with concern.

"Ransom notes?" she asked. "For the little boy whose mother was shot?"

Ian sank onto the step, keeping one hand on the banister. "Yes. A ransom demand came this afternoon."

"What do the cops say?"

Ian scoffed. "It's not like here. Kidnappings are sometimes negotiated by 'lawyers.' So far as I know, the police don't have any leads."

She raked her hands through her hair and tugged it. "Absolutely nuts."

"Archer says Marie's family is trying to come up with money, but they aren't wealthy, and she didn't have life insurance."

Gentry fell silent, her gaze cutting to Colt and then back. "How much?"

"Pardon?"

Her palms flipped upward. "What's the ransom?"

"Fifteen grand."

"Fifteen grand? For a woman's life and a kid's freedom?" Astonished anew, Gentry shook her head. "So much tragedy for a measly fifteen grand."

A *measly* fifteen grand?

"That's a lot of money for most people. Especially people in a country where the average per capita income is probably less than you spend on a pair of shoes."

Her face blanked as if it couldn't compute what he'd said, even as he regretted the nasty barb.

Colt cried out in response to Ian's voice, which had fired off like a machine gun. Gentry turned without a word and mollified her son, then walked to her purse, pulled out her checkbook, and wrote a check. She strode back to Ian, waving the paper. "Here."

He didn't take it, so she let it drop onto his lap.

"I can't take this." He tried to hand it back, but she tucked her hands under her armpits. "You don't even know these people. Don't do this to prove some point."

"Prove a *point*?" Her face puckered. "I don't need to know someone to want to save a terrified little boy who watched his mother die on the street. Take the fucking money, Ian, and send it to whomever so Timmy can come home. I might not have control over most things in my life, but *this* I can fix." Spinning away, she grabbed Colt and marched into her room, slamming her door so hard it rattled the pictures on the wall.

In the stillness of the empty room, he heard his heartbeat throbbing in his ears. Solitude didn't ease the tightness in his shoulders or back, either.

He stared at her loopy signature and all those zeros on the check. She wouldn't even miss that money, yet the poorest people in Haiti ate mud cookies to fill their stomachs. The gap between those who had access to everything and others who struggled to survive burned in his stomach. Irrationally, he considered tearing up the gift.

But anger wasn't fair, especially not when driven by envy of the fact that Gentry had the means to help when he could not.

She had been generous with her money and time since they'd met. Frivolous, perhaps, but she certainly didn't owe him—or Marie—anything. Ian couldn't let his bruised pride cost Timmy Ormont his life.

He stuffed the check in his pocket.

His thoughts turned to his dad and their fight. To his twenty-two-year-old self that had worried the path he'd been on would turn him into someone he might not like. Today proved that prophetic concern true. Ian had become much like his father. Unable to relax, accept joy, or be playful for any length of time. Unable to accept or share intimacy. Spending most of his time surrounded by suffering and loss had taught him to detach so goodbyes wouldn't hurt.

Gentry's bitterness came out through sarcasm. He now realized that *his* appeared as judgment, which he used to convince himself he wasn't missing out on the best parts of life. But he couldn't hide from the feelings Gentry had roused today. He couldn't pretend he wouldn't miss out on her.

Reluctantly, he went to her room and knocked on the door.

"Go away," she snapped.

"Gentry—"

"I'm pissed off, Ian. Trust me, now's not the time to talk."

"Okay." He took his hand off the doorknob. "I'm sorry."

She didn't answer or open the door, so he ordered an Uber and then texted Archer.

Only once seated in the car did Ian admit that he'd been sick with jealousy from the moment Hunter called with news of Smith. Jealousy, an ugly emotion, could fell any man, no matter how righteous.

Self-righteous was more apt, actually, and suddenly he felt very, very small.

Chapter Fourteen

Skydiving

According to *Merriam-Webster*: the sport of jumping from an airplane and typically executing a prolonged free fall before deploying a parachute

According to me: telling Smith he's a father

The distinctive, heavy click of the front door echoed throughout the condo. Sitting on the edge of her mattress, Gentry fell backward and flung her arms across her eyes.

Would Ian accept her help, or would she walk into the living room to find her check turned into confetti? As a mother, the thought of any child's terrified bewilderment provoked an urge to vomit. An unfortunate response when her stomach was already in knots because of Smith.

She propped herself up on her elbows. Wallowing wouldn't do jack shit to help. She forced herself off her bed and checked on her son. Colt's eyelids hovered at half-mast, heavy from exhaustion. He looked peaceful, drifting off to sleep in the bassinet he'd almost outgrown, blissfully unaware of the surrounding chaos.

Kneeling beside the bassinet, she traced his eyebrows with a feather-light touch. "Boo," she whispered. "Stop growing, please. I'm not ready to move you upstairs to the nursery. I need to keep you close."

He yawned before his eyelids closed. Her precious little boy amazed her every day. It was all she could do to keep from picking him up and squeezing him tight.

Whenever she decided to move Colt to his crib, she'd probably sleep in the guest room for a few weeks so she'd be nearby if he needed her. That wouldn't have been a problem before, but now that room would remind her of Ian.

Gentry didn't pretend to be good at personal relationships, but by God, he was worse. If she were wise, she'd walk away and not look back. But no one had ever accused Gentry of being wise. Nor did she ever back down from a fight. She wouldn't give up on Ian. Deep down beneath all their walls, they shared a connection. A horribly inconvenient one that terrified them both.

Colt shifted in his bassinet, drawing her attention. She'd have to wait to deal with Ian because, right now, she needed to contact Smith.

"I love you," she whispered before leaving her room and searching for the dossier on Peter Smith.

Address. Phone number. E-mail. There it was . . . the Gmail account that gave her cold sweats.

After pouring herself a healthy glass of cabernet, she stared at the cursor pulsing on her laptop's screen. How should she address him? Peter? Smith? Should she be businesslike or personal? Funny or serious? None of her choices sounded right.

Ian had suggested her bluntness would be best, and although she had no fondness for him or his opinions at the moment, he probably had a point. Giving herself permission to write whatever popped into her head, she let her fingers type out her stream of consciousness.

When she finished, she reread the note.

> Dear Peter,
>
> Welcome to a blast from your past. We met one evening last August in Napa. You knew me as Artemis, but my real name is Gentry Cabot.
>
> There is no easy way to say why I've tracked you down, so I'll just lay it out (you might want to sit down).
>
> You have a son (I've attached his picture, and you can see many more on this link: www.apronstringsandmommythings.com). His name is Colton Cabot, and he's got great lungs despite being born a few weeks prematurely, on April 15th.
>
> As you can see, he looks like your mini-me. If you want more proof, I'll provide whatever DNA sample you need.

She paused for a moment, wondering if she'd been too cutesy about Colt's colic. Deleting that line, she revised it to read that he was healthy despite his premature birth. Satisfied with that correction, she continued reading.

> To be clear, I'm not looking for financial support. In fact, I have no expectations or demands. I only sought you out because I realized that Colt would eventually have questions about his father. I wanted those answers for him, so I hired an investigator.

I'm sorry for the shock, which I remember reeling from when I discovered I was pregnant. For a brief time, I'd considered giving Colt up for adoption, but, ultimately, I couldn't do it.

While his conception was far from ideal, I'm a proud and happy single mom of the planet's most beautiful baby boy. I am also aware that, by not finding you sooner, you've missed precious months of his life.

I'm sorry for that and invite you to meet your son, if you wish. We live outside of Portland, Oregon, in Lake Sandy.

Please write back to me if you are interested in any further involvement. If I don't hear from you, I will not contact you again. When Colt asks about you, however, I will tell him what I know. I've made a vow to never lie to him, which I hope you understand.

Sincerely,
Gentry Cabot

How perfectly ridiculous that sweat trickled down her back and between her breasts despite the air conditioning being set at a brisk sixty-eight degrees. She chugged the rest of her wine and hit "Send," then snapped the laptop closed.

Oh shit. Shit, shit, shit.

She rocked herself, arms crossed over her stomach, bile fighting its way up her throat.

It was done. She rocked faster, tears pooling, frantic. She closed her eyes and conjured up Hunter, the ultimate control freak. If he'd read anything troubling, he would've told her not to contact Smith, right? Then she remembered the connection Smith might have to Alec.

She grabbed for her phone and dialed her sister. While the phone rang, she curled her body into a ball, hugging her knees to her chest beneath a hand-knit throw. When her sister answered, Gentry barked, "Colby, I need to talk to Alec."

"What's wrong? You sound panicked."

"I am! I need to know if he ever met a Peter Smith at the culinary school in New York." She grabbed a nearby throw pillow and tucked it between her thighs and her chest.

"What?"

"Peter Smith." Gentry then remembered that Hunter hadn't shared the fact that they'd found Peter with the family. "Smith, Colby. Colt's father is Peter Smith. He's a Master Sommelier in San Francisco. He's only thirty-two, but Hunter says he went to the same school as Alec."

"Holy Moses, that's a coincidence. Hang on!" Her sister must've dropped the phone, because Gentry couldn't hear her talking.

A minute later, Alec's voice came through the line. "Gentry?"

"Alec, please tell me you have good news."

"Would you settle for the fact that I've got nothing bad to share?"

Since when did Alec speak in riddles? "What's that mean?"

"I don't remember him well. You know I've never been extroverted." There was a brief pause, as if Alec was trying to remember something to ease her mind. "He seemed like a decent guy, but I can't recall more than that cursory impression. He had friends. I never heard anything negative about him."

Basically, nothing that the PI report hadn't essentially revealed. "I suppose that's good news, then."

"Small world, right?"

"Very." Suddenly she sat upright, letting the pillow and blanket fall away. Could Smith be googling her this very minute? Scouring his own contacts and, in this "small world," finding someone who knew her—or worse, knew of her?

Given her antics and indiscriminate past, he might get the impression that his son deserved a better woman as a mother. Maybe Smith had a perfect girlfriend or wife . . . a Lilly Pulitzer to his Brooks Brothers.

Someone like Sara.

Another cramp gripped her midsection.

"Gentry?" Alec asked.

"I'm here." She held her forehead with her palm. "Thanks for sharing what you could remember."

"Sorry I can't be more helpful. Here, your sister's grabbing for the phone."

Gentry heard the sound of a kiss before Colby got back on the line. "I can't believe you found Smith."

"Peter. Maybe I should call him Peter." She slunk back into the sofa cushions, weary. "Or Pete. Petey?"

"I doubt that one." Colby hesitated. "Did you call him?"

"No. I chickened out and wrote him an e-mail instead. Sent a photo of Colt."

"Has he responded?"

Gentry stared at the computer, which now resembled a weapon of mass destruction. "I don't know. I shut my laptop as soon as I sent it and then called you. I'm afraid to look."

"Do you want me to come over and wait with you? I can. The restaurant's closed on Sunday nights."

Gentry smiled at the offer. It was nice to hear the support and was surely more than she'd get from her mother. "No. I've got my big-girl pants handy."

"And you've got Ian."

Gentry glanced at the door that Ian had yet to come back through. "Yeah. He's . . . helpful."

"Take a deep breath. It's going to be okay. You're doing the brave thing for your son, Gentry. Be proud."

"Proud? Nope. Can't say that's how I feel. Sick. Doubtful. Frantic. But not proud."

"You should feel proud. These are tough decisions. You've got a lot on your plate, and you're managing it all."

Was she? The ChariTea work she'd planned on doing this evening would clearly not get done tonight. Her son might or might not have reflux, not that she'd even come up with that theory. She'd slept with a man who consistently promised to leave town. All she seemed to be managing well was digging her own grave.

"If you call alienating coworkers, fighting with my mom, and letting a stranger into my son's life 'managing well' . . . who am I to argue?" She laughed, and it felt good. Loosened the tightness in her chest so she could draw some oxygen.

"Are you sure you don't want me to come sit with you?"

"No. I think I'll do some googling of my own now and see what else I can learn." Of course, she should be working on those memes and media games for ChariTea, not surfing the web.

"Okay. Call me if you change your mind."

"I will." Gentry hit "Off," feeling energized by her new mission. A one-day delay on social media wouldn't make or break the campaign. She needed to prepare for meeting Smith. Needed to gain insight to handle the man who had the power to change her whole world.

She opened up her laptop and, without checking e-mail, googled "Peter Smith Master Sommelier San Francisco." That search returned dozens of mentions and a few blog posts written by Peter. Apparently, being a Master Sommelier was a BFD. Only 229 of them in the whole world? This was good. This meant he had discipline and ambition and passion. Three excellent traits that he might've passed on to Colt.

And . . . wine! Who didn't love wine?

With that reminder, she refilled her glass to prep for a long night of reading. An hour later, she'd scoured interviews, blog posts, and social media pages. He never referred to a wife, although she did see photos of him with a woman and a child. Could that be his sister and niece? Or did he have a family of his own already?

A family of his own would keep him occupied and less apt to glom on to her and Colt. Then again, that situation would make Colt be like her, having half siblings and a part-time family, which wasn't ideal, either.

She supposed she should take heart in the fact that everything she'd read reassured her that Smith could be a good role model. A modern man with a normal life, unlike Ian Crawford.

She stared at the Google search bar. With one finger, she tapped out "Ian Crawford Portland Oregon" and hit return.

Surprisingly, there were several Ian Crawfords in the area. Her Ian, however, left a nearly invisible digital footprint. A single years-old mention in a local paper for something connected to a prior EMT job. No active social media account that she could find. His father's obituary.

That got her attention.

She pulled up the post, which featured a prominent photograph of Brian Crawford.

As she'd suspected, Ian physically resembled his father, although more handsome. She read the obituary, noting phrases like "restoring community one person at a time" and "endless energy" and "service on community boards" and on and on. She suspected the funeral service must've filled an entire chapel.

Having grown up in the shadow of highly successful parents, she could imagine how Ian struggled to live up to his father's example. From the sound of things, his mother hadn't exactly overcompensated for his father's absence, either.

Gentry pictured Ian, young and wide-eyed, working his butt off to be like his parents instead of bucking them at every turn, as she'd done. They'd handled life differently, but she had no doubt that both she and Ian had never felt unconditional love. He could deny it all he wanted; she knew better. He needed love. And he needed it from someone like her, who understood why he pushed it all away.

The front door opened, rousing her from her thoughts. Ian stepped inside and closed the door. He stared at her, sighed, and shrugged. "I'm sorry I was such an ass."

◆ ◆ ◆

Gentry set down her glass and strode toward him, arms open wide, and embraced him without a word, once again defying his expectations.

He wrapped his arms around her and rested his cheek on the top of her head. "I didn't expect forgiveness."

"Someday you'll stop trying to predict my next move," she mumbled against his chest before easing far enough away to look up at him. "Oddly, the fact that you suck at intimacy makes me feel better . . . less alone in my fuckedupness."

If only that solved anything. "Glad to be of service."

"A role I know you enjoy," she quipped. "Please tell me you deposited my check."

"I didn't." He removed it from his pocket.

She scowled, stepping back. "Okay, now I'm getting mad again."

"Hold up." He stuffed the check in her pocket. "Archer said to wait. The family is making a counteroffer while the police are working with an informant who might lead them to the boy."

"You said the cops don't usually get involved. Are you lying to me now because you don't want to take my money?"

"Seems things have gotten a little better recently since some New York cop came and instituted some training to turn the system around." And if that cop could work miracles, maybe Ian could, too. Training locals. Empowering them, and making a difference that strengthened an entire nation. He had to believe the sacrifices he'd make would be worthwhile.

"I wonder how long that'll last?" Her cynical sigh followed.

"It'll last. Most people there want a better life. The Haitians are, by and large, determined, resilient people, and surprisingly hopeful despite the constant setbacks."

Gentry clasped his hand and led him to the sofa, then sat beside him, cross-legged. "I don't want to talk about Haiti. Let's talk about today."

"About Smith?" He'd been heartless to walk out on her after she'd been handed life-changing information.

"About everything. We can't pretend like nothing has changed. I know you have your mission, but isn't there any way this might work?"

"I think my failed engagement proves it can't." Ian quirked a brow. "And in case you missed the clues today, I'm not exactly good at relationships."

"Neither am I. I can't tell you how many guys I've cycled through."

"I'd rather you didn't, actually."

She poked him, smiling. "Look at you, McJ, making jokes."

Had he been joking? He wasn't sure.

She leaned against him like a puppy, tucking her head against his shoulder. "I'm good for you. Stick with me and you'll laugh more before you die."

"That's some sales pitch." He allowed himself a minute to enjoy the weight of her body resting against his.

He sensed danger when she fell silent, because no one could predict the direction of Gentry's thoughts, least of all him. She kept her head on his shoulder, avoiding eye contact. "Neither of us got much attention from our parents. Neither of us has had a healthy love life. Neither of us likes being vulnerable."

"None of those similarities are arguments in favor of this working, you know."

He felt her shrug. "I've got a thing for underdogs."

"Not a surprise." He held himself still, unable to give over to her will and throw caution to the wind. "But you're forgetting something important. Smith."

"Peter," she corrected.

"Peter shares a child with you."

"We accidentally made a baby. That's it."

"It's a big thing, Gentry." He set his index finger against her lips to force her to think before she spoke. After a second or two, he removed his hand.

"Maybe not," she said. "Maybe he'll want nothing to do with us."

"That's not what you want for Colt."

"No," she admitted quietly. "But coparenting isn't dating."

True enough. People coparented all the time without dating. Divorced parents managed it, too. Biology alone wasn't a good enough reason for Ian to run away from his feelings. "Did you contact him?"

She nodded.

"What did he say?" Ian simultaneously hoped Peter Smith had been eloquent and idiotic, because the best and worst thing that could happen would be for Gentry to actually like Smith.

"I don't know. I sent an e-mail a while ago and am too afraid to look for his reply." She grimaced.

Reluctantly, Ian asked for a summary of Peter Smith from San Francisco. After she finished reciting the mostly impersonal data, he said, "He sounds like a pretty good fit for your life."

She slapped his thigh. "More snap judgments."

"He's affluent. Likes to travel. Enjoys wine." Ian nodded toward her empty wineglass. "And you did find him attractive."

"You just described a helluva lot of men I've known, Ian. None of them fit so far." She pulled away and twisted to face him. "You know, I thought you were cute when I went into labor, but the timing wasn't right. Then you showed up here, all patient and kind, without expecting anything in return. You've helped me with Colt, Ty, work . . . even with my own doubts about whether or not I can do this whole motherhood thing. I've never had someone believe in me like that. Everything feels different, and now I don't know what to do with all of this." She motioned with her hands like she was trying to grab on to clouds. "Honestly, life was easier when I cared less."

He couldn't help but smile, because she'd been right about one thing. They were the same when it came to incompetence in the tricky world of romance. He cupped her face and kissed her. "I get it, but there's a lot at stake, mostly for you and Colt. You should see what Smith has to say before we consider possibilities."

She wrinkled her nose and stared at her laptop. Her in-box was like the wardrobe in that Narnia book. Once she'd opened it, life as she knew it could change forever.

Gentry shot him a "Here goes nothing" look and opened her e-mail account. Biting her thumbnail, she stared at the screen. Ian's heart thumped when he saw Peter's reply in the in-box. "I'll let you read it in private."

When he moved to leave, her hand landed on his thigh. "Please stay."

It seemed wrong to read a private note from a man who'd just learned, out of the blue, about his son. But Ian couldn't turn down Gentry's pleading gaze. "Okay."

"Thanks." After a deep inhalation, she muttered, "Okay, Smith, what have you got to say?"

Gentry,

Of course I remember you, Artemis . . . rather fondly. However, I didn't expect your email and am now sitting here in a state of shock.

Please don't take this the wrong way but, although Colt resembles my baby photos, I'd be foolish not to confirm his paternity. My quick research says we can get DNA results in 1–2 days.

That's not to say that I think you're lying. I don't . . . at least, I believe you believe he is mine.

The possibility that I'm a new father is equally terrifying and exciting. I adore my two nieces and have envied my sister for a few years. Unlike her family, though, our situation is not ideal. And while you've had time to get to adjust and adapt, I've got lots of catching up to do. Frankly, it may take a few days to catch my breath.

I won't share this news with my family until I confirm Colt's paternity and we have a chance to talk. However, I have a feeling my father will be thrilled to finally have a grandson despite the unusual circumstances.

Let's coordinate the test and, once we have the results, I will arrange to visit. I think the sooner, the better.

Smith

Ian didn't ask about the Artemis reference. He didn't ask if Gentry was insulted by the DNA-test request. He didn't even ask her to wait until he left to invite Smith to visit, although the selfish part of him wished she would. "Are you okay?"

She nodded, her eyes glued to the screen, apparently rereading the short note several times. "He seems rational, right? I mean, this is a pretty open, calm response. Almost friendly, even."

"Yes." In contrast, Ian was finding it difficult to remain rational and open to discussing this, which suggested that Smith must be a damn confident man.

"He's not angry or jerky, like he could've been." Her eyes were wide and still focused on the screen, teeth feverishly chewing her thumbnail.

Ian scratched the back of his neck, but it did little to help the itchiness taking over his body. "Nope. Not angry."

"This part about his sister and dad means he must be close to his family. That's a good sign, right?" She'd begun rocking herself, although he doubted she noticed. "If I have to share Colt, I want it to be with someone who loves his family."

Those last words came out with a choked sob, and then Gentry hunched forward in a mess of tears right there in front of him.

He threw his arm around her shoulders and pulled her close. "Sh, sh. It's okay. It'll be okay."

She sniffled and wiped her face with her hands, body trembling from the ebb and flow of adrenaline this e-mail exchange had wrought.

When she looked up, her brows were furrowed in a tight knot, worry lines fanning out from the corners of her eyes. "I don't want to share my son. I mean, I want Colt to have a father and more people who love him, but I don't want to send him away for long visits. I can't stand the idea of being away from him. I can't." Hysteria tinged those last words.

Ian wiped new tears away and gripped her shoulders, forcing her to hold his gaze. "Don't jump ahead. Take things one step at a time. First, meet Peter. Then, if he wants to take Colt to meet his family, you go with them. You don't have to hand Colt over until you're comfortable, okay? This guy doesn't sound like the type who plans to bully you or take you to court. Remind him that you two need to put Colt's interests first, and it will all be okay."

She wiped her nose with her shirt while mumbling, "This is the right thing to do. I'm doing the right thing."

He nodded, praying he hadn't inadvertently pushed her into a choice that might hurt her.

Chapter Fifteen

Catch-22

According to *Merriam-Webster*: a problematic situation for which the only solution is denied by a circumstance inherent in the problem or by a rule

According to me: building family ties for my son

Gentry wove through CTC's hallways in a daze, thanks to a whopping two hours' sleep last night. If the time she'd spent awake in bed had been with Ian, she'd be skipping through the office. To her chagrin, once he'd held her long enough to calm her down, he'd sent her to bed alone. Smith's reply had given Ian pause, and he insisted they take time to think. So she'd alternated between staring at the ceiling and then gazing at her son, praying for the strength to be stronger than her mom had been when it came to blending families.

"Gentry, where are the latest updates to the social media strategy and new graphics?" Her mom stood in her office doorway, having clearly been on the lookout for her arrival.

Gentry stopped, too tired to think of a snappy comeback. "I'll copy you when I send them."

Her mother shook her head. "They're not completed?"

"I got a little sidetracked this weekend." Gentry eyed her distant workstation-turned-prison, wishing she'd made it there before getting stopped by her mother.

"Sidetracked? The launch is less than two months away. Now isn't the time to get distracted by some new hobby, or the nanny."

"Mom, stop. I'd planned to finish it last night, but—" She glanced over her shoulder before muttering, "We found Smith."

Gentry watched the ice queen lean against the doorjamb, speechless. They stared at each other, neither moving. A silly fantasy, one involving her mom's open arms and supportive hug, drifted through Gentry's sleep-deprived brain. It died when her mom said, "Come into my office and close the door."

Becky passed by in time to catch that ominous command, so now everyone would know Gentry had messed up again. This time they weren't entirely wrong, though. She should've been working on Sunday instead of running around Portland with Ian.

Then again, she didn't regret that afternoon. Not even a little.

Ian, flawed man that he was, made her think. He made her want to be a better person. And he might not see it yet, but he needed her, because she had a lot to teach him about joy. Until last night, she'd never considered that she might've inherited a little of Grandpa John's gambler gene. But at three a.m., when she'd considered racing upstairs and going all in on a long-shot gamble with Ian, she understood more about the pull of addiction. Wisely, she'd folded and stayed in her room.

"Sit." Her mom pointed to the empty chair before taking her seat behind her beloved desk. The one Gentry had never been allowed to use for coloring or eating lunch or anything else that other kids got to do at their parents' offices. "Why didn't you call your father and me yesterday?"

"I didn't want everyone's opinions. Ultimately, this is about my son and, to a lesser extent, me. I e-mailed Peter—that's his real name—and he replied late last night."

"So it's done. You've opened your son's life up to a stranger." Her mother tapped her hands on her desktop. "What if he's a terrible influence? What if he wants joint custody?"

"And you wonder why I didn't turn to you for support." Gentry let her head fall back. Eyes closed, she prayed for patience . . . although she could've easily fallen asleep, too.

"I am supportive. I've picked you up after every mistake, Gentry. Don't pretend there haven't been many along the way."

Gentry counted to five in her head. Yes, she'd made mistakes. Maybe even some big ones, but nothing that'd ever ruined her life, or anyone else's.

"Do me the courtesy of looking at me," came her mother's exasperated voice.

Gentry complied. "Are you finished, or are there other criticisms you'd like to pile on before you ask me to go be creative?"

"As if you don't criticize *me* at every turn." Her mom rubbed her temples. "Despite your perspective, I've killed myself to give you every advantage and opportunity, including giving you a good man as a father. And when it comes time to battle with 'Peter' over Colt, who will be fighting for you each step of the way? Me, that's who."

"Please stop acting like you worked so hard to give *me* things. This fiefdom is about your ego, your needs. You never once asked what I wanted. But let me tell you, all I *ever* wanted was to matter to someone. How many Sundays did I wish Colby and Hunter would take me to Leslie's so I could be part of a real family . . ."

"What a rotten, ungrateful thing to say." Her mother's eyes glistened. "I gave you the kind of life I only dreamed of as a child."

Gentry hadn't seen her mom teary very often, so it threw her. She shifted in her chair, softening her tone. "Your dreams, Mom. Not mine. Now I'm asking you to back off a little. I'm sure I'll make mistakes with my son, but I don't need *your* parenting advice. Whatever resentments Colt might have one day, they won't be because I kept him from his father and a family that might love him. No matter how tough it is on *me*, Colt deserves to know his father."

Her mother flattened her palms on her desk. "And who, exactly, is Peter? Am I allowed to know that much?"

Gentry's head pounded. She craved sleep. Barring that, an escape from her mother's office would be nice, too. Robotically, she recited Peter's résumé and summarized their e-mails.

"When's he coming?"

"On Friday."

Her mother tapped her fingernails on her desk. "Will your father and I get to meet him?"

"I'd like to spend the first day alone with him and Colt. On Saturday, you and Dad can come over for dinner." Her home. Her rules. "Maybe Hunter and Sara can join us, too. Colby and Alec will have to work, I guess."

"Will Peter be staying with you?"

"No."

"So you're not interested in a romantic relationship?" The wheels of Jenna Cabot's mind had started to turn, judging by the twitching of her eyes.

"No."

"Why not? Obviously, you found him attractive. If he's a decent man and there's chemistry, why not get together so you don't have to worry about sharing custody? If creating a family for Colt is your goal, then dating Peter should be no-brainer. A priority, actually."

Gentry couldn't argue with the main thrust of that logic. It, however, didn't consider two important variables. First, Peter Smith's feelings and personal life might preclude romantic entanglements. Second, and more important, her feelings for Ian.

Gentry had never believed she'd fall in love—much less instalove. But something about Ian had her by the throat, even if she didn't tell him so. He was the first man she'd ever been open with. Surely that meant something. Maybe Ian would come to that conclusion, too. Maybe, like her, he'd believe he'd come into her life for a reason.

"How about we get to know Peter before you marry me off?"

"If you'd taken the time to know him *before* you got pregnant, you wouldn't be a single mother juggling work and childcare." Her mother sighed, while Gentry imagined a cartoon version of her mom's head exploding. "What's your plan for Colt after Ian leaves?"

"Day care." With Colt's infection cured, he could attend Miss Linda's once Ian left town.

"I thought you liked having help around the house. And what of the late nights we can expect to log here, with the launch?"

Gentry shook her head, wondering if she'd ever cross the line that would win her mother's approval. "I'll figure the rest out. Day care will give Colt other kids to play with instead of a nanny who's distracted by her phone."

"Is Ian always on his phone?"

"Ian's not really a nanny."

"No, he's not. He's a bit of a lost soul, I think."

Gentry's entire body tipped forward in shock. *"What?"*

"He doesn't know what he wants. The savior complex lets him avoid commitments. His fiancée must've called things off once she realized he had no plan for their life together."

"He's got a plan. She just didn't like it." In truth, Gentry liked it less and less the more she learned about the dangers involved. "Ian's goals have life-and-death stakes, but of course, peddling tea is a far more worthy pursuit."

Her mom touched her forehead to her desk. "Why can't we have a single conversation that isn't laced with sarcasm?"

"Habit?" Gentry shifted in the hot seat, eager to leave.

"That's not funny." The increasingly prominent lines in her mother's face deepened. "Even Hunter and I have less hostile conversations than you and me."

"Probably because you don't disapprove of everything he does and says."

Her mom raised a skeptical eyebrow.

Gentry conceded, "Okay, so you two rarely agree, but he's not bothered by it, because he doesn't care about your opinion."

If Gentry's brain hadn't been half-asleep, those words would *not* have slipped out. It'd be too much to hope that her mom missed the revelation that her opinions *did* matter to Gentry despite Gentry's lifelong insistence that they didn't. That truth filled her with self-loathing.

Rather than seize on a moment of triumph, her mom folded her hands on her desk. "Don't take this the wrong way, but I'm concerned that you've got too much going on now to adequately focus on your job. We should push some of your responsibilities to others until this Smith situation is resolved."

Resolved. Like a single answer or act would make everything clear. There'd be no such resolution. Smith would be a permanent fixture of sorts, requiring her to compromise for the rest of her life.

Her stomach turned over again, but she hadn't worked the past ten months at this job to fail now. Quitting would hand her family more proof that she didn't have the mettle to stick with anything. That she wasn't committed or ambitious or in any way like the rest of them.

"No." For better or worse, CTC was the tie that bound the Cabot family, and dammit, she was a Cabot. She needed to belong to her tribe, *especially* with Smith moving into the picture. "I'll get it done. I know I dropped the ball this weekend, but I can finish today if you let me get to work. Don't humiliate me in front of everyone."

"This can't become a habit."

"I get that." Gentry knew she shouldn't bug her eyes, but a lecture from her mother delivered the same full-body jolt as a fork in the toaster.

"I'll tell your father about Peter Smith." She inhaled through her nose, then blew a sigh. "I still can't believe you gave up control of your son's future."

Control. Gentry had thought about that all night to the point of making herself sick. Her conclusion? Relationships based on control never worked. Her mom should know this by now, because she'd never been able to control Gentry's behavior.

Ian had been right when he implied that doing the right thing was the only thing in anyone's control.

"Maybe, if *you'd* given up 'control' years ago and tried to blend our family with Colby and Hunter, my life would've been happier. My relationships with them stronger."

"I never prevented those kids from coming over."

"You barely welcomed them. You never reached out." When her mother opened her mouth, Gentry held up her hand. "We don't have to agree on that, or on Smith. All I'm saying is that my priority is to fill Colt's life with people who love him. I won't keep my son from Smith and his family because I'm afraid of sharing him."

"I hope you're not sorry."

Gentry bowed her head and left the room, wishing she could leave the building entirely. But there were memes and tags to create, and data to gather. At least none of her coworkers peeked their heads above the cubicle walls as she made her way to her workstation.

She fired up her computer to check on the stats and analytics from the latest rounds of Facebook ads they'd tested. Data analysis for her blog excited her more, but this had to be done.

Gentry made notes on another round of postcards from the art team while trying to quell her mother's warnings and her opinion that maybe Gentry was an ungrateful screwup who had no business being anybody's mother.

When her desk phone rang, Hunter's name appeared on its screen. Her stomach clenched because she hadn't finished her analysis. He'd be even more pissed about the delay than her mom. "Hello."

"Hey, can you swing by my office?" To the point and efficient, like always.

"Now?"

"Yes." His flat tone gave no hint of his mood.

"Sure." She glanced at the clock as she hung up. Earlier she'd sat down to work, blinked, and now it was twelve thirty. She pressed her fingers to her temples. If she didn't complete this soon, she'd cause delays for other people waiting on her.

She pushed back from her desk and walked the green mile to her brother's office. His assistant, Haru, barely looked up from her screen as she gestured for Gentry to enter his office.

Hunter sat at the round conference table, where he normally huddled over spreadsheets with Bethany, the comptroller. In other words, that table was a circle of hell.

At the moment, the takeout from Gab-n-Eat—his and Colby's favorite dive—caught her attention. With a slight smile, Hunter pushed a greasy burger and milkshake toward an empty chair and gestured for her to take that spot.

She stood still, dumbfounded, the scent of fried onions and bacon filling the air. Granted, many people might consider Gab-n-Eat's food a serious punishment, but Hunter considered it a reward. "What's this?"

"Lunch." He blinked, his literal interpretation of her question totally missing her point.

"I mean, why? Are you cushioning the blow before you fire me or something?"

He frowned, setting his burger down. "Why would you think that?"

"In all the months I've worked here, we've never had lunch." She'd never seen him eat lunch, actually. He worked tirelessly, the way a shark never stops swimming.

She'd bet he didn't realize he'd never shared Gab-n-Eat with her. Not ever. Not even as a kid. He and Colby always went without her.

"Sorry about that." Hunter pointed to the empty chair again. While she took a seat and unwrapped the food he'd chosen for her, he said, "I usually eat at my desk while I work. After yesterday's big reveal, I wanted to check in with you. I got you a burger."

The food coma from all this fat and carbs wouldn't help her work better, but she couldn't say no. His sharing lunch meant working here *was* bringing them closer. She'd suffer Bethany, deadlines, these damn boring work clothes, and more for that.

Cheeseburger grease coated the wrapper and her fingers, but she'd never complain. "I'm okay. Tired, mostly."

"You've looked better." He said this matter-of-factly, like he did everything else. That trait always intimidated and fascinated her and everyone else.

"Such a charmer. No wonder Sara loves you."

"At least you know you can trust me to be honest." His tongue retrieved a stray bit of onion from his lip. "I hate having to read between the lines. Say what you mean . . . it's always the best policy."

"Okay, then." She held her hands up, sending her bangles jangling down her arm. "But here's a suggestion. Try gilding brutal honesty with a little tact."

"Point taken." He grinned. The juxtaposition of his penetrating gaze and unexpected smile could be quite breathtaking.

She forced another bite of the sloppy sandwich. "The Smith stuff is scary, but after today, it won't interfere with my work. I've almost finished updating the teasers and am crafting a 'behind the scenes' campaign for the next phase of our social media strategy."

He slurped at his milkshake. "You're late with that."

"I know."

"You know what's riding on this launch." For weeks he'd been driving everyone hard, poring over stacks of memos and financial papers, meeting with partners, distributors, and designers. He shouldered the weight of the company's success like Atlas, and she hadn't done as much as she could've to lighten that burden.

"I'm sorry."

She braced for a scolding, but he nodded and changed the subject. "Sara swung by your house this morning to drop off some of Ty's hand-me-downs. Ian let it slip that you heard from Smith. He assumed you'd updated us."

"Well, now you know." She sipped her milkshake to avoid a bunch of questions for which she didn't have good answers.

"Sara's got it in her head that there's something between you and Ian." He studied her now as if she were one of his spreadsheets.

Gentry stuffed a fry in her face, unprepared to discuss her sex life with her brother. Maybe he'd drop it if she let the comment pass.

He sighed. "Uh-oh."

She looked up. "Why 'uh-oh'?"

"He's leaving, isn't he?"

"He says he is." She stabbed another few fries into a dollop of ketchup. Hunter was wise. Maybe he could help her plot. "I still have a little time."

"Time for what?"

"To convince him he could help as many people here as he can in Haiti."

Hunter shook his head. "Don't do that."

"Why not?" Whether due to childhood idolization or the simple fact that Hunter's decision-making skills exceeded hers by miles, she cared about his opinion.

He wiped his chin with a napkin. "Because he's obviously driven to honor his dad's legacy."

"Is that worth risking his life? Or throwing away a chance at happiness?"

"Maybe his happiness depends on seeing it through. I get that. For some of us, leaving a legacy is in the blood."

She sighed, remembering how close Hunter had come to losing Sara over the very same thing. If Ian's commitment to his project was even half as serious as her brother's was to CTC, she didn't stand a chance. "Well, I'd better tell Colby about Smith before she thinks I'm holding out."

"Dad will be in soon, too."

Gentry rolled her eyes. "My mom has probably already fed him her version."

"Her version?" He tore open another packet of ketchup and squeezed it on his fries. He ate as if someone might come steal his lunch any second.

"Can't you guess?"

Hunter loaded his mouth with a wad of fries while waiting for details, so Gentry mimicked her mother by folding her hands on her lap and speaking with condescension. "It's going to be a disaster that you'll regret forever. You're an impulsive idiot for giving up 'control.'" Gentry resumed her slouched posture and normal voice, shrugging. "You know, the basic pep talk."

Hunter wiped his hands with another napkin and then reached across the table to take her hand. They hadn't shared a lot of one-on-one time, so the intimacy froze her in place. "There's not much love lost between your mom and me, but I think, in this case, her fear is sincere and overwhelming her. You and I finally have a clue about how a parent's hopes and dreams and fears get tied up with their kids. Truth is, none of us has the best advice for your situation, and we're all a little anxious." He released her hand and sat back in his chair. "Do what you think is best for your son. I'll stand with you every step of the way."

"Thanks." Of everyone in her family, Hunter exuded the most power. If he said he'd be there to fix things, she believed it would be okay. She waved her hands in front of her eyes to stave off the tears, hoping he'd buy her lame excuse. "God, this burger has so much onion."

"They're good, aren't they?" He smiled, finishing his off in two bites. "I could eat these every day."

Gentry nodded, gulping the rest of her milkshake to cut the salt and grease, and fibbed, "Me too."

◆ ◆ ◆

Ian's mother sat on the edge of Gentry's fancy sofa as if she feared she'd stain it or, possibly, that it would swallow her whole. "Why don't you look happier?"

Timmy had been recovered, and the police had two suspects in custody. Ian should have been ecstatic at the prospect of justice for Marie's death. "Guess I'm exhausted."

"Infants will do that to you." The smile she offered Colt had nostalgia written all over it, too. "Can I hold him? I love babies."

Ian placed Colt in his mother's arms. He felt like a father; she looked like a grandmother. Her glittery eyes suggested she'd shared that thought.

"He's darling. Such striking blue eyes." She glanced at Ian. "When you have a child, I hope he or she has your green eyes."

Or Gentry's. That thought struck faster than lightning and twice as hard. "Don't get your hopes up."

He needed to heed his own advice. Each day he spent here with Gentry and Colt peppered his soul with laughter, fire, and an alarming yearning to be still. But his dad's dream remained unfulfilled, and he wouldn't be much of a man—or a son—if he let it die with his father.

"You never know." She tickled Colt's chin.

"A traditional family life doesn't fit with my plans, Mom." Not even if he wanted it with someone as untraditional as Gentry.

"You know what they say about God and plans. Trust me, dear, he's up there laughing right now." She spared him a wry glance before returning her attention to the baby.

"Gee, thanks."

"I'm teasing. But you're young. Plenty of time to settle down once you've finished what you've started. Somewhere out there is a woman who'll knock your socks off. Maybe that woman is in Haiti."

Ian stared at a photograph of Gentry and Colt, thinking that woman was closer than his mom realized. The picture had probably been shot with a self-timer, like the ones she'd taken of him yesterday, on the sofa where his mom now sat.

He leaned forward and rubbed his eyes. His head hurt from an all-night tug-of-war between what he wanted and what was best for everyone. If he thought Gentry could be happy despite his odd schedule . . . "Mom, did you ever resent Dad for leaving you so often?"

She let Colt clutch her forefinger while she made silly faces, encouraging some smiles. "Why would I resent someone who sacrificed so much to help others?"

"You never got lonely?"

"I had you, dear. My little man of the house." Her distant gaze told him she was replaying the past. "You were a good boy. Too good to be true, some might've said."

"Was I?" He searched his mind for evidence of a little misspent youth. A trip to the principal's office, shoplifting a pack of gum, swearing—anything to suggest that he'd been a normal kid with a carefree childhood.

Gentry's opinions about him and his family had been gnawing at him. Had he made the choices he'd made of free will? Or had his deep-seated recognition that the Crawford way would be the only way to be close to his father driven most of his decisions?

"Dad, can we hit the batting cages today?"

"Not today, Ian. There's been an earthquake in Cariaco, Venezuela, and I'm leaving to help deliver medical supplies."

Cariaco, Venezuela, sounded way more exciting than Portland. "Can I come?"

His father smiled. "You're only nine, son. You help your mom with the church fair this week. When you're older, then I'll bring you with me."

"How much older?"

"We'll talk about it with your mom." He patted Ian on the head. "Now go play so I can pack."

"But, Dad, I need to practice for next week's all-star game. Can't we go for a little while?"

"Ask your mother to take you."

"She's got a charity meeting." Ian scowled, his voice rough.

His dad knelt beside him. "I'm sorry you're disappointed, but you mustn't get angry when your mother and I work for the greater good. We're very lucky to live in a safe home, to have plenty of food and water, and to have clothes to keep warm. Some people in this town and around the world don't have these things, and it's our duty to help them. Baseball is a wonderful pastime, and I know you love it, but isn't the welfare of others more important?"

"I guess so." Ian looked at his feet, still wishing he could go to the batting cages.

"Good boy. It makes me proud when you make unselfish choices, Ian. That's the Crawford way."

The Crawford way. He'd heard that a million times before. "Will you be home for my all-star game?"

"I'll try." He ruffled Ian's hair again and then stood. "Now go see if your mom needs help before you meet up with your friends."

Ian nodded, but he didn't go find his mother. He picked up his mitt and a tennis ball and went to the backyard, where he threw the ball against the brick wall over and over, feeling ashamed that he still wanted his dad to take him to the batting cages instead of going to Venezuela to help all those strangers.

"Ian?" his mother asked. "You look upset."

"Sorry. An ancient memory."

"Of what?"

"A conversation with Dad that ended with a lecture about the Crawford way."

"The family motto." She smiled proudly.

"Uh-huh . . ." That came out as more of a grunt than an expression.

"What?" She rocked Colt while speaking to Ian.

"Sometimes I wonder."

"Wonder what?"

"He used that 'Put others first' motto to justify his personal crusade, but let's be honest. There were two people he never put first, weren't there?"

He'd never before criticized his father and now had the sensation of falling through the sky without a parachute. His mother's offended expression didn't help.

"Are you calling your father a hypocrite?"

"No, Mom. I'm just saying maybe he wasn't *as* selfless as everyone thought."

"He died trying to save a child," his mom sputtered. "That's the epitome of selflessness."

"Don't get me wrong. I loved him. If I hadn't, I wouldn't have followed him all over the world, or spent so much time with Archer and Stanley to see this thing in Haiti through."

Her expression turned pensive; then she frowned. "Has living here, in all this grandeur, made you second-guess our values?"

"No," he lied. Another first. Lying to the woman who made sure there was strawberry jelly in the house because it'd been his favorite. Who'd baked up a storm for every school fund-raiser. Who'd read countless books to him and taught him how to drive. "*You* brought up marriage and family. That made me wonder if life the Crawford way can truly make a woman happy." Specifically, Gentry. Not that his mom could answer that question. Only Gentry could, but asking her wouldn't be fair play on the cusp of Smith's arrival. He shouldn't add to the things vying for her attention.

"Happiness is relative. If people have some idealized idea of marriage and love, they'll be doomed to disappointment. I loved your dad, and the life and family we created. It might not be for everyone, but I'm proud of what we accomplished together. The good we've done. Those things make me happy." She patted his thigh, smiling. "Your dad and I managed to give you a good start, too, right?"

"You did." Ian rubbed his mother's arm, eager to reassure her of his love and admiration. "You did, Mom."

"Are you giving up on C-VAC?"

"No." Was he? The part of him that had laughed, loved, and been trusted in this home wanted to chuck it all and stay put.

"Good." Her relieved smile might as well have been a nail to the cross that was his life. "How's it coming?"

Better, actually, since he'd been in touch with Marcus Fairfax, the auto dealer. "I might have secured some sweet vehicles, but it's not nailed down. Still waiting on some conditions. I think the guy wants us to involve his son in the venture. We could use extra hands, but I don't know if the kid has what it takes."

"You'll figure it out." When his mother raised Colt in the air, the baby treated her to a wide, wet smile. Colt had been unusually pleasant this past thirty minutes. Was that a sign? "Will you miss this little one? He knows he's darling, doesn't he?"

Colt did seem to have inherited his mother's ability to recognize her own appeal.

"I'll miss him a lot." An understatement, although Ian wouldn't miss the poop explosions.

"Maybe Gentry will send you pictures. She sure has enough of them."

On cue, they heard the door to the garage open. The sound of Gentry's bag hitting the ground let them know she'd entered the house. Her heels clicked on the wood floor but weren't loud enough to drown out her voice as she made her way toward the living room.

"I survived the day from hell. I need sleep, although if you'd strip down and join me in—" She had rounded the corner to the living room, raising her heel to remove her shoe, and then stopped short when she saw his mother.

Ian froze, too, eyes closed, wondering what in the world his mother must think of him. Farrah had ended their engagement only a month ago, and he'd already slept with another woman. Seemed he wasn't quite as good of a man as he or his mother had always thought. Like father, like son.

"Oh, hi, Gloria!" Gentry set her shoes aside and resumed her approach, head held high. Her demeanor reminded him of that first morning when he'd caught her in her undies. *That* image wouldn't help him do the right thing where she, Colt, and Peter Smith were concerned. Right now she looked almost as irresistible as she had then, in her fitted summer minidress that showed off her legs and every single curve. "Nice to see you again. Sorry about that crack. I'm a little punchy from lack of sleep. Bad joke." She shrugged unapologetically, then gazed lovingly at her son. "He's beautiful, isn't he?"

"Adorable. I was telling Ian that I can't *wait* to be a grandmother." His mother traded smiles with Gentry.

"Oh?" Gentry's gaze sharpened, and an edge of jealousy honed her voice. "Is Farrah whatshername pregnant?"

"Goodness, no." His mom looked at him. "I'm just projecting."

Ian couldn't look at either woman, so he kept his eyes on Colt.

"Ian will be a good dad and make pretty babies." Gentry reached for her son, whom she smothered in kisses, like always. "Of course, no one will be as pretty as you, Boo. No one ever."

"Thank you for helping out the other day with the blessing bags, Gentry." His mom smiled. "We can always use extra hands and donations."

"You're welcome. It was enlightening."

"That's what my husband and I always believed." Ian's mom didn't look at him, but he knew that message had been directed at him, not Gentry. "Well, I'll take off now. Nice seeing you again."

Ian laid his hand on his mother's lower back as they walked to the door. "See you later, Mom."

"Okay." She kissed him on the cheek. "I'm so glad for your good news. Keep me posted on your other progress."

Once his mother left, Gentry asked, "What good news?"

"Timmy's been recovered and arrests made."

She jiggled Colt. "That's cause for celebration, but right now I can't keep my eyes open. I'll take Colt and see if he'll nap with me."

"He just woke up ninety minutes ago." Ian gestured for the baby. "Leave him with me."

"It's after six. I don't want to take advantage of you."

He cocked a brow. "Liar."

"Jokes! Will wonders never cease?" A saucy look lit up her tired eyes. "I like the effect I'm having on you, McJ. Maybe you should come nap, too."

Sorely tempted, he sealed his mouth shut and gestured for Colt with his hands. "You look like hell. Get some sleep."

Gentry stepped closer. "Remind me again why we're keeping our hands to ourselves."

It wasn't easy to remember why, especially when she stood so close it made him throb with the need to wrap his arms around her. "Because I'm going to Haiti, and you want a real family for your son."

"Oh yeah." She huffed, then settled her hand on his chest. "Sometimes, when I'm near you like this, I forget to care about all that."

Electricity in her touch bound them together. "Me too."

"So maybe we shouldn't ignore these feelings. I mean, what's the shortest length of time you could be in Haiti and get the center off the ground?"

He shrugged. "To cement relationships with local government and hospitals, secure donor money and an ongoing medical supplies relationship, train enough locals . . . another year. Maybe nine months."

"Maybe I could wait nine months."

He grabbed her hand and kissed her knuckles. "Smith will be here in a few days, and you could feel differently soon."

She withdrew her hand. "It's bad enough that my mom is pushing me to be with him. Now you?"

"Your *mother*?" The idea that her family might push her into Smith's arms punched him in the gut. He didn't know Smith, but he hated him already. "She doesn't even know the guy."

"If I'm with Smith, the shared-custody problem is solved." Ian's face must've reflected disapproval, because Gentry said, "I know. She's twisted. Although there's a certain logic to it. And, as *you* like to point out, Smith is Colt's dad." She snapped her fingers. "Instafamily."

Her words tumbled over him like ten gallons of ice water. Jealousy never suited him, so he pushed away from it hard. "Then take your mom's advice."

"Don't pretend you don't care. Even if you've decided that we're a lose-lose situation, I still have feelings."

"So do I." Strong feelings. Ones that couldn't stand the idea of Gentry with any other man. They stared at each other while he took Colt from her.

"Well, that's something, then." Free of Colt, she yawned, stretching her arms wide. "Let's not argue. I don't have a single working brain cell left. I need some sleep."

She kissed Colt's head and, without waiting for a reply, wandered to her room.

He stood there, holding her son, with a bunch of words stuck in his throat. Maybe they'd come out if he could answer one preposterous question for himself before Smith arrived. Was he already in love with Gentry Cabot?

Chapter Sixteen

Relief

According to *Merriam-Webster*: removal or lightening of something oppressive, painful, or distressing

According to me: Smith's demeanor

"Gentry, relax," Ian called from the kitchen. "Your heels will wear a rut in the hardwood."

Nothing irked her more than being ordered to relax. Especially following a long week of rising stress levels in the office and the anticipation of meeting Smith. Five days that had felt like ten. "I need wine."

"Not a good idea." Ian came out of the kitchen with a clean binky for Colt. Smart thinking, because Smith would be here any minute, and she didn't want him to be scared off by Colt's crying.

"Since when has that ever stopped me?" she scoffed, and started for the kitchen.

Ian blocked her. "You'll want your wits about you."

Wits? She'd lost those days ago. Who could keep her head together when navigating so much gray area? She and Ian had shared a few tender kisses that went nowhere because their circumstances hadn't changed. But there'd been moments when she, Ian, and Colt had felt like a perfect family. When the dream sparkled like pixie dust, and she thought she could will it to be. Then Archer would call, and Ian's wall would go back up.

Smith's arrival today would not improve matters.

"I wonder if he's already checked in?" She'd recommended the nearby B&B, Lakeside Cottages, and sent over a nice bottle of wine to kick things off on the right foot.

"Probably." Ian crossed his arms, looking rather grim. "I should go up to my room and give you two some privacy."

"Don't leave me alone. Smith should meet you, considering . . . everything." She waved her hand between them, unable to find the words to describe their current relationship. She only knew that her heart chased him like a dog did a butterfly.

Ian sighed and took up a position by the playpen.

She kept pacing, occasionally adjusting photographs and other knickknacks. Anything to keep in motion because, when she stood still, her stomach lurched.

The knock at the door caused her to flinch.

The evening sun streaming through the picture window cast Ian in shadow. Deep down, she'd hoped Smith's arrival would make Ian rethink his future. Ian's expression remained aggravatingly neutral, although his silhouette took on a superhero quality—legs in a wide stance, arms crossed. "I'm right here with you. Take a breath."

She nodded, as if convincing herself that this had not been a colossal mistake. Smith—Peter—stood mere yards away.

Her son's father. A stranger. The black metal door between them remained the only barrier between what was and what would be.

"Gentry?" Ian asked.

A second knock spurred her to action. She crossed to the door, her Manolos clicking like offbeat maracas. Would Smith like her home? Would he be patient with their son? Who were his friends and family? What the hell had she done?

She gripped the cold bronze handle, yanked the door opened, and nearly stumbled backward.

Smith's crooked smile flashed, although unlike before, this time he offered it up awkwardly instead of as a weapon of seduction. "Artemis."

Gentry crinkled her nose. "We should probably use our real names now, although it'll be hard to think of you as anything other than Smith."

He hesitated, both of them uncertain of the proper etiquette for this meeting.

"My friends call me Smith, so you can stick with that." He stepped into the entry, his eyes searching hers instead of exploring her home or hunting for Colt.

She'd forgotten how tall he was. Six three or four, and broad. Overwhelming, and as handsome as he'd been that night in Napa.

"Okay." She tried to smile. "But no one calls me Artemis."

"Got it, Gentry." Her name sounded funny coming from him. She'd reveled in their role-playing that night last year. Loved the anonymity. Now she'd have to expose herself, and that always wore her out.

After an awkward embrace, she gestured toward the living room. "Thanks for being so gracious about everything."

"I'm blessed—or maybe cursed—by having been trained by my mom to confront awkward situations with extreme optimism. Doesn't mean I'm not uncomfortable, or make me a pushover, though. But let's muddle through together and make the best of it. We got on well before, so I have high hopes we can manage this, too."

Gentry almost said something about his mother, knowing from the PI file that he'd lost her years ago, but she decided to wait until he wanted to share more. "I'll do my best."

Smith stepped down into the living room, at which point he noticed Ian. His brows rose and fell before he stepped forward and offered his hand. "Hello, I'm Peter Smith."

"Ian Crawford." Ian didn't smile or scowl when he introduced himself, nor did he specify his role in her life.

How could he, with it still so unclear? Humanitarian. Friend. Temporary nanny. Lover. Soon to be a memory. That thought lodged itself in her throat. She couldn't think of that now, though. Smith was here to meet his son.

"Nice to meet you." Smith mimicked Ian's aggressive posture. They stood there, each taking measure of the other, until Colt whimpered from behind Ian, drawing a sharp turn of Smith's head.

Smith's eyes sparkled—anticipation tinged with trepidation—as he parted his lips.

Gentry scooted around Ian to lift Colt out of the playpen. She'd dressed him in a gorgeous Armani Junior piqué and chambray shortall. The conservative outfit should appeal to Smith, whose taste in clothing apparently still leaned toward Brooks Brothers. She faced Colt outward, her grip a little more possessive than normal. "This is Colt."

Smith stood arrested, eyes wide, half-dazed. She flicked a glance at Ian, hoping he might intervene, but he never looked her way. He, too, remained stiff, his gaze trained on Smith. If she had to guess, McJ was compiling a list of snap judgments about Smith's French cuff shirt and polished shoes.

"Would you like to hold him?" she finally asked Smith, having confirmed with a quick sniff that Colt's diaper wasn't stinky.

She noticed Ian's jaw clench.

"I would." Smith gingerly reached out to accept the squirmy bundle.

"He fusses a lot, so don't take it personally," she warned, her arms a bit shaky.

"Got it." Smith stared, apparently still thunderstruck by the reality of this visit.

When Gentry placed Colt in his father's arms for the first time, she had to fight to catch her breath. Smith's frame dwarfed their son. *Their* son. Those words sounded odd after two months of Colt being only hers. But now they stood in her home, together, like a real family. Colt finally had his father.

She hoped to wipe her wet cheeks without being noticed. Smith was too mesmerized by Colt to see anything else, but Ian handed her a tissue, which then drew Smith's attention.

His eyes shone with misty tears, too.

"Sorry." She sniffled, relinquishing all pride. "It's a little overwhelming to see you two together, and *not* just because it's clear that Colt got none of my genes," she teased, but the joke didn't help her breathe any easier.

Smith cleared his throat. "Seeing him in person . . . even without the DNA results, I'd know he's mine."

He sniffed his child's moisturized skin, touched his chubby cheeks, and kissed his downy head. Colt fussed a bit, seeking the comfort of familiar arms. Smith tried swaying and speaking softly, but it only ramped up their willful son. With a half-cocked grin, Smith glanced at Gentry. "I think maybe he got a few of your genes, after all."

She welcomed the laughter that burst from her chest. It boded well that Smith joked with the easy repartee they'd shared last year. Earlier, she'd been unsure whether he'd arrive with latent anger and bitterness. His pleasant mood helped her relax, even if it proved that Colt's ornery side definitely came from her. "Let's lay him on the blanket and sit on the floor. He's probably a little nervous because he doesn't know you yet."

She took Colt, whispering lovingly in his ear, and laid him on the blanket she'd spread earlier. Smith watched them intently, as did Ian.

She tugged at her short skirt and tucked her legs to one side. "I should've asked if you're thirsty or anything."

"I'm good, thanks. Just tell me all about him." Smith's fascinated gaze studied Colt, even as he casually stretched onto his side nearby, propped up by one elbow.

Gentry recalled the earliest days following Colt's birth, when she couldn't tear her eyes away from him. Even with his constant crying, hours would pass where she'd done nothing but catalog the shades of his skin, count his tiny eyelashes, stroke the minuscule fingernails. She'd memorized the swirling pattern of his hair, cradled him to her chest, and marveled at the miracle of her own body's ability to have produced this tiny new life.

Colt had been, and continued to be, the most wondrous part of her life. She almost envied Smith for experiencing that novelty now, but guilt about how he'd been denied months of knowing his son tempered the feeling.

While she recited a long list of facts about Colt, Ian didn't speak. He stood to the side, his only movement being the rise and fall of his chest. In other words, he'd transformed into a living statue.

"Does he sleep through the night yet?" Smith asked.

"Not really. He'd probably sleep better if I put a little rice cereal in his bottle, but the pediatrician says to wait. Normally, I don't care much for rules, but I'm afraid to take chances with his health."

"My sister started her daughter, Mia, on solids ahead of schedule, but I think she was five months old at the time. I can't remember for sure." Smith held out his fingers for Colt to grasp and then smiled as he moved Colt's arms around. Colt pumped his legs a few times. "Mia's one now."

The fact that Colt had more cousins filled Gentry with warmth. "So your sister will give you tips?"

"Her name's Patty, and, yes, she will. She's older. More like a mother than a sister most of the time." He rolled his eyes in a good-natured way. "She's got a three-year-old daughter, too. Cammy."

"She must be busy." Gentry tucked her hair behind her ear, curious about his family but choosing to let him fill her in at his own pace. "You sound close."

"We are, but she and my dad live in Pasadena, where I grew up. I moved to San Francisco for work." He spared her a brief glance. "What about your family?"

"We're all here in Lake Sandy. I have an older brother and sister. For the most part, we all work together at the family business."

"Cabot Tea Company." He shook his head, although his attention remained on Colt's expressions and gurgling. The familiar mixture of pride and resentment arose whenever Gentry discussed CTC, the entity that had given *and* taken so much. "When I saw that online, I about fell off my chair for the second time. You're one surprise after another, Art—er, Gentry."

"Keeps things interesting, and fun," she joked. She didn't shoot Ian a pointed look, even though that comment deserved some emphasis.

Smith smiled beneath a warm gaze. "I remember that about you, too."

Ian cleared his throat. The sound oddly soothed her. It smacked of jealousy, which meant he wasn't nearly as unaffected by all this as he pretended. He cared, just like she wanted him to.

Smith glanced at Ian. "Sorry."

"If you'll both excuse me for a minute." Ian wandered around the corner without another word.

Once Ian disappeared, Smith lowered his voice. "What's the story with you two?"

"It's complicated." Nothing like the stark truth to slap her with reality.

"How so?"

"He's Colt's temporary nanny—long story."

Smith's expression grew more intrigued. "He lives here?"

"For now. He'll be leaving the States soon. Humanitarian work."

"So you aren't together?" He tickled Colt's belly while speaking to her.

"Like I said, it's complicated." Gentry picked at the threads of the corner of Colt's blanket.

"I'm not big on complicated. I prefer easy." He winked, but she didn't want to read too much into that remark. "Will you put Colt in day care once Ian goes?"

"Yes."

Smith's expression shifted. "Did you consider taking more time off from work . . . until he's a little older?"

Keeping a straight face, she replied, "Actually, I hoped you'd stop working for a few months and watch Colt so I can help launch my company's new product."

She fought a smirk while she watched Smith's reaction.

"Sorry." Smith flushed when he chuckled. "I forgot to mention my family's half Neanderthal. Didn't mean to offend you."

Big points, she thought. He got her dry humor and apologized easily. Two fine traits. All in all, things could be much worse. Now he studied her, wearing an odd grin.

"What?" She self-consciously tongued her teeth, probing for lettuce or a poppy seed from her earlier bagel.

He shrugged, humor lighting up his eyes. "You didn't strike me as so career oriented when we met."

In truth, she'd been undisciplined and untethered at that point in her life. Rather than confess that, she defaulted to her favorite old saying. "Sometimes you've got to break the rules and set yourself free."

Colt kicked and wailed, as if realizing he'd lost their undivided attention. God, he was exactly like her.

Smith pumped Colt's legs and made googly-eyes at his son. Then, with a serious expression, he said, "Except in our case, breaking the rules didn't set us free at all. In fact, it sort of tied us together for life."

◆ ◆ ◆

Even in the kitchen, Ian couldn't escape Smith's presence. The man's jovial, confident voice—his insufferable ego—consumed the whole condo. It'd probably linger after he left, saturating everything like cigarette smoke.

"I didn't expect to already be falling in love with him," Smith exclaimed from the other room, the note of pride obvious to anyone listening.

"He has that effect on people," Gentry replied. Ian couldn't decipher the tone of her voice. She teased all the time, but without seeing her face, he wasn't sure if it'd been a deflection or something warmer.

He crept to the kitchen door to spy on them.

Smith was sitting up now, holding Colt in the air like he was inspecting a melon. The man's crooked grin made him even better-looking.

All week, Ian had held himself on a leash. Separated his desires and fantasies from reality and fairness. Considered the time Archer had spent with him, and the money they'd already raised and committed. The community awaiting their help. He'd weighed all of that against his feelings for Gentry and Colt, the suddenness of which made them seem an illusion that would surely end up disappointing all of them.

And then there was Smith. His behavior suggested he might have some lingering personal interest in the mother of his child. If Smith was good for Colt and Gentry, Ian should walk away, happy that Gentry could create the family she wanted for Colt.

But no rationale lessened the ache in his chest from being on the outside of the little family.

Gentry and Smith caught him staring at them. Luckily, his phone rang, giving him something to do. He turned sideways, answering it without looking at the screen. "Hello?"

"Ian," came a familiar voice.

The timing seemed significant. "Farrah?"

"Yes." She paused. "Are you free today? I need to see you."

"What's wrong?"

"I've been doing a lot of thinking, especially after seeing you last weekend." Her voice wobbled. "We ended so abruptly I really want to talk. Can you come over, please?"

He'd promised Gentry he'd stay here in case things went south with Smith. But things weren't going south at all. In fact, he suspected Gentry thought things were rather looking up.

"Ian?" Farrah begged. "Please."

He closed his eyes. Talking with Farrah about what went wrong might help him better understand his feelings for Gentry, and whether a relationship with her could fare better than the one with Farrah. "I'll be right over."

He hung up and ordered an Uber before alerting Gentry. "I have to go."

"To see Farrah?" She raised that chin of hers like she did anytime she tried to hide her feelings.

"Sorry. It can't wait." Ian crossed to the front door, eager for fresh air. "Nice to meet you, Smith."

Colt started crying, possibly picking up on the tension in the house. Ian slipped out the front door to wait for the Uber driver. He'd barely had time to close the door before Gentry came outside.

"What's going on?"

He wanted to kiss her. To reassure her. To find a solution that didn't require him to walk away. But he couldn't make promises, so he said, "Farrah needs me."

"Why now?" Gentry's nostrils flared. "And why do you care? She *dumped* you."

"I was a shitty fiancé." He rubbed his forehead with the heel of his hand.

Her jaw set, but she didn't argue. "When will you be home?"

Home. That either of them thought of her condo as his home seemed absurd, yet true.

"I don't know." A black Kia pulled up to the curb. Ian reached out to touch Gentry, then let his arm fall. "You'll be fine. Smith seems like a good guy."

"First you tell me things didn't work out with her because she's too needy. Now you're ditching me because I'm not. Think about that, Ian." She turned and went inside.

Fifteen minutes later, the Uber driver dropped Ian at the circular driveway of Farrah's place on SW Harbor Way. The center island bloomed with clustered red flowers. He stared at the beige siding of the four-story apartment building. Its appearance, neighborhood, and tiny balconies paled in comparison with the grandeur of Gentry's condominium and setting. Still, he had warm memories here. It'd been a haven compared with his housing in Guatemala, Colombia, and Haiti. Farrah had always welcomed him home, her gentle touch and kind heart a balm to the horrors he often experienced while away.

Now he shaded his eyes with one hand and peered at her balcony, where they'd enjoyed their morning coffee. Farrah preferred peaceful routines. A bit of a homebody, she'd been content to bake or read or do whatever Ian suggested. Easygoing. The opposite of Gentry.

Doubts about his coming here assailed him. What the hell was there to say after he'd let her down in every way? Accepting his discomfort as penance for taking her for granted, he took the stairs instead of the elevator to buy himself a few extra moments.

He came through the stairwell door and turned left, passing Mrs. Montana's apartment. Farrah stood in the hallway outside her door. The pile of blonde hair on top of her head spilled over, partially obscuring her face.

"Thanks for coming." Her forced smile didn't cover red-rimmed eyes. He refrained from asking what was wrong, because he knew, and he needed another minute to prepare for whatever she had to say.

"Of course." He stepped inside and scanned the living space. Everything was neat and organized, like always. No picture out of place, no shoes discarded.

"I have a surprise, actually." She waved him toward the kitchen. "I made peach pie yesterday. It's really good."

Pie, his weakness, as she knew well. "Never could turn down one of your pies."

The praise earned him a genuine smile. While she busied herself in the kitchen, he took in the beige corduroy sofa, the simple oak dining table, the frilly drapes on the boxy little windows. It all looked exactly as it had last month, yet felt entirely different—foreign—after living with Gentry.

"Coffee?"

"Sure." He heard the Keurig hum.

"Seeing you standing here . . . it's almost like you never left."

He looked at his feet to hide the betrayal of having already moved on. He shoved his hands in his pockets, his chest hollow. "Not sure what to say to that."

"Maybe that was part of our problem. We talked about so many things, but never about us except when we fought." She plated a slice of pie. After setting it and a cup of coffee on the breakfast bar, she slid onto the stool beside him and watched him eat. It brought back memories of how she'd often sat there with him, smiling and chatting about her day. Her attention had been comforting and pleasant. A peaceful escape from the turmoil of his many journeys. He'd loved her—still did—but not the way a man should love the woman he planned to marry.

He cut through the flaky crust with the side of his fork. She watched him take his first bite, her scrutiny making him self-conscious. "How are your folks?"

"Fine." Her eyes bore into his. "But let's not waste time on that. Today I want to talk about us."

"Me too." He sipped the coffee, which she'd sweetened with one teaspoon of sugar, exactly how he liked it. "I'd like to learn something from our mistakes."

She reached for his fork and sampled the pie. She'd done that a million times, too. "After we got engaged, I always felt like you thought I was holding you back from your plans. Tell me, why haven't you returned to Haiti yet?"

"I bought a one-way ticket home because I couldn't afford the round-trip fare." He'd been sinking money into the foundation, and assumed he'd have the engagement ring to hock to buy a flight back. "I stuck around to make some money and scare up some new donors."

Farrah slid a cautious glance his way. "Your new boss is pretty."

Ian nodded, keeping his eyes on the pie.

"I didn't see a wedding ring." She shifted in her seat, dancing around the questions she really wanted to ask. "Is her baby's father in the picture?"

"He's in California, although he's here today visiting." Ian took another bite of pie. The image of Smith and Gentry playing with Colt soured the taste of the pie's sweet filling. "But I thought you wanted to talk about us, not Gentry."

"Sorry." She scratched a spot by her ear. "So you'll return to Haiti soon?"

"That's the plan." The words came out on a sigh. "What's really on your mind, Farrah?"

"Are you happy?" She tipped her head. "Happier than when you were home with me?"

He couldn't give her the answer she probably wanted to hear. "I don't know what you want me to say."

"I want to know if you're happy. Is C-VAC enough?"

That question sounded different coming from Farrah than from Gentry.

"Farrah . . ." He stalled, groping for the right words. "I'm happier knowing I'm not letting you down anymore."

"If you could do it all over again, would you do anything differently?"

He hesitated, but the truth came to him forcefully. He wouldn't have gotten engaged just to appease her. "I wouldn't have made you promises I couldn't keep."

"Was it me? Was I too boring or clingy or something? Is that why you were always running off?"

Only now, when comparing the reluctance he felt about leaving Gentry, could he see that his lack of passion for Farrah might've been there all along. But he'd never hurt her with the truth. Not now, with nothing to gain. "You know I'm on a mission. You've always known that."

"I do." She looked relieved when she clasped his hand. "I've wanted to apologize for the way I handled things, especially at the end."

"No need." He patted her hand and then eased out of her hold.

While she adjusted the loose knot of hair on her head, tucking stray bits behind her ear, he finished the pie. She cleared her throat. "Ian, I made a terrible miscalculation."

"Farrah—"

"Let me finish."

He dreaded where this conversation seemed to be headed.

"It wasn't easy to worry and pray for your safety all the time, but I did it. When we finally got engaged, I thought you'd spend more time here. Get a job at a hospital. Settle down and start planning a family." She frowned then. "When that didn't happen, I got frustrated, even though you'd never promised to change. It wasn't fair of me to expect that from you."

Maybe not, but Gentry had shown him that his expectations were hardly reasonable. "It wasn't fair of *me* to expect you to settle for a part-time partner. You deserve more."

"But that's just it. There isn't 'more.' I love you."

"Love isn't enough. We both know that." He squeezed her hand, which she then clasped with her other hand. "There's someone else for you."

She shook her head. "No, Ian. You're irreplaceable."

"That's not true. In time, you'll meet someone new who'll be a better fit for you and your life."

"I don't want someone new." She grimaced. "You know, I kept the ring because I thought you'd miss me and come begging for another chance. I never wanted us to be over."

As sorry as he was about her pain, he wasn't coming back. "I'm sorry."

"Me too." She swiveled to face him and gripped his thigh. "So you forgive me?"

"There's nothing to forgive."

Her round, blue eyes pled for a second chance. "Come home, Ian. I won't ever ask you to change. I'll stop teaching summer school and come with you for several weeks each summer, too."

Farrah was a sweet girl. The kitchen cupboards contained a menagerie of gift mugs and candles, proving how well liked she was by her students. She volunteered at her church and loved his mother. Had they stayed together, he'd have been faithful and content . . . maybe even happy, by his mother's definition. But he would never have been happy by Gentry's definition.

That complicated woman who'd fill her home with love as fierce as her temper had blasted into his life and stolen his heart. She provoked him, challenged him, surprised him. Even if nothing permanent came from his time with her, he knew, now, the passion he ought to feel if he ever decided to marry. "You're saying that now because you're lonely."

"I'm not just lonely. I miss you, Ian. Don't you miss *me*?" A tear rolled down her cheek as she hugged herself. Her weeping tormented him. If wrapping his arms around her would take the hurt away, he'd do it. But he couldn't ease Farrah's pain any more than he could give Marie back to Timmy, or his father back to his mom.

He didn't like to lie, but in this case a little fib would do more good than harm. "Sure, I miss you, but we can't pick up where things left off. We both know, eventually, you'd grow unhappy again." He clasped her hands after wiping her stray tear. "I'm sorry you're having a hard time, but the break has shown me that you made the right decision, Farrah. Deep down, I think you know that, too. So please, don't sit around here clinging to the dream of what you wanted us to be. Remember what we were and all the reasons you got fed up in the first place. We can't be together anymore, but I'll always love you, and I'll always be your friend."

Good speech, he thought, until she burst into tears. Then he knew he was in for a long night.

Chapter Seventeen

Juggle

According to *Merriam-Webster*: to handle or deal with usually several things (such as obligations) at one time so as to satisfy often competing requirements

According to me: an evening with Ian and Smith

At six in the morning, Gentry sat on the living room floor, finishing a collage she'd worked on the previous night for Smith. The evening had gone as well as she could have hoped, allowing her worry to fade like a dream at dawn.

Smith might've stayed into the night to give them a chance to learn more about each other and discuss parenting, but she'd sent him to the B&B after putting Colt to sleep. Had she known Ian would not return, she might not have shooed Smith away so early.

Ian's absence nettled, like a pebble in a shoe. His cryptic late-night text—Don't wait up—hadn't helped, either. She'd distracted herself by working on the ChariTea campaign and printing out a bunch of photos of Colt to make the collage for Smith.

By midnight she'd given up her vigil.

She needs me, he'd said of Farrah. Lying awake for most of the wee hours, Gentry had concocted forty-three potential explanations for why he never returned.

She certainly didn't *hope* for one involving an Uber accident. She preferred options that involved his mother, or happening upon another emergency and offering help, or Farrah tying him up and stealing his phone so he couldn't leave. But regardless of the varied and strained explanations she'd dreamed up, deep down she couldn't escape the most obvious one—he'd spent the night with his ex.

Total dick move, but also not *wholly* unexpected. Those two had been engaged until recently. Maybe old feelings resurfaced.

She'd wanted to believe that what had happened between Ian and her last weekend had meant something. Everything. Or, at least, a lot. He'd said so, and she'd thought him sincere. It'd been a long, long time since she'd been taken for a fool, and she didn't like the feeling.

She lumbered into the kitchen, dragging a week's worth of sleeplessness with her. Although not particularly hungry, she scanned the refrigerator's contents. Almond milk, pineapple yogurt, strawberries—all Ian's favorites. She opted for the yogurt, collapsed onto a kitchen stool, and stabbed her spoon into the cupful of lumpy protein.

While licking the spoon after her third bite, she heard the front door open and click shut. Ian's soft shuffle into the condo made her stomach flip.

She slid off the stool and stormed into the living area, catching him by surprise. "Look who decided to come back."

He stood there—hair matted on the left side of his head, rumpled shorts and shirt—staring at her. The deep lines around his mouth and between his brows revealed his exhaustion and no small amount of resignation. Contrition hovered around him like mist on the lake.

Her own emotions—rage, rejection, betrayal—pulsed through her in alternating bursts. Pressure continued to build inside, and if she wasn't careful, pain would explode out of her.

From the age of ten, she'd committed herself to never feeling this way. Obsessed. Possessive. Rejected. Hurt. It surely said something about her—something not at all good—that she'd broken her rule for the man least willing or likely to return her feelings.

"Good morning." He approached her, but she retreated.

She swallowed hard, tempted to pretend Smith was asleep in her room. Not long ago, that was exactly what she would've done right before sending Ian packing. "For some, maybe."

"Don't say that. I didn't sleep with Farrah. Not the way you think."

Whatever that meant. "Even if that's true, you bailed on me."

"I had to see her." He pulled an engagement ring out of his pocket, held it up as some kind of exculpatory evidence, and set it on the entry table.

Gentry pulled her thumbnail away from her mouth. "Why now?"

"Until several weeks ago, we were planning a life together, Gentry. It ended abruptly. There were things to say and sort out. She's hurting."

"She wants you back?"

"Yes."

Her gaze went to the engagement ring on the entry table. "And you said no?"

"I did. I felt like shit, with her sobbing all over my shirt, and me knowing I've moved on without much heartache at all." He scrubbed his hands through his hair. "I couldn't leave her alone like that, so I stayed. When she finally fell asleep, I spent the rest of the night in self-reflection, most of which made me feel worse."

"Because of me?"

"Because of *me*." Ian closed his eyes, shaking his head. "Because I don't want to repeat the same mistakes, or hurt anyone else." He glanced at the collage project on the floor. "You and Smith hit it off."

"He makes it easy, but I sent him home early so you and I could talk. Little did I know I'd be waiting in vain."

He reached for her hands, searching her gaze. "You don't like waiting."

His touch settled her for the first time in ten hours. "Patience isn't one of my virtues . . . if I have any at all."

He squeezed her hands. "I did a lot of thinking last night. As much as I care for you and Colt, I also care about my plans with Archer. Any relationship with me will require a lot of waiting around."

"Not if I give you incentive to return often." She wound her arms around his neck and kissed him. He responded like fire, but she could feel his fatigue, and hers. Ian cupped her face with his hands and touched his forehead to hers. She released a sigh. "I'm spending the afternoon with Smith and Colt. My family's joining us all for dinner here."

He eased away. "Oh."

"Would you like to join us?"

"I don't know if that's best." He yawned again.

"You might feel differently once you've slept." She motioned toward the stairs and watched him lumber up to his room. When she heard his bedroom door click shut, she turned. Sunlight sparkled off the small diamond ring he'd abandoned on the entry table.

She crossed to it, sneaking a peek over her shoulder before lifting it up for inspection. A half carat or so. Classic round cut in a white-gold setting.

Without thinking, she slipped it on her finger and held out her hand, imagining how it might feel to have someone—have him—make her that promise. Her ring finger tingled with warmth as she pictured Ian sliding something similar on her hand. She got so lost in her daydream that she didn't hear him come back down the steps until he cleared his throat.

"Oh!" She jumped, clutching her hand to her chest. "I thought you went to lie down."

"I did, but then I remembered the ring. I want to put it someplace safe until I can sell it." He stared at her finger. "Not exactly the place I had in mind, although it looks pretty on your hand."

She guessed her face must look like a maraschino cherry. Grimacing, she tugged at the ring, but it wouldn't clear her knuckle. "Sorry!"

He clasped her wrist and laid her hand on his, looking at the ring, then looking at her. His green eyes looked translucent in the light coming through the windows. "Let me."

He drew her hand up to his mouth and sucked the length of her ring finger to wet it, then twisted the ring loose and tucked it in his pocket.

"I'll miss you." The words fell from her lips.

"And I you." He stared at her. She couldn't tell if the intensity of his gaze was because he had too many or too few things to say.

"I wish . . ." What? That they'd met under different circumstances, sure. But she didn't wish away Smith and Colt, because Colt gave her life more meaning and purpose than anything or anyone.

He kissed her again. "We'll talk later, when my head's clearer."

She watched him go upstairs, and then wandered into the living room. She studied the collage, staring at father and son. Smith would be part of Colt's life no matter what Gentry decided. Would pursuing Ian make her a bad mother? Or did she owe Colt a chance at having the stability of two parents under one roof?

◆ ◆ ◆

When Smith entered Gentry's condo that evening, all conversation stopped, with the exception of Ty's "vrooming" his truck along the floor and Colt's whimpering. Those two didn't know who Smith was and, at this point, didn't much care. Ian wished he could say the same. He came to this awkward affair hopeful he'd learn something to help him make the right decision.

The only person—besides the children—who didn't look the least bit uncomfortable was Smith.

"Welcome." Gentry kissed Smith on the cheek.

He handed her a bottle of wine. "Didn't want to arrive empty-handed."

Ian didn't know much about wine, but given Smith's profession and the rich look of the gold-and-maroon label, it had to be expensive.

"2007 Valentini Trebbiano d'Abruzzo." Gentry grinned at Smith. "I hope this goes with pizza."

Smith laughed as if she'd been joking. When she didn't smile, his brows rose. "Oh, you're serious."

"Hell yeah, I'm serious. My cooking skills are limited to reheats and cereal. If you want fine food with this wine, we'll need to order from Alec."

Jenna groaned quietly, but Smith didn't appear to have heard her.

"Pizza's fine." Smith surveyed the room. "Is Alec coming?"

"No, he and Colby are working tonight," Gentry said. "Don't worry, though. My sister won't wait too long to meet you."

She then turned to face her family, all of whom literally sat on the edge of their seats, awaiting an introduction. Hunter's laser-sharp focus blazed from behind his glasses. Sara smiled warmly. Jed cleared his throat, and Jenna maintained a polite smile. The awkward scene would be perfect for another *Meet the Parents* sequel.

"Everyone, this is Smith. Peter Smith. Smith, this is my dad, Jed; my mom, Jenna; my brother, Hunter; and his wife, Sara. That's their son, Ty. And you've met Ian." Gentry's dad stood to shake hands with the man who'd screwed his daughter without even knowing her name. Ian doubted he could be so cool in either man's shoes. "While you all say hello, I'll go open this bottle. I'm sure everyone could use a hearty glass of wine."

Gentry ducked into the kitchen, leaving Smith to fend for himself. Jenna took advantage of Gentry's absence and patted the cushion beside her. "Sit here, Smith. Tell me what you think of our little Colt."

Jenna certainly treated Smith with more interest than she ever had Ian. He had to hand it to her, though. She wasted no time setting up the chessboard on which she planned to strategize her plan for Gentry to secure full custody. Would Smith be a pawn or a player?

Smith picked Colt up out of the playpen and then complied with Jenna's request. "I'm blown away by my son."

Those last two words landed like a punch to Ian's gut. After weeks of being responsible for Colt's well-being, Ian disliked his diminished role.

Gentry returned to the living room, balancing a tray with seven glasses and a full decanter. She set it on the ottoman and flashed a pretty smile at Smith. "This smells amazing."

"Good nose. That's a blend of lemon curd, Bosc pear, and hints of smoke. And the texture is fantastic." Smith poured glasses for everyone, swirled his own, dipped his nose inside the rim, and inhaled deeply.

Ian struggled not to roll his eyes.

Gentry downed a good chug. "Nice."

Smith laughed, which surprised Ian. He supposed he should be glad that Colt's father wasn't completely pompous, but Gentry's responding smile made it hard not to hate Smith. Jenna, on the other hand, splayed her hand on her chest, eyes wide with horror at her daughter's behavior.

Jenna turned to Smith. "I've done a little reading up on your profession. Master Sommelier. That takes a lot of discipline."

"It's pretty intense," Smith replied.

Kidnappings, cholera, earthquakes . . . those things were intense. Studying wine seemed easy in comparison. Ian's expression must've shouted his thoughts, because Gentry muttered, "McJ."

"You must be passionate about it." Jenna smiled as if she was *his* proud mother. Ian had never seen her treat Gentry so respectfully, and that made him scowl.

"Can't imagine enjoying any other job as well." Smith bounced Colt on his lap.

"Even with the long, late hours?" Jenna sipped her wine, acting like she gave two figs about Smith's job.

"Mm-hm," he replied.

"I imagine there's a lot of travel, too." Jenna tucked her hair behind her ear and leaned in, utterly fascinated by him and his career. Ian could've barfed in his mouth.

Smith lapped up the attention. "That's the best part, especially the trips to Europe."

"Must be exciting." Jenna lightly touched his arm, giddy.

"And fun."

"Sounds almost perfect." Jenna's head then tipped left, over a slight shrug of that shoulder. "Of course, all those hours and travel will make it difficult to keep Colt for any stretch of time, won't it?"

Boom! Ian hadn't seen that one coming, and he felt the corners of his mouth pull upward in response. *Well played, Mrs. Cabot. Well played.* The room seemed to brighten.

But Smith was neither naive nor an idiot. If anything, he appeared to enjoy this game. "Gentry and I will work those things out. Maybe they'll join me on a trip or two. Nothing like travel to educate a child. We can go anywhere and show our boy his roots."

Smith had done the impossible—he'd flabbergasted Jenna into silence. He winked at Gentry, who laughed. Ian, however, didn't laugh. If Gentry wanted Colt to see the world, he'd rather they travel with him so Colt would see the realities, not the resorts.

Her father interjected, "It's good to love your work. Jenna, Hunter, and I certainly do." As an afterthought, he added, "And Gentry, too."

Ian watched Gentry suppress the sting of that lag, although, in truth, Gentry didn't love CTC. She loved her family. Did they get that yet?

Smith nodded. "It's nice that your whole family works together."

"Not the whole family," Hunter added. "Colby's on her own, with minimal input from us. I understand you know Alec."

"Not well. He was a couple of years ahead of me and really focused. Obviously, he went on to do great things. I hope to get to know him better now."

"You'll have to stop by A CertainTea and say hello." Jenna sipped her wine. "Perhaps one day you could work for them so you can be closer to Colt."

"I suppose anything's possible, Jenna." Smith shot Gentry an inscrutable look.

Ian had never seen her at a loss for words, but her father stepped up to rescue her from the awkward moment. "How did your folks take the news? Must've been a shock."

"Yes." Smith's wide smile dimmed. "My mom died years ago, but my dad and sister had a lot of questions. Can't say they were thrilled by the circumstances—I suspect neither were you—but they're eager to meet my son."

"The situation's not exactly conventional." Hunter's tone had a bit more bite than the wine.

"The best things in life rarely are." Smith smiled.

Gentry's eyes lit with appreciation for that sentiment, proving a certain compatibility with her son's father. She also seemed to admire the fact that her family didn't intimidate him.

Meanwhile, Ian stood on the fringe of the group, arms crossed, fingers nearly white from their death grip on his elbows. Perhaps he shouldn't have come. Before anyone else spoke, the doorbell rang.

"Must be the pizza." Gentry slid off the arm of the sofa and trotted to the door, returning with a stack of pizza boxes.

Hunter gave her the thumbs-up. "I *love* Il Migliore's pizza. What are our options?"

"I got you sausage, cherry peppers, and mushroom." Gentry set the boxes on the edge of the table.

"My favorite!" He seemed both delighted and surprised that she knew him so well. Ian didn't understand why none of them seemed to notice how she always paid attention to those details.

Sara helped Gentry spread out the boxes down the center of the dining table, where she'd already set out plates and flatware. Ian, however, couldn't imagine shoving greasy pizza into his already-upset stomach.

"I'll get Colt settled to sleep." Ian reached out for Colt. "Start without me."

"Let me." Smith stood, still clutching his son.

Gentry held her breath, her gaze silently asking Ian to concede.

"Of course." Ian dropped his arms to his sides.

Smith rose from the sofa and started across the living room.

"I'll teach you the routine." Gentry excused herself from the group and led Smith toward her room.

Ian took a seat at the far end of the table, pretending to listen to her family's whispered conversation—a general rubber stamp of approval. Meanwhile, Smith's deep chuckle, big as the man himself, buzzed in Ian's ear like a gnat. Gentry's gentle laughter followed. Those two were like pigs in a blanket already.

Ian should be glad for her and Colt. It should also make his decision easier.

It didn't.

When the proud parents returned from Gentry's room, Smith's face glowed. The man wasn't bitter or trapped or angry. He seemed excited, or at least bemused, by the idea of being Colt's dad. And by getting closer to Gentry. Ian had never been a jealous man, but whenever he thought about how Colt came to be, it burned deep inside.

"Ian, Gentry tells me you're a do-gooder." Smith chomped a bite of pizza, grease from the cheese dribbling down his chin. "Must have a lot of stories."

"Most don't make for pleasant dinner conversation." Ian reached for his water, remembering a little too late to smile politely.

"When are you leaving?" Jenna asked.

He stifled a snort at the transparent remark. "Not sure."

"But soon, right? Now that Colt is well, you must be eager to get on with your plans." Jenna ate her pizza with a knife and fork. That bugged him, even though it was of no consequence.

"Your mom will miss you, Ian," Sara added.

"She's not the only one," Gentry said.

Jenna paused midbite, her gaze darting from Gentry to Ian and Smith, then to Jed, who shrugged as if to say, "What the hell do I know?" Hunter shot his sister an unreadable look that she seemed to understand, given her confessionary tilt of the head and nonchalant shrug.

"I won't be dead." Ian looked at Gentry. "I'll be back from time to time."

When her family all stared at her, Gentry deflected. "Pass the pepperoni."

"From what I've heard, Haiti's riddled with malaria and cholera. Could you be a carrier?" Smith's smooth voice belied the sharp edge of his question.

"I'd never put Colt at risk, if that's what you're asking."

"But how can you be sure?" The large man swallowed an equally large bite of pizza. In his folksy tone, he added, "My doctor's always asking me if I've traveled out of the country recently, so I'm guessing it's possible to be a carrier without knowing it."

"Anything's possible," Ian admitted, hating the way Gentry's round eyes widened at Smith's revelation. "But not probable. I get all available immunizations and take every precaution."

"From what little I've read so far, infants' immune systems aren't fully developed," Smith said, as if he were now an expert.

"I'm aware." Ian sensed everyone wanting to put a few extra inches between themselves and him . . . just in case. "I've gone back and forth between developing nations for a dozen years and never once contracted or transferred a serious illness."

Everyone's posture relaxed slightly, until Smith drove another wedge between Ian and the Cabots. "There's always a first time."

Smith covered his strategy with a congenial smile. The guy was smoother than his beloved wines.

Ian had done a little reading, too. Restaurants hired people like Smith to help guests choose a good wine and then empty that customer's wallet through a combination of expertise and showmanship. Clearly, Smith had mastered the showmanship part. Would Gentry see through him or be caught in his spell again?

"Let's change the subject," Gentry suggested, reaching for another slice of pizza while carefully avoiding both Smith's and Ian's gazes.

"I want to take a minute and tell my grandson what good manners he has." Jed flashed a proud smile across the table to Ty. "Your daddy wasn't nearly as neat as you at your age." He winked at Hunter, who had to wipe grease from his chin. "Still isn't, it seems."

Ty didn't react much to that praise. Ian had worked with kids like him who'd survived trauma. Who'd had a rough start in the world with poor nutrition and poverty and chaos. Gentry had temporarily burst through Ty's wall with her playfulness by the lake, but it would be years before he'd have the sense of security that would help him fully connect with this family.

"Sara's a wonder woman." Hunter rubbed his wife's shoulder. "I'm constantly amazed at how smoothly she keeps things running with Ty. The calendar is loaded with appointments, Mommy and Me classes, and playdates. She's teaching him to be organized and neat, have good manners. She's amazing."

"I hope you're taking notes," Jenna said to her daughter.

Gentry's body stiffened beside Ian, who was about to defend Gentry's parenting style when Smith spoke up.

"I'll take notes, too." Smith winked at Gentry. "Next time we get together, we should probably talk about parenting expectations and stuff like that."

A flush rose up Gentry's neck. "How do you mean?"

"Heck if I know. But my sister and her husband debate things all the time, like whether kids should watch videos, or if sharing is a good or bad thing, or if time-outs work better than other consequences. Now they're trying to figure out if public school is better than private school."

Gentry's nostrils flared, a reflex warning that she was about to end this discussion. "My take is real simple, Smith. I'm probably an outlier, but I'm of the 'Play it by ear' parenting school of thought, because Colt's an individual, not a robot. He can't be programmed with certain inputs to get some desired output, and even if he could, I don't want that for him. I want him to explore himself and the world, which he can't do if he's bogged down by too much structure and expectation."

Sara and Hunter exchanged a look. Ian knew Gentry hadn't meant to offend them. She'd merely had her own philosophy and didn't want Smith to muck it up.

"Interesting perspective." Smith nodded noncommittally. "You certainly started him off with a unique name."

"You don't like Colton?" Gentry now picked at her cuticles beneath the table. Ian reached for her hand and squeezed.

"I like it fine." Smith shrugged. "Of course, maybe we can talk about his last name."

Jenna cleared her throat. Gentry's grip on Ian's hand turned her knuckles white. In a deceptively light voice, she managed, "We can talk about anything."

A name change would not be easy for Gentry to swallow. Neither would Jenna's "told you so" gaze.

Smith wiped his mouth and tossed his napkin on the table. "It's only a suggestion. Didn't mean to bring the whole dinner to a halt."

"Don't apologize." Gentry attempted a brighter smile. "He's your son, too."

"That's still a shock," Smith admitted.

"We all love him dearly, no matter what name he has," Sara said, breaking the tension.

"My family will, too, once they meet him," Smith said.

The energy in the room downshifted, turning to superficial conversation. Gentry grew particularly quiet. A rarity that suggested she wanted everyone to leave as soon as possible.

Sara must've picked up on her mood, because she'd barely finished eating when she said, "I hate to eat and run, but Ty's bedtime is in twenty minutes, and as already established, I like to keep him on schedule."

"No worries." Gentry kissed her brother and Sara and hugged Ty. She turned to her parents. "You two might as well go relax, too."

Jenna might've fought to stay if Jed hadn't gripped her arm. "Of course, sweetheart. I'm sure you're tired. It's been an exciting weekend for everyone. Smith, it's been nice to meet you." Jed then turned to Ian. "Ian, in case we don't see you before you take off, good luck down there in Haiti."

"Thank you." Ian shook Jed's hand.

Jed ushered Jenna out of the house, leaving Ian alone with Gentry and Smith.

"I didn't mean to make everyone uncomfortable," Smith said. "And I'm not trying to disrupt everything, Gentry. I only want to catch up on what I missed and figure out the best way you and I can go forward to give our son a semblance of normality."

"You don't need to apologize for wanting a voice, or wanting your son to share your name." Gentry shrugged. "Once I decided to keep

Colt, I should've tried to find you. If I were in your shoes, I'd be a lot less nice about all this."

"Can't do anything about the past, and besides, it's not about you or me." Smith crossed his arms. "Let's focus on the future for Colt's sake. He's what matters most."

Gentry exhaled with a smile. "Agreed."

"Maybe you'd consider hyphenating his last name to Cabot-Smith."

Ian couldn't fault Smith for wanting his child to share his name. And he had to admit that, all in all, Smith had handled this life-altering situation with grace.

"A compromise." Gentry nodded.

"I'm pretty good with those," Smith said.

Ian didn't belong in this conversation, so he headed to the dining table. "I'll clean up."

"Thanks," Gentry replied, then turned to Smith. "Excuse me for a minute."

Ian suspected she needed a few minutes alone with her son, even if he was sleeping. She'd said all the right things, but the realities of no longer having Colt to herself could not be easy to accept.

Smith watched Gentry go and then followed Ian into the kitchen. "You might tell me to go to hell, but I'm curious about your relationship with Gentry."

Ian raised a brow but said nothing.

"You're thinking it's none of my business, but considering how it could affect Colt, I think I'm entitled to a little information. Like, do you plan on being part of their lives after you leave this house?"

"Whatever does or doesn't happen, I'm sure Gentry will fill you in."

"Not good enough, Ian." Smith reached out to touch Ian's shoulder but dropped his hand before he made contact. "Is it fair for Colt to get attached to you if you won't be around? And if you hurt his mother, how will that affect my son? I can't control who Gentry dates, but I hope she, and you, will consider the bigger picture when making decisions."

Ian stared at Smith, his own thoughts bundled in a lump of knots—Farrah's disappointed tears, Archer's expectations, Gentry's vivid smile. "I'll never do anything to hurt Colt."

"But you're not fully committed." Smith widened his stance. "Do you expect Gentry to wait around and handle all this on her own while you're off chasing your other dreams?"

"Gentry's capable of making her own choices." Ian tossed the flatware into the sink with a clatter. "She doesn't need either of us making them for her."

"No, I don't suppose she does. But wouldn't you agree she'd be better off in a relationship with someone in this time zone who also has a permanent interest in Colt's welfare?"

Ian swallowed. Smith dealt his hand like a croupier. The man's interest in Gentry seemed piqued by the twenty-four hours he'd spent with her this weekend.

"I don't presume to decide what's best for her." And if Smith were smart, he wouldn't, either, not that Ian would give him that heads-up. "Should I assume this is a warning? Do you plan to seduce her again?"

"I won't push. But I'll be here for her and our son. If you really care about her happiness, you won't ask her to wait around for you to decide if and when you can squeeze her and Colt into your schedule."

"It's pretty presumptuous to assume she'd be interested in you if I bow out."

Smith didn't pull his punches. "She was before."

Gentry meandered into the kitchen, eyeballing them both. "Everything okay in here?"

"Peachy." Smith clapped his hands together. "I'll leave you two alone for the evening. I'd like to swing by in the morning to say goodbye to Colt before I catch my flight. Maybe then you and I can discuss bringing Colt to visit my family after Ian goes to Haiti."

Ian's jaw hurt from all the clenching it had done tonight.

"Of course," Gentry replied.

Smith kissed her cheek. "See you around nine, okay?"

"We'll be here," Ian said, slinging an arm over Gentry's shoulder, sending his own message to Smith.

"Good night." Smith nodded at Ian. "I can show myself out."

"Don't be silly," Gentry said, shrugging Ian off. "I'll walk you out."

As soon as they left the kitchen, Ian viciously crushed the pizza boxes, pretending that each one was Smith's head.

Chapter Eighteen

Bittersweet

According to *Merriam-Webster*: pleasure accompanied by suffering or regret

According to me: falling in love

Gentry returned to the kitchen to find Ian scrubbing the counters with enough vigor to strip their sheen. "You okay, McJ?"

"Yep." He neither smiled nor tossed the rag aside to pull her into a kiss. Each circular swipe of his arm coiled his energy tighter, until he looked like a viper waiting to strike.

She reached out to still him. "I think they're clean."

Ian released the rag. Sighing, he raked one hand through his beautiful waves of hair. Something *she'd* love to do. "Quite an evening."

From her perspective it had been brilliant. No arguments or tears or threats. Everyone made it through the entire meal without storming off. Not something that could be said about every Cabot get-together, especially not one with these stakes. "You don't like Smith, do you?"

"I don't know him well enough to make that call."

Oh, please. As if Ian needed more than two seconds to make one of his infamous snap judgments.

He tilted his head, leveling his gaze, and added, "Neither do you."

And there it was. His sobriety stung like a snapped rubber band.

"Maybe not, but this weekend went well. Smith didn't dump a barrel of guilt on me or push for anything unfair." She mentally tested out "Colton Cabot-Smith" for the thirtieth time in fifteen minutes. "We got along great."

"You sure did."

She blinked at his tone. "If you're jealous, then maybe we should work out our own stuff."

"What stuff?"

"Stuff like 'I can't stop thinking about what happened last weekend,' or 'Why can't we give this a shot?'" She wrapped her arms around his waist, her nose brushing against his chin, and then kissed his neck beneath his jaw. "It's Saturday night. Colt's asleep. The house is clean. I have to work tomorrow after Smith goes to the airport. Right now I just want to be with you. After that, we can take it one day at a time."

Ian tightened his hold on her, one hand behind her head, the other on her butt. He kissed her so hard and swift she lifted onto her toes.

"Is that a yes?" Her heartbeat thumped like a happy puppy's tail.

He nodded, kissing her again. She could only assume that a bit of envy or possessiveness due to Smith's presence spurred his reckless about-face. Didn't matter. Right now she'd take what she could get and have faith that everything would work out.

"Let's go to your room so we can be noisy." She winked, clasping his hand and leading him upstairs.

They fell onto his bed, their hungry hands quickly undressing each other in between kisses and fondling and murmurs.

Ian's breath heated her cheek and neck. Urgent kisses fueled her desperation to be closer, as if she were feeding off his need for her. Skin-to-skin friction sent goose bumps tumbling across her body until she became sweat-soaked.

He set his teeth to the tender spot where her neck and shoulder joined and bit her—sending sharp pleasure tripping along her nerves. His eyes remained open, watching her. Demanding a connection. Wrenching emotions out of some hidden corner of her heart or brain or lungs, or wherever it was that those vulnerabilities were stored.

Arousal flooded her heart with excitement and with trepidation about her defenselessness. She groped his back, the sheets, dug her heels into the mattress, anything to gain purchase and brace against the waves of pleasure.

Their climax shattered her, body and soul, unlike the superficial gratification she'd known with other men, including Smith. As she lay there, breathless and overwhelmed, with Ian's body covering hers like a warm blanket, she held back the tears that would expose the unfamiliar, hot, sticky feelings boiling over like caramelized sugar.

She closed her eyes, memorizing this feeling. This moment of connection. The comfort in the dark. The sound of his heart beating in her ear. The scent of their coupling and the sheer warmth of his being.

"I'll miss you." He kissed her, stoking so much want.

"Then stay longer." Her impish remark could not keep her heart from sinking when he didn't concede.

He rolled onto his back and tucked her body against his while gently tracing the line of her hips and waist with his work-roughened hand. Despite the exhausted satisfaction seeping from her pores, she sensed his building tension.

"What's going on in your head?" Rather than meet his gaze, she walked her fingers down the ladder of his abs, hopeful he'd open up.

He grabbed her fingers and kissed the tips. "Being with you makes me happy."

Her heart lit up a like a birthday cake with fifty candles. "Then why do you look sad?"

He shrugged. "I'm being selfish."

"It's not selfish to allow yourself to be happy, Ian. We're not hurting anyone."

He kissed her head again and tightened his hold. "I wish I foresaw a better outcome."

She propped up onto her elbow, patting the bedding all around him as if searching for something. "Where is it?"

"Where's what?" His brows knit in confusion.

"The Magic 8 Ball, or crystal ball, or whatever voodoo trinket you've got that's showing you the future."

When she chuckled, he wrestled with her, pinning her to the pillows. He pulled back and stared at her, then planted a kiss so tender it made her want to cry. "I never expected this . . . you . . . I hate to leave."

"So stay. You know I'm a disaster without you."

"You have everything you need here and here." He placed two fingers at her temple and then lowered them to her breastbone.

"You mean my dirty mind and my tatas?" she joked.

"Those too." He grinned; then he rolled onto his back and stared at the ceiling.

She needed a quick fix to rescue the night from his darkening mood.

"I have a plan." Her pronouncement got his attention. "When you get to Jacmel, locate the best area for cell service so we can keep in touch with FaceTime and daily phone sex."

When Ian chuckled, his eyes turned the golden green of a Bartlett pear and crinkled around the edges. "I'll pitch a tent by the nearest cell tower."

"Nice pun." She chuckled, but deep down she knew that keeping these feelings alive with so little contact would be difficult, if not impossible. Then again, Gentry thrived on proving people wrong, and she was determined to prove *everyone* wrong where she and Ian were concerned.

She nestled back into the crook of his shoulder and stared through the window at the stars. Pinpricks of light suspended above the world for eons, connecting time and space, all the while inspiring generations of dreams and magic and hope. "Let's promise to look at the stars each night and think of each other. Maybe even make a little wish, like 'I hope Ian had freshwater today,' or 'I hope Gentry gets more than four hours of sleep tonight.'"

"How like you to ask for miracles." He squeezed her as he smiled.

Her entire body responded. "Every time you relax enough to joke, it feels like a home run. Better than that—a grand slam."

"Thank you for bringing out a side of me that no one else ever has. I feel free here with you." His voice fell to something of a whisper.

"I love that."

He brushed a fallen piece of her hair behind her ear. "Me too."

Gentry had never said the words "I love you" to anyone outside of her family, and even within that group, she didn't say them often. As far as she'd been concerned, falling in love ranked up there with swimming in a tank of sharks, and making that exclamation would be like tossing chum in the water. Chances of survival: almost nil. No man had inspired her to take that risk until now, but even so, she'd never say it first.

She'd heard about "lightning strike" love stories, like with Hunter and Sara. Was this how they'd felt, or were they more certain? She wished someone would invent a love meter, like a mood ring that turned a certain color when two people felt the same way about each other. A clear sign that it wasn't one-sided, or wouldn't fall apart.

Gentry believed herself to be in love. Worse, she wanted to shout it loud and clear because she sensed he needed to hear it almost as much as she wanted to say it. But for all of her bold moves in the past, she didn't dare utter those three words now, because if he didn't say them back, she'd be crushed.

The piercing sound of her son's rousing cry emanated from the baby monitor in the living room.

"I'll go," Ian said, easing out of bed. "You relax."

"Thanks." Gentry rested her head on her fist and watched his gloriously nude body in motion. Long-limbed perfection.

"You're welcome." He pulled his boxers on and left her alone. "Be back in a few."

She rolled onto her stomach and stretched her limbs across the mattress, inhaling the scent of the pillow where Ian's head had lain. She decided then not to wash his sheets after he left. That way, when she missed him, she could come up here, lie on the bed, and remember.

Looking again at the stars, she knew that her wish would be the same every night. *Keep Ian safe, and bring him home to me.*

◆ ◆ ◆

When Ian lifted Colt out of the bassinet, Colt gripped his finger and bounced his head off Ian's shoulder. The baby's face pinched as he whimpered. "You're too big for this little cradle, buddy." He grabbed Quackers and tucked it under his arm like Colby said Gentry used to do. "Let's get you something to fill your tummy."

Ian padded along the hallway to the kitchen and managed to use his teeth and one hand to fill a bottle and slide it into the warmer while keeping Colt safely nestled against his chest. While they waited for the formula to heat, Ian caught himself stroking Colt's hair.

He loved this child, who now trusted him completely. Who recognized him and his voice. It shouldn't have surprised him that Smith had been smitten. Nor should he resent the man for being protective of his son, or wanting a shot at Gentry. But resent him he did.

"If you really care about her happiness, you won't ask her to wait around . . ." Shaking off the memory of Smith's interrogation, Ian removed the bottle from the warmer and fed Colt while strolling through the living room.

That first day, when Ian had arrived with his duffel and ass-backward assumptions about Gentry and her family, he couldn't have predicted how quickly and completely his life would change. Incredibly, this palace felt like home.

Everything about it had Gentry's eclectic stamp on it, from the elegant sleekness to the quirky artwork—like that abstract bronze flutist—to the feminine floral throw pillows in the otherwise starkly modern space.

Original, like the woman herself. He smiled at Colt, thinking him lucky to have a mom like that. Ian wondered what life might have been like with a bit of a rebel influence guiding his outlook and choices. Who might he be now if he hadn't been brought up the Crawford way?

Colt's saucer-wide eyes stared up at Ian even as he sucked at the bottle's nipple with all his might.

It seemed as if the kid had grown six inches in mere weeks. In a few months Colt would be crawling, maybe even pulling himself up onto two feet. "Who will *you* become, little man? Will you take after your Uncle Hunter and become a businessman? Will you have more of a free spirit, like your mom? Will you be a charmer, like your dad? Will you remember me?" As soon as he voiced those words, he stopped himself. Or, more honestly, the rest of his questions lodged in his throat and made it impossible for him to speak.

It hurt to think—to know—that the likelihood of being in the picture a year or two from now was slim. Not because he wouldn't want to be, but because he'd been around enough to know that wishing for something wasn't enough.

Choices mattered. Commitments counted. And now, Ian was confronted with a bunch of important choices, some of which seemed decidedly against him, and some of which would define his character.

Before he'd met Gentry, he'd made a promise to Archer and to his dad's memory. What kind of man would he be if he walked away after others had committed time and money to their venture? After he'd pitched Marcus Fairfax and gotten that man's son involved?

He'd already failed to live up to the commitment he'd made to Farrah. Did he want his legacy to become a string of broken promises? His heart might yearn to stay here, but he'd never made any promise to Gentry. If he failed to finish what he'd started in Haiti, he'd lose his self-respect.

Colt finished the bottle in record time, so Ian burped him and changed his diaper before bringing him upstairs to sleep in his crib for the first time. He laid him on the larger mattress surrounded by padded railings, then tucked Quackers in the corner below Colt's feet.

Ian accidentally bumped the plush mobile overhead, which caused Colt to pump his tiny arms and legs.

Ian wound the mobile, which then rotated while playing the lullaby song. He stared at Colt, who deserved more than the threadbare mascot of love Gentry had clung to as a child. He'd need focused love and attention to thrive. He'd need a reliable, familiar, steady support system.

What Colt didn't need was a man who'd be even less present than Ian's own father had been. Who'd miss out on more of his young life than he'd ever see. Who'd leave all the hard work of parenting to Gentry instead of being there with her, regularly sharing the burden and the joy.

Smith had been right. Ian *shouldn't* stand in the way of a relationship that Gentry might have with any man who could give her the kind of family life she deserved. The kind he knew, deep down, she and Colt needed. All evening, he'd been thinking about only himself and what he stood to lose . . . not what Gentry might be passing up.

For all her feigned nonchalance, what Gentry needed most was the security of abiding love. Colt would flourish more if his mother's needs were met. If Ian loved them both, he needed to be strong enough to step out of the picture and let Smith, or someone else, step in.

"You look morose. Do you hate Brahms?" Gentry surprised him from behind, then bent over the crib and touched her son, whispering, "He looks so tiny in this crib."

"He's too big for the bassinet now." Ian's throat ached. "Time to move him."

"I'm not ready." Gentry laid one hand on Ian's shoulder, but her gaze remained lovingly on her son.

"We have to do what's right when it counts, not when it suits us."

"It's hard to let go. I like having him close." She smiled at Ian in a way that acknowledged an "I'm pathetic, aren't I?" clarity.

The pain of his own clarity struck with surprising force. It would be tough to follow his own advice, but he had to if he wanted to be a better man than his father. "Gentry, I'm leaving for Haiti in a few days."

Her lips parted slightly. "You have enough money already?"

"Farrah's ring will give me enough to return and get set up. Archer's been on me about losing momentum with the alliances we'd been building. Fairfax's son is ready to fly out. It's time for me to go."

"Do you already have your ticket?" Her eyes glistened.

He shook his head.

She twisted her arms around her waist like she might feel sick. "What happened in the last ten minutes to make this so urgent?"

He glanced down at Colt, whose eyelids had begun to droop as he drifted to sleep. Ian had spent his life helping to repair broken families all around the globe. Yet somehow, for a little while, he'd fooled himself into thinking he could stand in the way of one that could become whole. "Let's go talk in my room."

Gentry kissed her finger and pressed it to Colt's forehead before walking out of the nursery ahead of Ian. She plopped onto the edge of the mattress, arms crossed, expression hot. "What's going on?"

"This has nothing to do with my feelings for you."

"Oh, brother. That's a line of bull if I ever heard it, Ian." Her mouth fell into a grim line, and that chin began its slow, proud rise.

"It's not." He sat beside her. "Not long ago you suggested we were both sort of footnotes in our parents' lives. I didn't agree before, but now I see some truth to it."

"What's that got to do with you leaving?"

"Every day we pretend this can work—that we're some kind of a family—it only makes it harder to accept the facts."

"What facts?"

He clasped her hand, turning it over in his. "We've told some pretty lies to ourselves to justify taking what we wanted. The truth is that I'm not Colt's dad. Smith is. I'm not going to be in this country, let alone this time zone, for most of the next year or longer. Smith is. I'm not the guy with whom you should be trying to build Colt's family. Smith is. I can't ask you to wait for me. It's not fair to you or your son."

"Did I just land on the 'Go Directly to Jail' square in Monopoly? How are we right back to where things started *before* we got together?"

"We're not where we started." He squeezed her hand. "I *wish* I could go back there and have had enough self-control to avoid getting here, where we both hurt. I did this . . . to you and to myself. If I were the only one who'd have to pay the price down the road for rolling the dice, that might be okay. But I'm not. The last thing I want is to hurt you. But it's better to hurt a little now, when there's time for you to start things off with Smith on a strong foot, than for me to hang on and mess things up, and still end up like I did with Farrah."

"I'm not Farrah. Why can't you see that?"

"I know you're not Farrah, but she also didn't have a son." He looked through the door toward the nursery. "Look me in the eye and tell me that you want an absentee father figure for Colt."

Her gaze dropped to her feet for a moment, and so did her tone. "So now I'm supposed to swap you for Smith? It doesn't work that way, you know."

"I know. But with me clearly out of the picture, it'll smooth the way for a better relationship with Smith. He's got to be feeling territorial about his son."

Gentry's eyes narrowed. "Did he say something to you?"

"If I were any kind of man, he shouldn't have to. And if you're being completely honest, you'll admit that you want more than I can offer."

At least she didn't lie. This would be a real goodbye, and that ache settled in his chest like banked embers, turning his lungs to ash.

He kissed her temple. "The jealous part of me wishes Smith were a bad guy, but he isn't. It's wonderful for Colt that his dad is coming into his life, and that Smith's family will embrace you both. If there's even a slight chance that you three could be a real family, that's as good of a reason as any for me to step aside."

She yanked her hand free. "I hate that everyone else always thinks they know what's best for me."

"I'm not telling you anything you haven't basically told me yourself since we first met. This is Colt's shot at the kind of family neither of us ever had."

"*We* could give him one if you stay here." She reached for him, but he kept his hands tucked beneath his armpits. "Colt can have *two* fathers."

He shook his head. "You're putting too much faith in me, Gentry. The other night I was listening to Farrah cry about broken plans and missing me, but the whole time I was thinking of you. What does my moving on so easily say about me?"

"It says Farrah wasn't the right woman."

"Or maybe the reason I globe-trot is because, like it or not, I'm like my dad, and my life will be a series of ins and outs, here-and-gones. That's all I know, and I'm not so sure I'd be good at staying put, even if it appeals to me right now."

Gentry shot off the mattress. "Fine, then. Sell the ring, buy your ticket, and go save the world."

"Gentry—"

"Don't! Let me deal with this"—she motioned her hands in circles in front of him—"my way. Sorry if I'm not contained like you. This is how *I* process. I let it out, and usually not in the healthiest way. So, since you're here and all at peace, I'm going out for a bit while you watch Colt. Okay?"

He stared at her, red hair flowing, eyes lit with frustration, body fidgeting and eager to run. "Where will you go?"

She glared at him, eyes burning bright. "In a couple of days, you won't know what I'm doing or who I'm doing it with, so get used to it."

She stormed out of his room like a charging bull.

When she left, all the energy and light in the room went with her.

He made his choice; now he'd need to keep his word.

Chapter Nineteen

Conflagration

According to *Merriam-Webster*: a large disastrous fire

According to me: Ian's decision

Gentry raced her car along the lakeside road, hugging the centerline throughout the roadway's twists and turns. She imagined her car looking like a cartoon sketch, with swirls of leaves and smoke funneling in its wake.

Colby would still be at the restaurant, and Gentry's mom would be the last person to encourage her to change Ian's mind, or to offer comfort. Sara might be her best hope—she liked Ian. She'd also understand Gentry's feelings. After all, Sara had followed her heart from a young age to be with Hunter.

Gentry practically dive-bombed Hunter's driveway, only then thinking to call and warn them of her arrival. It *was* Saturday night. Given Hunter's and Sara's tendencies toward tradition and schedules, an unannounced nine thirty drop-in might be quite ill-timed.

"Sis, what's up?" Hunter's voice sounded relaxed, not strained. A relief. Perhaps she'd caught them before they'd disrobed.

"I'm in your driveway." She sucked the blood from her torn thumbnail. "Can I come in?"

"Everything okay?"

She scowled at the media screen of her dashboard as if he could see her, and snapped, "Would I be here if it were?"

If she guessed right, he'd probably yanked the phone away from his head and frowned at it. "Come on in."

She slung her purse over her shoulder and exited the car. By the time she hit the porch, Hunter had opened the front door.

"Did something happen with Smith after we left?" He might've just tried to hug her, but she was too intent on storming the entry to be sure.

"No. I need to talk to Sara." And then, upon seeing his perturbed expression, she added, "And you, too, if you want. Warning—it's girl stuff. About Ian."

"So *not* Smith?" Hunter crossed his arms, his brows rising above the rims of his glasses.

In a way, she supposed it was about Smith, too. Gah! She still had to see *him* tomorrow before he left, too. "Not directly."

Hunter slung his arm over her shoulder and began walking her toward the family room. Hunter reserved most of his affection for Sara and Ty, and sometimes Colby. Gentry had rarely been on the receiving end of his demonstrative side, although since she'd started working with him, he'd been better.

Still, his affection was like an ice-cream cone in winter . . . a treat but somehow "off."

Sara set aside *A Parent's Guide to Developmental Delays* when Gentry entered the room. She tucked her feet under her butt and patted the sofa cushion beside her. "What's happened?"

Gentry flopped herself onto the sofa, which triggered memories of the short time she'd lived here during the earliest weeks of her pregnancy. She'd been self-centered then, and as much as she liked to think that she'd matured, right now she had her doubts. She could've given

Colt all the stability he'd ever need if she'd simply handed him over to Hunter and Sara like she'd promised. Instead, she'd kept him. Now she was still looking to have it all—her son, his father, and her lover. "Ian's going to Haiti."

Sara and Hunter exchanged one of those secret-message looks that long-married couples share. Once they finished their telepathy, Sara turned her gentle blue eyes back on Gentry. She reached across the cushions and touched Gentry's calf, looking at her the way she'd seen Sara look at Ty when trying to teach him something. "Wasn't that always his plan?"

Gentry sat up as if singed and then hugged a throw pillow. "Yes, but . . ."

"You thought you could change his mind with the right . . . motivation?" Sara ventured, at which point Hunter covered his ears, his face pinched in a way that silently shouted "TMI."

He opened his eyes, still shaking his head to clear out the image. "I'll need some wine." He scurried to the kitchen to avoid hearing whatever Sara and Gentry might say next.

"I'm not stupid," Gentry insisted, despite the fact of her being there with this complaint proving quite the contrary. "I didn't think I'd keep him from leaving. I just didn't think it'd be so sudden, or so final."

"Ah." Sara tugged the small blanket over her knees. "Perhaps Smith's arrival nudged him along."

Hunter returned with some glasses and an open bottle of cabernet, which he proceeded to pour, giving himself the largest glass. He sat on the arm of the sofa nearest his wife and stared at Gentry. She knew he meant to be supportive, but he had a way of making her feel interrogated.

"Smith didn't help things, that's for sure." She focused on Sara, who'd repositioned herself to face Gentry more directly. "My mom's pushing me to make us a 'real' family so I don't have to share custody. Apparently now Ian agrees. It's like he doesn't even care . . ."

"He cares." Hunter chugged a bit of his wine.

Gentry shot him a questioning look, doubting Ian had confided anything in her brother.

"I watched him during dinner. He bristled anytime Smith opened his mouth, but his hands are tied, Gentry." Hunter tugged one foot across the opposite knee. "Biology aside, Ian's got his plans. You and I already discussed why that drive isn't going anywhere."

"What are you talking about?" Sara asked him.

Gentry waved a hand in the air. "Ian's insane commitment to building an EMT training center in Jacmel."

"Why do you think it's insane?" Sara pressed.

Gentry set down her glass so she could tick her fingers. "Because the living conditions sound abysmal. Because he could be kidnapped. Because getting the money and supplies and expertise together isn't the same as keeping them in play year after year. And most importantly, because I don't think this is *his* dream. He's giving up a chance at happiness here in order to chase a ghost."

"Careful, sis. Given some of our family's issues, I get why you might question Ian's motives. But his family was intact. He's an only child. He's got a real interest in keeping his father's memory and name alive. That's powerful stuff."

"Why can't he do it like a normal person—get married, have kids, do good works around here?" Gentry grabbed her wine a bit too hard, so it sloshed over the rim.

"Maybe what makes him so appealing to you is that he isn't normal." Sara smoothed the blanket, her voice soft but knowing. "You never did like anyone or anything traditional."

Leave it to Sara to stop Gentry's rant cold. Some truths could not be denied.

"Let's step back a second and talk about Smith." Hunter leaned forward to set his now-empty glass on the coffee table. "You two were joking around like old buddies tonight. He got along well with everyone, including your mom. Is there any chance that you two might turn coparenting into something more?"

"Oh God, Hunter." Gentry slapped her forehead. "If you agree with my mom, we all better head underground because the apocalypse is nigh."

"I'm not suggesting you force it, but it would be convenient if it worked out, wouldn't it?" He crossed his arms with a shrug.

Gentry wrinkled her nose. "I can't go there mentally. I like the way things are now, with Ian." *I'm in love, you fools! Can't you tell? Don't I look different?*

"But he's leaving." Sara folded her hands in her lap.

"I *know* that. It's why I'm here. I need advice, not a blow-by-blow of the obvious." She leaned forward, elbows on her knees, and buried her head in her hands. "Sorry. I'm a wreck."

"Do you honestly want my advice?" Sara asked, unfazed by Gentry's mood.

Gentry and Hunter both stared at Sara, and Gentry swallowed her dread. "Yes, please."

"Do you care about Ian . . . maybe even love him a little?" Sara leaned closer now.

Love! Yes, now you see. Now we're on the right track.

Cold sweat broke out along Gentry's hairline and forearms. She couldn't quite handle this much intimacy filling the space between them, so she nodded, eyes downcast.

"Then let him go."

Gentry shivered from the ice-water effect of Sara's words.

Still, Sara continued. "Guilt or manipulation won't make him care more, and either one could backfire. And even if you succeeded in convincing him to stay, he'd end up wrestling with doubts about that choice forever. Find the grace to let him go with love. What's meant to be will be, Gentry. Have faith in that and in yourself."

Hunter laid his hand on Sara's shoulder and kissed her head. "She knows what she's talking about. I almost lost everything before I figured out that I couldn't control fate. I can only control myself." Then he grinned like an imp—unusual for him. "Not that I don't still sometimes think the world would be better off if I could control everything."

Sara chuckled, stretching up to pat his cheek. "More efficient, maybe, but not necessarily better."

Gentry chugged what remained of her wine, mulling over Sara's so-called wisdom.

"Adulting" sucked.

Life before Colt had been simple. Gentry missed the freedom to run off, rant, make mistakes, and generally start fresh every morning. Now she had to be accountable. Her decisions all affected her son. Her reputation mattered because it would affect him, too.

Losing Ian before they'd had time to cement their relationship was a cruel joke. Who needed to feel this way? Maybe her mother *was* right. A pragmatic relationship with a relaxed, easy-on-the-eyes man like Smith would never hurt this much. It could be comfortable and fun, and provide Colt with stability. And everyone, including Ian and her, agreed Colt should be the priority.

Smith wouldn't be killed or kidnapped on the job. They'd have an endless supply of good wine, clean water, and laughter. Her son could have his father in his life on a regular basis. Would that all be better in the long run?

"Gentry?" Hunter asked.

"Hm?" The effect of the wine wound its way through her limbs.

"I have one last suggestion." He looked so serious, her stomach dropped.

"Hit me . . ." Gentry held her breath.

"Focus on Colt and work, and let everything else sort itself out. We need you to be on top of your end of the marketing campaign. The launch is literally around the corner. Its success or failure will have a huge impact on our kids' lives, too."

Work. She'd let that fall to the bottom of her to-do list. Unlike Hunter—and Ian—she didn't consider her job a legacy. It didn't give her a sense of identity. Her photography and blog better represented who she was and what mattered to her, but that seemed frivolous. Maybe that's, in essence, who or what she still was despite months of trying to be more. Frivolous.

No wonder Ian was leaving, like she'd always known he would.

Two hours ago, she'd been optimistic. Now everything seemed upside down and inside out.

She looked at her brother and Sara. They had it all: professional drive and respect, a lovely family and home, confidence and security. Everything she wanted.

"I'm going to do *exactly* what you say. I've got all afternoon tomorrow to address what I didn't quite finish last week. Monday morning, I'll hit the ground running. If Ian can walk away so easily, then he isn't worth waiting for anyhow."

That sounded more convincing than it felt, but she'd always subscribed to the "Fake it till you make it" theory.

Newly determined, Gentry stood. "Sorry I dropped in unexpectedly, but thanks for listening. I'll be seeing Smith off in the morning. What'd you all think of him, by the way?"

"Very amiable." Sara nodded, although her glum expression proved that she empathized with Gentry's struggle.

"He handled himself well under the circumstances. And he's not holding a grudge, which means he's more than fair." Hunter nodded thoughtfully. "He could be good for you and Colt. In any case, you'll have help with parenting now, which is huge."

Not as huge as having Ian's help, but still, in the long run, who knew? Who knew anything, really?

"All things considered, I lucked out with Smith's attitude. I guess I'll be getting on a plane soon to take Colt to meet his family. I wonder what they'll think of *me*?" Gentry picked up her empty glass to take it to the kitchen.

"Depends on your mood . . . and your outfit," Hunter teased. His comment was met with a gentle backhand from Sara. "She knows I'm kidding . . . sort of."

"Just for that, you can put this in the dishwasher for me." Gentry handed Hunter her glass. "I'm outta here."

She kissed him goodbye and returned to her car.

Thousands of stars lit up the black sky, as if the whole galaxy had shown up for a concert. An hour ago those stars had promised a connection to Ian, but now they were nothing more than a reminder of a magnificent dream that hadn't come true.

◆ ◆ ◆

"Are you sure you don't want to join me at the diner for lunch?" Ian's mother asked as they exited church.

"Not today." He squinted into the sunlight, watching dozens of parents wrangle their kids into their cars. Families bound for baseball games or birthday parties.

Last night after Gentry had run off to cool down, Ian had sat in the nursery, staring at Colt and thinking about his life. Before Gentry returned, he'd gone back to his room. From there, he heard her check on Colt, but she didn't come to Ian, and he didn't push himself on her.

This morning, she'd been quiet and polite, resolved to accept his decision. He'd left the house before Smith arrived, mostly because he didn't want to see that guy again. It had been hard enough to let go of Gentry, and harder to suggest that she be open to a relationship with Smith. He didn't need to torture himself by standing on the sidelines to watch that happen.

His mother squeezed his arm. "I've never known you to pass up apple pie."

"I'm not good company today." He'd barely mustered the energy to shave. Not even the thought of fries and pie made him happy.

"You're usually riding a high before you take off for Haiti." Her tone held no judgment, only a question.

"I know." He let out a sigh, wishing he could be carried away with that breath.

His mother's eyes looked older today. Tired. Even a little sad. "Care to tell me why you aren't more excited?"

He patted her arm and kissed her cheek. "Not at the moment, Mom. My flight leaves in forty-two hours. I'll swing by to say goodbye before I go. Right now I need some space."

She wrapped him in a hug. He held her and rested his cheek on her head.

"I love you, Ian," she said, her voice slightly muffled by his body. "You are your father's son. A man with a heart bigger than the earth itself. I'm proud of you, and I know your father would be, too."

His nose tingled, but he didn't cry. He didn't do anything other than give his mom an extratight squeeze and choke out a thank-you. A month ago that sentiment would've fed his pride. This morning he was too aware that being like his father might not be quite as wonderful as he'd always thought.

He released her and walked her to her car.

"Don't you want a ride?" she asked when he didn't walk to the passenger side.

"I think I'll walk a bit."

"You can't walk to Lake Sandy from here!"

He'd walked much farther, and under more harsh conditions, in his life. "I'll figure it out, Mom."

She nodded, taking the hint. "I'll take you to the airport on Tuesday. Let me know what time to pick you up."

"I can grab an Uber."

She went still, her eyes growing misty. "Ian, when you go off to these places, I never know if it's the last time I'll see you. Let me take you to the airport."

He stared at her, having never given any thought to the stress his choices forced on his mother. She'd already lost a husband to Haiti, and Ian was her only child. God, he could be stupid. "Of course, Mom. But you don't have to worry about me. I'm careful."

So had his father been, until he hadn't. Of course, people died every day in every imaginable way. Bizarre accidents and terrible violence occurred around the corner just as often as they did around the world. He wouldn't live his life in fear of danger that "might" happen. Having goals, experiencing new things, being grateful. Those made for a good life, no matter how long it lasted.

He kissed his mother's cheek and then closed her car door once she was seated behind the wheel. After she drove away, he walked back into the now-empty church and sat in a pew.

Eyes closed, head bent, he sought reassurance about the path he'd chosen. He sought strength to be able to do the right thing for Gentry, Colt, and those he, Stanley, and Archer hoped to help. He sought peace, too, but that one eluded him.

◆ ◆ ◆

Tuesday morning, Ian rose before the sun and packed his duffel. He gathered his towels for the laundry. Before leaving the room, he stood in its center, committing its details to memory. Not just the color of the paint, or the shimmer of the gauze curtain, but the memories it held. The first impression he'd had, the first time Gentry had kissed him, the restless nights he'd spent fighting his feelings for her, the afternoon he'd fallen asleep with Colt in this bed. A lifetime lived out in less than a month.

He wished things had been warmer between Gentry and him these past two days, but he respected her need for distance. Last night he'd almost gone to her room to satisfy the overwhelming need to be close to her, but that would've been another mistake and made things even harder today.

He left his things in the hallway and crept into Colt's dark room. Babies looked angelic in their sleep, arms overhead, faces turned to one side, features relaxed and peaceful. For Colt, that was a rarity.

Colt's slumber gave Ian an excuse to remain silent. Not that he could have found the words to describe the difficulty of leaving this young child behind or the hopes he had for Colt's future.

Ian had saved many lives. Befriended and assisted many children. But nothing compared with the awesome responsibility of having an infant depend on him for everything, day after day. Or seeing those dark-blue eyes drinking in every new experience. Or feeling the trusting weight of this baby against his chest each day.

These past several weeks had given him a taste of fatherhood. Some days he'd caught himself projecting ahead. Thinking about whether Colt would like baseball or football. Whether he'd be a good student. Whether he'd be artistic. In those daydreams Ian had been there by Colt's side, at a game or recital or spelling bee. Fanciful notions that came from a corner of his soul Ian had never explored.

He pressed the heels of his palms against his wet eyes and whispered, "Love you," before walking away and closing the nursery door. His mother would be arriving in fifteen minutes to whisk him off to the airport.

He heaved his duffel over one shoulder and gathered the towels. When he got down to the living room, he found Gentry in her robe, seated on the sofa, hair pinned up in some knot. It reminded him a bit of the first time he'd shown up here, when she'd been in that same robe—frazzled and overwhelmed.

"Good morning." She stood, hands buried in her robe's pockets. The first hint of sun peeked through the trees behind her, glinting off the gold highlights in her red hair.

"Good morning." Ian set the duffel on the floor and placed the bundle of linens on the sofa. "Didn't expect to see you this early."

"Thought you'd make a clean getaway, did you?" Her sly smile popped into place for a flash; then she dropped her gaze to the ground. Within another second, she recovered and raised her chin.

"I planned to leave a note." Ian took a few steps closer. "You've been quiet these past two days. I wanted to respect your space."

She nodded, blinking as if to stave off tears, and attempted another smile. "I've been thinking a lot, so it's no wonder if you've been confused."

Whenever she derided herself, it cut him up. He wanted to hold her, but he didn't think it'd be welcome. "I like your spontaneity. I hope this change isn't permanent."

Gentry shrugged. "I'd hoped to find brilliant words—or at least eloquent ones—to sum up all of my feelings. But I'm not Sara or Colby. I'm not good at it, so you're stuck settling for this." She walked to him, pulling Quackers out of her pocket.

He frowned, puzzled, as he looked at the matted toy she held out. "And what, exactly, can he say to me that you can't?"

"Everything." She pressed the plush toy to his chest. "I want you to have him, Ian. He's pretty good company when you feel alone . . ." Her voice was strained now, so she forced him to take hold of the duck and then dropped her arms.

He trembled. Of all the expensive and extravagant things Gentry owned, Quackers was, by far, her most precious. He thrust it back at her. "I can't take this, Gentry. It means so much to you."

Twenty-plus years of love, to be precise.

She shook her head. "Please take him. I want you to have him. I want you to know . . . just that. Just know . . ."

His phone pinged. No doubt his mother was outside in her car, waiting to drive him to the airport. He cursed under his breath. Gentry sucked her lips inward, biting down hard to keep from speaking or crying or both.

Unable to resist any longer, he grabbed her into a hug and squeezed her so tight she coughed. "If I didn't love you, this would be much easier," he said, right before he kissed her. He cupped her wet cheeks, and she wiped at his as he stared into her eyes. "Be happy. Don't doubt yourself. Don't settle for less than you want. And don't forget to wish on those stars, Gentry."

She sniffled and kissed him again, then pushed him away and touched her fingers to her mouth. "Don't take this wrong, but I'm going to try to forget all about you, Ian Crawford."

She would, too, of that he was sure. She'd spent a lifetime building that defense mechanism, and he could hardly begrudge her whatever she needed in order to ease her pain.

His phone pinged again. "I have to go."

"I know." Her chin wobbled, and new tears fell from her eyes. She followed him to the door. He'd gotten a few steps down the walkway when he heard her call out, "I love you, too."

He stopped and looked over his shoulder. The joy from hearing that declaration became muted by guilt. He'd encouraged her feelings for him even though he knew what it would cost her. A terrible thing to do to a person, especially to one with so little faith in love. Shame cascaded over him, killing any temptation he might've otherwise had to drop his duffel and run back for another kiss. "Goodbye, Gentry."

He watched her nod and swallow whatever words were stuck in her throat. She stepped backward and closed the door between them. His body ached, but he forced his legs to carry him to the car.

His mother didn't say anything until they'd merged onto I-5 North. "It's not easy, is it?"

He stared at the pavement ahead, a luxury not found in most byways of Haiti. He thought of all the times he'd left Farrah with a quick kiss and a care package neatly tucked in his bag. It had never gutted him. Then again, he'd assumed that she'd be there waiting for him when he returned. And by the time Farrah had grown tired of him and his choices, he'd grown used to life without her. He doubted he'd be able to say the same about Gentry.

"No." He had nothing more to share. If his mother had questions about Quackers, she kept them to herself.

"If it helps, I doubt Gentry and her son are going anywhere. Her family is here. She's busy being a mother. You can keep in touch. If it is meant to be, it will be, Ian."

But Ian knew better. Nothing in life happened in a vacuum. The choices people made affected outcomes. He'd made a choice, and he would live with the fallout, no matter how painful.

Chapter Twenty

Catalyst

According to *Merriam-Webster*: a substance that enables a chemical reaction to proceed at a usually faster rate or under different conditions (as at a lower temperature) than otherwise possible

According to me: Miss Linda

The first week Colt had spent at day care with Miss Linda, the woman had been patient, blaming his fussiness on the transition. The second week, Miss Linda became determined—for surely someone with her extensive experience could solve the problem better than Colt's young mother. By the end of the fourth week, Miss Linda admitted defeat.

At four months old, Colt had yet to outgrow colic. Even the Cucumber, Dr. Evans, had expressed some surprise with its persistence, although she'd had a few other young patients like him in the course of her practice.

"Ms. Cabot, I'm sorry, but I can't have Colt here until he outgrows this phase. There are only two of us managing eight young children. Colt requires too much attention. It's not fair to the others. Plus, his constant crying affects the other kids. Perhaps in another two months or so, we can try again." Miss Linda stood, hands clasped in front of her body, resolute in her decision.

Gentry held Colt while glancing around the light-filled walkout basement–turned–day care, with its butter-yellow walls, multiple easels, carpeted play area, and miniature library. As on the day when she'd first visited, several toddlers now played together with colorful cardboard blocks. The homey environment and intimate group of children had seemed like the perfect solution for Colt. Miss Linda, a middle-aged woman with cherubic cheeks and a friendly smile, had appeared to be an ideal caregiver. Apparently not so, on either count.

Gentry was accustomed to being spurned, but witnessing her *son's* first rejection flayed her calloused heart. "No, we won't try again. If you can't handle Colt before he's even able to crawl or walk or get himself into real trouble, how can I trust you to care for him later?"

"It's not a matter of my abilities, Ms. Cabot."

"I disagree." Gentry flashed back to memories of Ian patiently tending to Colt, even when her son had cried for hours. "I've seen a competent caretaker not only manage Colt but help him thrive. If you and your assistant aren't intuitive, ingenious, or interested enough to engage him, that is definitely not *Colt's* fault. Own up to your own shortcomings, for Pete's sake."

"There's no need for insults."

"Isn't there? You just told me my child is too nerve-racking."

Gentry almost hoped for a nasty retort so she could unleash more of her fury. Unfortunately, Miss Linda's solemn exhale signaled her retreat from battle. "I assume, then, that I can give Colt's spot to another child on my waiting list?"

"By all means." Gentry glared at the woman before spinning on her heel and storming out of the home. As she buckled Colt into the car seat, she mentally composed a scathing blog post about Miss Linda and her so-called day care. On her drive home, however, she realized that going public with her complaints could ultimately make Colt an object of debate. She wouldn't satisfy her own need for vengeance at his expense.

If Ian hadn't left, they wouldn't be in this trouble. Of course, Ian didn't aspire to be a lifelong nanny, and Gentry still wanted Colt to be with other kids when she wasn't with him. Now she had to find alternative arrangements.

Perhaps—and she was loath to admit it—Miss Linda had a bit of a point. Would other day care workers also tire of Colt's wailing? Might they shake him or do some other awful thing? How the hell would she figure this all out by Monday morning?

Her phone rang while she was stopped at a red light. "Hello."

"You left work early," her mother said without any pleasantries.

"Colt's day care called." Wouldn't Gentry's mother have loved to witness another "I told you so" moment? It would surely be added to the long list she liked to cast up as often as possible.

Her mother's tone shifted to concern. "Is he sick again? I told you day care is a petri dish, Gentry."

Yes, you told me, all right.

"He's fine." No way would she confess that Colt had been kicked out of day care. Once she found a new solution, she'd present it as a better one. "Anyway, what do you need? I thought I'd tied up all my loose ends for the week."

"We got a call from the producer in charge of filming those launch-week videos. Rich . . . Rick? Apparently, there's a problem coordinating filming with some of the bloggers you'd contacted, so you need to jump on that ASAP. Also, Becky isn't sure the Snapchat "limited time" contests are having the impact you'd projected, so you need to take another look at those as well."

Colt cried from the back seat. Gentry stifled the scream building in her chest to keep from crying right along with him. "I'll call Rich when I get home. I'll take a closer look at the Snapchat data, too."

"Promise you won't let it sit. In fact, I'd love for you to update me tomorrow."

For the love of God. "At the company picnic?"

"Yes."

Gentry glanced in the rearview mirror before switching lanes to hang a left. "You know a picnic is supposed to be about fun, not work."

"For the employees, maybe. For the owners, it's always about work, Gentry."

Was it? Was work a person's most important purpose in life? Her parents thought so. So did her brother. Ian too. Yet, for Gentry, putting "work first" was like wearing a dress that was two sizes too small—no room to breathe. That triggered a memory of a conversation with Ian one night when she'd come home grumpy.

"There must be something wrong with me. I hear people talk about an endorphin high from exercise, but I've never felt it. I see Hunter and the rest of my family get that same high from work, but I don't feel it. Maybe I don't produce endorphins. Or maybe I'm lazy?"

"You're not lazy." Ian glanced around, pointing at the photographs of Colt. "Did the hours you spent taking, cropping, and framing these feel like work?"

She pulled a face. "Of course not. I love taking pictures."

"That's the difference." He peeled a banana. "When you do what you love for a living, it never feels like work. Maybe you ought to find a way to turn this *into your work."*

"I can't."

"Why not?"

"You wouldn't understand."

"Try me."

"CTC is who Cabots are and how we connect. If I leave . . ." She couldn't finish because, even to her, it sounded like an excuse.

"I understand better than you realize." And then, as if he'd surprised himself, he grimaced, took a last bite of banana, and walked out to the deck.

Poor Ian. He was so deep in denial, he might be worse off than she was. She hoped not, though. She wanted him to be happy.

She pulled into her driveway, grateful for the excuse to end the call. "I'll update you tomorrow. Now if it's okay with you, I have to feed my son, prepare for Smith's arrival tomorrow, and take care of these items."

"I'm glad Smith is coming to the picnic." Her mother's voice turned syrupy.

"No kidding?" Gentry rolled her eyes. Her mother's agenda had gone into overdrive ever since Gentry had taken Colt to California to meet Smith's family two weeks ago. Smith's father and sister must've mentioned the fact that Colt looked exactly like Smith at least two hundred times. They'd been gracious and pleasant to her, too. Her visit confirmed that Smith had grown up in a loving family and should know how to create one for his son.

Meanwhile, Smith continued to check in on a regular basis. He hadn't been back to town since his first visit, though. Until this past week, Gentry hadn't extended an invitation. Anytime she thought of Smith at her home, it reminded her of how his first visit had hastened Ian's departure. That memory might as well have been an ice pick to the chest.

"You are managing this new situation very well. Colt's very lucky," her mother purred.

How quickly she'd forgotten that, two months ago, she'd berated Gentry for searching for Smith. But Gentry refrained from getting snitty. She was getting too old for that kind of thing. "We do what's best for our son."

"I think it's also good for you."

Colt cried again. "Listen, much as I love a good mother-daughter chitchat, I need to go. See you tomorrow." She hung up and let her head drop back against the seat, drawing a deep breath.

Fortunately, Smith had never once pressed Gentry into anything romantic. He remained patient and open. Friendly. She didn't know if she could ever love him, but she did love the way he'd fallen for their son. And she didn't want to go to the CTC picnic alone, so she'd invited Smith for a visit. Bringing him would help cement them as sort of a family, and her as a responsible mother.

She opened her door and freed her son from his car seat restraints. Once inside, she shed her boring work attire and slipped into comfy pajamas, despite it being only five o'clock. It took five seconds to stop herself from reminiscing about coming home to Ian's friendly smile and a well-made meal. To having an adult—a friend—to talk to each night.

Like anytime she thought of him, which was often, she alternated between wanting to cry and wanting to hit something. Right now, she wanted to talk to him about Miss Linda, yet she was also pissed because he wasn't there to listen.

They'd decided a clean break would be best, so they'd had no contact. Instead, she wasted hours each week composing e-mails that sat in her "Draft" folder. She'd broken down once and asked Sara if she'd heard anything about him from Gloria, but she hadn't. Gentry's only consolation was that no news must be good news. If anything happened to Ian, surely Gloria would say something.

Enough. She couldn't afford to add worrying about Ian to her miles-long to-do list. She glanced around the living room, noting the unfolded blanket, last night's empty popcorn bowl, and a bunch of new photos of Colt splayed across the sofa. Sighing, she set Colt on his belly and put a few toys at the edge of his reach before she began to straighten up.

◆ ◆ ◆

At ten o'clock, she closed her laptop and stretched, pleased with herself, thanks to a comment left on her blog. Some days her followers came through with a well-timed compliment or thank-you for something she'd written. Those notes wrapped her entire being in a luxuriously soft, warm robe.

Only one task remained for the night. One she'd been dreading. She climbed the stairs and went to the linen closet to retrieve a set of clean sheets; then she went into Ian's room. The guest room, she corrected.

She set the sheets on the nightstand and then threw her body, facedown, onto the mattress, grabbing a pillow and inhaling. Very little of his scent—of him—remained. Maybe nothing but her memory and imagination at this point. Still, she'd kept these sheets untouched for four weeks.

But she'd invited Smith to spend the weekend at her condo instead of the B&B. A small step toward a stronger friendship and, possibly, someday, something more. Smith had been good to her. He deserved clean sheets, even if it meant erasing the last trace of Ian from this room.

Her nose tingled as tears formed. If only falling out of love would happen as swiftly as the dive in.

◆ ◆ ◆

Ian sprayed himself with deet before leaving the shower, a habit he'd formed through years of working in mosquito-riddled communities. It might be overkill near the beaches of Jacmel, but vaccinations couldn't prevent every disease, and he'd never been one to take unnecessary risks. Except for the hottest of days, whenever Ian had to travel into rural areas, he wore lightweight pants and shirts with sleeves, too.

Even now, though, he itched with the nagging feeling he'd had every day since he'd returned . . . as if he didn't belong here anymore. The pride in his mission didn't quite fill the hole in his heart, no matter how much work he took on or how many patients he helped.

Archer should be arriving soon for another meeting with administrators at Sainte Michel Hospital. Although the Crawford Volunteer Ambulance Corps wouldn't be operated by the hospital, they were working to foster cooperation and coordination between the entities.

Ian's shadow followed him through the narrow streets of Jacmel, which were lined with colorfully painted old buildings whose architecture—embellished with porticos and balconies—one would find in New Orleans. In certain gaps between buildings and byways, one could glimpse the turquoise waters of the Caribbean. If he had time, Ian might've strolled along the *promenade du bord de mer*—a kilometer-long walkway decorated with elaborate, colorful mosaic tiles—to catch a breeze and pretend, for an instant, that this was a vacation instead of a mission. Sometimes he'd stand there and imagine Gentry and Colt playing in the surf, similar to that day they'd spent at Lake Sandy. An impossible dream, of course.

Today he didn't have time for dreams, detours, or playing *osselets* with kids on the street. He had to get to the garage facility they'd been renovating. Archer had suggested they model their private operation on the Centre Ambulancier National in Port-au-Prince. CAN, the brainchild of the Haitian minister of public health and population, had come about through major involvement of the Brazilian government (which had donated thirty-five ambulances), the Canadian Red Cross, and a multitude of other partners. It was growing but still wasn't available everywhere.

C-VAC would be small and privately operated, like the Ship of Hope marine ambulance program, thanks to a number of donors. Of immediate necessity, however, was Marcus Fairfax, who kept dangling the donation of five Land Rovers along with funds to convert them to basic life-support ambulances—or BLSs. In this part of Haiti, where most roads were unpaved, rocky, and pitted, and where certain residents were barely accessible by vehicle, Land Rovers would work much better than the old vans Ian and Archer could find.

The sticking point? Fairfax wanted *his* name on the NGO. Ian couldn't let that happen, even though Archer had pressured him to bend.

Fairfax's son, Jeremy, was coming to Jacmel with Archer this morning. Apparently, the twenty-three-year-old EMT could also service automobiles—a bonus. The only drawback was that Jeremy didn't have much field experience in places like Haiti. Ian's goal for their initial meeting was simple: convince Jeremy to secure the Rovers without forcing a name change.

Before Archer arrived, Ian needed to assess where things stood with supplies to outfit the vehicles. He also needed to finalize the training materials for the first wave of students.

He ambled into the garage area of the aging brick-and-plaster building near the outskirts of town, close to the hospital and a fuel station. Although damage to the area from Hurricane Matthew had been somewhat repaired, work always remained to be done. "Morning, Stanley."

Stanley Delbeau looked up from the tables where he'd been cataloging supplies. A Haitian, born and raised in this part of the peninsula, Stanley was a muscular man in his thirties, with a shaved head and goatee. He favored colorful shirts, like the lavender one he wore today, and had a toothy grin that put people at ease.

"Ian." He immediately returned his attention to the five piles of packaged supplies he'd been stacking.

Ian assumed he was sorting one pile per BLS. Those piles marked another not-so-subtle bit of pressure on Ian to cave to Fairfax's demand. Around here, BLSs were a tenfold improvement over the norm. Ambulance sirens were a rarity in Haiti, but that was slowly changing. Once C-VAC got up and running, the quality of health care in this community would improve.

"Where are we today?" Ian quickly scanned some of the packages.

"We have most standard types of bandages, immobilization devices, infection-control supplies, and defibrillators needed to start. But we're missing some ventilation and airway equipment. No portable oxygen apparatus. Could use more tubing, too, and bag-valve masks." He used his hands to mimic the hand-valve motion needed to operate the bags.

Ian flipped through some of the burn sheets, cold packs, stethoscopes, and cervical collars, then looked along the wall behind Stanley. "Backboards?"

"We got the long ones but need short boards, too."

"You're keeping a list, right?"

Stanley held up the clipboard, tapping it. "Yes."

"Archer will be here soon. He's got someone helping him reach out to Global Links and other potential donors. When we get together with the administrators at Sainte Michel, I'll see if they know of other sources for those tanks." He noticed another two boxes at Stanley's feet. "Need help unpacking those?"

"I got it covered, Ian." Stanley waved him off.

Ian sighed, shoving his hands in his pockets. "Guess I've run out of excuses to procrastinate the paperwork, then."

Stanley smiled. "*Wi.*"

◆ ◆ ◆

Three hours later, Ian, Archer, and Jeremy Fairfax were saying goodbye to Kathleen Falbo, a hospital administrator, and Dr. Merat. They exited the small office and strolled through the crowded waiting room of Sainte Michel, a like-new facility that had been rebuilt after the earthquake, with its whitewashed walls and vivid purple, orange, and green trumpet-flower mosaic wall mural.

"I still think we should push to load up the Rovers with advanced life-support gear." Jeremy kicked a stone across the parking lot, such as it was. The kid reminded Ian of an exuberant Labrador. Blond, jumping out of his skin with interest in everything around him, taking on challenges he didn't fully comprehend. In other words, exhausting.

Ten years ago, Ian had been the same. Hell, in the immediate aftermath of his father's death, he'd been bitten by a furious need to do the work of seven men. Today, not so much. These past four weeks had been the least focused of his career, thanks to constant daydreams about what he'd left behind in Oregon.

"It's hard enough getting this stuff," Ian sighed. "Most calls will be injuries from motorcycle crashes, falling out of trees, and shootings. BLSs will be a huge improvement compared with what they have now."

"Trees?" Jeremy looked to Archer, as if Ian had been pulling his leg.

"They climb to get wood for charcoal. There's never enough wood." Archer rubbed his chin. "Even with the Rovers, there will still be places we can't reach, at least not quickly enough. The roads around here are practically nonexistent outside of town, as you noticed on our drive here from Port-au-Prince."

Ian knew that hours-long drive along the spiny backbone of a mountain range, on a road that, in large part, was mostly dirt and large rocks. On the upside, passengers had water views on either side of the range.

"We need to secure the basics, like oxygen and fuel, before we worry about more. In fact, we need to secure those Rovers." Ian scrubbed his head, itchy from the heat and dust. "The fact that you're here and prepared to stay awhile suggests your family is making that donation."

"My father wants to make sure there's a long-term plan here. He doesn't want to ship vehicles that will end up idle or sold for parts in a year." Jeremy folded his arms and looked at Archer. "You keep saying it's tough just to get to this point. Keeping funding going month after month, year to year, will require serious muscle and the help of people with money and connections."

"It'll be a challenge." Archer nodded, cocking one brow at Ian.

"My dad can help with that. He's connected to everyone and raises money for lots of causes." Jeremy looked at Ian. "This initial donation of vehicles and conversion costs is well over six figures, plus what he can raise annually. But in exchange for all of that, my family wants its name on the organization."

Ian avoided Archer's gaze. "We appreciate your generosity. Surely, however, you can appreciate that this is *my* brainchild, to honor my father's work and life. I initiated it, with Archer's help, of course. I'm the one who's spent time here throughout the years and who committed everything I have to seeing this through."

"I'm ready for an adventure, and this looks like a good one. There's nothing pulling me home, so I can work side by side with you." Jeremy shrugged. "Without our trucks and money, you might not make it work. Certainly not anytime soon."

"No offense, but I think my father's life is worth at least as much as your family's spare change." Ian knew he'd crossed a line. Frankly, that was something Gentry might've said. He should regret it, yet it had felt good to be blunt.

Archer laid a hand on Jeremy's shoulder, already setting the stage for an apology. "Jeremy, do you mind giving me a minute alone with Ian?"

"Sorry, Ian. I didn't mean to offend you. But *my* dad has conditions. He's willing to do this for me because this is what I want." Jeremy nodded. "Okay. I'll go hit the head."

He disappeared back into the hospital, leaving Ian and Archer outside. Ian had seen Archer and his father work together in the past—men with sober faces, rarely disagreeing on anything of importance. Ian's recent attitude probably shocked the man.

"Don't queer the pitch over a name, Ian." Archer scowled.

"The name is the whole reason I'm here." Ian raised his arms heavenward.

Archer shook his head. "The mission should be why you're here. To hell with vanity. You want to honor your father? See this through. If Brian were standing here, he'd let Fairfax have the marquee in exchange for five brand-new, high-end vehicles that can handle this terrain. They're better than anything you and I can buy, which leaves us more money for supplies and salaries for newly trained EMTs. Come on, Ian. Think with your head, not your heart."

Those words also reminded him of Gentry, who'd likely give him the opposite advice. Her way of viewing the world had affected his. "I've given up a lot for this cause only to spend my days behind a desk instead of in the field helping people. Now I'm supposed to roll over for some guy I met once, and his inexperienced son?"

"That paperwork's just as vital as being in the field and training the locals." Archer clapped his hand on Ian's shoulder again. "Your father would agree, Ian. He might even be chuffed to see you tucked safely behind a desk out here." He waved his hand in the general direction of the village and mountains beyond.

Ian shrugged. His mother would be happier, that was certain. And Gentry, too, if she knew.

Even if everything Archer said had merit, none of this felt right. It hadn't for weeks. He couldn't access the old fervor. The joy. The sense of accomplishment and contentedness.

Every night he'd lain awake missing Gentry. Wondering about her and Colt . . . and Smith. Lately he'd had one thought looping through his brain, each rotation cinching the thread tighter: was this worth giving up Gentry and Colt? In the darkness, over the buzz of mosquitoes circling his net, he could hear his heart whisper, *No*.

Archer sighed, snapping Ian out of his reverie. "Well?"

"I hear you, Archer." He glanced over his shoulder. Jeremy had yet to reappear. "I'll meet you and Jeremy back at the garage in thirty minutes. Need to make a quick pit stop first."

"Where the heck are you going?"

Ian had already started trotting away, so he waved over his shoulder, calling out, "I'll have an answer when I see you."

Ian jogged the roughly half mile to Hotel Florita, which provided free Wi-Fi in its bar.

The beautiful little tavern boasted pretty exposed brick and beams and a tin roof. He stood in the corner—near the open arched doorway—uninterested in a drink or anything else going on. He searched for Gentry's blog site on his phone. Something he'd done many times this past month.

He'd kept up with Colt's growth through Gentry's online journal. He'd checked the site, each time holding his breath, fearful of seeing some personal post about Smith. But so far, she'd referred to him only twice, both times in the context of being Colt's dad.

Her antics and the opinions she'd share with other working moms who followed her and asked for advice usually made him chuckle. Her wisdom usually had the theme of following one's gut. Leading with the heart. Breaking from the crowd.

It seemed to him that Gentry had lived her life that way until she got pregnant. Then she'd forced herself into a mold of her family's making. The constant friction between her natural state versus the "expected" state of motherhood and being a Cabot had her chafing from the inside out. Someone ought to tell her to follow her own advice.

Choices. It always came back to choices and consequences.

Now Ian had another choice. He had long thought his heart was here in Haiti, with his dad, and with the Crawford way. But at some point this summer, his heart had shifted its allegiance. Whether that was a good or bad thing didn't matter. It was what it was, and it couldn't be undone.

When her site finally loaded, his heart sank to his toes.

Letting Go

If you google quotes about letting go, you'll find hundreds. Some are funny. Some are rather obvious. And some cut so close, your heart bleeds. But I think each of us has to come to that point of letting go in our own way, in our own time, and with the knowledge that no amount of hand-holding or wise words makes it any easier.

For me, that time is now. There's symmetry to it, seeing as how I fell in love in a month, and now it's been a month since he left.

I wish I could be bitter. Anger makes it easier to say goodbye. Yet I can't even regret the time we shared because it opened my eyes to the possibility of something I'd never believed in before, and I think that's a good thing for my son.

With my new outlook, I can let go in peace, with hope for my future and the family I'll someday create. Next time I fall, it'll be with someone who wants the same things I do. That wasn't him, although a piece of him will always be with me in my dreams.

I need to compile a "Letting Go" playlist, so leave song suggestions in the comments and wish me luck. Now Boo and I are off to a picnic. Happy weekend, all!

He reread the post twice, his throat tightening each time, making it hard to breathe. He could call and tell her that he thought about her every single day. Ask her if she and Smith were taking their relationship to a new level. *"Next time I fall, it'll be with someone who wants the same things I do."* Was he ready to leave all this behind? He pushed away from the wall, phone shoved back in his pocket.

On his way back to the garage, he took that detour along the promenade, his head pounding. He sat on the border wall near a thatched umbrella and stared at the sea, watching the tide lap against the rocky sand. This beach had survived earthquakes and hurricanes. It'd been here long before him and would remain long after he died.

What made a life worthwhile? Duty and service had a place, but so did love and laughter. So did joy. Gentry had shown him that, and those memories glittered like the sun on the sea in front of him.

He'd given years of his life to the Crawford way. He didn't regret them, but he no longer viewed that credo quite the same way, either. His father had done what had made him happy. So had Ian's mother.

Could Ian be happier with Gentry than with living up to his dad's example? Could he have a family *his* way and still make a difference here and elsewhere? Serve his community, wherever that might be?

He glanced down the promenade, hand on his chest as if it could calm his erratic heart, watching a young mother with two small children enter a building. *I don't want to chase ghosts anymore.*

He hopped off the wall, antsy but invigorated. Decided.

Breaking the chains of guilt and duty that had been weighing on him all month, he ran to the garage like a man with the wind at his back.

"Finally." Archer said, looking at his watch. "I need to get back to Port-au-Prince. Have you made a decision?"

"You're all in? You're going to stay here for a year or more, come hell or high water?" Ian asked Jeremy.

"Hell yeah," he replied.

"Good." Ian nodded, still panting slightly from his exuberant run. "Because I've made a decision."

"We can move forward under the new name?" Archer's brows rose, and Jeremy's gaze sharpened.

"Yes, but I have my conditions. I'll complete the program paperwork, the manual, and show Jeremy the ropes, but then I'm going home. I'll return for two-week trips every few months to help, but I'm not going to live here." Sensing Archer's dismay, he looked at his father's old friend. "Jeremy's an EMT. He can run the training classes. Between Stanley and him, I don't also need to be here full-time. After all, the whole point is to train locals to do this so they don't need us at all. Within one to two years, there will be others who can help, too."

When neither spoke, Ian shrugged, hoping not to overplay his hand. "That's my offer."

Even if Jeremy didn't agree, Ian would work hard to find some other willing partner to take his place. Getting this off the ground would have to be enough of a nod to his father. It was time to get on with *his* life.

"Sounds good to me," Jeremy replied, his expression evidencing a bit of shell shock.

"You've got a lot to learn about this place, its people, its customs," Archer warned.

"Don't worry. I'll help him get up to speed ASAP." Ian rested his hands on the table where Stanley had been working earlier.

"Your father would never abandon this project, Ian." Archer's sharp tone expressed his disdain. "I'm gobsmacked."

"I'm not my father. And I'm not abandoning anything. I'm reducing my role. I've brought it this far and can handle paperwork and fund-raising from Oregon. I'll stay involved, but I don't need to live here, especially if it's *his* name on the door."

Archer stared at Ian. He must've sensed Ian's resolve, because he simply said, "Oh, sod it. Jeremy, there's a lot to do."

Jeremy shook Archer's hand. "Don't worry. I'm up for it."

Archer nodded and then headed outside to the waiting car. Ian followed him.

"I'm sorry you're pissed. I've given a lot of my time here and to this project. But I'm one guy. It doesn't all have to rest on my shoulders."

"I hope you don't cock this up, Ian." Archer slid into the back seat and closed the door.

Ian stepped back and watched the old Jeep drive away, then returned to the garage. He found Jeremy in the small office. The one where he kept Quackers on the olive-green metal desk that looked like something from the 1960s.

Quackers could be left out in the open because no one in his right mind would steal that thing, and Ian liked the reminder nearby.

"And what, exactly, can he say to me that you can't?"

"Everything."

Jeremy gave it a cockeyed stare. "What the hell is that?"

Ian crossed his arms. "A gift . . . from a friend."

"Not a very good friend, apparently." Jeremy chuckled.

Ian didn't respond. He wouldn't try to explain the priceless gesture Gentry had made when she gave him Quackers, or how often he'd replayed the last words she'd said to him the day he left her home. "You hungry?"

Jeremy patted his belly. "Starved."

"Let's go." Ian nodded and took him to a nearby café. While he listened to Jeremy prattle on, his mind wandered. He expected more cognitive dissonance about his decision. Its absence made him more certain.

Now he'd have to persuade Gentry that he'd changed. That he wanted the same things she did. A phone call wouldn't be enough to prove anything. He needed to show her that he could be spontaneous. That he could fill her life with happy surprises, too.

That blog post meant the clock was ticking, if he wasn't already too late. Time for drastic measures. He'd raid his small savings to fly home tomorrow, then come back and transition Jeremy for a few weeks. After that, he'd return to Oregon for good.

He swigged his beer. "Jeremy, are you up for a challenge? 'Cause I've got an emergency, and I need your help."

Chapter Twenty-One

Freedom

According to *Merriam-Webster*: the absence of necessity, coercion, or constraint in choice or action

According to me: the only way to live

Gentry pushed the empty stroller across the lawn, past the majority of employees at the picnic, to the CTC patio, where some of her family was sitting. Smith walked beside her, proudly carrying their son. Although Colt had been calm this morning, he grew wide-eyed at the noisy, bustling crowd, and started to cry.

"Come on, Colt. Don't be scared of these nice people." Smith's deep voice might melt the panties off dozens of women, but Colt wasn't soothed. Smith offered Gentry an amazed smile. "You've got an iron will to deal with this every day without jumping off your deck. He's tough."

"He's perfect." She wiggled Colt's foot. "He's just particular and sensitive. It makes him special. He'll learn to manage it, eventually."

"Manage what?" her mother asked, reaching for Colt as they approached.

"His inability to control himself." Gentry parked the stroller beside the table.

Her mother tossed her and Smith a look and snickered. "*You* didn't."

Smith chuckled, but Gentry had grown tired of the digs. Granted, she'd waged as many battles as Spartacus with her mother, so she'd earned her rep. But how long until she got credit for *any* change? Ten months of doing everything she could think of to prove herself hadn't made a dent.

Her dad enveloped her in a hug before shaking Smith's hand. "Welcome back to town. Gentry enjoyed her trip to Pasadena the other week. It's great to see you two working together to give Colt some family time."

Exactly what hadn't been a priority during *her* childhood.

"He deserves the best." Smith tipped his head, leveling Colt with an adoring smile. Colt kept fussing, though. Then again, he was in Gentry's mother's arms. Not the most comforting place.

"Here, Mom. I'll take him." Gentry plucked him from her mother.

"Actually, let his father take over." Her mom gestured to Smith. "I want to talk to you about the campaign for a second."

"I just got here," Gentry sighed.

"Let's get it done so we can enjoy the party." Her mom smoothed her skirt. "Come inside for a minute."

Gentry shot Smith an apologetic grimace. "Sorry. This should only take ten minutes."

"Take your time. I'll hang with your dad," he replied amiably.

"I'll introduce you to Colby," her dad offered. "You didn't get to meet her last time you were in town. Come with me."

Off they went. Seeing her own father strolling down the lawn with her son and *his* father should've made Gentry's heart go pitter-patter. It didn't, though. Her heart hadn't quite returned to normal since Ian had left.

She didn't want to think about Ian now, although the harder she tried to forget him, the more he invaded her thoughts. Hence her blog post today about letting him go. The public declaration would be an incentive to make it happen.

"Gentry," her mom called from the door.

Like a prisoner being led to the guillotine, Gentry followed her mother inside.

Her mom rested against an empty workstation. "Well, was Becky right?"

"The numbers aren't great on the Snapchat campaign." Gentry sent up a silent prayer that Becky hadn't heard that admission.

"Why not?"

"Honestly? I don't know. I thought they'd be better."

"Based on what?" Her mother crossed her arms and drummed her fingers against her bicep.

"My experience. Things I've read." She shrugged. "A hunch."

"Gentry, you may have survived twenty-six years living on hunches, but in business, we make decisions based on data." When Gentry didn't respond, she added, "When you started last fall, you were focused and determined. What's happened since then?"

"Seriously?" Gentry laughed, but then realized her mother didn't know the answer. "I had a baby. I've been a little preoccupied—and tired." Not to mention how she'd been grappling with her priorities ever since Colt's birth.

"If you'd let me help, I could teach you how to juggle the demands of your job and your child, like I did."

Juggle? Hardly. Gentry closed her eyes and blew the stray hair away from her eyelashes while counting to three.

"What are you doing?" her mom asked.

"Trying to let go of yet another criticism."

"Criticism? I'm only trying to understand what's going on with you."

"You can't, Mom. You'll never understand me because we are very different people with very different needs. I don't want to argue anymore. I hear what you're saying, so I'll pull the Snapchat plan and sink more money into Instagram, Facebook, and YouTube, where we *are* seeing traction." Gentry nodded toward the door. "Now can we enjoy the picnic?"

Before her mother could toss out another question, Gentry turned and stalked outside into the sunlight. The heat and brightness made her think of Ian toiling under the tropical sun. Or treating some dehydrated cholera patient. Maybe dodging mosquitoes? Thinking of her? *Oops. Let him go.*

Across the lawn, Smith sat in a tight circle with her sister, Sara, and her father. Hunter stood twenty yards off to one side with a group of accounting guys who looked more like they were at a meeting than a picnic.

She trotted down the lawn, wishing she could kick off her shoes and feel the blades of grass between her toes. Her mother would probably follow closely behind, so Gentry soaked in her few free moments until she caught up with her family.

"Looks like you finally met my sister." She smiled at Smith, wishing his handsome face gave her those tingles it had that night long ago.

"Yes. Unfortunately, Alec isn't here." Smith tickled Colt's tummy. At least her son wasn't crying at the moment. "We'll have to catch up some other time."

"Saturdays are tough for us. Alec's already at the restaurant, prepping. I need to leave soon, too." Colby lifted Colt off the blanket and snuggled him. "I don't get to spend near enough time with this little one."

"Me neither," sighed Sara.

Gentry noticed Ty sitting peacefully in the circle with a coloring book.

Other kids were running around, getting their faces painted, watching the clown make balloon animals. "Hey, Ty. Want Aunt Gentry to take you to get your face painted?"

He shook his head.

"Come on. I'll do mine, too." She crouched to his level and wiggled his shoes. "We can be panda bears or something."

He shook his head again.

"It's okay, Ty. You don't have to." Sara patted his leg, then smiled at Gentry. "He's still crowd shy. Besides, I'm not sure he'd love the messy face paint."

What kid didn't like face paint? But she wouldn't push. "Smith, do you think Colt would look cute as a bandit?"

"He won't tolerate a single swipe of the sponge." He chuckled. "I guess he'd be a cute smudge, though."

"Poor restless thing." Colby kissed Colt's head. "Smith told us about Miss Linda. What will you do now?"

"What happened with Miss Linda?" Her mother's voice crawled up Gentry's spine from behind.

Nothing sucked more than having them all looking at her like they were bracing for her next screwup.

"She can't handle Colt's colic, so I need to find an alternative." Gentry chose to look at her dad, who wrinkled his nose.

"That's outrageous," he said, showing surprising solidarity.

"Trust me, I let her have it." Gentry sat beside Smith.

"Well, great," her mother sighed. "Now what will you do?"

"I can watch him for a while." Sara clapped her hands together.

"Perfect solution." Her mom squeezed Sara's shoulder. "Thank you."

"I couldn't ask that. You've got Ty to chase after." Gentry hoped that hadn't come out too harsh, but she didn't want Sara bonding with her son on a daily basis. What if he found out that Sara could've been his mother and resented Gentry later? What if Sara handled him better? Although irrational, those thoughts proliferated like the wisteria climbing the patio columns.

"Actually, having Colt around will teach Ty about patience, sharing, and a bunch of other things. Plus, they'd bond as cousins." Sara reached for Colt, and Colby handed him over. "Oh, please. I love this little dove."

"Sounds like a pretty good temporary solution." Smith nodded and laid his hand on Gentry's knee.

Sara's plea and Smith's uninvited familiarity made her uncomfortable. She nudged Smith's hand off her leg and looked at Sara. "No, thank you."

Sara stilled, and even Colby held her breath. "Sorry."

"Gentry, what's wrong with you?" her mother asked. "Sara's family. She's compassionate, smart, and you know she'd never harm Colt. She might even be able to get him on some kind of schedule."

"Because I'm too much of a screwup to do it. That's what you think, isn't it?" She stared at the ground, heat rushing to her face.

"Watch your language." Her father glanced over his shoulder at the employees while Gentry realized Ty had probably heard her.

Colt started crying. Sara hugged him to her chest, swaying him. "Sh, sh, sh . . . it's okay."

Her mother shook her head. "Now look at what you've done."

A bee or wasp tore through their little circle with a loud buzz. All around her, the music and laughter became muffled. Perspiration rolled from her hairline down her neck.

Her body tensed as her thoughts turned to how much she wished she wasn't being compared with Sara. How she wished she'd never tried to be someone she wasn't by working at CTC. How she wished she hadn't wasted so much time on false bravado and insecurity.

Seems she hadn't changed as much as she'd hoped.

"Stop staring at me!" she snapped, glancing around at her family. "You think I don't know that you all think I should've let Hunter and Sara raise Colt? But he's *my* son. I want to raise him *my* way, and—"

Smith's hand landed on her shoulder, but before he could say anything, she batted it away. "Stop that."

She jumped up and reached for Colt. Sara handed him over without a word, and Gentry stalked off. Other employees were watching, whispering. As she left, she noticed her brother striding across the lawn toward the family circle.

Her nose tingled, but she would not cry. She rounded the side of the building and found an empty bench. Nestling Colt, she rocked him, flashing him her wobbly smile and humming. She'd left his diaper bag with his binky back on the patio, so she rubbed her finger along his gums and let him gnaw on that for a moment.

"I'm sorry, Boo. I swear I'll do better. I'll give you everything I have. You're the only one who matters." Tears formed but didn't fall. She conjured Ian up, replaying the way he'd reassured her about her mothering. He'd promised that love was enough. That mistakes didn't make her a bad mother.

"Gentry?" Sara's shadow fell across the bench.

Gentry closed her eyes and took a breath. "I'm sorry I snapped at you."

Sara sat beside her. At first they didn't speak. Then Sara said, "I only came to say that you're wrong—"

"Of course I am. Haven't you heard?" Gentry faced Sara. "That's where I excel."

"Stop." Sara laid her hand on Gentry's thigh and squeezed. "Just stop. You're wrong to think that we question your decision to keep Colt."

"Come on," Gentry snorted. "I remember what Hunter said that night in Dad's family room."

Those words had haunted her more than once. She'd expected his anger when she decided to keep Colt, but Hunter had hit her with her worst fear. *"I'm sorry, too. Sorry for that child you're carrying who had a chance to have Sara for a mother but now will be stuck with you."*

"He was hurt and angry." Sara shrugged. "We all say things in the heat of the moment that we regret."

"*You* don't," Gentry conceded.

"I do. Ask my sisters." Sara smiled and patted Gentry's shoulder. "You're the perfect mother for Colt. He's part of you, and you're part of him, and that love is all you need. Stop comparing us, because nobody else is. There's no *one* right way. But you've got to believe in yourself if you want others to believe in you, too."

That echoed the advice Gentry dispensed on her blog, yet, like with most advice, it was easier to give than to follow. "It's not that simple."

"It actually is, I think."

"Not when everything I do is picked apart by my mother. When every opinion or choice is judged immature or wasteful."

"You and your mom have had an unhealthy dynamic forever. I see you trying, though. She should give you credit for the ways you've matured. But maybe you need to stop assuming the worst of your family, too. Take Hunter. He has a hard time understanding people who don't think like him, he's bossy, and he's always going to see you as his baby sister. It's not personal, though. He loves you, and he'd be the first one there if you needed him."

"Maybe you're right." Gentry kissed Colt's head, grateful she had him to cling to during this sweet but awkward exchange. "I am sorry I lashed out at you. You make me feel insecure because you always have your shit together, and I rarely do."

"I have help. Hunter takes care of me. He handles a lot of the day-to-day details, so I can focus on Ty. You're doing it all on your own. Working. Motherhood. Now dealing with Smith. Give yourself a break, Gentry." Sara inhaled, and her gaze wandered to the trees. "I suspect you still miss Ian, which probably makes everything harder."

"It does." Gentry bit her nail. "But that's not the immediate problem."

"What is?"

Gentry wrinkled her nose. "I don't like working at CTC."

Sara's brows rose high on her forehead. "Then why'd you strong-arm Hunter into hiring you last year?"

"Because, for the first time, *my* voice finally mattered. Voting with Hunter was a way of making up for how I hurt you both, and a way into my family. I thought if I worked here, I'd connect with them and their drive." She grimaced. "I'm not ungrateful for everything it's given me, but CTC just doesn't mean to me what it does to them."

"I'm not surprised," Sara chuckled. "You've never been conventional . . . and that's not an insult."

Gentry stared at her son, praying that he'd have more direction than she'd ever found.

Sara gripped the edge of the bench on either side of her legs. "Maybe you should focus on what you love. How about photography? Maybe start with family portraits or architectural shoots or whatever. Or your blog. Where could that lead if you gave it more attention?"

"I don't know."

"You should trust yourself much more than you do."

"I told you, my mother always makes me feel stupid." Gentry grimaced.

"You're a little old to blame your parents." Sara bumped shoulders with Gentry. "Besides, we all make mistakes as mothers, don't we? Sit down with Jenna and work stuff out. It'd be better for you that way, and that will be better for Colt."

Gentry let her head fall on Sara's shoulder. "See, this is why you're better at life than I am."

"Hardly. Look at how I almost lost everything last summer. I only see *this* clearly because we're not talking about *my* family."

Gentry raised her head and sighed. "We should go back."

"Will you quit?"

Gentry bit her lip. "I'm finally closer to Hunter. If I leave, it'll go back to how it was before. He won't respect me."

"That's not true." Sara frowned. "Think of it this way—if your family didn't love you, then they wouldn't worry about you. As long as you come up with *some* plan for your future, they'll respect that." Sara stood. "Come on. Let's go."

"Wait." Gentry stood and handed Colt to Sara. "Is your offer to watch Colt for a few weeks still good?"

"So you're *not* going to quit?"

"Not until after the launch." Gentry wouldn't bail in the eleventh hour. "It'll give me time to make some new plans for my future."

"Might that future include Smith?" Sara bit her lip.

"I like him as a friend, and he's already a doting father. But I don't feel more."

"Because of Ian?"

"Ridiculous, right? He showed me what I'm missing, and now I can't pretend or manufacture it. If I get lucky enough, maybe I'll find it again one day, but I don't see it happening with Smith."

Sara smoothed her hand over Gentry's head. "I hope you find it.

"Me too." They walked around the building together, and Gentry stopped short. Colby must've taken off for A CertainTea. Hunter and her dad and mom looked like they were having some kind of powwow. "Oh boy. Wish me luck."

"You'll be fine."

Gentry charged up to Smith first. "I'm sorry I snapped at you."

"Thanks," he said, hands stuffed in his pockets.

Her whole family looked on. "Can you take Colt with Sara and Ty for a minute? I need to talk to my family."

"Sure." He took Colt and the diaper bag, and Sara led him up toward the buffet tables on the patio.

"What's up now?" Hunter asked, his arms folded across his chest.

"I'm sorry for my outburst, and I've already apologized to Sara," she said.

"Good," he replied, rising off the ground as if planning to go after his wife.

"Hold up. There's more." She didn't know whom to look at, so she closed her eyes and blurted her plans. "I'm resigning from my job, effective after the launch."

"Why, honey?" Her father's concerned expression took the sting out of her mother's arch one. "I've loved having another Cabot walk the halls and seeing you and your brother working together. It's what I'd always envisioned when I started this place."

Hunter's eyes narrowed while he waited for her explanation.

"That's the whole reason I wanted to work here, Dad," Gentry assured him. "I thought if I could make myself love it as much as all of you, we'd be closer. But I don't love it. I can't see myself there in five months, let alone five years. It's not my passion."

"Your passion?" Jenna asked.

"Jenna, let her talk." Hunter gestured for Gentry to finish.

"Yes, passion. That's why you're all so good at it, and why I'm not."

"You've done a good job here," her dad said. "You're still learning."

"I'm not sure everyone agrees." Gentry didn't look directly at her mother, but she didn't need to. "And it's beside the point. I want to wake up and look forward to my work like you all do. I think I can do something with photography. And I've got my blog."

No one spoke for a few seconds, like a game of chicken. With nothing left to say, Gentry accepted that they never would understand her. "I'm sorry I've let you down."

"You haven't let us down." Hunter reached out and squeezed her hand. "You deserve to love what you do."

"Thank you." She swallowed the lump in her throat. "Dad?"

"Baby, I just want you to be happy."

When her mother remained silent, Gentry said, "I should go catch up to Smith."

"Hang on," her mom said.

Gentry waited, bracing herself for disappointment.

Her mom reached over and clasped her hand. "I don't want you leaving here thinking that I wasn't proud of your contributions."

"That's not why I'm leaving."

"Maybe not, but you need to understand that I've always pushed you because I believe in you, *not* because I think you're a failure. I wanted you to see how much you could accomplish, and hoped that success would give you confidence." Her mom laid one hand on her stomach. "I'm not a warm person. I know that. I could blame my dad, but what's the point? I can't change who I am any more than you can change who you are. I'm sorry my methods hurt you, but I swear my heart was in the right place. I love you, Gentry. I always have, and I always will. I hope, one day, we can find a way to talk to each other without all the sharp edges."

Gentry's dad smiled at his wife. He'd loved her for years—admired her chutzpah, her drive, her smarts. And he seemed to understand her motives and moods in a way no one else ever did. Perhaps Gentry should try to see her mom through her father's eyes.

In a way, she and her mom weren't that different from each other. Both hid their vulnerabilities behind a hard shell. Grandpa John had stolen her mom's ability to give love without fear of abandonment, just like he'd stolen money from the family bank account. Through that filter, maybe Gentry could give her mom a break now and then, or at least count to five before engaging in a battle of words.

Right now she thought about what she'd want Colt to say to her if she were in her mom's shoes. It didn't take long to know exactly how to respond.

She hugged her mom, waiting for her to relax. "I know I never made anything easier for you. I'll try to be more understanding. I love you, too."

Her dad hugged them both. "Now I've got to get in on the action."

Hunter stood outside the circle, awkwardly patting his dad on the shoulder.

Gentry swiped a tear from the corner of her eyes and chuckled. “Okay, okay. People are watching. This is getting weird.”

“Go find Smith,” her father said. “When’s he leaving?”

“He’s got a late flight tomorrow night. He wanted to spend as much time with Colt as possible.”

“Maybe we can join you for lunch tomorrow?” he asked.

“Sounds nice, Dad.” She smiled, then scanned the lawn, spotting Smith, Sara, Ty, and Colt in the distance. “See you in a bit.”

She bounded across the grass, unburdened. The world hadn’t ended. Her family hadn’t berated her. She was free, and something like happiness bubbled inside. She gave a quick thought to Ian and hoped he, too, was finding his way.

Chapter Twenty-Two

Zen

According to *Merriam-Webster*: a Japanese sect of Mahayana Buddhism that aims at enlightenment by direct intuition through meditation

According to me: my new habit

After getting Colt to bed for the night, Gentry emerged from her room to find Smith in the kitchen, pouring them each a glass of Barolo. She lifted one off the counter. "Thank you."

He raised his glass. "Cheers."

She eyed him over the rim while she sipped. Its rich perfume helped boost the flavor explosion in her mouth. "Wow, is that licorice I taste?"

"Such a quick study. Sip again and see if you can taste the truffle and rose." He grinned and watched while she tested herself. "When Colt's a little older, we should take a trip to Piedmont. If you liked Napa, you'll love Italy."

Napa. She had loved it, and that trip had clearly been life changing. But the mischief in his eyes hinted that he was thinking about their tryst more than the wines. She smiled but set her glass down. "I think we should talk, Peter."

"Ah." He finished his drink, then refilled his glass. "How about you spare me the 'You're a great guy, but' speech and we just skip to the end, Artemis."

She stroked his bicep. "You make things too easy."

"What can I say?" He shrugged. "I'm an easygoing guy."

"You are. I couldn't ask for a better dad for Colt." She nodded toward the living room. "Let's take this to the sofa."

Once seated, he said, "We'll need to figure out some kind of custody arrangement when Colt gets a little older, but for now, let's keep things loosey-goosey."

"Sounds more than fair." She'd dreaded that idea a month ago, but now that she knew Smith, it didn't bother her. He was a good man with a kind heart. He loved their son, and Colt would thrive from time spent with Smith and his family.

"Truthfully, I'm not set up to handle him on my own yet. I basically keep the same work hours as your sister and Alec." Smith sipped more wine. "It's easy for me to come up here, although I'll have to shift to Sunday–Monday visits because I can't keep taking time off work. If you bring him down every couple of months, too, it'll be enough this year."

"I'll do whatever works for you. I swear. The last thing I'd ever want is to stand in the way of you two bonding." She reached across the table and squeezed his hand. "It'll be easy for me to be flexible after the launch."

"Mind telling me why you quit?"

She didn't want to rehash it, and frankly, she'd grown a little sick of herself and her issues. The bottom line should be enough explanation. "Remember how you said once that I didn't strike you as the corporate type?"

"I do."

"You were right. I think I'll be a better person and mother when I do my own thing. I've always loved photography."

Smith glanced around at all the pictures. "You're great at it. I love the way you put together collages."

"Thanks. Let's hope others do, too. I'll use my blog to create a gallery page. I need to do a little research about pricing and stuff."

"I'll be your test model," he teased, turning to show off his profile with the slight raise of his chin.

"No joke! You and Colt would be perfect models. I'm going to hold you to it." When he smiled at her, her chest ached with gratitude. "Smith, when we met in Napa, I never would've predicted we'd end up here, with our son sound asleep a few yards away. But I can't imagine a life without him. And you've been so damn nice about everything. I owe you big."

"You owe me nothing. You could've chosen not to have Colt, or to give him up. Hell, you took a big risk when you set out to find me. *I'm* the lucky one. I'm only a little sorry we won't be a more traditional family, like I had growing up."

"We'll be okay, and so will Colt. Someday he'll have two more parents who love him, too. But you'd better choose wisely." She pinched his leg in jest.

Smith turned a little quiet and set his empty glass on the ottoman tray. "I'd say the same, but I get the feeling you already know who you'd choose. What are the chances I'll be seeing Ian around here again?"

"Slim to none. He's gone." She cleared her throat. "I'm not ready to date, but when I am, I promise I'll never pick someone who isn't good for Colt."

"I trust you."

Gentry smiled. Those weren't words she'd heard often in life, but it felt damn good tonight.

"I think I'll go shower and read a bit, if you don't mind." Smith stood. "I'm a little worn out from the long day with your family."

"They are draining," she teased. "Go ahead. I think I'll do a little work and get to bed early, too."

Smith kissed the top of her head before going upstairs.

Gentry checked her phone. No messages. Never the name she hoped to see. She tossed it back on the ottoman and stretched her legs, staring at a photo of Colt.

Her family had built something they could be proud of. Now she would, too.

She went out to the deck, where crickets sang their tinny song. Looking at the cloudless sky, she chose a star. Stars were something she could still share with Ian, like they'd promised. She pretended its twinkle was his smile. Imagined his reaction to her latest news. When tears pricked behind her eyelids, she held them back.

Time to really let go.

◆ ◆ ◆

Ian stood on the sidewalk outside Gentry's condo remembering the first time he'd seen its impressive black door. His life had changed when he'd walked through it, and he hoped it would do so again, today.

He hadn't called. Hadn't asked her if he was welcome. Now, standing on the sidewalk with the ridiculously oversize stuffed dog he'd bought on his way here, he drew a deep breath.

Ian started down the walkway just as the door opened. He halted, his heart leaping, when Smith pushed Colt's stroller out the door.

"Oh," Smith said, stopping short, gawking at the powder-blue plush dog that dwarfed the stroller. "Ian."

"I found it!" Gentry called from inside before she appeared and nearly ran into Smith. "Here's the clean binky."

Then she looked up and her face drained of color. "Ian."

Her mouth fell open. Her gaze remained locked on him. If she noticed the dog, she didn't say.

"Sorry. I should've called. I . . ." Ian turned, his body a mishmash of tendons and muscles that forgot how to coordinate so he could walk.

The dog. He should leave the dog for Colt. His mind and body wouldn't work together, so he ended up turning in a circle.

"Hold up," Smith called.

Ian's eyes fell on Colt, who looked the same yet different from how he remembered. He couldn't tell if Colt recognized him, but he didn't dare overstep his boundaries with Smith standing there. His heart squeezed at the realization that he'd let that child and Gentry slip through his fingers. He set Brutus—as he dubbed the gift—on the ground. "This is for Colt."

Gentry blinked as Ian pulled Quackers out of the deep pocket of his camo shorts.

"I'll take Colt for a walk while you two talk," Smith offered, with no trace of anger or smugness.

The binky dangled from Gentry's fingers. "Thanks," she said, without sparing Smith a glance, her eyes tracking Ian's every move.

Smith snatched the binky from her and then pushed the stroller past Ian, hanging a left toward the park.

"You're home." Gentry bit her nail.

"Yes." Despite his reunion plans falling apart because of Smith, seeing her made him smile.

"Do you . . . do you want to come inside?" She hitched her thumb over her shoulder.

He should go. He'd waited too long. She'd moved on with Smith and was putting a family together for Colt. "It's okay. I don't want to cause trouble."

"Trouble?" She tilted her head, her red hair like fire, lit by the late-afternoon sun, tumbling around her shoulders.

"With Smith." God, he should've called. He should've *called* before upending his life and barging in on hers. She'd let go. He'd read it and then ignored it because he hadn't wanted it to be true.

Her brows pinched and then rose. "Oh no. We're not . . . he's not . . . he's only here to spend time with Colt."

The vise around his chest loosened. "So you two . . ."

"No." She shook her head, lips pressed together.

Relief exploded inside him, making him dizzy. He bent over, hands on his knees, and blew out a breath.

Gentry rushed forward. "Are you sick?"

Without thinking, he wrapped his arms around her, holding her tight and swaying slightly to the sweet music flooding his mind. He couldn't speak, so he kissed her temple, her cheek, her neck, and then, finally, her mouth.

She tasted like citrus and honey. He dug his hands through her hair, kissing her as if she were his last breath, stopping long enough to inhale, keeping his forehead pressed to hers.

"What's happened, Ian?" She tipped her head back, cupping his jaw in her hands. "Why are you here?"

He smiled at her confusion. "I'm here for you."

"Me?" She blinked.

"You and Colt." His face hurt from smiling, but he couldn't stop. This was right. Everything was right, now, and life promised to be an entirely new adventure.

"I don't understand." Her expression turned more solemn. "Now, you think we can handle the distance?"

"No more distance."

She dropped her hands, twining her fingers. "Did something happen with the project?"

"Sort of."

"So it didn't work? That's why you're back." She eased away.

"No, it's working fine, but it won't have the Crawford name."

"Why not?"

"I traded it for some trucks and the chance to work from Oregon. Jeremy Fairfax will stay in Haiti to oversee the day-to-day operation. I have to go back for a few weeks to prep for the first class of trainees. I'll also make a few short trips throughout the next two years or so. But I'll be living here, in Oregon."

"Why, Ian?"

"Because of you."

She shook her head, resting her palm against his cheek. "What about your dad? Your mission?"

He fingered the hair around her face, brushing the back of his knuckles against her cheek. "You were right. Ghosts won't make me happy like you and Colt do. It took me a few weeks to understand why I couldn't shake my mood, but then it struck me. I missed you. My dream has changed."

"Is your mother disappointed?" Gentry frowned.

"She'll be okay when she sees me happy."

"I can't believe you made that snap decision. It's so . . . unlike you." Without warning, she jumped him, her legs straddling his waist. He used his arms to support her while she kissed him.

"Maybe we should get off the sidewalk," he suggested. "And take Brutus inside, too."

"Brutus." She giggled, looking down at the dog. "I'm a shopper, Ian. I know this thing cost a pretty penny. Quite a *frivolous* gift, you know. This dog's price tag could feed a dozen people, maybe more. I hope you haven't changed everything about yourself, McJ."

"Not everything. But I kept looking at Quackers and thinking about what he meant to you. Given the way I left, I thought I'd better go big so you couldn't ignore me."

"I could never ignore you." She released her grip and slid down his body, then lifted Brutus. "You're not the only one making changes. I quit my job to make a go of photography."

"That can't have been easy."

"No, but I feel so much better now that I'm being honest."

"Me too. Hopefully, I'll land a steady paramedic job at a hospital."

"I can't tempt you back to being Colt's nanny?" she teased.

"No, although I'd like to be here for Colt, and you, on a regular basis."

"Well, you're in luck, then, because we'd love that, too." She threw her arms around his neck and kissed him. "Besides, now that I'll be working from home, I'll manage Colt in the mornings, schedule portraits in the afternoon, and edit photos at night. Just need a part-time sitter each day."

"I've always known he was a lucky kid." Ian kissed her again, because he could. Because he didn't want to stop kissing her.

"Let's go inside." She opened the door and set Brutus on the floor. "Smith will be back soon."

"I can take off until he leaves, if that's easier."

"No way. I'm not letting you out of my sight, Ian Crawford." She hugged him, resting her head on his shoulder. "When Smith gets back, we'll talk about how to be the best kind of family any kid ever had."

Epilogue

Two Months Later

Family

According to *Merriam-Webster*: a group of individuals living under one roof and usually under one head

According to me: my new normal

Crisp, light breezes swept over the lakeside lawn on the evening of Colby's wedding. The sky—a lilac canvas crisscrossed with pink and orange brushstrokes—perfectly accompanied the romantic event. Only the bushels of lilies and pink peonies decorating A CertainTea's flagstone patio were more remarkable.

Gentry waved goodbye to the sitter who was taking Ty and Colt home to sleep. She then meandered through the elaborately set tables, each with candlelight flickering from the hurricane lanterns, to find her spot at the family table.

Ian had already seated himself beside Sara. Leslie was flanked by Hunter and Colby, with Alec's and Gentry's parents filling out the rest of the table. Tonight the entire family rallied, putting on its best behavior so as not to disrupt Colby's big day. Even Gentry's mother had been friendly to Leslie—a first, and possibly a turning point.

"Didn't my sister look beautiful at the altar?" Gentry kissed Ian as she took her seat between him and her mother.

He squeezed her hand, leaning close and whispering, "Not as beautiful as you."

"Good answer." She toyed with the bow tie of his rented tuxedo. Another first, no doubt. If he was uncomfortable in the suit, he didn't say. "I'm not sure which Ian I like best. Casual T-shirts or this Hugo Boss thing you've got going on."

"Hopefully not this, because I can't wait to take it off."

She wiggled her brows. "Me neither, come to think of it."

In a continued effort to make peace with her mother, she turned to her right. "You look nice, too, Mom."

"Thank you." Her mother touched the side of her hair, which had been swept up into a sophisticated French twist. "I meant to tell you Marion Leckie mentioned how much she loved the collage of her grandchildren's portraits you made."

"I love working with kids. They're easy to win over. Such spontaneous, happy little creatures."

"Ignorance is bliss, I suppose." Her mother raised a brow and sipped her water. "Life makes us all cynics eventually."

Gentry might've made the same crack a few months ago, but now she knew peace and hope. A glance across the table gave her a clear shot of her sister's exuberance. Colby and Alec whispered something to each other, and then he kissed her as if no one else existed. Moments like these made it hard to be cynical.

Ian wrapped one arm around the back of Gentry's chair. Having him in her life had made her ecstatic, like the children she photographed.

Gentry replied to her mom, "Even the most cynical of us can be changed by love, though, can't we?"

Her mother looked at her own husband. "I suppose so."

The waiters roamed the reception, filling everyone's champagne glasses. Gentry's father then stood and tapped his glass with a fork. The guests all quieted themselves in anticipation of the father-of-the-bride speech.

Jed Cabot cut a dashing figure in his tux. His salt-and-pepper hair, still thick and closely cropped, lent him sophistication tonight. His best accessory had always been his smile, which shone like the stars starting to dot the sky overhead.

He beamed at Colby and Alec before speaking. "Thank you all for coming tonight. It's my honor to host you at this amazing restaurant that these two built with their imaginations, sweat, and hearts. I can't think of anyone more deserving of its success, or of the love that brought us here tonight."

He glanced at Alec's parents, Frank and Julie Morgan, and nodded before continuing. "Thirty-plus years ago, when Hunter was still in diapers, Leslie fell in love with a little Craftsman on Forest Street and badgered me into buying it. I wasn't sure I could pay that mortgage, but the neighborhood was perfect for kids, so we took the plunge. Who could've known then that that decision would've yielded not only a lifelong friend for my son but also a husband for my daughter?

"Alec, you've always been one of the kindest, most loyal, and patient men I've known. My daughter has never been happier in her life than she has this past year, and that's almost entirely thanks to you and your love. Hunter has always viewed you as the brother he never had, but I'm damn glad it's now official. Welcome to our family, and we wish you both decades of happiness to come."

He raised his glass of the Egly-Ouriet champagne Smith had recommended for the event, and everyone clanked their flutes and chugged down the bubbly.

Everyone except Sara.

Mr. Morgan and Hunter both gave short toasts as well, and again, Gentry noticed Sara raising her glass but then setting it aside without taking a sip. Had they tried another IVF in secret and succeeded?

Ian elbowed her side. "I think it's your turn."

"Oh!" She winced. "Sorry!"

Instead of facing the guests, she looked directly at Colby.

"Everyone else has already used all the good words in their toasts, so I'm going rogue. Those who know me well will not be surprised." A smattering of chuckles rippled through the crowd. "Alec, you owe me a lifetime supply of your curried shrimp dish as a thank-you. If I hadn't flirted with you so obnoxiously, Colby might never have faced her true feelings. And on a more serious note, Colby, I am so lucky to have an older sister who embodies grace and courage. You've taught me that strength comes from love, not pride, and I'm so glad you've found someone equally wonderful to share your life with. Now get busy making babies, because Colt needs more cousins." More laughter erupted, but Gentry noticed Hunter and Sara exchange a knowing look. "Cheers."

Gentry swallowed her champagne and eyed Sara, who yet again refused to drink her champagne.

She sat and said, "Hunter, you look like you're about to burst with some good news. Care to share?"

Her brother started at being put on the spot, pushed his glasses up his nose, and pivoted. "Well, our first few months' sales figures on ChariTea are on target with projections. No major hiccups yet. I think we can expect to see a lot of growth going forward."

"That is good news. We should drink to that as well." Colby raised her glass. "I love seeing my whole family together, and happy."

"And growing," Hunter said.

Gentry clinked her glass with Ian and watched Sara clink hers and set it aside. "Sara, you aren't drinking tonight?"

"Sorry?" Sara's eyes widened.

"I've noticed you haven't taken a single sip during any of the toasts." Now, everyone's attention shifted to Sara and Hunter. "You aren't feeling sick, are you?"

Sara and Hunter shared another look. He whispered something, and she shrugged.

Colby spoke up, eyes widening with understanding. "Don't you dare keep a secret just because you think I can't share this day with anyone. If you've got more good news, you'd better tell us right now."

Hunter smiled at Colby, and Gentry didn't even feel left out for a change. "Okay, then. Sara's pregnant."

The table erupted with clapping and hugs. Leslie's eyes began to leak, and Gentry's dad asked, "How did it happen?"

"Apparently, it's not completely unheard of for people to be unsuccessful at IVF, and then, when they stop trying or thinking about it, for everything to come together. We're only at ten weeks, but I'm keeping my fingers crossed."

"Congratulations." Alec wore a giant smile and then whispered something to Colby before kissing her again.

Excited chattering broke out all around Gentry as the waiters set the amuse-bouche in front of everyone.

Ian leaned close. "More cousins for Colt, indeed."

"It's the best news ever."

"I can think of something better."

She popped the sweet fig with creamy ricotta in her mouth. "Like what?"

"Like a brother or sister."

Gentry's whole body warmed. "That would be perfect."

"I think so, too." He kissed her.

She brushed her fingers through his bangs. "It seems unfair that I'm getting everything I ever wanted, but you didn't get to fulfill your dad's wish."

"Don't worry. I'm happy with my choice." Ian squeezed her hand.

She believed him, but it didn't lessen the discomfort of knowing that she hadn't had to make any compromises. Ian deserved some kind of gesture from her to show him how much he meant to her. "If we ever have a son, let's name him Brian. That way your dad's name will live on for another generation."

"I'd love that." Ian's face lit with a smile, his eyes bright with tears. "I wish my father had met you."

"Me too. But I wish more that he'd seen what an amazing father you are. Thank you for loving Colt and me, and making my family complete."

"Thank you for giving me a life better than anything I'd ever dreamed for myself."

ACKNOWLEDGMENTS

As always, I have many people to thank for helping me bring this book to all of you, not the least of which are my family and friends for their continued love, encouragement, and support.

Thanks, also, to my agent, Jill Marsal, as well as to my patient editors, Megan Mulder and Krista Stroever, and the entire Montlake family for believing in me and working so hard on my behalf. I've been eager to stretch into new territory, so I'm grateful that they've supported these Cabot stories.

A special thanks to Mimi Falbo, a hospital administrator who spent many weeks volunteering at the Hôpital Albert Schweitzer Haiti throughout the years; and Kathleen Hower, CEO and founder of Global Links, who educated me about Haiti, NGOs, and some of the conditions and challenges of its people and health-care system.

Thanks, also, to a special reader and his wife, Steven and Joan Walton, of Brooklands, Sale, England, for helping me craft Archer Cooke's dialogue.

I couldn't produce any of my work without the MTBs and, in this case, Lisa Creane, who help me plot and keep my spirits up when doubt grabs hold.

And I can't leave out the wonderful members of my CTRWA chapter. Year after year, all the CTRWA members provide endless hours of support, feedback, and guidance. I love and thank them for that.

Finally, and most important, thank you, readers, for making my work worthwhile. Considering all your options, I'm honored by your choice to spend your time with me.

MENU ITEMS CREDITED

Le Coucou in NYC

Queue de Homard Grillé (whole poached lobster tail, grilled romaine, citrus, sauce lauris)

Jean-Georges in NYC

Gulf Shrimp with Fiddlehead Ferns

The French Laundry in Yountville, CA

Almond Wood Grilled Japanese Wagyu

AN EXCERPT FROM

THE MEMORY OF YOU

(THE FIRST BOOK IN THE NEW SERIES SANCTUARY SOUND)

EDITORS' NOTE: THIS IS AN EARLY EXCERPT AND MAY NOT REFLECT THE FINISHED BOOK.

Chapter One

On her deathbed years ago, Stef's mom had imparted one final piece of advice: never regret anything that once made you happy. That lenient perspective had comforted Stef in the wake of many mistakes. Today those words drifted back as she turned down Echo Hill Lane, the narrow, tree-lined cul-de-sac where her next appointment, and many happy memories, lived. Then again, that old lesson didn't quite apply to her current predicament, because her regret had nothing to do with the time she'd spent here with Ryan Quinn and his family, and everything to do with leaving them all behind.

She parked her Chevy van across the street from the white Dutch Colonial that had been like a second home in her teens, leaving the driveway open in case Mr. Quinn had to come or go. Once she killed the engine, she sat in the driver's seat shaking out her hands.

Jitters at thirty. How ridiculous! She hadn't had a real conversation with Mrs. Q. in a decade. Ryan wouldn't have wanted her visiting, and she'd forfeited his family's comfort after she'd ghosted him in college.

But today wasn't about comfort. Today was about a job—one she and her childhood friend–turned–business partner, Claire, needed to keep their Lockwood & McKenna home remodeling and decorating business growing.

"Here goes nothing," she said aloud while still behind the wheel, then blew out a breath and opened the door. After buckling her tool belt, she trotted across the lawn to the shade of the home's small portico and knocked on its apple-red front door. The briny scent of the nearby Long Island Sound helped to calm her nerves.

Seconds later, Mrs. Q. opened the door, wearing an apron. Her lively face broke into a smile, curling the edges of her wise blue eyes. The tall woman exuded a no-bullshit vibe, although she now had a decade's worth of new wrinkles, and gray strands frosted her blonde hair. Nostalgia rushed forth, fanning pinpricks of joy across Stef's skin.

The aroma of freshly baked snickerdoodles wafted outside while the two women faced each other for the first time, each assessing the appropriate decorum for this odd reunion.

"Stefanie, good to see you. Come on in. I've got to get the last batch out of the oven before they burn." Mrs. Q. waved Stef inside—minus the hugs of yesteryear—and then strolled ahead, straight back toward the kitchen.

Assaulted by familiar sights and sounds—the creaky, old wide-plank floors, the sisal carpet running up the stairs that led to Ryan's room—memories overwhelmed her, causing her to bump into the cardboard moving boxes stacked near the base of the stairwell. "Oof."

"Watch yourself!" Mrs. Q. called.

Stef noticed an oversize, handsome photograph of Ryan with his daughter, Emmy, displayed on the mantel. His smiling brown eyes and curled cocoa-colored hair still as handsome as ever. Suppressing a tiny pang of envy, she made her way to the kitchen.

Molly gestured toward the platter on the counter with her spatula. "Have one."

"Thanks." Stef nabbed a thick, warm cookie, then stood in the kitchen feeling sixteen years old again. A quick look at the cherry cabinets and jade-colored granite counters proved that nothing had changed much since she'd been a frequent guest.

Then an uneasy feeling took root. Did those boxes mean the Quinns were moving? Was this renovation an attempt to make the home more attractive to a buyer? It shouldn't matter, yet the idea of anyone other than the Quinns living here seemed as grim as setting fire to her favorite scrapbook.

She couldn't say that, of course, so she opted for pleasantries. "You look great, Mrs. Q."

"Thanks. You too." She finished transferring the last batch of cookies to a cooling rack. "We're both adults now. Call me Molly."

"Okay." Stef attempted a smile despite the surreal exchange.

Molly turned off the oven. "So tell me, how are you?"

"Same as always." Not exactly true, but she wouldn't burden Molly with the changes ten years had wrought.

Molly crossed her arms. "Happy to be back in Sanctuary Sound, or is it too sleepy after life up in Hartford?"

"I think I've had my fill of city life for now." Idle chitchat, or was Molly fishing for something? "It's nice to be home."

Her hometown—three thousand residents nestled on the Eastern Connecticut coastline—certainly differed from city life. She'd returned about two months ago, eager to surround herself with the familiar after . . . everything.

"No boyfriend left behind?" Molly's even gaze betrayed no bitterness, but Stef didn't like the conversation heading in that direction, or the rising shame from her guilty conscience.

"No." Her cheeks turned as hot as that oven, thanks to the cruel way she'd dumped Ryan. It seemed like a good time to change the subject. "No time for much social life. Claire and I are super busy getting things off the ground."

"It's brave of you girls to start your own business."

"Given the local mini renaissance, this seemed like the right time to be my own boss."

"We've certainly seen an influx of newcomers." Molly's tone carried the same hint of sadness that Stef had heard from other longtime residents who bemoaned the armada of wealthy young families who'd sniffed out the undervalued aging homes near the beach. To Stef, however, those buyers were target customers.

Molly set the empty mixing bowl and spoon in the sink, along with the cookie sheet. "I miss the old days. Speaking of, how's Peyton?"

Peyton Prescott, the childhood friend who, along with Stef and Claire, had formed the middle-school triumvirate known as the Lilac Lane League. They'd all remained close friends until recently. Now Claire hated Peyton, and Stef was stuck in the middle. All because of a lousy man. "Writing for travel magazines keeps her on the move. I haven't seen her in a year."

"Most of the old gang has up and gone." Molly's gaze turned distant, and Stef guessed she wished Ryan hadn't moved to Boston. "It's the curse of a small-town childhood. You feel stifled and become convinced the rest of the world is more exciting, learning too late that deep relationships are what make life rich."

Stef had certainly come to understand *that* better with age. She almost asked about Ryan, because not talking about him seemed damned awkward. Something stopped her, though. Antsy to fill the silence, Stef asked, "Do you mind if I take a look at the back porch? It's been a while, and I want to familiarize myself with it again so I can figure out the project's scope."

Converting a screened porch to a family room would be a straightforward job, and a nice addition to the gallery of work she could show prospective clients.

"Of course. I'll come with you so we can talk through my ideas." Molly untied her apron and hung it neatly on its hook. She cast a hesitant glance at the dirty bakeware abandoned in the sink, but then let it go.

Stef covered a smile, having forgotten about how nasty-neat Molly had always been. Ryan had driven her crazy with his piles of shoes, clothes, and sports gear.

They stepped through the kitchen door onto the screened porch. Clusters of terra-cotta pots sat on the flagstone floor, overflowing with sunny-yellow begonias. A faux rattan outdoor sofa and two gliders had replaced the old wrought iron furniture Stef remembered. She estimated the patio to be a sixteen-square-foot footprint, which would make a comfortable family room.

"Tell me, what kinds of finishes do you envision?" Stef asked, whipping her small notebook and pen from her belt.

"Nothing modern, given that the rest of the house is eighty years old. I'd like the windows and floors to blend in, if possible. Same with the exterior."

Stef opened the screen door to go outside and look at the structure. Molly followed her. Together, they squinted in the August sunlight. "Shouldn't be hard to match these double-hung windows and shingle siding. Are you thinking we pull out all the floor-to-ceiling screens and build half walls and windows, or maybe you want French doors all around?"

"I like it to be bright and have views of my garden." Molly pointed to her massive pink polyantha rose bushes. "Maybe just one set of doors and as many windows as you can put in here without making it impossible to heat in the winter."

The distant wail of an ambulance siren split the air, interrupting their conversation.

Stef suddenly became blinded by the sunlight. Time shifted down to a slow pulse while short, sharp breaths chafed her lungs. *That's wrong. There shouldn't be sunlight. Should be blackness. No sun. Not even moonlight. Something—a shadow—lurking at the edges . . . stabbing, grunting, cigarettes and pain . . .*

"Stefanie?" Molly's touch broke through Stef's haze. "Are you okay?"

A trickle of the perspiration gathering along Stef's hairline rolled down her temple. "Yes."

"You looked panic-stricken." Concern colored Molly's eyes.

Stef shrugged off Molly's unspoken questions. She couldn't answer them even if she wanted to, which she didn't. "Lost in thought, I guess."

"About what?"

Stef flipped a new page in her notebook. As always, remembering any detail of her zone-outs was like trying to catch fog. "Dunno."

Molly hesitated before speaking. "Maybe we should go inside and get you some water."

She followed Molly inside, choosing to wait on the porch and catch her breath. She'd been losing track of time now and then for the past few months. Her hazy moments didn't follow a discernible pattern, so she chalked them up to the aftereffects of her most recent concussion.

She'd had a few concussions during her high school and college soccer career. Then, three months ago, her head had taken another harsh blow when some assholes jumped her in an alley, beat the crap out of her, and made off with her purse.

A sudden burst of acid surged up her esophagus, but she breathed through the burning discomfort. Molly returned and handed her a glass of water, which she chugged.

Determined to wipe that worried look off Molly's face and be professional, she said, "I think we should open it up into the kitchen, and also here." She pounded on the wall that she believed would lead into the hallway beside the stairwell. "That'll give you better flow."

"Good idea." Molly checked her watch, suddenly looking antsy. "Ballpark me . . . how much and how long will it take?"

"I need to check on some prices, and we also need to decide whether to connect to the home's HVAC or go with the new portable units, and stuff." She put her notebook away and withdrew a tape measure to verify her estimates.

"I'm not that picky. Functional and basic, that's all I need. What's the timing on all of this?"

"Maybe eight to ten weeks. We're working right on the slab, which saves a lot of time and expense."

"That's good." Molly opened the kitchen door, preparing to go inside while Stef continued measuring. "Let's get it started ASAP."

Stef remained on the porch, tape measure retracting. "Molly, I haven't even given you a bid."

Molly waved. "Honey, I know you'll be fair."

Stef felt her brows rise. "Do you mind if I ask what's the rush?"

Molly remained standing in the open doorway and cast Stef a peculiar look. "Ryan and Emmy are moving in. We'll need the extra space sooner than later."

"Ryan's moving home?" A steady rush of heat rose from Stef's toes to her head. Why would Ryan be moving in? And why hadn't Molly mentioned Val?

Before Molly could expound, the front door slammed open, and a young girl's voice called out, "Memaw, I smell cookies!"

Five seconds later, young Emmy Quinn raced into the kitchen and skidded to a halt.

◆ ◆ ◆

Ryan tossed his keys on the walnut entry table and kicked off his flip-flops, keeping the damp, sandy beach towels slung over his shoulders. He didn't relish moving in with his parents but couldn't deny the comfort of coming home to fresh-baked cookies and his mom's support. He needed help with Emmy now, and Emmy needed a stable, positive woman in her life.

"We're home," he called out, as if Emmy's dash to the kitchen hadn't already warned his mom of an oncoming storm. And Emmy was a storm these days—a raging sea of emotion that could turn from frothy giggles to waves of hysterics without notice. Val's decision to run off with her new lover had done a real job on their daughter, leaving him and his family groping to fill the void.

He glanced at the unpacked boxes, sighed, and kept walking. Those could wait another thirty minutes. Sharing warm cookies with his daughter would be a better use of his time.

The transition from their eclectic suburb outside Boston to this tiny beach community wouldn't be a cakewalk. Next week he would start his new job, and Emmy a new school, which was sure to bring another round of highs and lows while she struggled to make new friends. Between now and then, he hoped he and his parents could swaddle Emmy in some old-fashioned love and discipline. Something Val had never quite managed to provide.

He rounded the corner and spotted Emmy standing in her flamingo-pink swimsuit, brunette curls springy as ever as she tipped her head from side to side while staring out to the porch.

"What's up, buttercup?" Ryan swiped a cookie for himself and took a giant bite.

"Who's that?" Emmy pointed outside, past his mother, to a woman on the patio—*to Steffi Lockwood*?

He nearly dropped the cookie as his hand fell to his side. Why the hell was Steffi hanging out with his mother? Before he realized what was happening, he ended up standing in the middle of the patio. "What's going on here?"

Those gruff words erupted, reopening wounds from the scarred part of his soul.

"What kind of greeting is that, Ryan?" his mom admonished, giving him "that look" she gave when she expected him to behave. "Emmy, this is Miss Lockwood, and she builds things. She's going to turn this porch into a room for you to hang out in with your friends."

Steffi fiddled with her tool belt, looking like she'd rather be anyplace other than in Ryan's sight line. "Hi, Emmy. You can call me Stef."

"Miss Lockwood is fine," Ryan said without thinking. A quick glance at her ring finger suggested she'd never married. No surprise. Commitment hadn't been her strong suit, and he didn't need his daughter getting overly familiar with another woman who didn't keep her promises.

"Hi." Emmy gave Steffi a serious once-over, her gaze snagging on the tool belt before lingering on the black-and-turquoise work shoes. Quite a different look from Val and her friends, none of whom would be caught dead sporting overall shorts, a freshly scrubbed face, and a ponytail. Emmy then turned toward his mother. "Can we paint the room pink, Memaw?"

"I don't think so, Pooh. But maybe your dad will paint your bedroom pink." She smiled at Emmy, who bounced on her toes.

"Daddy, yes. Yes, yes, yes! The same pink room as my room at home." Her big hazel eyes pleaded. If he dared say no, the waterworks would start.

Not that he had time to paint a picture, much less a bedroom. "We'll see, princess."

"Maybe Mommy will help." Her hopeful smile shoved his heart through a meat grinder.

He wouldn't discuss Val in front of Stef, so he said, "Let's leave these two out here to finish their discussion."

"Actually, hand me those dirty towels before you get sand everywhere." His mother bundled the towels in preparation for her sprint to the laundry room. "I've already given Stefanie my thoughts. Why don't you weigh in? I'm sure you have an opinion about space for a big-screen TV or some such." She glided past him, patting his cheek on her way. "Emmy, come sit at the table and I'll pour you some milk for those cookies."

He thought to turn his back on Steffi, because even unpacking those moving boxes would be preferable to dealing with her. Then he decided he better not give her the satisfaction of seeing him agitated.

That'd only give her the misimpression that she held sway over him, which she didn't. She hadn't in many years.

If memories of how she'd blown him off still nicked his heart like a razor blade, it was only because he might mourn the fact that the girl he'd cherished had turned into a bitch.

He widened his stance and crossed his arms, reminding himself to play it cool. "I'm shocked to see you here."

"Yeah, well. I was surprised to get the call."

"I'm sure you were." He hated that she was here to witness the failure of his marriage. He tilted his head, the litigator in him coming to the fore. "What made you come? Morbid curiosity?"

"No." She stood still, unflinching now. "I need the work. Claire and I just got our company off the ground. I can't afford to say no to anyone."

"That must be uncomfortable for you, given how much you like your freedom." *Damn.* Guess he couldn't keep his cool. The sarcasm constituted the first blow of an argument they should've had years ago. Now it'd be pointless. He should change the subject. "How *is* Claire?"

"She's well." Stef's expression remained alert and somewhat wary.

"Is she? I'd heard about how Todd dumped her and ran off with Peyton." He shook his head, disgusted. "So much for the Triple L's infamous loyalty."

Steffi, Claire, and Peyton had been inseparable—living up to their "Men Come and Go, but Friends Are Forever" motto—until last fall. He empathized with Claire's pain from the duplicity, having been in her shoes himself more than once.

"Peyton didn't set out to seduce Todd, and I know she feels horrible about hurting Claire."

"Are you actually defending Peyton's disloyalty?" Actually, that shouldn't surprise him. He clenched his jaw and released it.

Steffi heaved a sigh. "I'm not happy about what's happened, but Peyton didn't get together with Todd until weeks after he left Claire."

"Left Claire for Peyton," Ryan reminded her.

"I love Peyton like a sister, so I'll forgive her even though it's hard. As for Todd, Claire is better off not to end up with someone who didn't love her completely. When she realizes that and meets someone new, maybe she'll forgive Peyton so we can all be friends again."

"Don't count on it."

They stared at each other, their entire history now ringing in their ears at a pitch not audible to any other human. How naive of her to think that moving on erases the pain of lost love. Or perhaps that was what she told herself to erase her own guilt for how she'd treated him.

This pause gave him an opportunity to study her. The ponytail—reminiscent of her soccer days—suggested she still wore her chocolate-brown hair in a simple, long blunt style. Her hazel eyes, flecked with gold and framed by heavy, dark brows, flashed her emotions like always.

She couldn't claim any singularly beautiful feature, but taken all together, she nailed the athletic girl-next-door appeal. Those work shorts proved years of playing soccer and doing manual labor had kept her legs toned as ever, too.

She swallowed before clearing her throat. "Your mom wants the finished space to have lots of windows and a French door. That's as far as we got."

"Well, it's her house, so I have no opinions." He turned to leave before he did or said something even less kind.

"Ryan."

Hearing her say his name stopped him for a second, but he didn't turn around.

She sighed. "I think she wants this to be someplace you and your daughter can be comfortable, so if you want a big TV or whatever, I'd like to know so I can plan for it."

He glanced over his shoulder. How many evenings had he and Steffi hung out here, candles lit, listening to rain on the roof while making out? Every spot in the whole damn house contained a shared memory, some better than others. There'd been a time when he would've bet nothing could've come between them. He'd considered himself the luckiest in love until she'd humbled him.

Between that and Val's recent whopper, he'd taken a hard look at his judgment lately. "I won't be here long enough for that to matter."

He didn't know how true that was, but he'd hoped he'd find his own place in six or so months. For now, he needed to conserve money to pay for his divorce. In his mind, Val didn't deserve one cent of his hard-earned paycheck, especially not after leaving her daughter behind while she moved in with her sugar daddy. The court would probably disagree.

When Stef had left him, he'd cried and prayed and secretly hoped for a reconciliation. When *Val* bailed, he'd shed no tears. Instead, he put their house on the market the next day rather than waste emotional energy on a woman who didn't want him. He'd found a new assistant public defender job in Hartford, and was moving in here to live rent-free until he had a better idea of what to expect. In the meantime, his mom wasn't just the cheapest after-school day care around but also the most reliable.

"I'm sorry about your marriage . . . ," Steffi sputtered.

She should be sorry. He wouldn't have met Val if he hadn't been on the rebound from Steffi's head games. Granted, Val's unplanned pregnancy at the end of senior year had pushed that relationship someplace it probably shouldn't have gone, although he couldn't regret having Emmy. His daughter gave him purpose and filled his life with immeasurable love. "My marriage is off-limits. I advise you to let it lie."

"Noted, Counselor." The sharp edge in her voice surprised him, so he faced her fully for another stare-down. Being a lawyer who regularly contended with criminals and cops made these kinds of contests too easy. She dropped her gaze, then looked up again. "Listen, it looks like I'll be here working for a couple of months, so it'd be nice if we could get off on a better foot. Maybe we could even be friends."

He snorted. "No, thanks. Friendship requires trust, and I don't trust you. So you can go back to treating me exactly like you did in college. Pretend I don't even exist. It gutted me back then, but now it suits me fine."

Bam! For three seconds, the overdue release of pent-up anger made him feel ten feet tall. Her slumped shoulders and red cheeks reversed his high, sinking him as low as a man could go.

"I'm sorry I hurt you, especially since it seems to have changed you into someone I might not like." She unwound her tape measure and started walking along the far edge of the patio. "I'll do my best to stay out of your way."

He'd changed, no doubt. She'd started that ball rolling; then his wife and his job had exposed him to even more injustice, making him cynical and, sometimes, bitter.

Steffi had been just shy of twenty when she'd blown him off. A decade ago. They'd both been different people then, and maybe she'd changed, too. Maybe she even regretted how she'd handled things. But he certainly had more important things to worry about than her or any lingering hurt feelings. He couldn't quite apologize for snapping at her now, so he pointed to the right corner of the room. "Might be nice to have my fifty-five-inch screen mounted over there."

She paused and glanced at him. "I'll be sure to factor that in."

"Thanks." He needed a shower. The damp, sandy suit had started to make him itch. "See you around."

He walked into the kitchen to find Emmy fingers-deep in a mug of milk and soggy cookie crumbles. Little sugar puddles lay scattered on the table all around her.

"You'd better wipe all that up before Memaw comes back. She won't stand for that kind of mess." Unlike Val, who never cared much about the messes Emmy left. In fairness, he hadn't trained his daughter to be tidy, either.

"Okay," Emmy said, dunking another cookie.

"That's enough, princess." Ryan removed the platter, although he was probably too late to prevent a tummy ache. "You're going to get sick. When you finish here, come up and help me unpack some of our boxes, okay? Then I need to work for a while. But maybe we can go to town and get pizza."

"Yay!"

"I'll take you to my old favorite, Campiti's. You'll love it."

Emmy kicked her feet beneath the table. "Memaw says Miss Lockwood used to hang out here a lot."

"Yeah." He scratched the back of his neck. "She grew up here in town, like me."

"Memaw says she was a special friend."

"Did she?" Ryan now suspected his mother had an ulterior motive with this remodeling plan. She'd always loved Steffi. Back when Steffi'd blown him off, his mom had made excuses, claiming she just needed to grow up a little. "Give her time and space," she'd said.

If his mom thought Ryan had any interest in women right now, she'd lost her mind. He'd have to be extra careful to make sure Emmy didn't make room in her heart for Steffi, because being disappointed by Steffi Lockwood was as certain as the sugar high those snickerdoodles were about to give his daughter.

ABOUT THE AUTHOR

Photo © 2016 Lorah Haskins

National bestselling author Jamie Beck's realistic and heartwarming stories have sold more than one million copies. She's a 2017 Booksellers' Best Award finalist, and critics at *Kirkus Reviews*, *Publishers Weekly*, and *Booklist* have respectively called her work "smart," "uplifting," and "entertaining." In addition to writing, she enjoys dancing around the kitchen while cooking, and hitting the slopes in Vermont and Utah. Above all, she is a grateful wife and mother to a very patient, supportive family.

Fans can learn more about her on her website: www.jamiebeck.com, which includes a fun "Extras" page with photos, videos, and playlists. She also loves interacting with everyone at www.facebook.com/JamieBeckBooks.